A STRANGER ON HER DOORSTEP

JULIE MILLER

SEARCHING FOR EVIDENCE

TYLER ANNE SNELL

This book is produced from independently certified FSC™
paper to ensure responsible forest management.

For more information visit: www.harpercollins.co.uk/green

Printed and bound in Spain
by CPI, Barcelona

MILLS & BOON

First Published in Great Britain 2021
by Mills & Boon, an imprint of HarperCollins*Publishers* Ltd
1 London Bridge Street, London, SE1 9GF

www.harpercollins.co.uk

HarperCollins*Publishers*
1st Floor, Watermarque Building,
Ringsend Road, Dublin 4, Ireland

A Stranger on Her Doorstep © 2021 Julie Miller
Searching for Evidence © 2021 Tyler Anne Snell

ISBN: 978-0-263-28345-7

A STRANGER ON HER DOORSTEP

JULIE MILLER

For my hubby and fellow author, Scott E. Miller.

Thanks for helping me brainstorm this one, hon. I knew I could count on you to know your high fantasy info.

Chapter One

Sabotage.

Luke Broughton pumped his brakes as the center line on the asphalt was gobbled up beneath the wheels of his SUV, in case it was the sharp curves and steep inclines of this mountainous highway that had caused his brakes to fail. But he knew better. He knew it in his bones.

Somebody wanted him dead.

A clearing in the trees to his left gave him a glimpse of the two black SUVs on the road above him. They were in hot pursuit, maybe a half mile behind his location. Another hairpin curve and they'd be on his tail. Until then, it was only a matter of time before his unchecked speed sent him flying off the edge of the road at the next turn he couldn't make.

He'd raced LAVs on the sand-swept roads in the Middle East and over the sparse terrain of the Afghan mountains. But this was no Light Armored Vehicle, and the Teton mountains in northwestern Wyoming were a different sort of beast. Higher, steeper elevations. Better roads but sight lines blocked by towering pines and aspen in the full leaf of summer. His knuckles whitened as he gripped the steering wheel and careened around the next curve, his rear tires fishtailing onto the shoulder before he regained control. Beyond the guardrail, there was a steep drop to the next cutback on the road. Or maybe it fell off into a rocky creek bed. Or an endless chasm filled with trees and granite outcroppings.

He tried downshifting, but his transmission had locked up on him. Definitely sabotage. Done by somebody who knew their business around ways to *accidentally* silence anyone who got in their way.

Luke laid on his horn when he saw the turkey vulture feasting on the carrion at the side of the road. The large black bird spread its enormous wings and reluctantly hopped back and floated out of harm's way as Luke plowed through the carcass. That was going to be him in about sixty seconds if he couldn't come up with a way to slow down the out-of-control SUV.

He cursed his own damn luck before risking taking one hand off the wheel to tap the front pocket of his jeans. The mini thumb drive was still there. Thank goodness he'd made himself a copy. Everything else he'd done since yesterday morning had been one rookie mistake after another. He'd been thinking like the civilian he'd been for a mere eight months, not the seasoned warrior who'd survived tours of duty overseas and fought his way through tangles of bureaucratic red tape when he'd been stationed stateside, putting together security units for the Marine Corps. Whistleblowing was a dangerous business. He should have known the illegal dealings he'd uncovered went deeper than his initial suspect.

That next turn was coming up fast. He checked his rearview mirror. The two SUVs were on the straightaway with him now, bearing down on his position. He knew what was coming—what he'd do himself if their positions were reversed and he'd been given the assignment to stop the escaping enemy by whatever means necessary.

The irony of it all was he'd been hired by Bell Design Systems to be the man driving one of those black SUVs. He hadn't realized he was the odd man out—that the enemy was someone he'd trusted, one of the men or women on his team, someone who should have had his back instead of chasing down his runaway vehicle on a remote mountain road with the express purpose of taking him out.

He steered around the next curve, careening into the guardrail and peeling the paint off the passenger side of his SUV as metal screeched against metal. He wondered if the guardrail was secure enough to stop his momentum, or if he'd have better luck turning the car into the ditch and rock face on his left. Risk sailing into the unknown or smash into solid granite? He didn't like his options. Even if he survived a purposeful crash, he'd have to pray he didn't flip the vehicle, and that he could get out fast enough to take out the other men or lose them in this vast, verdant wilderness he wasn't all that familiar with. Although he wore a gun strapped to his belt and another in an ankle holster, he had no idea how many men were in those vehicles besides the drivers. He could shoot. He could fight hand-to-hand. But one man against a potential army was never good odds.

He swerved into the oncoming lane, overcorrecting the curve, and glanced ahead at the road signs indicating a trio of tiny towns and a descent that was only going to get steeper.

"Think, Broughton." *How do I survive this?*

He should have checked the SUV before starting the engine and leaving the Ridgerunner Lodge, the fancy executive resort retreat owned by BDS on the southern end of Jackson Hole between the Snake River and Bridger-Teton National Forest. Less than a year out of the Corps and he was getting soft. Why had he agreed to meet the security chief, CEO and other company muckety-mucks in the remote location instead of corporate headquarters in Cheyenne?

And neither of those had been his first mistake. He'd handed over the evidence he'd uncovered to a source he hadn't checked and checked again. This wasn't the Corps. In the Marines, he'd trusted his senior officers without question. But he was a civilian now. His supervisor? The company bosses? His coworkers at Bell Design Systems? He hadn't personally vetted them. They hadn't gone through the same training he had at Quantico or Lejeune. They hadn't shared the same deployments or worked with a smooth-running team at Camp Arifjan or Fort Leonard Wood. The chain of command was clearly a lot sketchier in the civilian world, and he'd exposed his position like a damned private who hadn't seen battle yet.

He swore again as the speedometer crept past the eighty-mile-per-hour mark. More than thirty miles above the recommended speed limit.

The SUVs behind him were picking up speed, too. Tinted windows and the need to control his own runaway vehicle kept him from identifying his pursuers.

He suspected he'd stumbled onto something big when he'd run his security check on the executives visiting from China. He was too good at his job. Too thorough to ignore the red flags of classified communications that indicated someone within the company had a private agenda for meeting with their guests this weekend. Although he hadn't been able to pinpoint the source of the communications, the cryptic emails had been clear enough. This meeting was more than a scenic tour of Yellowstone and Teton National Park, with a couple of days set aside to lay the groundwork for a legal trade agreement. Someone intended to *illegally* sell BDS weapons technology to the Chinese. Maybe not the Chinese government. But there were enterprising souls on both sides who intended to turn a tidy profit at the expense of military and civilian lives right here in the US and among its allies. Technology meant to improve the side Captain Luke Broughton, USMC Retired, had fought for going on fifteen years before the old injury to his right leg and one concussion too many had forced him into early retirement. They'd offered him a desk job until he made lieutenant colonel, but he couldn't see staring at four walls and paperwork for another four years. He'd been raised in the Missouri Ozarks. Hunting, fishing, hiking, camping, anything outdoors, had always been his calling until a savvy recruiter had sold him on four years of college and a career serving his country.

Taking the job on the security team at Bell Design Systems had ticked all the right civilian boxes. He couldn't beat the Wyoming-based company for a location this close to the mountains and all the outdoor activities he loved. And, in a way, he'd felt like he was still serving his country, working for a firm that developed technology used primarily by the military and law enforcement. He wasn't the brains of designing the tech. But his recent military experience made him an experienced consultant, and his background with base and advanced guard security gave him the perfect skill set for being part of the multibillion-dollar company's security team.

Luke sailed around the next curve and felt his inward tires leave the road.

"Options, Broughton," he ground through clenched teeth. He needed options.

He was screwed unless he found an exit ramp or gravel road that would take him back up the mountain at an easier slope, slowing his speed enough to jump from the vehicle.

He felt the first tap to his bumper. The SUV skidded from lane to lane, but Luke fought to maintain control.

Oh, yeah. These bastards wanted him dead.

He'd survived explosions, a knife fight and a shattered leg. But you blow one whistle on someone who's supposed to be one of the good guys and there was hell to pay.

Maybe this was how he was going out.

But damned if the enemy got to win.

He had the backup evidence in his pocket. Even if he was dead on the side of the road, those maniacs would pat him down and take whatever they wanted so that not even the undertaker could trace their illegal activities. Or maybe they'd plant something on his body. Make him the scapegoat in case their scheme became public knowledge.

He needed to protect himself. He needed to get the information through to an outside ally who could help. He needed to complete this mission.

Luke pushed his gun aside and dipped his fingers into his pocket to pull out the thumb drive. This was going to hurt like a son of a gun going down, but it was the only way to secure the evidence. He jammed the data stick into his mouth and swallowed.

When the first black SUV tapped his bumper again, Luke only had one hand on the wheel.

And that was all she wrote. There was no recovering from the skid this time. He slapped both hands on the wheel, but it was too late.

The SUV tilted onto two wheels, hit the guardrail and bounced back across the road. He steered into the skid but sped off the shoulder into the ditch. A tree ripped off the side mirror and the front fender glanced off the rock wall, flipping the vehicle back onto the road.

Luke smacked his head against the window despite the airbag deploying. The seat belt locked up across his chest, stealing the air from his lungs. The crunching sound of metal was deafening. Sparks on burning asphalt stung his nose. His vision blurred as the SUV tumbled and tumbled. He blacked out for a few seconds before the SUV rocked to a halt.

He was nauseous, disoriented when he came to. Sharp, bruising pain made it difficult to catch his breath and his head felt like a spongy mess. Two men dragged him away from the wreckage. But he was sentient enough to know that this was no rescue.

The men dropped him with a thud on the side of the road between the twisted bulk of his SUV and the mangled guardrail. He tried to raise his eyelids and peer through his lashes, but he couldn't focus. He was on his back, looking up at a platoon of men gathering around him.

Faceless men in suits and ties. Even in his groggy state, he knew that wasn't how the enemy dressed. Had he been taken hostage? Had he been tortured and lost consciousness? Had his LAV hit a roadside bomb? Where was the rest of his team?

There were hands on him, and he was being searched. They removed his phone. He nearly retched when they rolled him and took his wallet. He felt a pinch at the back of his neck and knew they had ripped off his dog tags.

His eyelids were too heavy to keep open now. But he was still conscious enough to mentally assess his injuries. Another concussion. The coppery taste of blood at the corner of his mouth. Something stabbing him inside.

Radio for backup. Extraction! Extraction!

He had a vague notion that help wasn't coming. The enemy had him at their mercy. But the color of the world he'd glimpsed through his lashes was too green for Afghanistan or Iraq. The Hurt Locker never had a cool breeze like the one whispering across his face.

Suicide bomber must have made it past a checkpoint. Snider! Martinez! Sound off! Where were the rest of his men?

"It's not on him," he heard a voice say. "Maybe he didn't make a copy."

"He's too smart not to." That sounded like the man in charge. "I don't want anyone to link the body to us. Grab his gun, too. If the authorities ever find him, they'll be able to track him by the serial number."

"What about his car?"

"I'll take care of it." A third voice. Who were these men? Soldiers? Guards?

"It's a company loaner. Take it apart in case he stashed it there. We'll erase his name from the records."

That wasn't military talk. This wasn't right. He wasn't in the Corps anymore.

But damned if he could force any of this to make sense.

Gravel crunched the pavement beside his ear as someone stood over him, casting a shadow over his face. "I could have used a man like you. Too bad you couldn't see my point of view. I could have made you very rich." The shadow left and sunlight washed over his face again. "Put a bullet in his head and make this all go away."

Shake it off. Clear your head. How are you going to survive when the enemy captures you?

He heard multiple footsteps and a car engine turning over. He heard someone calling for a tow truck. They didn't do that out in the field.

Where was he?

What was happening?

Who were these men?

How did he get hurt?

How are you going to survive?

His CO's advice echoed in his head. He'd been trained to fight. To give the enemy grief. To do whatever it took to stay alive and complete his mission.

Forcing his leaden eyelids open to a swirling blur of blue sky and green treetops, of twisted metal and rocky outcroppings and pinpricks of light that pierced his brain, he took in his surroundings. Car wreck. A sliver of understanding warred with the pinpricks of light for control of his brain.

Shadows of men walked to another vehicle. There was nothing to his left beyond the grassy edge and some wild-flowers beneath the shredded guardrail that had done its job to save him from certain death. He could feel the bulk of metal in his boot. A gun. If he could reach it… The world spun into oblivion when he tried to move. He quickly squeezed his eyes shut and breathed deeply, willing himself to stay conscious. Staying awake was the only way he could fight.

Put a bullet in his head and make this all go away.

He needed options. Now.

Option A. Was there any way he could reach his gun and stand his ground here on the road? Hell, he wasn't even sure he could stand.

Option B. What lay in the abyss below his line of sight? Was he physically able to make a run for it? Was escape a possibility?

A shadow fell over him again. He heard the unmistakable sound of a bullet being loaded into a chamber.

"You're awake?" His would-be killer hesitated. Yeah. It was a hell of a thing to look a man in the eye when you pulled the trigger.

The man squatted beside him and pressed two thick fingers to his neck. Then he muttered a curse at determining he hadn't cooperated by dying for him. "Nothing personal, Captain. Orders are orders."

The man pushed to his feet and took aim.

Option B.

Luke rolled. He bet every heartbeat left in him that he wasn't plunging to his death as he slipped beneath the guardrail and tumbled off the overhang into the abyss.

The man with the gun swore.

He heard the crack of a gunshot, felt a burning hot poker drill through his shoulder. And then he was falling.

He dropped a good ten feet until he crashed into the

first ledge. But loose gravel and his momentum carried him over the edge, and he hit another rocky outcropping, jarring a fresh wave of pain through his side. He instinctively snatched at a sapling growing out of a fissure between the rocks, then tall grass, flowers, rocks, anything he could claw his grip into.

He heard more bullets.

The answering whiff of air and sharp pings of the tiny missiles hitting a rock or tree or dirt created a cacophonous symphony that chased his crazy fall down the mountain.

By the time he slammed to a stop near a copse of trees at the bottom of the ravine, his battered body and jumbled brain made him think he should be dead.

He prayed the man with the gun on the road above him thought the same.

HE'D BEEN RUNNING for hours.

Well, *running* was a relative term, considering how often he'd stumbled or fallen. But he'd kept moving. He hoped to hell it hadn't been in circles. It was hard to get his bearings with all these trees and no compass. Yet even with throbbing gelatin for a brain, he knew enough to keep going downhill. Away from the bullets. Away from the option of winding up dead. He'd followed the current of the creek, had even walked through the icy, rushing water itself for half a mile or so to avoid leaving footsteps and any scent that could be tracked, in case whoever was after him had dogs.

At least the cold water had stimulated his senses and kept him conscious when every weary bone in his body begged him to lie down and sleep. He'd torn up the button-down shirt he'd been wearing to tie off a bandage for the hole in his shoulder. He'd stemmed the bleeding for a little while, but now his shirt was soaked and the blood was trickling down his arm again, leaving a distinct trail of red droplets for anyone who had the skills to track him through the trees, scrubby grass and exposed gray rock of the mountain. He hoped he hadn't attracted the attention of some bear or mountain lion—they'd be able to follow the blood trail, too.

He'd sustained an injury to his head. Although his hair was cropped close to his scalp, it was matted with blood. But without a mirror or proper med kit, he had no way of assessing or treating the wound.

He could feel cognition slipping away as steadily as his life's blood was ebbing from his body. Only his training was keeping him alive.

Imminent threat. Behind enemy lines. Keep moving.

Why was he running? How did he get hurt? Was he being followed?

He'd never heard any footsteps or vehicle pursuing him. Only a serious climber or someone willing to break his neck and fall like he had could make that descent quickly. He'd avoided anything that resembled a road or even a hiking path, so trailing him in a vehicle was next to impossible. Why did he think he was being chased? Someone tried to kill him. Someone nearly succeeded.

Who was the enemy?

Keep moving.

He caught the toe of his boot on a rock and stumbled. He paid dearly for the instinct to catch himself. Pain ripped through his wounded shoulder and bum knee, and his lungs seized up in his chest.

Medic. He needed to reach a medic.

If he didn't get help, he would be dead soon. He rolled onto his back and gazed up at the dark green of pine needles and the lighter green of deciduous leaves arching high over his head. Trees like that didn't grow in the sand. And he was wearing jeans, not a uniform. He mentally shook off his confused thoughts. "You're stateside, Captain. You're out of the Corps."

Captain. The Corps. That meant he was a Marine.

That didn't mean he knew where he was in the good ol' US of A.

He had a feeling there was a lot he didn't know.

He squeezed his eyes shut against the dapples of light dancing through the trees. Every now and then, the lights hit his retinas straight-on, piercing his brain like shrapnel. He'd taken a hard blow to the head. He fought the urge to surrender to his fatigue or succumb to the dizziness that made him want to puke.

So he dragged himself to his feet and kept moving.

Find help. Survive.

He felt the ground change beneath his feet before he recognized the clearing in the trees. The grass, dirt and pine needles gave way to the crunch of tiny rocks beneath his boots. The uneven terrain became a relatively flat surface. A gravel road. No, a driveway.

Driveways led to houses or businesses.

Driveways led to help.

The gravel was evenly distributed and there were no ruts in the road, making him think it hadn't been used very often. He'd made a pretty fair assessment of how isolated this place was long before he crested a rise and saw the two-story log cabin with an attached garage and a heavy-duty pickup truck parked out front.

The porch ran the width of the house, and there were big pots of colorful flowers on either side of the steps he tripped up. He heard a dog's loud, deep barking before he ever reached the front door and knocked.

Maybe he should rethink this. Guard dog? Sounded like a big one with that booming voice. Unknown location? What if he'd circled back to the very doorstep he'd been running from?

He swiped his palm across the bristly buzz cut of hair on his head and came away with blood on his fingers, making the desperate decision for him. He braced that bloody hand against the doorjamb, falling weakly against it before pounding the door with his fist again.

The dog's bark vibrated the door beneath his hand. It definitely didn't sound friendly. But the grain of the wood beneath his hand was spinning into bizarre patterns, and he wasn't sure if it was his eyes or his thoughts that couldn't keep things straight anymore.

He heard a chain scrape across the inside of the door. A dead bolt flipped open. There was a sharp, sotto voce command and the dog fell silent a split second before the door swung open.

"Sorry to bother you, but…"

He stared into the twin barrels of an over-under shotgun.

The dog was a big, white furry thing with black markings around its eyes and muzzle. But the dog wasn't what captured his attention. He was caught by a pair of blue eyes, dark like cobalt and twilight skies and every hushed, intriguing fantasy he'd ever had about a woman.

"I don't like surprise visitors. What do you want?" She was a little younger than him, probably in her thirties, but there was no mistaking that she had the advantage here.

"I'm wounded. Need help. Can you call an ambulance?"

"Is this some kind of joke? Who are you?"

"My blood and your shotgun are a joke?" Who had a sick sense of humor like that?

"How do I know that blood is real?"

He had no answer for that.

She shook her head slowly from side to side, stirring the long cascade of coffee-colored hair that hung in a loose ponytail over one shoulder and revealing the long, thin scar that curved from her cheek to her jaw. If the gun wasn't evidence enough, he could see that this woman was a warrior. "You run along. I don't sign books for desperate fans who trespass on my property. And I won't reward your cleverness or diligence in tracking me down by writing you into one of my stories."

Her words made no sense. He must have taken a really hard blow to the head. "What are you talking about?"

"Call 9-1-1 yourself. Don't bother me again."

He was leaning heavily on his good shoulder now, the sturdiness of the house about the only thing holding him up. "No phone," he managed to eke out. "Please. I need… sanctuary. Place to rest…to think…"

She shook her head, but the gun never wavered. "The last time a stranger asked for my help…"

He saw the muscle of uncertainty twitching in her jaw, the fear and compassion warring in her expression. Yet he knew the moment her eyes hardened like dark ice that she'd made the decision not to help him.

He pushed away from the door, willed his legs to hold him upright, even though that made him a good six inches taller than her and probably looked like he was trying to threaten her. "I fell down the mountain, lady. I've been shot," he argued. There was more to tell her, but he couldn't find the words. "I swear I won't hurt you."

"I've heard that before, too." That's when he saw the other scars. Through the spinning haze of his vision, he spotted the matching puckers of healed skin on each hand. There was another at the vee of her tank top beneath the long-sleeved blouse she wore. He recognized marks like that. She'd been tortured. Some time ago, because every mark had healed, and he glimpsed the patch of what had been a skin graft along the underside of her arm, beneath the cuff of her rolled-up sleeve.

Fists of anger and compassion squeezed around his

heart at the suffering she had endured. "Whatever happened to you, I won't—"

"Town's that way." She inclined her head to the left. "They've got a clinic." With the shotgun still aimed at him, she tossed that beautiful ponytail behind her back and retreated a step. "Maxie, heel."

The dog retreated with her and she closed the door in his face.

The decisive click of the dead bolt and the scrape of the chain locking him out sent the clear message that he wasn't finding refuge here.

When he didn't immediately leave, she shouted through the door. "I'll call the sheriff if you don't go."

Yes. Do that. The sheriff can help me. He needed to say the words, but his body was shutting down. His brain was refusing to work.

If he were one hundred percent, he could bust down the door and overpower the woman. But he was closer to ten percent, probably less than that, and the pellets from that shotgun would be embedded in his chest before he could even break through a window, much less get to her phone.

He turned, looking for the next option, but the forested mountainside swirled into a miasma of greens and grays. His knees buckled and the world faded away as he collapsed onto the porch.

Chapter Two

Ava cringed at the thud from the other side of the locked door. "Don't do that. Do not need my help."

She peeked through the window beside the door and saw dusty, grass-stained jeans and a broad back sprawled across the edge of her porch and top step. He looked different from this angle, unexpectedly vulnerable and deceptively harmless without the stern line of his bearded jaw and piercing silvery-green eyes. A bloodstained wad of material had fallen loose from beneath the shoulder seam of his missing sleeve. Trickles of blood mingled with lines and curves of an intricate tattoo adorning his upper arm and circling the firm muscles of his biceps and triceps. More blood seeped from a gash and goose egg above his left ear, soaking into the collar of his blue shirt. With trembling hands, Ava hugged the shotgun to her chest and pressed her back against the door, turning away from the man on her doorstep. "Oh, damn. He's really hurt."

Or was this a really convincing charade?

She'd fallen for that once before. And it had nearly cost her everything.

A blow to the head. Waking up blindfolded and cold. Strapped to a wooden chair that left splinters in her back and thighs because she was wearing nothing more than her bra and panties. But that discomfort was only the beginning of her pain.

Just as panicked thoughts clouded her vision, she felt a soft bump against her hip and a cold nose nuzzling her hand where she held the shotgun. Ava blinked away the traumatic memories that threatened to overwhelm her and looked down into the big white dog's steady black eyes. Ava dropped her hand from the butt of her shotgun to smooth her palm across Maxie's warm head and bury her fingers in the dog's thick white-and-black coat.

"Good girl, Maxie." Although she'd gotten the Great Pyrenees as a guard dog to give her advance warning of anyone coming within shouting distance of her isolated cabin, the gentle giant had turned out to be a natural therapy dog. More than keeping Ava company while she avoided the world that had nearly killed her, Maximillia Madrona Draconella Reine—named after the lead dragon character in the books she wrote, and answering to the more practical Maxie—had sensed, even as a puppy, when Ava's post-traumatic stress was kicking in and the waking nightmares were filling her head. The big, furry caretaker had learned to touch Ava, even crawl into bed and lie down beside her if necessary, to offer strength and comfort—a warm body to cling to and dark eyes or a gentle touch to focus on whenever the panic attacks threatened, or the flashbacks dragged her into the terrors from her past. With Maxie at her side, Ava had learned to handle the simple intricacies of human interaction again—when it was on her terms and in small, planned doses.

Surprise visits from dangerous-looking men who were bleeding on her front porch hadn't been checked off her list of encounters she was comfortable with yet. After the weekend two years earlier that had changed her face, her life and her ability to trust, she might never be comfortable with things she couldn't control.

Weekly check-ins with her online therapist assured her she was improving, that she was more than capable of returning to *normal*, given enough time. Dr. Foster had promised Ava that trusting her own instincts was the first step to learning to trust others again. She trusted Maxie. She trusted her therapist. She trusted her editor and agent in New York, so long as she didn't have to travel there to see them in person. She trusted that leaving Chicago and moving to her late grandparents' isolated cabin in the mountains near Pole Axe, Wyoming, where she'd spent the summers of her childhood was the right decision for her. Here she could find the space and healing surroundings she needed. She'd found comfort and security in the dog by her side. She'd found confidence in the weapons training and self-defense courses she'd taken. And with every cautious foray into town, she'd reconnected with old friends and was on her way to making new ones. Given enough time, she'd learn to interact with the real world as easily as she did the fictional world of fantasy creatures and noble quests that she wrote about. She hoped.

Ava concentrated on the soft texture of Maxie's fur beneath her fingers and inhaled deeply. She could do this. Here in Wyoming she was the anonymous Ava Wallace, big-city transplant turned small-town girl who'd inherited her grandparents' cabin. Despite her quiet, cautious life, she was accepted in Pole Axe because she was Jim and Myrna Wallace's granddaughter, not because she was A. L. Baines, the *New York Times* bestselling author who'd disappeared from the limelight at the peak of her success. Here, she wasn't the obsession of a depraved kidnapper. She could answer her front door to help a neighbor, or even a tall, desperate stranger with silvery-green eyes and intertwining tattoos she was far too curious to identify.

Every survival instinct that made her a well-armed recluse, who lived as far off the grid as her necessary links to technology allowed, warred with her innate compassion. She knew better than most what it was like to be desperately hurt and at the mercy of another. The old Ava wouldn't have hesitated. But caring had gotten her into trouble before. Compassion had nearly gotten her killed. She rubbed her cheek against the gun's cool steel barrel before clutching it in a firm grip once more. "Damn it, Maxie, we have to help him."

A soft, deep woof backed up her resolute vow to help the man outside.

"This better not be a trick." Ava unhooked the chain and dead bolt and opened the door, urging Maxie out ahead of her. Tucking the butt of the gun against her shoulder, she kept it aimed at the intruder's back as she crossed the wood planks of the porch. Although she wielded a gun instead of a bow and arrow, she could put on a tough-chick facade like Willow Storm, the heroine in her books. Ava nudged her toe against the man's boot, as far away from the blood and potentially grabbing hands as she could get. "Hey, mister? Are you dead?"

Right. Because he'd answer that question with a yes if he was. With no reply to either her voice or her boot, Ava exhaled a resolute breath and propped the shotgun just inside the door, beyond the man's reach if he came to. Maxie sat with curious eyes near the man's head, panting, as Ava knelt beside him and checked for hidden weapons and identification, a hard-earned skill she wished she'd known two years earlier.

Starting at his leather boots, she dipped her fingers inside. No hidden knife. She found an ankle holster with a short-nosed Springfield Armory pistol, which she removed. After discovering it was loaded, but that there was no bullet in the chamber, she tucked the weapon into the back of her jeans. Unless she squeezed the trigger, she knew the safety was engaged. Teaching literature and

composition at a small college in Chicago, and attending
Renaissance fairs and Comicons to get ideas to make up
spells and to portray her fictional costumes and weaponry
with accuracy in her books, she never would have expected
that she'd become an expert in modern guns, knives and
homemade torture devices. Her reaction to the stranger's
weapon was clinical—identify its potential threat, neu-
tralize it, move on to the next task. Allowing herself the
luxury of feeling shock or fear would only delay her reaction in ensuring her own safety. That sort of discipline had
been a hard lesson to learn. Now those routine assessments
were second nature to her. It was the only way she could
get through personal encounters anymore.

But there was something about running her hands along
the man's warm, muscular calves and thighs, then cupping
the back pockets of his jeans to find he carried no wallet with identification on him, which spoke to something
purely female and purposefully forgotten deep inside her.
Lord, she hadn't touched a man with anything other than a
handshake since... She squeezed her eyes shut as a phantom pain sliced across her cheek. "Damn it, Ava. Stay in
the moment."

Maxie moved to sit beside her, leaning against her and
nearly toppling her over. Ava laughed before the tears
could take hold and hugged her arms around her furry
caretaker's neck. "I'll be okay, girl. Come on. Let's turn
this guy over."

Not that she needed the help, but it reminded Ava she
wasn't truly alone when the big dog propped a paw on the
man's uninjured arm and seemed to pull him with Ava off
the top step until he lay flat on his back on the porch. Then
her curious dog lowered her head and sniffed the stranger,
nuzzling his neck with her cold, wet nose before slurp-
ing her tongue across his abraded jawline. "Maxie!" she
chided, nudging the dog back to a more sanitary distance.

But the raspy stroke of the dog's tongue roused the man a little. A deep-pitched moan vibrated in his throat and he repeated the last word he'd heard in a husky whisper. "Maxie…"

"Mister? Can you tell me your name?" It was then that she realized that her truck was the only vehicle parked in the driveway. Maxie hadn't alerted to a car driving up. The dog had heard his footsteps on the gravel and jumped up, barking an alarm while Ava pulled her shotgun from the gun safe. "How did you get here? How did you get hurt?"

It wasn't hard to assess his injuries from this angle. Blood in a beard that was longer than the hair on his head. Scrapes and bruises along almost every sharp angle of his face and body—knuckles, elbows, knees. He'd taken a bad fall—or several of them. The hole in his shoulder was from a bullet. She picked up the wad of sleeve material he'd torn from his shirt and gently wiped the blood from his arm, giving her a clearer look at the tattoo he bore. An eagle sitting atop a globe with an anchor behind it. The words *Semper Fi* and numbers she assumed were a significant date circled the hollow of sinewed skin beneath the jut of his shoulder muscle. Muscles. Lots of muscles. He was big and built like a prizefighter…or a medieval swordsman. This man had been trained for battle. Despite her own self-defense instruction, if this guy were more cognizant, he'd easily be able to overpower her.

Just imagining the possibility of their positions being reversed, with her at his mercy and him armed and towering over her, sent a chill rippling down her spine. She rocked back onto her heels, needing to put some distance between them and get her head right again. "Come on, Ava. You've got Willow Storm's spirit running through your veins. You can handle this."

"Willow Storm—" he echoed, never opening his eyes "—can handle anything."

"What?" He wasn't exactly parroting her words this time, but he wasn't making sense, either. Ava squeezed the man's chin, carefully avoiding the scrape there, and turned his undeniably masculine face to hers. "Are you awake or not? Sergeant? Lieutenant?"

Mr. Dying on Her Front Doorstep.

She couldn't let that happen.

"Need medic…call team for extraction…"

"Extraction?" Oh, wow, was this guy out of it. "You have a team around here?" Of course not. Even if he were part of a National Guard unit starting their weekend drill, they wouldn't be on maneuvers in blue jeans and dress shirts. Would they? And though neatly trimmed, that beard would be the first thing to go, right? This man was alone, and he was in trouble. She'd been too suspicious to believe his plea for help. Now she hoped she hadn't waited too long to act.

Ava tossed the soiled cloth to the ground and uncurled her legs to dash inside the cabin to retrieve clean towels and a first-aid kit. When she returned and knelt beside him again, she could see that the wound had reopened without the cotton material he'd packed it with if, indeed, it had ever stopped bleeding. And that puffy bruise and split in his scalp above his ear, along with the various scrapes she spotted on his hands, arms, face and through a tear in the knee of his jeans, indicated he'd been in an accident and had lost enough blood to pass out. Unless floating in and out of consciousness had something to do with the wound on his head?

She folded a towel and pressed it against the wound in his shoulder. He caught his bottom lip between his teeth and moaned at the pressure, the only signs that he was aware of her ministrations as she unrolled a ribbon of gauze and lifted his arm to tie the towel into place. Then she bent his arm and fitted him with a sling made from a dish towel. Since she hadn't seen an exit wound, that meant the bullet was probably still in him. She needed to immobilize the injury as best she could to prevent the projectile from traveling through his body.

By the time she was done, he was breathing more deeply. That was a good sign, right? But he still wasn't opening his eyes and responding to her in any way that indicated he was aware of his surroundings and what she was doing.

Ava gently dabbed at the wound in his scalp, relieved to see that there was no blood coming from his ear, a sign of a skull fracture. She wasn't a doctor, but she'd had basic first-aid training, had endured numerous injuries of her own and was highly suspicious of a concussion. Instead of applying any more pressure to the swelling, she lightly covered it with a gauze pad and activated a chemical ice pack that she placed against the injury, loosely wrapping a towel around his head to keep it in place.

"Come on, mister. I need you to wake up and tell me your name." A cursory search of the pockets of his shirt and the front of his jeans revealed the only clue she had to the man's identity. He had no cell phone with a list of contacts or screen name, but she pulled a ring of keys from his jeans and found a stainless-steel key ring with the same Marine Corps emblem and the initials *L.B.* etched into the polished surface. "L.B.," she read aloud. "L.B.? Hey, L.B.?" she called to him. But clearly it wasn't a nickname he answered to. "Open your eyes, Sergeant? Colonel?" She had no clue what rank a man who appeared to be in his late thirties or early forties would be. But the fact he was military explained the gun and the buzz cut of hair, the mumblings about an extraction team and his ability to hike to her place from wherever the shooting event had occurred. With the mountain and trees reflecting sound for miles, she would have heard shots fired if they'd been anywhere close to her cabin. How much ground had this guy covered?

"Listen up, Marine." She tried another tactic to get a lucid response. "I need your name, rank and serial number." That didn't work, either. She exhaled a frustrated breath, studying the key chain for some other clue that refused to reveal itself before stuffing it back into his pocket. "With my luck, you're probably some Larkin Bonecrusher wannabe."

He moaned again. "Bonecrusher…"

"I need you to do more than repeat everything I say."

Was that a nod? The slight movement of his head could have been something else, but there was no mistaking the lines deepening beside his eyes as he squeezed them tight against a new wave of pain. *"The Bonecrusher Chronicles,"* he spat out, fighting to articulate every syllable. "Good books…"

"You've read my books? *Those* books?" she hastily corrected.

He was finally communicating in a way that made sense, and it was on the one topic she didn't dare talk about.

But even with an addled brain, he hadn't missed the slip she'd made. "You? You write Bonecrusher…? Sweet. When's the next book…? Why so long…?"

She went back to work, finding scissors in the first-aid kit and cutting away the denim around the cut on his knee and cleaning it. "That's right. You think I'm the lady who writes the books. You found me. It's been two years since the last release and it ended on a cliffhanger between the rebels and the Fey alliance. You want Larkin and Willow to have sex. You want Maximillia to find a mate, so the dragon line continues. You want me to kill off Lord Zeville because nobody likes the new villain." Ava worked in sharp, sure strokes as sarcasm leaked into her tone. About the same time she realized he would need stitches in his leg and regretted her less than gentle touch, she realized that the man's eyes had opened in slits, and he was watching her. Lousy timing. Of course, he'd focus in at just the time she was revealing more than she should. Ava ignored his assessing study of her and concentrated on bandaging the cut. "I can't make any of that happen for you. You've wasted your time coming out here. You've got the wrong woman."

"Good books. Buddy put me on to them…last deployment… Willow's hot… Series got me through rehab… Wait." His eyes opened wide and he pushed himself up. "*You* write the books?" But he'd sat up too fast. The color quickly drained from his face. His arms buckled and he swayed.

"Whoa, mister." Ava moved quickly to slide her arms beneath him and catch his shoulders before he struck his head again. "Easy." His head rolled onto her shoulder and his nose nuzzled her neck beneath the collar of her shirt. Suddenly, she had a lapful of man collapsed against her.

One thousand one. One thousand two. One thousand three. Why wasn't she pushing him away?

He was heavier than Maxie's cuddles, but the contact was completely different from the dog's soothing comfort. The shoulder-to-chest contact and scrape of his beard against her neck and collarbone wasn't soothing, but it wasn't completely horrible, either. The urge to shove aside his unexpected touch didn't immediately spike through her, and that should have alarmed her. He smelled of musk and heat from his ordeal, and of something spicy and uniquely male as his short, spiky hair tickled the underside of her jaw. Deployment? Rehab? She smoothed a comforting hand across his clammy forehead and savored the unfamiliar assault on her senses. "What am I going to do with you?"

What *should* she do? Call the sheriff's office? Sheriff Brandon Stout had been one of her childhood friends, a local boy who'd grown up in the area. They'd reconnected every summer when she'd visited, maturing from kids to teenagers. Brandon had been her first kiss during that last summer before she headed off to college at Northwestern. Even then, she'd sensed he'd wanted something more from her, but she had college degrees to earn and had wanted to travel the world and extend her adventures beyond the realm of Wyoming's Wind River Mountains and the Chicago suburbs. She'd made it to forty-two states, ten countries and even the fictional world of Stormhaven before the night she'd been taken from the parking lot outside her campus office and everything had changed. Now she was back in Wyoming, and she knew Brandon would be more than happy if she called and asked him to do her the favor of removing this man from her property.

But she didn't want Brandon to think she wanted something more. She didn't want him to think he was welcome to drop by whenever he wanted. He'd see a phone call from her as an invitation to take their relationship to the next level—to be something more than a friend to her. She needed a friend far more than she needed *something more*. And what she desired more than anything was to be left alone.

Because she couldn't make a mistake then. She couldn't be hurt.

Should she call the volunteer fire department? They'd descend en masse from all corners of the county. She hated crowds of people—there were too many possible threats to keep an eye on.

Maybe she could tell this man to take a hike. Keep the towels, bandages and ice pack. But he was in no shape to send him on his way by himself. And as damaged as she was inside, life had made her fearful, not cruel. She couldn't send an injured man out into the woods on his own to possibly die.

As always, she looked to the clarity and reassurance of the dark, soulful eyes she trusted more than any other. "Maxie, girl—you know what we have to do." The dog tilted her head in that responsive way that made Ava imagine the dog understood what she was saying to her.

She'd already made her scheduled trip into town.

But the thought of this man dying in her arms was even less appealing than facing the friendly people of Pole Axe for a second time this week.

So she scooted out from beneath the man's weight and laid him on the porch before gathering the first-aid supplies and climbing to her feet.

The last thing she needed was an entire platoon of weekend warriors here, looking for their missing buddy—or the sheriff's department and state police swarming the area for a crime scene and asking her questions about a gunshot victim.

Dumping the first-aid supplies and soiled bandages in the kitchen, she pulled a spare blanket from the linen closet, looped the long strap of her bag with her keys and wallet over her neck and shoulder, grabbed the shotgun from inside the door and locked the cabin.

"Maxie? Let's go, girl. Up." Ava marched to her truck and opened the door for the big dog to jump up onto the bench seat. Then she secured the gun in the rack in the back window and turned to find her mystery man had pulled himself up to a sitting position and was leaning heavily against one of the giant ceramic flowerpots at the edge of the porch.

"Maxie's ze dragon in your books…" His eyes were open in slits against the afternoon sun as he nodded toward the dog. "Better 'n a tank for backup…"

Ava hurried back to kneel on the stair in front of him,

checking the bandages to make sure they were still in place. "She's not a dragon. That's my dog, Maxie."

"Maximillia Madrona Draconella Reine. Queen Mother of the Dragons."

Yep. He'd read the books, all right. "Come on, Larkin. Can you stand if I help you?"

"I want a pet dragon." He straightened as she sat beside him and draped his uninjured arm over her shoulders, holding tight to his hand and circling her other arm around his waist.

Ava grunted as she pushed to her feet, pulling him up with her. "Maximillia's not a pet. She's a comrade in arms. Part of the team."

He leaned his hip against the railing, gritting his teeth and breathing through his obvious pain. "Dog or the dragon…?"

The man couldn't remember his name. Why couldn't he forget her alter ego?

"Lean on me," she ordered, bracing her legs to take his full weight. "We're going to walk over to my truck, okay?"

He nodded and dropped his foot onto the next step with her before sitting back against the railing. "Where's the rest of my team? Did they make it back to the base?"

Ava tugged at his waist, hooking her fingers around his belt to keep him upright and moving with her. She couldn't be rescuing a welterweight? Still, while she wasn't exactly an Amazon, she wasn't a petite woman, either. And ever since the assault, she'd worked hard to get herself into fighting shape and stay that way. She could do this. With a little coaxing. "Right now, I'm your team. But you're too big for me to carry, and I don't want to drag you, in case it reopens your shoulder wound."

"Willow, Larkin and Maxie, off on a quest. Jus' like the books." She felt his chest expand against her and his grip tighten on her shoulder as he steeled himself against the pain and dizziness. She had to admire his sheer will and determination as he made it down the stairs and around to the passenger side of the truck with her. "You got a wizard and a thief hidden somewhere? Didn't know I'd stumbled into Stormhaven."

Shaking her head at his refusal to let the story elements of her books go, she propped him against the truck while she opened the door. "You're delirious."

Shielding his head, she got him inside the truck and covered him with the blanket. Ava jogged around the hood and climbed in behind the wheel to start the engine, secure in the knowledge that ninety-five pounds of Great Pyrenees sat between her and the man who had closed his eyes and leaned back against the corner of the seat. She pressed on the accelerator, speeding down the drive as fast as she dared on the gravel.

She turned onto the asphalt road that led past a line of summer homes and rental cabins nestled in the trees against the side of the mountain. Since they were all currently occupied, the fact that he hadn't stumbled onto one of their front porches meant he had come through the wilderness, not from the direction of civilization or even the main highway. But there was nothing in that direction for miles. He certainly wasn't dressed for mountain climbing. Even the dress shirt and what had once been nice jeans weren't what people wore to go hiking unless they were novices. And she had a feeling, judging by that fit, muscular body and those silvery-green eyes that saw more than someone who was dazed and confused should, that this guy wasn't a novice at much of anything.

But he was awfully quiet. Maybe she'd better keep him talking until she got to the clinic and handed him off to the emergency staff. "Hey, mister. You awake over there?"

He was awake.

When she reached the two-lane highway that would

take them down the mountain into Pole Axe, she stopped for a black SUV that was moving at a touristy pace up the mountain toward a scenic overlook above the next ridge. The man flinched, groaning at the sudden movement, and hunkered down beneath the blanket.

"Why did you do that?" Ava turned left and followed the blacktop that hugged the curves of the granite slopes, anxious to get the man to the hospital and relieve her conscience of the burden of caring for him. It took him a couple of minutes to sit up straight and lean back against the headrest again.

"I'm not sure." His slitted eyes were studying the sideview mirror. Ava glanced in the rearview mirror and watched the black vehicle disappear around the bend in the road before he continued. "Something about a black SUV. I wrecked my car."

That explained the blow to the head. Possibly the other cuts and scrapes, depending on how the accident happened. "How do you explain the bullet wound?"

His chin dropped to his chest and he studied the sling and bandage she'd rigged, as if remembering the injury for the first time. "You patched me up?"

She nodded. "You didn't leave me much choice. I couldn't have you dying on my front porch. I'm driving you into town to the emergency clinic. It's a satellite facility from St. John's Health in Jackson."

"Wyoming?"

Poor man. He wasn't even sure of that much? "Yes. I'm driving you down to Pole Axe. We're south of Jackson Hole and Grand Teton and Yellowstone National Parks, if that helps."

"Pole Axe," he repeated. "Sounds like a thriving metropolis. I think I'm a long way from where I started this morning."

Was that a clue? Was he recalling his home? "Where

did you start this morning?" she asked, slowing to take the next curve. His legs straightened and his right arm shot out, bracing against the dashboard. Odd. "Are you getting carsick?"

Instead of answering, he pulled his limbs back, as though he, too, questioned the instinctive reaction. "I checked out of a hotel room and went to work. Bad day to go."

Although some of the color had returned to his rugged features, he still wasn't making sense. "What hotel? One of the lodges around here? Sounds like you travel for work. Did you drive? Fly into Jackson?"

He considered her questions, although his tight expression made her wonder if concentrating on his missing memories was hurting him. He put a hand on Maxie's back, using the dog's strength to push himself upright and turn toward Ava. She wondered what those eyes looked like when they weren't narrowed in pain and confusion. "Can you tell me my name?"

"I never met you before today."

"You called me Larkin Bonecrusher. That's a fictional name. Why Larkin?"

"Because you're a big bruiser like he is? A warrior? You have an L.B. engraved on your key chain. No wallet or ID on you. Not even a phone. If we were in Chicago, I would think you'd been mugged. I needed to call you something besides 'mister.'"

He released the dog and sank back against the seat. "Larkin's cool. Got started on those books on my last deployment. Until everything went FUBAR."

Ava frowned at the acronym. "What does FUBAR mean?"

He started to answer, then snapped his mouth shut. "Fouled Up Beyond Any Recognition, Repair or Recall is the polite way to explain it. Suicide bomber made it through a checkpoint. I lost a team of MPs. Busted up my leg. Got sent stateside."

At least some of his ramblings were starting to make sense. "I can tell you're a Marine. Your tattoo and the *Semper Fi* say as much. Are you a veteran? On leave? Do you know where you're stationed?" No answer. "You went to work this morning. Was it a military base? The Air Force is the only branch I know of with a base in Wyoming."

"How did a Marine wind up in the middle of Nowhere, Wyoming?"

Since she had no answer for him, she kept pushing for something to click into place inside his head. "So, you went to work this morning, and everything went FUBAR."

He chuckled, a soft, husky sound that skittered across her eardrums. "You pick up the lingo fast. I'm guessing with these injuries that's pretty accurate."

"Do you answer to Colonel? Gunny?" No response. "General?"

"I wish." There was one fact he knew. He wasn't a general. "Captain. I remember someone calling me that. I'm a captain…" His chin sagged to his chest before he raised it again. "I'm out of the Corps now," he said with a degree of certainty. "My injuries—the leg pain is chronic." He stroked Maxie's fur, as though he found the same calming comfort from the dog as she did. "But I talked to a buddy of mine yesterday who's still in."

"That's great." Ava seized on the flash of memory. "What's his name?"

He swore. "I can't even tell you what we talked about."

"It's okay. You'll figure it out."

"I'm a damn invalid. And I don't like it." He curled his hand into a fist and thumped it against the door, startling Ava and eliciting an alarmed woof from Maxie. "Sorry, girl." He stroked the dog before sinking back into his seat. "I hate being at such a disadvantage."

Ava shrugged, feeling the tension in the truck. Logically, she knew none of his anger was directed at her. But still, she knew enough about violence that seeing others express it could sometimes trigger one of those dreaded flashbacks. Automatically, she reached for Maxie and stroked her fingers through her long hair. The big dog switched allegiances, and they both relished the familiar contact. "I already know more about you than I did twenty minutes ago, Larkin. You're a veteran Marine. You probably haven't been out for too long, judging by that haircut and the fact that you talked to a friend who's still on active duty."

"You called me Larkin again. I like it. It feels familiar." When he inhaled a deep breath to force some of the tension out of him, Ava found herself relaxing a fraction, as well. "I know *The Bonecrusher Chronicles* are fiction, but those are details I can remember. There's a little bit of comfort in knowing my brain isn't complete gelatin." Twisting his body again, he reached over to brush his fingers over the scar on the back of her hand where it still rested on Maxie's back. *One thousand one...*

Oh, hell, no. Ava flinched away and squeezed her grip back around the steering wheel. Even though she'd developed a rule of three with her therapist—allowing someone to touch her for three seconds instead of jumping at even accidental contact—she was already over her quota of human contact today. She couldn't help it. Getting touched without knowing its intent was still a hot button for her.

"Larkin" splayed his fingers apart in a silent apology and pulled away, letting his hand settle into Maxie's fur instead. He scrubbed his knuckles around the dog's ear and beneath her chin, and the big dog leaned into that caress, as well. Maxie seemed to have her own rule of three, four, five, ten—*however long you want to pet me*—where this man was concerned.

Traitor. You're my therapy dog. Not his.

"Sorry," the man apologized. "Didn't mean to startle you. I can see where you get some of your inspiration. Your scars remind me of Willow. She's freakin' hot."

"Scars are not hot."

"She can kick butt. She's royalty, but not a girlie-girl princess. Real woman."

Willow Storm was another member of the Bonecrusher Brigade who used sorcery, swordplay and a team of allies to defeat their enemies and complete their quests. "I'm nothing like her. She's brave and beautiful."

"So are you." If he was waiting for a thank-you for a compliment she didn't believe in, he'd be waiting a long time. He pulled his hand away from Maxie and leaned back against the seat, his eyes drifting shut again. "Glad you didn't shoot me."

"It creates too much paperwork when that happens. Brings too many cops to my front door."

Without opening his eyes, he arched a golden eyebrow and hooked up one corner of his mouth. At least his temporary amnesia didn't impact his ability to understand her sarcasm. "Is that why you're driving me to town instead of calling 9-1-1? You don't like people in uniform? Or is it company, in general, you have an aversion to?"

They passed the road sign indicating they were within a few miles of their destination. Ignoring his probing questions, Ava tried one more time to help jog his memory. "*The Bonecrusher Chronicles* are fantasy stories. I need you to come back to reality and tell me your name. Why someone shot you. A coworker's name. Anything."

They passed another mile marker before he answered. "I don't remember."

"How did you get to my cabin?"

"Followed the road."

"From where?"

His growing agitation evident in the drumming of his fingers on the armrest, he sat up straighter. "I don't remember."

"Who shot you?"

Whatever amusement he'd enjoyed a moment earlier had faded. "I don't remember." She jumped when he snapped his fingers. "I took Option B."

"Option B? What does that mean?"

"A bullet to the head or rolling off the edge of the cliff. I remember that much. Someone was trying to kill me. I chose Option B."

Rolling off the edge of a cliff? On purpose?

"I'm driving you to the hospital—the clinic we have in Pole Axe. They can do more for you than the first aid I gave you. You've lost a lot of blood. And I'm worried about that head wound. It's probably why you can't recall details. Once the swelling goes down, I'm sure you'll remember everything you need to. Then you can call someone. A friend. Your wife."

He studied his left hand where it hung from the edge of the sling. "No wife." He propped up his wrist and twiddled his fingers in the air, explaining his certainty. "No ring. Not even a tan line where I used to wear one."

"That's hardly definitive proof."

He unhooked his broken utility watch, revealing a distinct pale line on his forearm. "Look at me. I spend a lot of time outdoors." He tucked the watch into his shirt pocket. "Nope. No little woman at home waiting for me."

"Not if you call her the *little woman*."

He chuckled. "I suppose not." His eyes narrowed to slits again. "You're really A. L. Baines? Don't think I didn't catch that slip you made earlier. That's why you chose Larkin instead of Larry or Lance or any other name you could have guessed for me. I've read all your books. You're good."

Yeah. She wrote the *New York Times* bestselling fantasy series.

She was A. L. Baines.

At least, that was the name millions of readers around the world knew her by.

"Baines" came from the Latin root for *bones*, the star of her books. Although the initials had originally been an homage to her parents, Alice and Leo, they had come to represent so much more. A.L. *Ava. Lives.* Despite one very sick bastard's attempt to keep that from happening. No one knew her by her pen name here in Wyoming.

"As far as anyone around here knows, I'm Ava Wallace. That's my real name. If you don't remember anything else about today, remember that."

"Yes, ma'am. Ava Wallace. Keeping secrets." He seemed to be drifting off again. "You should be proud of those books."

"I am. But I also need my anonymity."

"Why?"

Too many questions. Ava shook her head. "I liked you better unconscious."

"You're funny. A little prickly. But funny." His chest expanded with a deep breath and he sank farther into the seat. "Why are we keeping secrets?"

Survival. Hopefully, if he let anything slip, the clinic staff and anyone else they ran into in town would dismiss it as the ramblings of a man with a head injury. "Once you tell me your secrets, then I'll tell you why I need to be Ava Wallace."

"*Need* to be. Interesting choice of words. Deal." Not really. She intended to be long gone and out of his life by the time he remembered anything.

He drifted off again. But he was smiling. It softened his hard, masculine features and made him almost handsome. Annoyingly so because she didn't want to be attracted to a man again. Ever. She certainly didn't want one interested in her.

"Eyes on the road, Willow."

She snapped her gaze back to the windshield. "Ava."

"If I'm Larkin, you're Willow. Dog's the dragon."

"Fine. Go with that when you get to the hospital. They'll call in a psychiatrist." Thankfully, they'd reached the city limit sign with the whopping population of 103, a number that could multiply ten times during tourist season. She slowed her speed to drive the main drag to the clinic on the far side of Pole Axe. "And if you're going to look at me, would you open up your eyes so I know when you're doing it? That whole slitty-eyed stare is a little unnerving."

"Light hurts my eyes." The lone stoplight changed to red and she stomped on the brake. They both jerked against their seat belts and he moaned in pain. "That hurts, too."

"Sorry. I don't mean to hurt you. I…" *Have issues.* Maybe even more than this man who was in such obvious pain and suffering from partial amnesia.

"This is Pole Axe, hmm?"

Thankfully, he hadn't asked her to finish that last sentence. "Just another three blocks and I'll have you at the clinic. I know the doctor there. He'll take good care of you."

"You've taken good care of me, Ava. Despite our rocky introduction. And I'm grateful."

"I hope you'll be okay."

"I hope you will, too. I'm looking at you now, by the way." She glanced across the seat and caught him grinning, despite the effort he was making to keep his eyes open and readable for her. But the grin disappeared as the light changed and she drove through the intersection. "Whatever secrets are haunting those beautiful blue eyes— I hope you'll be okay, too."

Chapter Three

Ava sat in her truck in the farthest corner of the clinic parking lot, playing the voice mail one more time.

"Hey, Ms. Wallace. Detective Charles, Chicago PD, here. Hope you're doing well."

Gabriel Charles had been the first detective on the scene after she'd stumbled into a local trucking office in the warehouse district where she'd been held, and collapsed after her three-day ordeal. He was still the only man she trusted enough on the force to maintain this regular contact with once or twice a month since moving to Wyoming. The man with the gold studs in each earlobe had been supportive and dedicated yet frustrated with her inability to identify the man who'd taken her. She knew her attacker's voice, his general build and the feel of his hands on her body. With her research into weaponry for her books, she'd been able to give Detective Charles a pretty good idea of the different knives he'd used on her. She knew her kidnapper's smell, a pungent blend of garlic, grease and sweat. But she'd never seen his face.

"Sadly, I have to report that there was another abduction earlier this month. This guy's been like clockwork these past five years. Including you, he's taken someone every summer. Makes me wonder if he's transient like a truck driver. Or a tourist who comes to the city to visit fam-

ily or see the sights. I'm sorry to share bad news, but you asked me to keep you in the loop. We found the woman..."

Even hearing it for the third time, when the detective hesitated, her stomach cramped with dread.

"She'd expired. Excessive blood loss. The ME said one of the stab wounds nicked her heart."

Ava shook her head, her fingers buried deep in Maxie's fur. Even if her grip pinched, the dog didn't shy away from her post. "He's not sloppy like that." It would end the torture too quickly. And for the man who had kidnapped her, it had been all about the torture and the sick release he got from making his victim suffer, not killing her. Even now she could hear the moans of satisfaction he got each time the blade had pierced her skin. "She must have gotten her blindfold off. Seen his face."

Or it could be a copycat killer. But she doubted Detective Charles would call if he suspected that was the case.

"The MO matches yours and last year's abduction," the detective's message continued. *"I've got a couple of forensic leads I'm following up on. You're still my best witness. Hell, you're my only witness who's been willing to stay in touch. When we catch him, we'll need you to come back to Chicago and ID him."*

When, not if. Detective Charles was always positive that CPD would make an arrest. Or maybe that was the party line to keep survivors like her from giving up hope that they could one day stop greeting visitors with a shotgun and start leading a normal life again.

"As always, if you think of anything else that might help our investigation, give me a call. We'll catch this guy. I promise. Meanwhile, you take care and stay safe—"

Ava screamed at the sharp rap at her window and Maxie jumped up. The dog stepped right onto Ava's lap and barked at the man in the white lab coat. When she recognized Kent Russell, the lone doctor who was working the clinic this weekend, she ordered Maxie back to a sit and rolled down the window. "Sorry about that." She punched off her phone and held it up to explain her reaction. "I was listening to messages. Are you ready for me?"

A toothy smile appeared in the middle of the doctor's curly, salt-and-pepper beard and he lowered the hands he'd raised in apology. "I'm the one who's sorry for startling you. I appreciate you waiting around until we could talk."

Ava breathed deeply, slowing the rapid thumping of her heart against her ribs, before nodding. "I take it 'Larkin' survived?"

The doctor stepped back onto the curb and waited by the landscaping of granite boulders and pine trees that framed the multiuse lot that also served a dentist's office, a chiropractor and an optometry shop in addition to the clinic. "That's one of the things we need to talk about. He's answering to it, but that can't really be his name, is it?"

Ava avoided making any mention of her books and shrugged. "It's a nickname, I guess. I take it he's still a little addled in the head?"

"You could say that. I want to keep him overnight for observation. But he's fighting me on it. Don't know if he's afraid of the cost or getting another shot. Some men can't handle the needles."

Ava tried to picture Larkin backing down from any threat, even one as small as a syringe. "He seems pretty tough to me."

"Sometimes, the tough guys are the biggest babies." Uh, no. She definitely couldn't see the man on her front porch being compared to a baby.

Dr. Russell opened the front of his white lab coat and pulled the pager from the belt of his jeans. He read whatever the message said and tucked it back onto his belt. The Pole Axe clinic couldn't exactly afford cutting-edge technology, so she didn't question his use of a pager. She'd missed Detective Charles's call because there'd been no cell-phone reception inside the hospital itself. Better reception was the excuse she told herself for moving her truck so far from the clinic's sliding front doors. Other people would understand that reason over her desire to hide the fact that Ava Wallace had come to town.

"Physically, your friend only needed outpatient surgery. I removed the bullet and stitched up his shoulder and scalp. Gave him a shot of tetanus and antibiotics, an analgesic for the pain and a blood transfusion. We'd be life-flighting him to Jackson if you hadn't stepped in to stop the bleeding and get him here when you did."

"Thank goodness for my first-aid training."

Dr. Russell scoffed. "You patched him up like a field medic." Coming from a former Army doctor, she supposed that was high praise. "Kept him from going into shock. Probably saved his life."

Ava summoned a smile. The men at that trucking center two years ago had done the same for her before the ambulance and police had arrived. "I'm glad I could help."

"My nurse is moving him to a curtained-off section of the waiting room until we can get a room fixed up for him. Frankly, I'm more worried about the less obvious injuries. X-rays didn't show a skull fracture, but he really needs someone to keep an eye on him the next twenty-four to forty-eight hours. Wish I knew who to call, in case somebody's worried about him."

Kent Russell didn't know her history or her pen name. But as Pole Axe's only full-time doctor, he knew she'd been the victim of an attack before moving to Wyoming. Although she'd started the long healing process with doctors in Chicago, she'd transferred the final stages of reconstructive and cosmetic surgeries to the hospital in Jackson. Dr. Russell had been tasked with changing her bandages and inspecting skin grafts and the newer, less obvious scars for signs of infection as she healed from the procedures.

Ava shrugged. "I'm not sure what else I can tell you. He seems to recall more distant memories, actions rather than names and places. He doesn't remember much about yesterday or today. That will all come back to him, won't it?"

"Possibly. Right now, his brain is like Swiss cheese. He can tell me he's a Marine Corps brat who moved around a lot as a kid, could name bases where they lived, but he doesn't know his parents' names or even if they're still alive." His gaze swept the parking lot beyond her truck before coming back to her. "Could we finish this conversation inside?"

"Sounds like you've already found out more about him than I did." Ava tunneled her fingers beneath the dog's collar. "I need to get Maxie home to exercise her."

And she needed some time alone in the great outdoors to decompress from all the violence and mystery and maleness that had intruded on her life that afternoon.

Another thing she appreciated about Dr. Russell was that he didn't mince words—not about her medical visits, and not about today's events. "Ava. It's a gunshot wound. I had to report it. Sheriff Stout was delayed at the scene of an accident, but I just got word that he's on his way. I don't think you want to have that conversation out here in public. I know how you feel about town gossip. Not that I blame you. If one more of those old biddies tries to set me up with her daughter…"

Ava didn't hear the end of his complaint. She was focusing in the rearview mirror at periodic traffic moving slowly along the main drag, the tourists strolling along the sidewalk window-shopping and the locals who were heading into town for drinks at one of the two bars or dinner at the barbecue joint on Main Street. No sign of Brandon Stout and his official black-and-white SUV. Yet. She needed time to prepare for this meeting. She didn't do well with surprises to begin with, and she'd had far too many unexpected encounters already today.

"Bring the mutt in with you." Dr. Russell brushed his fingers against her arm, quickly pulling away as soon as he had her attention. "I know she's your security blanket. You ought to get a therapy dog vest for Maxie, so no one questions why she's with you 24/7. She's well-trained. Probably wouldn't have any trouble getting certified."

Compliments about Maxie usually made her smile. But she was in more of a panic when she swung her gaze back to Kent's. "You called Brandon?"

Not wasting time on an apology, Dr. Russell continued. "I know you two have history. But he's going to have questions for both of us, and I don't want to report to Stout's office any more than you do. Larkin's not my only patient. It's after-hours and I don't have anyone watching the front desk." He tapped the pager on his belt. "Mr. Garcia's already coded once. I need to stay close by until we can get him stabilized enough to move him to Jackson."

Shaking her head at the inevitability of the reunion vibe Brandon attached to any conversation with her, Ava hooked Maxie's leash to her collar and climbed out of the truck with the dog heeling beside her. Ultimately, she wasn't going to let her trust issues and need for isolation jeopardize someone else's life. Together, they strolled across the nearly empty parking lot. "I'm sorry to hear about Mr. Garcia. He was a friend of my grandfather's. Will he be all right?"

"For an eighty-eight-year-old man, he's holding his own." He opened the automatic door and stood back for Ava to enter the clinic's waiting area ahead of him. "Your friend Larkin has been asking about you."

"He's not my friend."

The doctor chuckled behind her. "Tell *him* that."

Ava tightened her grip on the leash and let Kent pass her to the reception counter. "Has he been…talking about me?" Larkin wouldn't have bragged about meeting her alter ego, would he? She'd made it clear how much she relished her privacy.

Dr. Russell picked up a laptop from the counter and typed in some tidbit of information. "Are you kidding? First, he wanted to know if you've ever shot at someone with that gun of yours. Then he went on about how lucky he was to faint on the right front porch, since you had the knowledge and means to patch him up." He arched an eyebrow and grinned. "He also wanted to know if you were seeing anyone."

"I'm not."

"I suspected as much. But as your local physician, I told him I couldn't reveal that kind of information."

"Thank you."

"I numbed the areas where I gave him stitches. I couldn't risk a normal sedative with that head injury. Although he's physically fit, he's pushed his body to the limit." He inclined his head as the nurse pushed a wheelchair with the very patient they'd been discussing down the hallway. "He'll be out of it for a while. I want to put him to bed and keep him under observation for at least twenty-four, preferably forty-eight, hours."

Larkin's chin rested against his chest and his eyes were closed. Or maybe he was doing that squint thing again, where it looked like he was asleep, but in reality he was aware of everything and everyone around him. At least his color was better—a healthy tan instead of that blotchy pallor he'd had when he'd been sliding in and out of consciousness. There was a neat white bandage over the gash in his scalp, and they'd changed him from his torn, bloody shirt into a hospital gown with a blanket draped across his lap. The sling that cradled his left arm rested on a plastic bag that held his scuffed boots, socks and folded-up jeans.

Despite her resolve not to have any interest in the enigmatic stranger, Ava's brain couldn't help but note three things. The angles of his rugged face were even more compelling without the blood streaming down the side of his head and matting in his golden beard. His shoulders stretched the thin cotton of the hospital gown to the point it could barely tie behind his neck. And what was he wearing underneath that blanket if he was barefoot and holding his pants? Her palms itched where she clutched Maxie's leash as they remembered how she'd clinically molded her hands over his legs and buttocks when she'd been tending his wounds and searching for ID.

Her observations seemed to heat her blood, making her feel far too aware of the scars marking her face and body, and the emotional inadequacies that were even more crippling. What she might once have embraced as a healthy interest in the opposite sex, the frissons of lusty awareness that bubbled through her veins and fed her imagination with possibilities now made her self-conscious. She twisted her fingers into her ponytail and pulled it over her shoulder, instinctively hiding the most noticeable mark that branded her as a victim—that told the world she was *less*.

Her eyes went out of focus as she dropped her gaze to the clinic's vinyl floor. This was wrong. Being attracted to any man was wrong. Her therapist had said if the right man came along, one day she'd be able to move past her trust issues and form a healthy relationship. But she couldn't trust a man she'd just met. And there was nothing *right* about this Larkin Bonecrusher in the flesh. She only felt this pull toward him because he was hurt, and he'd needed her. The scars and the hang-ups and the big white dog plastered to her side hadn't mattered when he'd collapsed into her lap and huddled against her. She'd been strong enough to be his match in his time of need. She'd been whole enough that he hadn't looked at her with pity or awkward politeness or even fear. He'd simply needed her to be there for him. And no man—no one—had needed her for a very long time. It felt almost…normal. But *normal* was a scary possibility for her. *Normal* had left her life the night she'd stopped to help another stranger.

At least Larkin, as she was coming to think of him, wasn't afraid to show her his face or let her look him in the eye when she demanded it. And it was such an interesting face…

"No." Ava muttered the admonition, needing to focus on what was important here.

"No?" Kent Russell frowned, looking up from his laptop, not understanding the directive was aimed at herself.

Ava snuffed out that flare of awareness buzzing through her veins and tilted her chin back to Dr. Russell. "Sorry. I had something else on my mind. You do good work, Doctor. He looks a lot better."

"I promise you won't have to be here much longer. I waited until the sheriff called to say he was on his way before I went out to get you." The nurse wheeled Larkin beside a gurney that was already enclosed on two sides by curtains. As the nurse moved the bag from Larkin's lap to the foot of the bed, Dr. Russell tapped something else onto his laptop and then closed it. "If you'll excuse me a minute."

He strode across the waiting area to where the nurse was setting the brakes on the wheelchair and moved in beside Larkin to help him stand. Ava glanced away as the blanket fell to the floor, revealing far more tanned skin down the back of the hospital gown than she was certain Larkin—or anyone—would want to show the world. As the nurse hastily scooped up the blanket and wound it around Larkin's waist, Ava found herself glancing back with a naughty fascination and spotting the distinct line where the tan ended, and a curve of much lighter skin peeked into view.

Feeling the heat creeping up her neck, Ava turned to face the opposite wall. What was wrong with her? True, she hadn't seen a man's seminaked body in several years, but she wasn't a virgin, either. The only man she lusted after these days was the title character of her books. And although they'd shared a few dramatic, life-celebrating kisses, Larkin and Willow had yet to consummate the frustrated desire simmering between them. Ava couldn't bring herself to write that scene. The idea of sex had been perverted by the kidnapper who'd used his power over her to satisfy his own sadistic needs.

However, the tragic incident hadn't killed all sense of longing inside her. Why couldn't she stop noticing and, worse, reacting to the Marine on her doorstep?

Was she transferring her dormant desires onto a manifestation of the fictional hero she'd created?

"Ava?" a deep, husky voice called to her. She held tight to Maxie's leash as she spun toward the man being tucked into the hospital bed. Larkin's eyes opened wide and met hers across the waiting area. He pushed himself up off the pillows and smiled. "You stayed."

Dr. Russell pressed against his patient's uninjured shoulder. "Mr. Larkin, if you could just—"

"Wait." Larkin Bonecrusher pushed back. "I want to see her."

"Close the curtain," Dr. Russell ordered.

"I didn't know she was still here. Ava?" Before the nurse could reach the curtain, Larkin swung his legs off the edge of the bed, banged his stitched-up knee on the wheelchair, then cursed the state of his undress and sat back on the bed. "Why am I so damn groggy? Where are my clothes?"

"Lie down before you fall over."

Larkin rose again, clinging to the edge of the bed, the

pleading expression in his eyes sending a message she didn't understand. "Ava? I need you."

Ava shifted on her feet, wondering at the urge to say or do something to calm him down. The instinct to help was almost as powerful as the need to bolt from this place. But the battle between the woman she used to be—the woman who wouldn't hesitate to help someone in distress—and the hypercautious woman she'd become ended abruptly when the outside doors opened again and a man in dusty jeans, wearing a gun and a tan uniform shirt, strode in.

Chapter Four

"Ava! There's my favorite gal." Sheriff Brandon Stout took off his cowboy hat and raked his fingers through his dark, sweaty hair before tossing it onto the reception counter. With the same outstretched motion, he wound his arm around Ava and pulled her into a hug against his stocky chest. He held her so tightly that the corners of the badge pinned above his pocket pinched into her cheek. *One thousand one. One thousand two.* She inhaled a panicked breath, drawing in the smells of smoke and perspiration and something more pungent like gasoline. Ava was mentally suffocating in even this casual embrace. "How are you holdin' up? He didn't hurt you, did he? I checked your truck before I came in. There was blood on the front seat."

One thousand three.

Maxie jumped to her feet as Ava wedged one arm between her and her old friend and shoved at his chest. "Too much, Brandon. We talked about this."

"Right. Your three-second rule." She wasn't sure if that was amusement or irritation, or maybe even pity, in his tone, but he didn't let go. He rubbed his palm in circles at the center of her back. "You must have been terrified. A trespasser, bringing violence right to your front door. You should have called me."

"Brandon!" The tension exploding inside Ava must have

traveled right down the leash because Maxie rose on her hind legs, propping her front paws against Brandon's shoulder. The big dog used her full weight to knock the sheriff off balance and give Ava the chance to finally free herself.

"Down, girl." Brandon grinned, pushing the dog off him, and wrestling a bit around her ears to show there were no hard feelings between them. Once the dog had plopped down into a sit between them, Brandon retreated a step, accepting Ava's need for distance, if not necessarily understanding it. "My bad. When I get a call that says 'Ava Wallace' and 'gunshot victim' in the same sentence, I worry."

"I'm fine." Calming herself at the familiarity in his warm brown eyes, Ava even managed a smile. "I was surprised more than anything. I don't get a lot of visitors."

"And whose fault is that?" Brandon had grown a few inches and certainly filled out from the teenager she'd once known, but the boyish smile that had charmed her at seventeen was still evident. Undeterred by the distance or the dog between them, he reached out and tapped his finger beneath her chin. "Always working. My brainy English professor, writing that big dissertation."

Ava glanced over to the curtained-off area, and saw the drape still billowing and the nurse's white clogs returning to the bed as they finally closed off the space and gave Larkin his privacy. Since there were no bare feet in view beneath the curtain, Ava assumed the nurse and Dr. Russell had gotten him back into bed. Good. He needed to rest.

But the tight grip on Ava's stomach hadn't eased. There was so much wrong about this day, so much uncertainty surrounding that stranger that she felt it, too. Was this her empathy kicking in? Was she buying into the whole Willow Storm/Larkin Bonecrusher alliance he seemed to be clinging to? Did she simply want the man who seemed so alone against the world to understand that she hadn't always been such a jumpy, antisocial freak? With that curtain closed, she'd probably seen the last of Larkin, and that was for the best. She didn't need to get any more involved with his trouble. She had enough of her own she was struggling to overcome.

Brandon was still talking, and since there was no one else around, she politely smiled and faced him again. "I'd love to take you out sometime. Give you a break from all that work." He winked. "Say the word, and I'm your man."

Not. Going. To. Happen. The sabbatical story was the reason she gave anyone around here who bothered to ask why she kept to herself so much. The citizens of Pole Axe thought she was on an extended break from her university in Chicago, needing the quiet time and distance of her grandparents' cabin to conduct her research. She already had her PhD and continued to publish an article here and there. But her books were her bread and butter. She'd earned enough on them that, even if she never finished the seventh one, she could live on what she'd saved and invested. So long as she lived frugally. And other than the calorie-laden specialty coffee she splurged on every Monday at the coffee shop, *frugal* and *hermit* went together. She hadn't gone back to a classroom since the kidnapping. She probably never would. She'd loved teaching. Loved tapping into the creativity of her students and challenging them to create stories of their own. But she couldn't do busy parking lots and campus crowds anymore. She couldn't handle young men with hoodies and downturned faces that masked their expressions gaping back at her from the classroom.

Ava could control her fantasy world. Dragons and great battles, sword fights, curses and noble quests were all safer than the reality of her world back in Chicago—safer than even here in Pole Axe. Maybe if she never finished her book, she'd never have to return to the reality that was so hard for her.

"I wish you lived in town so I could keep a closer eye on you." Brandon caught her hand where she clutched Maxie's leash and squeezed it. "You know how much I care. When Doc Russell said you were involved in this mess…"

"I'm fine. Truly." She squeezed her fingers around his before pulling away. Ava seized upon the acrid odor and smudges of soot and dust clinging to his clothes to distract him from focusing on her any longer. "But you, on the other hand, smell like smoke. Did you trade in your badge and become a firefighter?"

"Oh, that." He swatted at his short sleeves and chest, stirring up a cloud of dust, then frowned and wiped at the streak of grime on his shoulder. But his effort to clean the rusty brown swath of mud and grease only spread the stain onto his chest.

"Stop," Ava chided with a slight smile, grabbing his wrist and pulling it away. "You're making it worse. You need to rinse off that mud and rust?—blood?—then put some pretreatment on it and wash it before the stain sets."

She released him almost as soon as she'd touched him. The man really did need a woman to reel him in and take care of him, but she wasn't volunteering for the job. Still, his smile broadened at even that most practical of attention she paid him.

"Thanks. I'll do that as soon as I chat with our mystery man." He picked up his hat and worked the brim between his hands. "There was a fire at Old Man Harold's junkyard. Nobody hurt. But what looked like a late-model SUV and the cars on either side of it are a total waste. I did what I could to contain it before the VFD got there, but I doubt he's even going to be able to salvage parts. The three vehicles must have been burning for a while before he sobered up enough to crawl out of his recliner and call it in. I'm tempted to cite him for willful destruction of property."

"But if it's his junkyard?"

Brandon could look dead serious when he needed to, and he wasn't joking about this. "We've had plenty of rain this summer. But we're coming up on fire season. I doubt we'll get any more precipitation until snow falls. That fire had ignited the grass. If it got beyond his property line, we might be talking forest fire and I'd be out setting up roadblocks and diverting tourists back into the valley."

"Was it deliberately set?" Why was she asking? Why wasn't she on her way home right now? What curious suspicion kept prolonging this conversation?

Brandon nodded. "An arson investigator will need to confirm my observation, but yeah. There were pour marks. Unless Mr. Harold dropped his bottle of whiskey and a lit cigarette before he went inside and passed out, I'd say somebody set those cars on fire. The perp wanted them burned beyond recognition." He looked over her head toward the curtained-off area and acknowledged Kent Russell joining them at the counter. "That's another reason I want to chat with the guy you brought in."

"You think he had something to do with the fire?"

"He could have been destroying evidence."

Ava hadn't smelled smoke or any kind of flammable liquid on Larkin, the way she had on Brandon's clothes. But a man setting a fire wouldn't stick around to fight it the way Brandon apparently had been battling with the flames and its aftermath. "My place is a good twelve miles from Mr. Harold's junkyard. That's a long way to hike in his condition. You can't place him at the junkyard."

"Not yet." Brandon reached around her to shake Dr. Russell's hand. "Doc."

"Sheriff. I heard about the fire. Is Mr. Harold okay? I'm running out of beds in my clinic."

"That old coot's fine. The volunteer firefighters were still there when I left, making sure there were no stray hotspots. I fixed him a pot of coffee and warned him to drink it instead of the whiskey, or he could lose his whole place next time. He was too far out of it to even notice any trespassers." Brandon directed his smile at Ava. "I go a month dealing with nothing but speeding tickets and running rowdy teenagers home to Mom and Dad—and in one day I get hit with a mysterious fire, a gunshot victim and Ava comin' to town when it ain't even Monday. That, in itself, tells me this guy is trouble. You're sure he didn't hurt you?"

He reached out with one finger to brush aside a tendril of hair that fell over her cheek. Although his indulgent smile never wavered, she saw the exact moment his gaze fell to the scar that bisected her cheek. She felt the hesitation in his touch and did him the favor of turning her head and pulling away. She supposed Brandon still saw her in his mind's eye the way she'd looked twenty years ago, and the imperfections on her skin now were jarring.

Why couldn't he see that she was a different woman from the girl he'd professed to love and move on? "Positive. Any blood you saw in my truck is his, not mine."

"And you've got no idea where he came from or who he is?" She shook her head. Brandon propped his hands at his waist, beside his holstered gun and handcuffs. "We've got a lot of tourists this time of year. Maybe he had a car accident or crossed somebody at Dolan's Bar and got in a fight."

Ava's tolerance for answering questions and pretending she was okay being around so many people was wearing thin. "I really need to get Maxie home. I don't know this man. Can't you leave me out of your investigation? He showed up on my front porch and collapsed. End of story. I don't know anything about burning cars. I didn't hear any gunshots. I'm just the good Samaritan who drove him into town."

Dr. Russell reached into his pocket and pulled out a small, plastic bag. "You're the good Samaritan who saved his life." He handed the bag to Brandon. "Here's the slug I took out of John Doe's shoulder. It's a 9 mil."

Brandon inspected the bloodstained projectile inside the bag before tucking it into the pocket of his jeans. "That's good."

"Good?" The doctor and Ava echoed together.

"Yeah. I was worried you were going to tell me Ava had shot him for coming onto her land. But since she favors buckshot, I can clear her of any suspicion." Had she really been a suspect in Brandon's eyes? Or was this more of his effort to show how well he thought he knew her, and how close he wanted them to be? Her distress must have shown on her face because he winked. "I'm teasin' you, Ave." He finally pulled a pen and notepad from his shirt pocket and jotted some information. "Anything else either of you can tell me?"

"The patient's other injuries are contact wounds," Dr. Russell explained, perhaps even less amused by the teasing than Ava was. "He took a bad fall."

Ava nodded. "He told me he remembered rolling off the edge of a cliff."

"Tumbling down a mountainside would certainly account for the injuries I stitched up. He's lucky he didn't break anything. He's got plenty of bruises, inside and out, though." With a weary sigh, Dr. Russell pulled back the front of his lab coat and hooked his fingers into the pockets of his jeans. "He said his name is Larkin Bonecrusher. What do you make of that?"

Brandon snorted a laugh. "That's an alias if I ever heard one."

"Obviously. But why not come up with John Smith or Bob Jones if he wanted to hide his identity? Bonecrusher is a little dramatic, don't you think?"

"Is he on something? Delusional?"

"I didn't detect any drugs in his system. But he took

at least one good blow to the head, so I believe his amnesia is real. Now whether it's permanent, I can't tell you. If he's not lucid in the next twenty-four hours, I'm going to refer him to a neurologist in Jackson. I'd prefer it if you allowed him a good night's sleep before you question him. He might remember more then."

"You know the drill, Doc. Procedure says I've got to talk to him as soon as possible, while his memories are still fresh."

"What memories? My patient needs his rest. Trust me, you'll get better answers in the morning."

"I need answers now. What if I've got a shooter running around my county? Or another accident victim who wasn't as lucky as this guy to see the inside of a hospital?" She felt the focus of both men shift to her. "Ava, did he say anything to you?"

Um, loves my books. Says I have beautiful eyes. Thinks my dog is a dragon. None of which she would share with these two men. "He was in and out of consciousness. Sorry I can't—" She jumped at the beeping of an alarm from the computer behind her.

Kent Russell dashed around the counter and checked the monitor on the desk. "Damn it. Garcia's coding again." He shouted toward the nurse behind the curtain as he ran down the hall. "Leslie! I need the crash cart in Room One. Stat."

The nurse popped through the curtain surrounding Larkin and raced down the hallway after Dr. Russell. The two medical professionals disappeared into separate rooms a few seconds before Leslie pushed the crash cart across the hall as they rushed to save Mr. Garcia's life.

Ava stroked her fingers over the top of Maxie's head. "Poor Mr. Garcia. Does he have any family left in the area?"

But there was no one listening to her concerns. When she turned to see why Brandon hadn't responded, she saw him striding over to the privacy area. With a tug on the leash, Maxie fell into step beside her as she hurried across the room to catch Brandon by the elbow. He'd pulled back the edge of the curtain, but stopped when he saw the battered patient, propped up on the bed, fast asleep. At least, the veteran Marine with the bruised temple and crisp white sling resting atop his chest seemed to be sleeping. His arm and chest moved up and down in deep, even breaths, but she couldn't help but wonder if those silvery-green eyes behind those dark gold lashes were fully aware of being watched. Ava dropped her voice to a whisper and tugged at the sheriff's arm. "What are you doing?"

The long breath that hissed between his teeth spoke of frustration and fatigue. "Realizing that my long day is about to get even longer." He pulled the curtain to again and patted Ava's hand where it rested in the crook of his elbow. "I'm going to have to hang out here until he's able to answer some questions."

"Dr. Russell said he needed to sleep tonight."

He tapped the badge on his chest. "I took an oath to protect this county."

"And the doctor took an oath to protect his patient." Having passed the three-second mark, Ava pulled her hand from his skin and straightened his collar, which had gotten stuck in the muddy mess on his shoulder. "Why don't you go home and clean up, put this shirt in the wash and then come back. By then, maybe Mr… Bonecrusher…will be awake and you'll have better luck. I'm guessing you haven't eaten dinner yet, either."

Brandon grinned. "Is that an invitation?"

"I need to take Maxie for a walk before we hit the road. It's been a while since she's done her business."

"I'll walk you to your truck. I'll come back later when Doc Russell can be here, so he won't accuse me of bullying his patient."

He put his hat on and led the way to the door to open it for her and Maxie. He fell into step beside her as they crossed the nearly deserted parking lot to the pine trees and boulders where she'd parked. The mountain air had cooled a few degrees from when she'd arrived. But the sun was already forming a pinkish-red glow over the peaks of the Wyoming Range to the west. She wasn't going to make it home before dark.

Brandon moved to the back of the truck, where he opened the tailgate to access Maxie's kennel.

"She'll ride up front with me."

"You spoil that dog."

"I know." While Brandon closed the tailgate, Ava pressed her key fob to unlock the door, and reached behind the seat to retrieve a plastic waste bag for the dog. "If you need me to make a formal statement, you can call me."

"I'll do that." When she turned around, she found Brandon blocking the triangle formed by the open door and truck frame. Thank goodness Maxie was there, forcing a bit of distance between them. Had he meant to trap her here? Or was he unaware of his actions and how they affected her? "Unless you let me take you to lunch tomorrow? I'll get my report typed up, and we could handle the paperwork then. I'd be happy to drive out to get you and—"

"No." She tamped down on the urge to tell him to back out of her personal space. He didn't understand her anxieties, and she didn't have the time, energy or interest in explaining them to him again. "Call me. I can stop by your office on Monday if you need me to sign something." She shook the waste bag in the air, emphasizing that she was ready to focus on other things now besides the upheaval of her day.

"All right. Whatever you say. I've got your number." Although it was obvious he was disappointed by her refusal, Brandon still smiled and leaned in to kiss her. Wondering if she was even interested in remaining friends with a man this thickheaded, Ava turned her head to offer him her cheek. He hesitated at the scar, then kissed her forehead instead. "Good night, Ave."

"Good night."

He finally retreated far enough to allow Maxie to rise to her feet and tug on the leash. Walking the dog wasn't just an excuse for ending the conversation. "Good night, girl." He scuffed his hands around Maxie's ears and patted her flanks. "Enjoy your walk." Finally, he circled around her truck and headed back to his black-and-white SUV. "I'll let you know if I find out anything about this guy."

"Sounds good."

Once he was inside his SUV, Brandon pulled out his cell phone and tucked the hands-free earpiece into his ear, probably calling in his location to his office. His headlights went on as he pulled out of the parking lot, reminding Ava that she needed to get moving. "Come on, Maxie. Let's make this fast."

But, of course, when she wanted to settle for a short walk around the perimeter of the parking lot, Maxie insisted on stretching her legs and sniffing all the town smells that weren't evident in the woods around the cabin where she usually roamed. They stopped at nearly every rock and tree and revisited a couple of them twice. Since Maxie had been such a trouper with the day's unusual events, and had had her back more than once throughout the day, Ava couldn't begrudge the dog the exercise she needed. Even though the sun was setting and their stomachs were grumbling from missing dinner, at least they were alone now. Ava felt her nerves relaxing and the stress of the day melting away beneath her feet. Today had been an anomaly. Tomorrow she could go back to being safe. Isolated. A little bored, perhaps. Frustrated by a book that wouldn't write itself. Emotionally paralyzed and driven into seclusion by a sadistic serial abductor who continued to elude the police. Frozen in a life that no longer seemed to be going anywhere. But safe.

After dropping Maxie's mess into the public trash can and cleaning her hands with a disinfecting wipe from her purse, Ava led Maxie back to her truck. She made her routine safety check underneath the truck and peeked through the windows before she opened the door. "Maxie, up."

While the big dog stretched out across the seat and rested her head on Ava's thigh, Ava buckled up and drove away. Nearly every angled parking slot on Main Street was full, and lights were blazing from Dolan's Bar, the more touristy Cowboy Bar, Buckskin Barbecue, and even Kris DeKamp's Koffee Shop. The newspaper office and Sue Schulman's General Store, full of practical clothes and gear as well as almost any souvenir a tourist could want, were closed for the night. The sheriff's office, volunteer fire department, a small grocery and other local businesses were a block to the east. Farther up the road, and down into the valley in the opposite direction, away from the hub of town, were rental homes, ranches and resort lodges. Some catered to skiing, others offered spa services or outdoor activities or a conference center. Closer to the tree line at the top of the peak was a lodge owned by a company called BDS. Unless they worked there, most of the locals never saw the luxury stone lodge because the best view of the Wind River Mountains and Hoback River Basin came with a steep price.

Ava inhaled a deep breath of the night air coming through her open windows. Music from the bars and voices from open doorways and the sidewalk filled the air as Ava cruised through downtown Pole Axe.

It was a charming town that felt as far away from her life in Chicago as she could get.

She made it through the first stoplight. But when she

stopped at the intersection to turn onto the highway, a shadow fell over the ambient light reflecting in her rearview mirror. She looked up, thinking a truck had pulled up behind her. Instead of another vehicle, the shadow was rising right from the back of her truck. Something was moving beneath the tarp that she'd anchored over Maxie's traveling crate. "What the…?"

Everything in Ava tensed. Someone was in the back of her truck. The shadowy figure grew larger, took the shape of a man, vaulted over the side onto the road. The doors were locked. She pushed the button to raise the windows. But the figure was moving forward, not running away.

She eyed the red light. Cursed the cross traffic that wouldn't allow her to stomp on the gas and leave the hitchhiker on the side of the road.

The damn windows were taking too long.

She reached for the glove box where she'd stowed Larkin's handgun, but she cowered back as a strong arm reached over the top of the window, unlocked the door and climbed inside. Maxie pushed to her feet and spun around, filling the cab of the truck. But a hushed command, a gentle touch, and she plopped her butt down beside Ava as the man pulled the blanket she'd used earlier over his shoulders and hunkered down as much as he could between the seat and the dashboard.

Larkin Bonecrusher.

Ava swore as silvery-green eyes bored into hers. "I knew you weren't asleep."

"I can't stay there," he whispered in a tight, deep-pitched voice. His breathing was as noisy and labored as her own, although she suspected for different reasons. Her so-called guard dog stretched out across the seat, content to have him back in the truck.

But Ava saw the real danger. The gun she'd taken off him was clutched in his very capable hand, pointed at her.

She glanced from the barrel of the Springfield Hellcat to the glove compartment and back to those fascinating eyes, which narrowed but never blinked.

"Yeah. I found where you stashed it. I've got the cartridges for that shotgun in my pocket, too." Ava's grip pulsed around the steering wheel. She felt light-headed. Sick to her stomach. This couldn't be happening to her. Again. "When the light changes, drive."

Chapter Five

Every muscle in Larkin's body ached. His brain felt like it was in a fog from whatever the doctor had given him for the pain. His bum leg was screaming at him to untuck from this awkward position, squeezed out of sight between the dashboard and the dragon-size dog. He could feel the chill of his zipper pressed against parts of his body that didn't like to be touched by anything cold. And he felt like a son of a bitch for doing this to Ava.

He'd seen the flare of fear in her eyes when she'd spotted the gun he'd retrieved during this impromptu escape. Even without the weapon, he would have found a way to commandeer her truck and get away from that hospital. His brain might not be running on all cylinders, but his gut was telling him that he wasn't safe there. Her knuckles were white where she gripped the steering wheel, but her jaw was set like stone, and her delicate nostrils flared with every breath. That was anger, not fear. She was probably already plotting his demise, or at least a way to escape. Anger was healthy. He could deal with her being angry at him.

He couldn't deal with being at the mercy of someone knowing more about what had happened to him than he did—and having no clue who his enemy might be. Ava

Wallace and her dragon dog were the only safe haven he believed in right now.

Ava's gaze shifted down to the corner of the truck where he crouched. "You're not coming with me."

"Don't look at me," he ordered, making her gaze snap back to the intersection. Her right hand came off the steering wheel to stroke Maxie's coat. That was a coping mechanism he'd seen her use several times today. Well, he was coping the best way he knew how under circumstances he didn't fully understand, too. "Don't let anyone see I'm in here with you. Don't do anything to signal other drivers. You're not in any danger unless you give me up." The glow of the traffic light that tinted the dog's white fur through the windshield changed from red to green. "Drive."

Her foot didn't move off the brake. "Where am I taking you?"

"Your place."

"No." She had both hands back on the steering wheel.

More teddy bear than dragon, Maxie stretched out across the seat, resting her snout on her big paws, close enough to him that she could sniff his face and shoulder without lifting her head. Couldn't Ava see that the dog she trusted so well thought he was okay? Shouldn't that reassure her? "Turn the corner. Go."

Only when bright lights flooded the cab of the truck from the road behind them, indicating they were no longer alone at the intersection, did she flip on her signal and make a left turn. The truck's powerful engine hummed as they picked up speed, merging onto the state highway that zigzagged up the side of the mountain toward her cabin. "You know, I could drive you out to the wilderness and leave you stranded in the middle of nowhere."

"I don't think you will. Gun aside, you're a woman with a heart. Or a conscience at least. You don't want me to get hurt."

"Now who creates fiction?"

While he appreciated her sharp wit, this wasn't the time for playful banter. "Did I read things wrong at the hospital?" The sling he wore made it difficult to push himself into a more comfortable position or avoid the dog's curious nose. It had also made it impossible to load the gun he held on Ava. If he'd had a few more seconds before retrieving the weapon and diving under the tarp in the back of her truck, and the challenge of focusing on completing the task in a moving truck hadn't made his head spin to the point of nausea, then he'd be posing a real threat. But Ava didn't need to know the magazine of bullets was tucked into his back pocket. He hadn't wanted to put her in that kind of danger, anyway. Not when he'd sensed an ally in her. "I thought you were helping me when you sent your sheriff friend home after the doctor and nurse were called away."

"I wasn't aiding and abetting a criminal. I felt sorry for you, thought you needed to rest. I regret that now." He felt the truck slow as they rounded a curve, then pick up speed on a straightaway.

Since he hadn't seen any lights coming through the windows for several minutes now, and their steady climb told him they were headed in the right direction, Larkin moved the gun to the hand at the end of the sling. He used his good arm to nudge the dog up into a sit and push himself onto the seat beside her because his knee couldn't take another second in that cramped position. He allowed himself a couple of deep breaths to let the pain in his battered body dissipate before he buckled himself in. Visually assured that she was driving toward her cabin, he tugged at the strangling neckline of the hospital gown he'd hastily tucked into his jeans, and patted his flat belly to confirm the presence of the medical printout he'd stuffed inside the gown. His left hand was strong enough to maintain control of the gun, although it was no longer pointed at her. "Look, all I'm asking for is a few days of refuge. Your place is isolated, yet you've got good sight lines to see anything coming up the road or out of the woods."

"It's my refuge, not yours. If you didn't have that gun, I'd be dumping you out on the side of the road."

He lightly touched the side of his head. "There's something…wrong in here. I didn't get shot by accident. I need someplace safe to stay while I get my head on straight. I need time to figure out who shot me. I have a feeling he's coming after me to finish the job, and I don't know who to look for."

Ava shook her head, stirring the long ponytail over her shoulder. "I don't do company. I'm the town recluse. The weird lady with the dog. Ask anyone. I keep to myself."

"The sheriff doesn't know that. He was all over you, and you didn't like it." Her head swiveled toward him, her reaction confirming his suspicions about that relationship. He pointed her attention back to the road as they neared another curve. "You told me not to grab you. I thought it was because I was a stranger. But you've told Sheriff Touchy-Feely that before, haven't you? He doesn't listen."

Her grip tightened, eased, then tightened again. Was she upset because he'd struck a nerve? Or was she plotting an escape? Although Maxie seemed like a gentle giant, was it possible she could order the dog to attack him? Sic the dog on him. Skid to a stop. Shove him out the door and drive away. It was a plan he might try if their situations were reversed and he had what he thought was an armed stranger in his vehicle.

"Brandon is a friend from childhood. We reconnected when I moved back to Pole Axe. He wants to be something more. I'm not interested." So, not hatching a get-rid-of-Larkin plan. But one more reason to back up the instinctive distrust he'd felt toward the sheriff after seeing his actions and eavesdropping on his conversation with Ava and the doctor. "If you're in danger, you can't get much safer than a hospital. You should have stayed there."

He watched another mile marker reflect in the headlights and pass by in the darkness of the night and thick trees rising above the drop-off at the edge of the road. The sense of unease he felt watching the pine trees and guardrail meant something. But he wasn't sure what his subconscious was trying to tell him about this drive any more than he could pinpoint the alarm he'd felt at the hospital. "I felt exposed there. In more ways than one. I had a feeling your sheriff wouldn't listen to what *I* had to say, either. He thinks I'm responsible for setting that fire at the junkyard."

"Are you?" He started to answer, but she already knew his response. "You don't remember."

"The answers are here, Ava, I know it. I need time to figure them out." He seized upon the most likely explanation for the bond he felt toward the frightened, angry woman sitting across from him. "You and Maxie are the only people I know here."

"Maxie's a dog."

He looked into the Pyrenees's soulful dark eyes. "I noticed."

"Earlier, you called her a dragon."

"See? I can tell the difference now. I'm better already, just being with the two of you."

"You're better because Dr. Russell took care of your injuries." He hunkered down behind the dog as they passed an oncoming vehicle. "I don't even know what to call you."

He thought of the key chain engraved with an L.B. tucked into his pocket. "Larkin Bonecrusher will do for now."

"I will not be your Willow Storm."

He pushed himself up straighter as they passed through the darkness again. "No. You're Ava Wallace. You saved my life, so that makes you the closest thing I have to a friend in this town."

"I am not your friend, and I'm not going to be your nursemaid. I'll stop at the next turnaround and call the sheriff."

"Empty threat." He understood that he had a knack for reading people—everyone, that is, but himself. "You don't want to ask that guy for any favors. Whatever he wants from you, it's not mutual, and you're worried that engaging him will send him the wrong message." He tilted his head back to look around Maxie's shoulders. "Or is it that you don't want any man touching you?"

"Now you're some kind of psychic?"

"My eyes work fine. I know what I saw when he hugged you." He scuffed his palm along the dog's muzzle and scratched beneath her ears. "It took Maximillia here to push him away."

"You and your eyes."

Although he wasn't sure what she meant by that, the dog hadn't been the only one to recognize the flare of panic she'd had when the sheriff had wound his beefy arms around Ava and hugged her tight. "Am I wrong about the sheriff? Hell, if I could have gotten up, I would have stopped him myself."

The nostrils weren't flaring anymore. Her fingers weren't pulsing around the wheel. He was right about the sheriff stomping all over her comfort zone. He prayed that, in his desperate need, he hadn't done the same. "Ava, please. Someone's trying to kill me. I don't know who. I don't know why. But I *know* you're not my enemy."

"How can you be sure?" Her chin pointed up with a stubborn resistance that was more than bravado and unexpectedly sexy. "Maybe I'm the one who shot you."

He couldn't help but smile in admiration of her strength. He tilted his head toward the shotgun anchored in her back window. "You favor that Browning stackbarrel, not a 9 mil." He tamped down on the ill-timed attraction he felt. If she wasn't interested in an old friend with a badge, she wasn't going to be interested in a stranger who'd brought a ton of trouble right to her front door. "You're the only person I'm certain *isn't* the bad guy. You could have shot me and dumped me out in the boonies, and no one would have been the wiser. Hell, I was unconscious on your front porch—you could have smothered me with a pillow. If you wanted me dead, I'd be dead. You wouldn't have worked so hard to save my life. That makes you the only ally I trust right now. Please."

They drove another mile in silence before she answered. "I can't. I'm sorry, Larkin. I'm alone for a reason. You don't understand."

"Then explain it to me."

She shook her head. "I don't wish you any harm. But I can't be your ally. I'll drop you off somewhere. I can turn around and drive you down into Jackson if you're not comfortable with the local cops or medical facility. I can float you a loan if you need money for airfare or a place to stay."

"I don't need more cops. I don't need a hotel full of strangers or to put more distance between me and what I suspect is the scene of the crime somewhere around here. I need to hide out with someone I can trust."

The truck swerved onto the shoulder as she turned to him. "You trust *me*?"

Larkin didn't question the instinctive clench of every muscle as they veered toward the guardrail. "Eyes on the road. The last thing I want to do is crash again."

"Again?" He'd blurted out the word without thinking. But she'd picked up on the slip. "You were in an accident? *And* you got shot and fell down a mountain?"

Black SUV. Racing down the road. The next curve flying up at him. "They sabotaged my car." The glimmer of the memory played through his head like a TV channel that was out of focus. "That's how they stopped me. They forced me off the road. They wanted something from me."

"Who are *they*? What did they want?"

The channel went dark before he hit upon the answers he needed. "I don't know." He tore at the neckline of the infernal hospital gown and reached inside. He pulled out a folded X-ray printout. He turned on the cab's overhead light and opened the black-and-white image. He held it up to avoid Maxie's shadow and pointed to the small rectangular object below his rib cage. "I'm guessing it has something to do with this."

"You stole that from the hospital?"

"It's *my* x-ray. The doc was checking for internal injuries. He found this instead. Asked me about it. I didn't know what to tell him." Maxie showed an interest in the picture by sniffing it, and Larkin suspected that told the dog about as much as he knew, which wasn't a lot. "The nurse left it in my cubicle when she ran out to help with the other patient."

"What is that little thing in the middle of the picture?"

"Looks like a thumb drive to me."

"What's it doing in your stomach?"

"I'd like to know that myself. Doc Russell gave me something to help it pass smoothly. Still might take a day or two."

"That's gross."

"That's a necessity. I need to know what's on it."

"Maybe you should go back to the hospital until you… get rid of it."

He folded up the printout and tucked it back inside the gown. "If this is what the man who shot me was after, then I don't want to be lying in a public facility with no real security, waiting to pass a key piece of evidence."

"I'm sorry for your trouble, but I don't want to get involved." Although she'd seemed briefly interested in solving the mystery, Ava's shoulders stiffened with a resolute dismissal. "I have issues of my own I have to deal with."

"I can see that." Her hand flew to her cheek, hiding the scar that had already seen some reconstructive surgery. He turned off the overhead light, hating that she thought she had to hide the mark from him. "Not your scars," he explained. "Your reaction to things. Your attachment to this big brute." He smoothed his fingers into the dog's fur, wishing he could test the weight and softness of Ava's ponytail instead. "I can tell Maxie's more than a guard dog to you. Sure, I'm curious about your injuries. I'm human. But I'm not going to pry. You've been hurt. Terribly. You have all the habits of someone with post-traumatic stress. I've been there. A bum leg isn't the only reason I had to leave the Corps."

"You have PTSD?"

"I was a career Marine. My last deployment ended with a literal bang." Before those graphic images could surface, he mentally repeated the mantra some headshrinker on some military base had taught him. *Acknowledge. Compartmentalize. Replace the guilt with a more positive feeling and keep moving forward.* "That's one thing I wish I could forget."

"You remember getting hurt?" she asked, as if that might be a trigger for her.

His was something different. "I remember the team under my command getting blown to bits."

Her hand fell away from her scar. She even brushed a wavy tendril of coffee-colored hair away from that cheek and tucked it behind her ear. The moment she ventured out of her own head, she became open, compassionate, brave. A woman he'd like to get to know. Under different circumstances. "I'm so sorry."

He didn't need pity. He doubted she did, either. "I can

tell you're afraid of something. Probably whoever cut you like that." He set the gun down in his lap. Maybe there was a better method than coercion to earn her cooperation. "You've already helped me, just by listening and asking the right questions. I'm trained military police. If we could keep talking like this, triggering some of my memories, I'd be happy to help secure your place while I'm there."

"How do you know you're an MP?"

"Body condition. Reflexes and stamina. Weapons knowledge. An instinct to observe the hell out of the details and people around me." A few distinct memories he wished he didn't have. "I may not remember much about today or yesterday, but I remember serving. Training other men and women under my command. Wearing a uniform." He hesitated at that one vivid memory he couldn't forget. *Compartmentalize. Move on.* "If you still feel threatened, let me help you. In exchange for a place to hide out for a few days."

"No."

"But you *are* afraid of something?"

"Larkin…" She slipped him a glance that revealed… hesitation? Fear? Weariness? But then she turned her eyes to the road again. "I'll drive you anywhere else you want to go. Beyond that, I can't help you."

Coercion—no. Hooking her curiosity—no. Revealing they were both damaged souls—no. Bargaining—no. Hell. He only had one option left to secure her cooperation. "I'll tell everyone in Pole Axe that you're A. L. Baines, famous author, probably rich enough to buy that whole town outright."

"You wouldn't."

"Even if you deny it, just putting the rumor out there in the universe is bound to stir up one or two hundred internet searches on you. I bet you'd have fans coming out of the woodwork."

She released her breath in an audible gasp. "First kidnapping, now blackmail?"

"You leave me no choice. I'm sorry I have to resort to that." If the tattoo wasn't evidence enough, he knew by his scramble to survive and the resolve he felt in making this difficult decision that he was, in fact, a military man. He had a mission to complete, and he needed her on his team to do it. "I won't do anything to hurt you, Ava. But I need an ally, and you're it."

She shook her head. "How can you need someone like me?"

That was self-doubt, not a protest. Something in his heart tugged at the captivating dichotomy of Ava's personality. Strength and vulnerability. Bravery and insecurity. A wildly creative imagination and a stone-cold grasp on reality. A legit talent in the art of sarcasm, and he had yet to hear her laugh. He carefully considered his answer. "Something about you makes me think you know exactly how I'm feeling right now."

"The last time I tried to help a man who needed me…" The truck gained speed as she shot him a sharp look. But she swallowed whatever emotion had darkened her eyes and spilled a truth he hadn't expected to hear. "I was kidnapped two years ago." Guilt, instant and overwhelming, weighed heavier than the gun lying in his lap. "Not like this. He didn't need a gun. I voluntarily went to him. He was lying in a parking lot on campus, next to a beat-up old car. I thought he was a student who was hurt. Then he was smashing my head on the pavement. I woke up in my underwear, blindfolded, cold, strapped to a chair…and he… kept me. For three days, he tortured…" She ended with a blunt, "The scars are all from him."

Shock numbed him for a few moments. "I'm sorry. I had no idea." And then the anger kicked in. He swore. Repeatedly. "And here I am, kidnapping you." Survival had been his only goal. Truth was the key to reaching that goal. Ava Wallace had unwittingly offered him a way to achieve both. But there was a limit to who and what he'd sacrifice to complete his mission—and he'd just reached that limit with her confession. The end hadn't justified the means. There was so much wrong with what she'd shared that Larkin felt like an ass for reaching out to her, for demanding something she couldn't give him—something she shouldn't have to give anyone. Whatever hell had screwed up his day, she'd been through worse and didn't need to be a part of his world. When they sped past a forestry department sign indicating a stopping place up ahead, he pointed to it. "Pull off at that scenic overlook."

The truck wasn't slowing down. "You won't be able to see anything at night."

"I'm not interested in the view. Pull off." He winced against the seat belt as she stomped on the brake to make the turnoff.

Gravel crunched beneath the tires before she pulled into a parking slot facing the sidewalk and low rock wall that probably revealed a picturesque photo op of the lush, tree-covered mountains in the daylight. She shifted into Park and set the brake. "Are you not feeling well?"

Nope. He was suffocating. Suffocating from the weight of guilt at subjecting Ava to any part of his trouble, and frustration that he hadn't seen it coming and he couldn't seem to do a damn thing about it. Except this. He had to tuck the gun into the back of his belt and push the curious dog out of his face to reach his seat belt and free himself.

Maxie, no doubt picking up on the stress that was rolling off him in waves, leaned against his stitched-up shoulder. Larkin grunted at the ache that shot across his chest and down through his arm. But the pain was what he needed to clear his head to coordinate his movements and shove the door open.

"Larkin?"

Another sharp pain jolted through his knee and spiraled up to his brain when his feet hit the pavement. He had to cling to the open door for a few seconds to find his balance. Damn it. Why was he still so dizzy? He was in better shape than this. The day had taken its toll on him, leaving him feeling weak as a puppy. Determination had gotten him through everything else today. His stubborn will would get him through this, too. Once he felt like he could walk without face-planting, he closed the door and headed toward the sidewalk so that the path would be clear for Ava to drive away.

She called to him through the open window. "Where are you going?"

"Away from you." He reached the rock wall, thought he might sit for a moment, then retreated a step at the thought of losing his balance and crashing over the edge of a mountain again. He headed back toward the road instead. He'd thumb down a ride and hitchhike to…somewhere. "It was a mistake to get you involved. I didn't realize how fragile you were. I'll figure this out on my own."

"Fragile?" He could tell from the tone of her voice that she didn't like that. "Is that how you see me? Do you think that's how everyone sees me?"

"Poor choice of words. I meant…" He came back to the passenger window to explain that he was trying—possibly too late—to make things right between them. "You're still working through your trauma. Getting involved with me isn't going to help that." That military resolve to get the job done, no matter the toll it took, faded in the shadows of those striking blue eyes aimed at him. "You saved my life. At the very least, I shouldn't make things worse for you."

Her nostrils flared again, making her look a little pissed. "I'm already involved with you. Get back in the truck."

He pointed to the highway. "I'll hitch a ride with someone else."

"How will you know if the person who picks you up isn't the one who wants you dead?" She waved him back in. "I can handle this."

"Ava, you don't have to prove to me how tough—"

"Get in the damn truck."

He was beginning to see where a lot of her fictional inspiration came from. "That's Willow Storm talking."

"Don't say that. I'm Ava Wallace. I'm a real person. I'm a fighter. I don't…want to be a victim anymore." Her flare of temper faded, and she released the steering wheel to wind her arms around Maxie and bury her face in the dog's shoulder. The stalwart pooch sat up straight, rubbing her head against Ava's, giving her mistress the support she needed.

"Honey, the woman who greeted me with a shotgun and tended my wounds is no victim. The woman who barely batted an eye when I pointed a gun at *her* is no victim." He couldn't tell if she was crying or inhaling deep breaths to get her through the emotions he'd stirred up in her. But he knew he couldn't walk away and leave her feeling raw like this. He waited for the silent sobs to pass and found himself wishing he were in the dog's place, absorbing her tension, allaying her fears, reminding her of her strength. He had one last card he could play to earn her cooperation. But he didn't feel like he was making this deal for himself. When she raised her head again and met his gaze, he made his offer. "Do you think that helping me could aid your healing? Would it prove something to you that you need to believe in?"

"I don't know. I…" She stroked her fingers through Maxie's fur. "I'm tired of being afraid and suspicious all the time. I never used to be. I'm an accomplished woman. I have skills. I've earned three college degrees. Written six books. The last five made the bestseller lists. There's a filmmaker who wants to option the whole series. I have a dissertation and a dozen published articles under my belt. I can handle myself in the outdoors. I'm smart. I'm a good person. I used to help all kinds of people. Cared for my parents when they were sick. Tutored students. Mentored budding authors."

"You sound like a fighter to me to make all that happen."

"I made one wrong decision. Nearly paid for it with my life." She leaned back in her seat, tipping her head back as if sharing her story had exhausted her. "I'm not sure why I'm telling you all this. Why aren't I running over you with my truck and getting away from you as fast as I can?"

"Because you and I get each other. I made a mistake this morning. Nearly paid for it with my life." He repeated her words that rang far too true for him, too. "You're telling me because you understand how that one mistake can change your life. And you'd give anything for a chance to correct that mistake. Maybe I'm that chance."

She nodded. "Nobody here or back in Chicago gets that. People want to take care of me. Or fix things for me."

"Which makes you feel even more like a *fragile* victim."

Yeah, he got that. Even though he'd been tempted to take care of her, too, he could see that that wasn't the kind of help that either of them needed.

"It's another reason I stick to my own company. Then I don't have to see those looks of pity. Even Brandon hesitates when he sees this." She softly brushed her fingers across the scar on her cheek.

Another reason to relegate Sheriff Touchy-Feely to the jerk category, as far as Larkin was concerned. "There's a fine line between compassion and pity."

She agreed. "I can't tell anymore. I haven't been able to trust my instincts since then. That's why there hasn't been another Bonecrusher book. I write and write, but I don't trust that I'm taking the story in the right direction. I live like a hermit because I don't trust people."

"The man who hurt you—was he caught?"

It took her long enough to shake her head that he already knew the horrid, unjust answer.

"Is he here in Wyoming?"

Another headshake. "Chicago. I don't know if he lives there, but he's been there every summer for the past five years. That's where it happened."

"That's why your anonymity is so important to you. You're hiding from him." Larkin turned his head and swore into the night. Then he grabbed the edge of the open window and leaned in, wanting to judge her reaction. "Do I look like him? Remind you of him in any way?"

"You're both men." But her attempt at humor fell flat. Her voice was soft, broken, as she reached for Maxie again. "That's the hell of it. I never saw his face. He kept me blindfolded. Detective Charles, a friend of mine in Chicago PD, thinks he has a lead after a recent attack. I'm not the only woman he's hurt. But apparently, I'm the only survivor who's willing to work with CPD. Try to identify him. By sound. By touch and smell."

"Touch and smell?"

"He…had scars, too. I could feel the puckered skin on his arms and chest when he touched me. He had one on his neck, too." Larkin's hand was curled into a fist, ready to punch someone, when she tried to make light of her suffering again. "If you were a diesel mechanic and had the smells of grease and hot metal on you, I don't think I could have helped you."

Probably another reason why she chose to live in the fresh air of this natural habitat. "And his voice?"

"I'll never forget the things he said to me. The way he said them—as if the scar on his neck had damaged his throat, too. But I wouldn't know him if I passed him on the street."

Sounded a little like a suicide bomber back in the Middle East. The young man who'd driven his delivery truck up to their checkpoint had been little more than a boy. Although his team had begun their routine check of the vehicle, they'd taken a few minutes to chat with the kid because they hadn't seen the imminent threat. Hell of a way to live, not having anyone you could trust—not even herself. "He'll know you before you know him. You don't know who your enemy is."

"I guess that does sound familiar." She sat up straight and studied him. "The only difference between us is that I'm trying to forget my past, while you're trying to remember yours."

"I can't do this to you." As much as this woman's books had gotten him through dark times, and her actions today had saved his life—as much as he was drawn to her wit and honesty and strength—Larkin turned away from Ava and started walking.

"Who's going to help you if I don't?" He stopped at her words. Now, who was trying to convince the other that they should be working together as a team? Larkin turned to find her looking at him. Ava's eyes were as dark as the twilight sky. The dashboard lights twinkled like stars reflected there. Larkin felt the impact of her beauty like a punch to the gut. Yeah, he supposed men like Sheriff Touchy-Feely saw the scars first. Or they overlooked her because she hid her femininity by dressing like a boy in those baggy clothes. But there was a light inside this woman that beamed straight into the murky shadows of his soul and illuminated the foggy nothingness of his memories. "It's not realistic to think I can snap my fingers and go back to the person I used to be. But you...need me...to be that person again."

And who was arguing that they'd be better off apart? "I'm not forcing you to help me, Ava. I'll find another way to get to the truth. I was wrong to threaten blackmail. I won't tell a soul you're A. L. Baines. I'm grateful for all you've done for me." He tapped the door with his palm and retreated a step. "You take care of yourself. Be safe."

He spun around too quickly and swayed. When the black night and black asphalt swirled into one, he grabbed the bed of her truck and leaned against it to steady himself. Ava was out her side of the truck in a second, hurrying around to help balance him. With one hand at his elbow, she steadied him against the side of the truck. When she opened the passenger door to help him inside, he discovered he was a little stronger than he'd been that afternoon and planted his feet and pushed away her steadying hand. "I'm not asking you to get involved with this."

Why the hell would anyone think this woman was weak? She grabbed his belt and turned him toward the opening. Larkin grasped her wrist with his usable hand and pulled her grip loose. When he stepped to the side, she shifted. He settled his hand at the curve of her waist and pushed, but she palmed the center of his chest and pushed back.

"Stop fighting me," she chided. "I don't want to hurt you."

He suspected that even with his aching shoulder, he could lift her off the ground and set her aside. But with his wonky sense of balance they'd probably both end up flat on the pavement. This time when she pushed, his knee buckled, and his hips landed on the edge of the seat. She tumbled into the vee of his legs, the brace of her hand the only thing keeping them from full body contact. Larkin froze, not wanting to frighten her once she realized how close they were.

He didn't want Ava, for even one second, to fear him the way she must have once feared her abductor.

She stared at the hand splayed against his chest, and he wondered if she could feel the heat of that touch through the ridiculously thin cotton of his hospital gown the way he could. He wondered if she had any idea that she was close enough for him to inhale the herbal scent of her shampoo on her hair. He wondered if she understood how attracted to her he was.

Her fingertips flexed against the cotton, briefly pressing into the skin and muscle underneath. Even that little pinch was a turn-on for him. Could a blow to the head make a guy this hot for a woman he'd known fewer than twenty-four hours? The nurse at the hospital had been pretty, in a delicate, feminine sort of way, but she hadn't even turned his head. Maybe he was into Ava Wallace because this woman's stories had already filled his imagination, distracted him from months of pain and rehab and touched his soul. She reminded him of the strong and sexy Willow of her books. It felt like he'd known her a lot longer than twenty-four hours.

"Maybe I need someone to ask for my help." He could see the wheels inside her head turning behind her eyes. And then she blinked and turned her face up to his, and he knew he'd agree to whatever deal she had in mind. "I make no guarantees about how much good I'll really be to you. And I can't promise I won't have a panic attack and flip out on you, possibly make things even worse." Her chest expanded with a deep breath. "My instincts tell me that I can trust you, and that I'm the only person who can help you, until you regain your memory. Clearly, you think the same thing."

"Ava…"

Just as he covered her hand with his against his chest, she reached behind him and took the gun from his belt before pulling away. He'd been briefly distracted by feelings and chemistry when he should have been bracing to face the barrel of the gun. Ah, hell. Had this whole conversation been a distraction so that she could regain the upper hand? He wouldn't have protested her right to defend herself. But she tucked the Hellcat into her own belt. "I have a three-second rule."

"Huh?"

"I panic when people touch me, especially when I don't see it coming." A hazard of her ordeal, no doubt. "But when I control the touch, or okay it, I've worked up to keeping it together for three seconds before I have to break contact."

He'd been worried about the gun, while she'd been worried about him touching her. Although he felt like she'd been leaning into him a good deal longer, he respected her directive. "Three seconds. I'll remember that."

"Maxie. Move over." He no longer fought her efforts to help him inside the truck because he didn't want to fight her. "You can stay with me until you can look at that thumb drive, or you regain your memory—whichever comes first."

"Ava—"

She held up a finger to shush him. "I need to be able to do this. I need to be able to trust my instincts again. Yes, I made a mistake that night. But I am not the mistake. I need to believe that again." She closed the door and walked around the truck to get in behind the wheel. "The way I live, it should be fairly easy to keep your presence at my cabin a secret for a few days." She reached over to lock the gun in the glove box before starting the engine. "But I am keeping all the guns and ammo with me. Even the magazine that's in your pocket."

Impressed with her observation skills, he pulled out the

rack of bullets and handed it to her. "When did you know the gun wasn't loaded?"

"Just now. I suspected earlier when you held it in your weak hand. But I confirmed it when I felt the weight of it." A blush crept up her neck and warmed her pale skin. "And I may or may not have checked out your backside when you stumbled." He arched an eyebrow. Although he couldn't imagine worse circumstances to launch any kind of relationship between them, it was nice to know he wasn't the only one fighting a little chemistry. "You step one foot out of line, though, and I will shoot you myself," she warned.

"Yes, ma'am. I wouldn't have it any other way." He was smiling as she shifted the truck into gear. "You're strong enough to do this, Ava. I know you are. If I can help you in any way with your situation, I will. I owe you everything."

She pulled back onto the highway. "Just get your memory back."

Chapter Six

Light flickered through the treetops higher up the mountain, sharp and blinding enough that Ava shielded her eyes and looked away. It wasn't the soft glow of the rosy gold sunrise creeping through the forest like a warm fog on the eastern side of the mountain. That flash was harsh and cold. Possibly, the sun was reflecting off the window of a rental cabin or the windshield of a car parked at a scenic overlook. Only, the reflection seemed to be moving. She couldn't tell if it was the swaying of the trees, or the reflection itself that was shifting. Then, as suddenly as it had appeared, the discordant light vanished.

"Aliens," Ava muttered out loud, frowning at the anomaly. If only she could truly dismiss such aberrations in her life so casually. She paused in her morning hike to take a quick assessment of her surroundings. Bird calls. Pine boughs creaking in the wind overhead. Soft splashes of water tumbling over the rocks in Panner's Creek down the bank below her feet. The lodgepole pines and smaller deciduous trees were thick enough on either side of the path to block the sounds of the highway higher up the mountain and any view she had of civilization below her in the valley. These things were all familiar to her.

A flash of light through the trees above her was not.

If she'd only seen the flash once, Ava would have dismissed it as a trick of light and brainstormed a story about an alien invasion. But she'd spotted that reflection high in the sky twice now. Logically, she knew she wasn't going to run into whoever was behind that periodic flash unless she hooked up her rock-climbing gear and started an ascent up the mountain. But logic had little to do with the sensation crawling over her skin that said she wasn't as alone on her walk this morning as she liked to be.

"Come on, girl. Leave that critter alone. All you're doing is getting wet." Ava whistled to draw Maxie's attention from the frog she'd followed to the edge of the creek. Since they were still on private property, she could let the dog off leash. Seeing the pooch she demanded so much from enjoying her free time gave Ava pleasure, too.

Third flash. Slightly different location.

Was that simply because the angle of the sun changed as it climbed higher into the sky? Or had whatever been making that reflection moved?

And then she heard the hum.

A drone.

Of course. The latest technology for professional and amateur photographers alike. Someone must be trying to get that perfect picture of a sunrise over the mountains. Or maybe it was a geological team, or the forestry department or a conservationist, a scientist mapping out topography or tracking the movement of a flock of birds or herd of mountain goats or…

Tracking?

Ava shivered despite the pleasant morning temperature. She tilted her face to the sky once more. The flashes of light were the drone changing directions, the lens of its camera or another shiny component catching the unfiltered rays of the mountain sunrise.

Ava was in the best shape of her life following two years of physical therapy, fitness training and self-defense classes. She hiked these paths every day and barely broke a sweat. Now, she rubbed her palm over her chest, struggling to catch her breath as the mountain air thinned.

The mountain air hadn't changed in the last thirty seconds. *She* was the one who was making it difficult to breathe.

With such dense tree cover and the relatively steep angle, could whoever be up there see her down here? It wasn't as if she were wearing bright colors in her worn jeans and her grandfather's faded plaid shirt that she'd rolled up to the elbows. She turned back along the trail beside the creek. It was one of many paths she'd followed through these woods over the years. Almost every path led back to her cabin. But surely that was too far away for anyone higher up on the mountain to be tracking *her*.

Not for the first time, she wondered how long the hooded scar-face man had watched her before the night of her abduction. Had choosing her been an impromptu decision? *The lady professor is working late on a Friday night—I can take her.* Or had he been watching her for days, weeks, specifically choosing her as his next victim long before he created the opportunity to strike?

"Breathe, Ava," she coached herself. "They're watching the scenery. Not you." Still, a sudden sense of urgency poured adrenaline into her legs. She needed to get back to the cabin to make sure Larkin was still asleep in the guest bedroom. Still safe, still secret. *She* needed to get back to her security zone before paranoia got the better of her.

Maxie was splashing her big paws in the water, getting ready to jump in after the living toy she'd been playing with. Ava thumped her walking stick down on the dirt path. "Maxie! Come. We need to go." The big dog stopped, raised her spotted head and looked up at Ava. Maybe Ava gave off a unique scent when she started to panic. Maybe Maxie could hear the edgy timbre in her mistress's tone.

In one instant, she was playing like an overgrown puppy, and in the next, she was loping up the embankment to lean against Ava's thigh. The dog's weight and warmth snapped Ava out of her spiraling mood. Ava lowered her hand to Maxie's head. "That's my good girl." Reassured that she wasn't alone, that she was safe, Ava hooked the leash to Maxie's collar, and they headed back to the cabin.

Thinking she was being watched could be due to any one of a half dozen upheavals she'd gone through yesterday, from greeting an injured stranger with her shotgun to sharing more details about her kidnapping with Larkin than she'd shared in any one conversation with her therapist over the past two years. Yes, he was a kindred spirit who understood PTSD. Yes, he stirred up desires in her that hadn't responded to any man since her abduction. Not that she was ready to act on those impulses. But even the fact that she was aware of a man, and that she suspected he was aware of her as a woman, had thrown her isolated, well-ordered world into chaos.

She'd agreed to help him because it's what the old Ava would have done, because her isolated, well-ordered world was a lonely place to be—because safe wasn't the same as happy, self-confident or even content. Helping Larkin was the biggest risk she'd taken since her life had been cut to bits two years ago. She had to shake things up or she'd never be free of her frightened, lonely life. She'd never be able to complete her book. She'd never be able to live or love again.

But change was hard. It was scary. Taking that risk with her own Larkin Bonecrusher in the flesh was probably what made her see a drone as a threat and pick up the pace. She reminded herself that she had made the offer to help a wounded veteran regain his memory and true identity. He'd offered to walk away and take his trouble with him. But she'd wrestled him back into her truck and made up the bed in the guest room because she was afraid she'd be making another life-altering mistake if she refused to help and something happened to him.

Willow and Larkin had been reluctant allies in her first book. But by book two they'd forged a tight bond of complementary skills and an unshakable trust that one would always have the other's back. Maybe there was something in the stranger's obsession with her books that spoke to that same need in her. They were stronger as a team. She'd keep him at her cabin for a few days because she'd become an expert at safe and secret. In return, she might learn to believe in herself again—and she might learn that there was someone else in this world who believed in her, too.

She unhooked Maxie when they cleared the trees and chased the dog up onto the porch in a game of tag that left the dog panting, and her a little winded—this time from true exertion, not panic. "You win!" With Maxie thoroughly personified in her imagination, Ava pressed a shushing finger to her lips. "We have to be very quiet, Queen Dragon. Larkin might still be asleep. Our wounded warrior needs his rest."

Maxie cocked her head from side to side, reacting as if she understood the words. But as soon as she unlocked the door, Maxie was all dog, dashing past Ava and heading to the kitchen for a noisy drink from her water bowl.

Ava locked the dead bolt and leaned her walking stick in the corner beside the door. She paused a moment to listen to the stillness inside the cabin. A quick walk through the kitchen revealed the mug and glasses she'd set out for Larkin's morning coffee, milk or orange juice remained untouched. She spotted the light beeping on her answering machine on the landline next to the fridge. Not even a ringing telephone had awakened him, apparently, since no one was moving about the house.

Swallowing the trepidation that always seemed to crop

up when she got an unexpected message, she pushed the Play button. "Hey, Ava. Kent Russell here. My patient, Mr. Bonecrusher, left the hospital last night. I know you said you were just the good Samaritan who helped him out, but I was wondering if you knew where he had disappeared to. I really need to find him. Give me a call."

Give him a call? And tell him what? Just how good was she at lying through her teeth and pretending she wasn't harboring his missing patient? Not answering would only make the doctor call again—or worse, stop by to speak in person. Although he might dismiss any nervous behavior because she was the town eccentric, she needed some time to practice playing dumb before that conversation happened.

In the meantime, she'd better check on said patient. She hurried up the stairs and peeked into the bedroom across from hers.

Pushing the door open without a sound, she tiptoed across the rug to the bed to make sure Larkin was still breathing. Although he'd said Dr. Russell had told him rest wasn't a bad thing, she still felt the old-school concern that a head injury and sleeping for so long meant something was wrong.

There was nothing wrong with the way this man slept.

Ava felt a skitter of awareness chase across her skin that was completely unlike that sense of being watched she'd experienced on her walk. Sometime in the night, Larkin had shed the hospital gown and tossed it onto a chair. He'd rolled over onto his back, pushing the covers down to a precarious position below his belly button and over the points of his hips. She glanced at the floor beside the chair and felt another skitter waking her senses. He'd shed his jeans, too.

Ava studied his exposed chest long enough to make sure it was rising and falling with even, normal breathing. She studied it a bit longer because she hadn't really looked at a man in a long time for any reason other than to assess whether or not he was a threat to her.

This was therapeutic, she reasoned, being able to feel safe indulging her rusty hormones. She made a clinical assessment of Larkin's chest and torso and reached the conclusion that she didn't need to buy him any shirts. The muscular hills and hollows of his shoulders, chest and stomach revealed colorful bruises, a sprinkling of much older scars and some intriguing mileage on her guest. The hair that dusted his chest and narrowed into a straight line that disappeared beneath the top of the sheet was mostly a golden color, mixed with a darker shade of bronze and a few sprinkles of silver, just like the close-cropped hair on his head and the beard that was filling in across his jaw and neck.

She moved closer to touch his forehead and cheek. The skin that had been cool and clammy yesterday afternoon was now a warm, healthy temperature. Without any clothing or injury to impede her view, she studied the ink on his shoulder. The fictional Larkin wore a tattoo that had been branded into him by the first master he'd served before defying his tyrannical rule and joining Willow and her band of rebels fighting to bring rights to all people and the magical creatures of Stormhaven. She suspected the Marine Corps tattoo represented a different kind of loyalty to his comrades and a cause. Touching her fingertips to the dark lines, she wondered at the significance of that date embedded in the stylized links encircling his bicep. She traced the curve of the eagle's head up to the top of his shoulder and over the sharp angle of his clavicle, skirting the crisp white square of gauze taped over his stitches.

A deep-pitched moan hummed in Larkin's throat. She snatched her fingers away and snapped her gaze up to his face to make sure he was truly asleep and not squinting through nearly closed eyes, watching her ogle him like a woman who'd never seen a half-naked man before. Since there was no bemused grin or sudden effort to cover himself, she exhaled a silent breath, relieved to see he was truly resting. He might even wake up remembering his name and who had tried to kill him. That's what she should be thinking about, not her wildly errant hormones. She needed to go. Therapy session over.

Ava grabbed the shopping list he'd made for her off the bedside table, pulled the covers up to his chest and hurried downstairs to retrieve her purse and the dog. Locking the door behind her, she hustled Maxie into the truck and climbed in beside the Great Pyrenees. She wanted to get into town to run Larkin's errands and pick up groceries before it got too crowded with tourists on a Saturday.

With one last glance at the cabin to make sure her temporary roommate was still locked inside, and another glance up the mountain to ensure the flashing lights of the drone hadn't followed her home, she started the engine and headed down the road.

Forty minutes later, Sue Schulman, a lifelong Pole Axe resident who'd outlived two husbands, knew everyone in the county and ran the ironically named Hole in the Wall General Store, was helping Ava gather the items on Larkin's list. After the initial gush of welcome and surprise that Ava had left her remote cabin and come to town on the weekend to shop for new clothes, the older woman with the short, bright white hair had literally shushed herself, unwrapped a rawhide treat for Maxie and proceeded to move around the store to retrieve items and bring them to the front counter where Ava waited. Everything Ava needed, from a disposable cell phone to toiletries, was on the shelves at Sue's. If Larkin had wanted a pair of off-season snowshoes or a lime green foam ax with *Pole Axe, WY* emblazoned on it, she could get him that, too, without ever leaving this warehouse of a store that took up one side of the block between the clinic and the town's second stoplight.

Sue didn't mind Maxie coming into the store along with Ava, and she didn't mind carrying a conversation. With anyone. Not with Ava. Not with the tourists who delighted in her stories about the area's history. Not the locals who remembered her daddy's ranch or went to school with one of her two sons. But the two men in suit jackets and sunglasses who chatted for a few moments at the door before one of them left, made Sue pause for breath.

"I wonder what they want." She laid a stack of men's long-sleeved work shirts on the counter in front of Ava. "You go through these, dear," Sue directed. "They're all the size you asked for and will go with those new jeans. Still don't know why you won't let me put you in a pair of women's pants. Your tomboy casual style simply doesn't show off your shape."

That was the whole idea of dressing the way she did. Drawing attention to herself was the last thing Ava wanted.

The older woman turned her focus back to the man in the suit and frowned. "We won't make a sale off him."

Ava noted the high-school girl walking over to the burly man, who removed his sunglasses and smiled at the teenager as she offered to help him. "Maybe he's lost and stopped in to ask for directions," Ava suggested, although a curious suspicion was tickling the back of her neck. Her reaction could be attributed to her instinctive reaction to strangers. But the only time she'd seen a man with a chest that stocky was Detective Charles when he'd worn a Kevlar vest beneath his shirt the day he'd walked her through the crime scene, from the campus parking lot where she'd been taken to the warehouse district where she'd been released. Either the man at the door was training for a bodybuilding competition, or he was armed beneath that suit jacket. She dropped her voice to a whisper. "Do you know him?"

"I don't think so." Sue tapped a bright pink fingernail against her bottom lip. The older woman had spent her whole life in the area, while Ava had only been a summertime resident, so if anyone could place a face, it was Sue. They watched the dark-haired man strike up a friendly conversation with the teen before pulling his cell phone from inside his jacket and showing the screen to the girl.

"Maybe he does just want directions." Ava picked up a green chambray shirt that reminded her of the color of Larkin's mysterious eyes.

"Ava." Suddenly focused on her again, Sue clicked her tongue in a gentle reprimand and plucked the green shirt from Ava's hands. She pulled out a pink-and-gray plaid instead. "I think it's time you zhush up your look a bit. If I can't get you to wear women's clothes, at least try something a little more feminine. Pink was your grandma Myrna's favorite color." She held the shirt up to Ava's chin and frowned. Then she reached into the stack of men's shirts and pulled out a different one to hold up. "The soft blue, I think. It draws the attention up to your eyes. Away from the marks on your skin."

And just like that, Ava was done with the whole shopping experience. Not because of Sue's comment—after all, her scars were a part of her she could hardly deny. But because of the rest of the conversation she knew would follow. "The blue is fine. I think I'm finished—"

"I feel like I have to take up Myrna's cause since she's not here to help you. I know you came to Pole Axe runnin' from something—a lot of folks do. Why else would you come to this godforsaken town if you weren't born to it."

"I came to work."

Sue waved off that explanation. "Work, schmerk. It's not right for you to be alone so much. You're never going to get yourself a man staying so far outside of town all by yourself and dressing to hide every pretty thing there is about you. You always look so sad, dear. I remember how bright and funny you are. I know Jim and Myrna would want you to at least make friends your own age." The older woman punctuated the grandmotherly lecture with a sigh and threw her arms around Ava in a tight hug. "They'd be worried about you, too."

She patted the other woman's back. "I'm fine, Sue."

One. Two. The hug wasn't ending. She needed to be able to move.

"I think that cute Sheriff Stout has his eye on you."

Ava felt the panic welling up inside her, constricting her throat, blanking out her thoughts. "I need you to let go..."

Ava didn't know if it was the soft woof of Maxie going on alert, trotting over to Ava's side, or something else going on in the store behind her. But Sue abruptly released her and circled around Ava. Ava turned, as well, to see that the man in the bulky suit jacket had moved over to a couple standing at the rack of souvenir T-shirts. He was chatting them up with an amiable smile and showing them something on his phone screen. When they shook their heads, he moved on to another couple.

"What is that man up to?" Sue traced her finger around her lips, as though making sure her lipstick was still in place. Even through the haze of Ava's mini-episode, she recognized the signs of putting on armor and gearing up for an attack. Not that the septuagenarian was going to physically take on a man twice her size. But this store was her territory, and Sue wasn't afraid to speak her mind to anyone. Thankfully, the sorry state of Ava's social life had been forgotten. "If he starts chasing away my customers..." Sue squeezed Ava's arm. "Will you excuse me, dear?"

With the reprieve, Ava could genuinely smile. "You go ahead."

Ava set the jeans and shirts she wanted with the rest of the items already in her pile on the counter. All that was left on Larkin's list was a package of boxer-briefs, which Ava was more than happy to pick out herself, so that Sue wouldn't give her a sales pitch about lacy bras and silk panties, or feed the rumor mill about some of the more unusual items she was buying. She flagged Monica down, and the teen met her at the counter to check her out.

She was helping the teenager pack her items into two reusable bags when Ava heard a gravelly voice from behind her. "I heard you met a mystery man yesterday."

Ava jumped inside her skin and reached for the reassurance of contact with the dog.

At least the older man with the receding hairline and wire-rimmed glasses had been considerate enough not to touch her. His hands were raised in apology as he moved around to stand beside her. "Oh, dear. I'm sorry, Miss Wallace. I forget how sensitive you are. I didn't mean to startle you."

Last night Larkin had called her *fragile*, and now she was *sensitive*? Add in Sue's mothering and she really needed to work on her reputation around Pole Axe instead of living down to everyone's expectations of her. Willow Storm would be insulted. And frankly, Ava was getting tired of it. Last night's conversation with Larkin had been cathartic. Mentally, she was ready to change, but regrowing her confidence and her faith in the world wasn't going to happen overnight.

But it was going to happen.

Ava fixed a smile on her face for the widower who ran the local newspaper. "It's all right, Mr. Middleton. I'm working on trying to be more comfortable around other people. Coming to town on a busy Saturday is good practice for me." *This is miserable practice for me, but what else can I say? I'm jumpy about hiding a man at my cabin?*

I was assaulted by a man who's never been caught, and I think anyone who sneaks up behind me could be that guy? Better stick to the excuses she'd rehearsed and divert attention from her by saying something "normal." "How are your grandkids?"

The older gentleman smiled as she hit on a favorite topic. "Ginny just got engaged. She's asked me to walk her down the aisle."

"Congratulations. You'll look smashing in a tuxedo."

"Thanks." He leaned in a tad and winked. "Her brothers aren't too thrilled about putting on suits and ties, but they're excited about the wedding, too. It'll be back East where they all live. A year from October. It's going to be quite a production."

Ava took the receipt from Monica and tucked it into her purse. "Do you miss living back in DC?"

"Not really." He slipped his hands into the pockets of his khakis and shrugged. "My blood pressure needed the slower pace of life out here. After losing my son and wife, I was ready for a fresh start. Though I do miss tracking down the leads on an interesting story."

And now they'd come full circle to the reason the editor and chief reporter for the *County Gazetteer* had struck up a conversation with her in the first place. Sly. "And you think a mystery man is an interesting story?"

"You tell me."

Even living on the fringes of town, Ava had heard the story about James Middleton's son, a Navy ensign who'd been killed in a training accident. His wife had died soon after from a prophetic blood clot to her broken heart. Ava understood better than most about how a lifestyle change and relocation could help one recover from an emotional upheaval. But once a newshound, always a newshound, she supposed. After retiring from a career at a metropolitan newspaper covering political intrigue, Congressional committees and Supreme Court rulings, the occasional events to drive tourism and agricultural news here must seem pretty tame. Especially with a paper that only came out once a week. Still, Ava wasn't about to indulge his curiosity.

"There's not much to tell. He stumbled out of the woods, fainted on my front porch. I drove him to the hospital and left as soon as Sheriff Stout took my statement."

"You have no idea what his name is? Where he works?"

Ava looped her purse back around her neck and shoulder. "Sorry."

"My sources say he left the hospital without checking out."

"You have sources in Pole Axe?"

He chuckled. "The town gossips. You know how they love to talk. I've heard everything from this guy being shot in the head to being attacked by a mountain lion. While I imagine the truth lies somewhere in the middle, it sounds to me like he needs to be under a doctor's care. Makes me curious about why the man would wander off from the hospital. What if he's a danger to himself? Collapses again, and no one's around to help? What if he's a danger to someone else?"

Ava got a whiff of a woodsy cologne and cigarette smoke a split second before she heard the man's voice behind her. "You're not talking about this man, are you?"

The advanced warning kept her from gasping out loud. Ava turned to see the big man in the gray suit holding out his cell phone. Thankfully, her eyes were downturned when she saw the image on the screen, or he might have seen a flash of recognition there.

Sue had linked her arm through his to escort him to the counter, steering him away from a group of tourists who'd descended upon the section of Wyoming souvenirs. "This is the woman I was telling you about, Roy." Roy? Sue sure could make friends quickly when she put her mind to it. "Our local heroine, Ava Wallace."

The dark-haired man stuck out a meaty hand. "Nice to meet you, Ms. Wallace. I'm Roy Hauser. Security chief for Bell Design Systems. I've been looking for this man."

She barely touched his fingers as they shook hands. "Who is he?"

"He used to work for BDS. Luke's gone missing."

Luke? Bell Design Systems? Larkin's key chain had an L.B. carved in it. *Luke Bell?* Great. Had the heir to a tech fortune stumbled into her life yesterday? No wonder this man was looking for him.

The older man beside her introduced himself, as well. "I'm James Middleton. I run the local paper." The two men shook hands. "BDS. Isn't that a high-tech company? You have contracts with the military?"

"I'm not at liberty to say, sir." He showed them both the picture on his phone again. "You're sure this isn't the man you met?"

The man in the picture staring back at her was fresh out of the military. He was clean-shaven, and she could see his scalp through the close shave of his hair. But even wide open instead of narrowed in scrutiny, the eyes were unmistakable—silvery-green and piercing in their intensity.

A quiver of excitement stirred in Ava's belly. This man knew Larkin. But she had to respect Larkin's request that no one know he was hiding at her place. As long as he kept her A. L. Baines persona a secret, she would do the same for him. She wondered if anyone gave out acting awards for playing dumb. If people believed she was *sensitive* and *fragile*, maybe they'd believe she was clueless, too. This would be good practice before she called Kent Russell back.

"I don't know." She combed her fingers into her ponytail and made a show of twirling it between her fingers.

"The man I saw had a beard and longer hair than that. Plus, he was beat-up from his injuries—bruises and swelling. His face wasn't shaped like that." She studied the image on Roy Hauser's phone, hoping to get a glimpse of any sort of identifying information. But in the split second before he swiped it away, she saw no name with the picture, only a code of numbers and symbols across the bottom of the image. Ava glanced up into Mr. Hauser's brown eyes, the way any normal woman would. "From that picture, it's hard to tell."

"Your sacks are full of men's clothes," he observed, perhaps not buying into her helpless, eccentric persona the way the folks of Pole Axe did. He peeked into the tops of Ava's bags. "You know it's a crime to aid and abet a fugitive."

Ava's head shot up. "Is he a fugitive?"

He grinned. "Well, right now he's just a missing person." He pulled the green chambray shirt from the top of one bag. "The men's clothes?"

Okay. So, she hadn't played dumb enough if this man was suspicious of her guileless responses. Allowing the irritation she was feeling to rise to the surface, she snatched the shirt from his fingers and stuffed it back into the bag before flicking her collar and patting the baggy fit of her jeans, indicating the clothes were for her.

"Ah. I forget that women are as rugged as the men in this part of the country. Sorry to have bothered you." As he pulled back the front of his jacket to tuck his phone inside, she confirmed that not only was he wearing a protective vest, but there was a gun holstered at his waist.

This man was no fool. And even if he was, he wasn't anyone Ava wanted to mess with. Maybe the gun and vest were standard issue for a security chief at a tech company. But was this the man who had tried to kill Larkin? Or was he a friend who was trying to save him before the would-be killer found him?

Before Ava had to make an excuse to escape any more questions, the other man dashed back into the store. "Roy. I've got the doc in his office at the clinic. He's free to talk for a few minutes."

"Thanks." Roy started after his coworker, then paused and reached inside his jacket before turning back. She was relieved to see that he'd pulled out nothing more dangerous than his wallet. He handed her his business card. "In case you run into that man you rescued again. Or think of anything that might help us." She took the card and tucked it into the pocket of her jeans. Roy handed one to James and Sue, too. "If any of you see him, give me a call." Then he hurried to lead the other man out the door. "Let's go."

Sue helped Ava gather her shopping bags. "What can I do for you today, James?"

The balding man smiled. "You free for lunch?"

Sue winked. "For you, sweetie, I am."

Not one to be caught in the middle of anyone else's budding romance, Ava made a beeline for the door. "That's my cue to leave, too. Thanks!"

"Don't be such a stranger," Sue called after her.

The door was swinging shut behind her as she saw the two men in the black SUV pull out and drive the whole block to turn into the clinic's parking lot. The black SUV wasn't unlike the one Larkin had instinctively recoiled from as it drove past yesterday. Had Roy Hauser and his armed sidekick been searching for Larkin then? What was Larkin's connection to BDS? Were they friends or foes? Or had it simply been a coincidence—a sense of being hunted that had made him duck and hide in her truck yesterday?

And if it was just a coincidence, why did Ava get the sense that someone was now watching her, too?

Although the two security men were headed in the opposite direction from her cabin, she decided it would be smarter not to go straight home. Let them settle in with Kent Russell and that interview before they or anyone else decided to follow her.

After locking her bags inside the truck, Ava tugged on Maxie's leash and crossed the street to Kris DeKamp's Koffee Shop. The moment she pushed open the door, she heard a friendly greeting from the dark-haired woman behind the counter. "Hey, there, stranger. And it isn't even a Monday."

Ava held up the end of Maxie's leash before coming inside. "Do you mind?"

"Not at all. Maxie's always welcome here. I've even got a treat for her." As Maxie trotted up and propped her big paws on the counter, Kris tossed her a crunchy treat. Maybe it was just as well that Ava didn't come into town often. Maxie might become a big tub of lard with all this spoilage. Once the dog was chomping on her treat, Kris wiped off the counter and smiled. "What can I get you?"

Ava read the chalkboard behind the counter for the day's selections, and chose a frothy, chocolate-flavored concoction. She almost ordered a second coffee for Larkin. But if she'd had a close call explaining her sacks full of men's clothes and toiletries, then she'd have an even harder time explaining two drinks for one homebody. Instead, she chose a bag of coffee beans to brew at home. If Larkin felt cheated out of a mocha latte, he'd have to be satisfied with this.

"Digging in for the weekend to work on that dissertation, I can tell. I don't blame you stocking up on caffeine. This is my own roast. I've added a touch of vanilla and hazelnut, cooler flavors for the summer."

Ava inhaled the heavenly brew before taking a sip. "It's delicious. Thanks, Kris."

While Kris rang up her purchase, the coffee shop owner

nodded to the Hole in the Wall across the street. "What is Roy Hauser doing here? I figured we were beneath him and his big-money, high-tech ways here in Pole Axe."

Ava nearly dropped her coffee. But she managed to hang on to the insulated cup and casually say, "I just met him at Sue's place. Do you know him?"

The other woman nodded. "I've catered a couple of luncheons up at the lodge BDS uses when they have imported guests."

"Imported?"

"They do a lot of business with foreign investors. When they come to the US, they like to show their guests the all-American sights like Yellowstone and the Grand Canyon. They use the Ridgerunner Lodge up on top of the mountain. Great views. Luxury rooms. Plenty of privacy, yet easy access to the Jackson Airport and parks." She handed Ava her receipt. "Roy and his people do security checks on anyone they hire to work with their executive staff and investors."

"And Roy checked you out?"

Kris pushed her glasses up on her nose and rolled her eyes. "In more ways than one. He asked me out to dinner. Picked me up and flew me in the BDS jet to Cheyenne."

"Wow."

"Well, it would have been *wow* if the company had been more interesting. He's attractive enough in that manly man kind of way. But I'd have paid my own way just to get a real conversation out of him."

Ava's opinion of the security chief was leaning toward suspicion again. *I'm not at liberty to say* had been his response to Mr. Middleton's question about Larkin's picture and working with the military. "Did you think he was lying to you about something?"

"Yeah, but I couldn't tell you what." Kris handed Ava the bag of coffee beans. "I know Bell Design Systems works with some government stuff, so he can't say much about his work. But I'd have been happy with a story about growing up on the mean streets of the city, fighting to make something of himself until he enlisted in the Army and finally found a family in his comrades in arms."

And Ava thought *she* was the one who made up stories. "Is he a soldier?"

"Roy talked more about the money and perks he got with BDS, and how he worked closely with Gregory Bell, the company's founder and CEO. Like that was supposed to impress me." She eyed the door, as if the burly security chief was headed this way. "He seems like he could be military, doesn't he?"

"I didn't talk to him long enough to know." Ava had automatically turned when Kris's focus had shifted. Fortunately, there was no sign of Hauser, his sidekick or the black SUV. She hid her sigh of relief behind another sip of the decadent coffee. "It's good to chat with you, Kris. Thanks for the coffee."

"Good to see you, too. Feel free to stop in more often."

Ava held her cup up in a friendly salute, then headed back to her truck. She set her coffee in the cup holder and loaded Maxie onto the bench seat. She had completed her mission to buy supplies for Larkin and had engaged in more conversation than she had since moving to Wyoming. Was she getting clues to piece together Larkin's forgotten life? Or was she merely taking in a lot of useless facts that might mean nothing?

She was climbing in behind the wheel when she noticed the flyer tucked beneath her windshield wiper. "What now?"

She stood on the running board to pull the colorful advertisement free and noticed similar pieces of paper had been put on the windshield of every vehicle parked in the downtown area.

"Come to the cookout." A group of local ranchers made some good money every summer taking tourists on a ride in a mock wagon train, culminating in a fireside cookout for dinner. The wagon train had been a staple every summer she could remember. She'd even ridden in a Conestoga wagon and gone to the cookout with her grandparents once herself.

She was smiling at the pleasant memory from her childhood until she turned the flyer over and saw that someone had scrawled a message on it.

I will always find you.

Ava's senses suddenly stopped working. Cotton filled her ears, muting the sounds of traffic and voices on the street. Spots swirled through her vision, her breath locked up in her chest and she was suddenly cold. So cold.

But then adrenaline spiked through her system and she jumped down. She ran to the truck beside hers and pulled off the flyer. No message. She pulled out three more flyers with pictures of a Conestoga wagon and bonfire. Dates. Times. A blur of other printing. But no handwritten words.

Words that shouldn't be here.

Words that could only be meant for her alone.

I will always find you.

If she hadn't felt a cold nose nuzzling her hand at that exact moment, she might have fainted. Or screamed. Instead, she knelt and hugged Maxie tight around the neck, oblivious to the voices of concern, shaking off the hands that tried to help.

"I'm okay," she lied to the disembodied voices that were worried for her, letting Maxie pull her to her feet. "I have to go." She brushed aside the circle of strangers and friends alike who had rushed over to help her and climbed into the truck right behind the dog.

She started the engine and backed out, barely hearing the tires squealing on the pavement as she stomped on the accelerator. She hadn't had an attack like this in months. She'd pushed herself too hard. Made contact with too many people. That drone this morning had put the idea of being watched in her head, and she'd never really shaken that sense of someone tracking her. She'd dropped her guard and hadn't seen the threat coming. She was having a full-blown panic attack in the middle of Main Street, but she couldn't do a damn thing to stop it.

I will always find you.

Ava wadded up the flyer and tossed it onto the floor of the truck. She needed to get out of here. Needed her sanctuary.

Needed someone who didn't see her as a victim.

Now.

Chapter Seven

Larkin heard a vehicle crunching over the gravel road and shot up from the stool in the kitchen where he'd been thumbing through the skinny county phone book, wondering who he could call to locate Ava without giving himself away. He knotted the silky ties of the snug, flowered robe he'd found in the bathroom over his jeans, and picked up the carving knife he'd set within arm's reach on the stone countertop, in case an intruder showed up. He'd prefer his gun—the loaded version—but he could defend himself with a knife if he had to.

When he peeked through the curtains beside the door and saw Ava's pickup pulling up to the house, with Maxie's big, panting snout hanging out the passenger window, he exhaled a sigh of relief. "About damn time, woman."

He paused with his hand on the doorknob. Although he wanted to know why she'd been gone longer than a trip into Pole Axe should take, according to his calculations, and ask if she'd considered the importance of having a backup plan or even a way to contact each other if either one of them got into trouble, he thought better of rushing outside and greeting her with a knife in his hand.

While she unleashed the hound and unloaded several bags from behind the seat, Larkin jogged back to the kitchen to return the knife to the butcher block from where he'd pulled it.

Chances were, he was overreacting to her lengthy absence. She had agreed she'd shop for him today so he could have some clothes that fit and a blessed pair of underpants. She'd told him she rose early to walk the dog and might be out when he got up. But he'd slept in later than he had in years, no doubt a side effect of his injuries and the medications working through his system. The list he'd jotted last night was gone from the bedside table, so he knew she'd come in to see him. He'd been half-aware of her presence as he'd slept—floating around his bed, gentle hands checking his vital signs, tending him in a way that made him feel someone cared. Or maybe that had all been a dream conjured by his jumbled brain.

The ringing telephone had jolted him awake nearly two hours ago. When it became clear that Ava wasn't around to answer, he'd grabbed his jeans and run downstairs to hear a message from Kent Russell, asking on his whereabouts. Was the doctor really that concerned about his recovery? While he was being nosy, he listened to an earlier message from Dr. Russell, and another from Sheriff Stout. Was that why Ava had been gone so long? Had one or the other cornered her in town and pressured her with their suspicions that she knew something she wasn't telling them?

He'd been worried that something had happened to her, and he'd had no way to confirm or disprove his worst suspicions. Even more unsettling had been admitting he'd been worried for himself. Ava Wallace was his lifeline to the world. His best chance at survival. Without her, he was a sitting duck, with no clue who his enemy might be or when that enemy would strike again. He felt guilty enough asking her to help him, to help them both recover from the mistakes that left them feeling so vulnerable and alone.

But even more than the guilt was something unfamiliar twisting around his heart. He'd been worried that she'd wrecked her truck on the twisting drive. Or that Sheriff Touchy-Feely had ignored her boundaries and upset her again. Or that whoever wanted him dead had put two and two together and gone after Ava instead of him.

That's what scared him the most.

He liked Ava Wallace. Liked her big galoot of a dog. He'd admired her talent long before he'd even met her. Her bravery was unquestionable. He loved her sense of humor. He could look into those deep blue eyes all day long and, if he was lucky one day, he hoped to taste those full, sensual lips that so rarely smiled. He'd lost too many people who mattered already. Of all the memories he was certain of, the loss of the men and women who'd served with him, trusted him, had been as close as family, was crystal clear. The fact he could feel that loss so much more viscerally than anything else from his past made him think he didn't form many close attachments to people anymore. But in less than twenty-four hours, he'd made a connection to Ava. And the thought of anyone, anything, hurting her hit him like another bullet to the chest.

So, running to the door, swinging it open to meet her on the porch might be overreacting. But since he wasn't exactly in his right mind at the moment, he wasn't going to argue these instincts where Ava was concerned.

"Where the hell have you been?" he demanded before he could temper the emotion out of his words. The dog lumbered past him, but he scooped two grocery bags out of Ava's arms and blocked her path. "You were gone longer than you said it would take you. I had no way to call you. You couldn't leave a damn note? Why didn't you wake me up? I was worried about you."

"You needed your rest." Her voice sounded used up. She stared at the middle of his chest for a moment, but her gaze never reached his eyes.

Then she shouldered past him and walked into the kitchen, where she set two cloth bags onto the counter. Something was off. Something was way off. Avoiding people was one thing, but the Ava he knew was antisocial with an attitude. This robotic tone and distant focus were something else.

"Ava?" He locked the door and followed her to the kitchen to find her studying the knife block before she pulled out the blade he'd used and reset it into its proper slot. What? No freak-out about the knife after the kidnapping nightmare she'd shared last night? No joke about the robe with the pink flowers that reminded him of his grandma's garden? He preferred a slap across the face for greeting her like such a scary jerk to this spooky quiet. He set the sacks on the center island. "I'm sorry. I shouldn't have jumped on your case like that. I let my uncertainties get the better of me. We don't have a backup plan in case this cabin gets compromised or one of us gets into trouble and needs an Option B to stay safe." He circled the island as she unpacked the groceries and turned to the refrigerator to put them away. He made his voice as gentle as a Marine who was used to giving orders could make it. "I was right to be worried, wasn't I. What's wrong? What's happened?"

No reply. No acknowledgment that he'd even spoken. She unpacked a bag of coffee and a disposable cell phone. She pushed the cell phone across the countertop toward him and turned to put the coffee away in a cabinet. This woman had bossed him around six ways to Sunday, pulled a gun on him and ogled him with an unabashed appreciation he wondered if she was fully aware of. He certainly was. That was the fighter she wanted to be—the fighter he suspected she had once been before tragedy had stolen her trust in the world and her faith in herself. Today, she was slowly, methodically going through the motions as though her brain didn't fully realize what her hands were doing.

And it was killing him.

"Ava, I'm going to touch your arms. Okay?" If he hadn't been studying her so closely, he'd have missed the subtle nod. When she didn't flinch at the cup of his hands around her shoulders, he turned her to face him. He hunched down to study her pale skin and her unfocused eyes. "You drove home like this?"

Instead of offering an explanation, she raised her hand and touched the point of his chin. Her gaze followed her fingers as she rubbed her palm against his jaw and curled her fingertips into his beard and gently tugged. He cooled his body's response to her curious exploration. Whatever was going on, she didn't need it complicated by the punch of desire heating his blood. He lifted his chin to give her access to the side of his neck. And when she slipped her fingertips beneath the edge of the silly robe, he understood that she was touching him in the places she'd said her abductor had had scars.

There were no reassuring words he could offer. She had to discover the truth and believe it for herself that he was no threat to her. Eventually, her shoulders lifted with a weary sigh and she slowly walked into his chest.

Larkin wrapped his arms loosely around her. When she didn't instantly bolt at his touch, he slid one hand up beneath her silky ponytail at the nape of her neck and splayed the fingers of his other hand at the small of her back. *One thousand one.* Even with her arms folded between them, she fit perfectly against him. But she was shaking. He felt her breath come in stuttering gusts against the skin of his chest exposed by this ridiculous outfit he wore. *One thousand two.* Ava was usually a prickly touch-me-not, and now she was melting into him. She nestled her head beneath his chin, some of the long strands of her dark hair tangling with his golden beard. Her fingertips slipped into the front of the robe and she palmed the thumping beat of his heart. Seeking warmth? Taking comfort? Ensuring he was the same man she'd made a dangerous bargain with last night? *One thousand three.*

It took a considerable will to relax his arms and step back.

"You counted to three, didn't you." She tilted her blue eyes to his and he breathed a little easier at the clarity he saw there.

"This is *your* sanctuary. We play by your rules."

Even in that simplest of embraces, several strands of dark hair had come loose from her ponytail and drifted in curly wisps against her eyelashes and cheek. "It's nice to have the option to snuggle in or break contact if I need to. Thank you for understanding."

"You know me—I'm all about Option B." He reached out to capture those stray tendrils of hair and brush them off her cheek. But then he pulled away, despite having discovered an affinity for burying his fingers in the sable-colored silk. "If breaking contact is what you need, then that's what will happen."

"And if I don't want to break contact?"

He swallowed hard at the implication that she might want his touch, that she trusted him with that gift, at least a little. "I'd be game for that." No sense denying his attraction to her. "But no pressure. Like I said—your house, your rules."

She crossed to the center island and picked up the discarded sling that he'd never bothered to put on once his mission had been to locate her. She held it out to him. "You're supposed to wear this."

"And you're supposed to be okay. You're not."

She dropped the sling on the island top and went back to unpacking the groceries. "I wasn't always like this, you know. Tentative. Jumpy. *Fragile.*"

"I didn't think you were. Willow Storm is a passionate

woman. And I'm guessing there's a lot of you in Willow." Larkin reached into the sack closest to him and pulled out a carton of milk. "Talk to me, Ava." When he handed her the milk, he held on for a few seconds until she made eye contact again. "Last night you said you wanted to be a fighter. Fight through whatever's hurt you this morning and tell me what happened."

She carried the milk to the fridge before she spoke. "I had a panic attack in the middle of downtown."

"Because of me?"

She shook her head. "Because of this." She pulled a crumpled piece of shiny paper out of the second sack and set it on the counter.

He unfolded the advertisement and read the message. "'I will always find you.'"

She carried the sacks to a crate by the back door and stooped to pet Maxie where she'd stretched out in one of several beds Larkin had noticed around the house. "I don't know how many people saw me. But it's the height of tourist season. They were shocked or feeling sorry for me. It's humiliating to lose control of my senses like that. Even worse is how vulnerable I am when that happens. I couldn't see faces. I heard voices asking if I was okay, and I think someone called 9-1-1, but…" She'd been deprived of her sense of sight when she'd been kidnapped. Losing her ability to focus in on anyone had probably fed her panic. "I had to get out of there. No wonder everyone I know walks on eggshells around me." When the big dog rolled onto her back, Ava obliged by rubbing the dog's tummy. "If Maxie hadn't been there, I don't know what I would have done."

"You would have figured it out. You *did* figure it out because you're here now. You're safe." Her hand paused on Maxie's belly. "Clearly, this note triggered something in you. What does it mean?" Nothing good, he could guess from her seeming need to maintain contact with the dog. Although his instinct was to go to her and offer the same support she got from Maxie, he gave her the space she insisted on. "Honey, I'm so sorry this happened. What do you need from me?"

She rolled to her feet and came back to the counter. "Right now, I need you to go away and leave me alone. And maybe you'd better not call me honey. Here." She tossed him the bags of clothes and finally commented on the robe he'd borrowed. "My grandmother would be honored that you like her robe, but I hardly think the pink peonies are something Bonecrusher would wear. There are towels in the hallway closet if you want to shower."

He looped both bags over his good shoulder, wondering if she had truly recovered from the panic attack, or if this was a brave front meant to keep him at a distance. "If I had on my own underwear right now, this conversation wouldn't be over."

She rewarded him with the shadow of a smile. "I can't share my backstory with a man who has no underwear."

She was back with him and she was okay. But there was definitely something wrong when her gaze slid over to the message on the counter. He'd been serious about trading his military police skills for her protection. Even if that note had nothing to do with him, a panic attack was no joke. If he could do anything to prevent another one, he would. However, he sensed that pushing her to talk to him wasn't going to get him an explanation. He'd best give her what she'd asked for. Distance.

As he backed into the living room, he looked over at Maxie, who'd laid her head on her big paws. "You keep an eye on her, okay?" Then he nodded to Ava. "I'm leaving the dragon to watch your back."

A soft smile rounded her lips a little further. "I'll be fine, Larkin. Go."

One thing Larkin hadn't forgotten from his military training was how to take a five-minute shower. Since he was skipping shaving these days, he was stepping out of the guest bathroom in three. But with his bum shoulder making it difficult to lift his arm over his head, it was taking him five times that long to towel off and get dressed.

That's why he was standing at the foot of the bed in nothing but his briefs and his unhooked jeans hanging low around his hips when he heard a startled, "Oh," from the open doorway.

He spun around to see Ava beating a hasty retreat into the hallway. "Ava?"

"Sorry." She tried to pull the door shut after her, but each hand held a mug and she couldn't grab the knob or the door.

Larkin buttoned his jeans and hurried to catch her. "What's wrong?"

When he reached the doorway, she gaped at his chest, then turned her back to him. "I'm sorry. Your door was open. I thought... I can't seem to stop looking at your naked body. I mean... I keep seeing you without your clothes on. And I'm not looking away." She muttered a curse. "Why am I still talking?"

He laughed at the unintended compliment. "Not the worst thing a woman's ever said to me. Especially for a guy who's a little beat-up around the edges."

When she faced him again, her cheeks were that healthy shade of pink he enjoyed putting there. "That makes you interesting."

And now he was the one blushing. Nice to know the attraction he felt wasn't one-sided. But this was hardly the moment to act on it. Time to move on from any further discussion of his seasoned attributes. The fragrant steam rising from the mugs she held reached his nose and he breathed in the rich, toasty smell. "Is one of those for me?"

She held out a mug, which he gladly accepted. "I saw you hadn't helped yourself to anything in the kitchen. Thought maybe you could use some caffeine."

"Desperately." He breathed in the aroma, then sipped the steaming, revitalizing brew. "Mmm. That's good. Thanks."

After another drink, he carried the mug to the bedside table and set it down so that he could pull on a T-shirt. When it got caught beneath his arm and he groaned at the twisting motion of trying to free it, he suddenly felt an extra pair of hands on his shoulder and back. "Try not to lift your arm." His muscles jumped at the stroke of Ava's hands. There was nothing tentative about her touch. And though he knew she was acting as a nursemaid, there was something about her fingers against his skin that felt familiar...and arousing in an ill-timed, moving-too-fast-for-this-woman way. "Do you want the sling? I can run downstairs and get it," she offered.

Why would he remember her touch when he couldn't come up with his own name? Plus, it was a dangerous sign that he wished she'd been taking *off* his shirt, instead of pulling it down his torso. With his *naked body* removed from her view, he moved away from where her hand lingered on his shoulder, although moving away from Ava was the last thing he wanted to do. "I'm not wearing that thing anymore. Makes me feel like I've got one arm tied behind my back. I think the stitches will hold as long as I don't overdo it."

He drank another sip of coffee before pulling on a pair of socks. When he groaned at the resistance of tugging on his work boots, Ava knelt in front of him to help with that, too. "I pegged you for a black coffee kind of guy. Although I do have sugar, half-and-half and four flavors of creamer if you want."

Yep. A man who couldn't properly dress himself needed

to stop thinking about the whole sexual tension thing simmering in his blood. "Straight up will do fine." He took another drink a little too quickly and nearly scalded the roof of his mouth. But it was enough of a metaphoric pinch to pull him back to what was important here. "I've got it. Thanks." He took over tying his own boots while Ava rolled to her feet and retrieved her own mug of coffee. "You ready to talk about that note?"

"How's the rest of you feeling this morning?"

So that would be a no. Fine. She wasn't the only one who needed a few minutes to shake off the feeling that their lives had crashed into each other and were irrevocably changing. "I finally shook that groggy feeling. Makes me wonder what the doc gave me for it to hang on so long. Shoulder and knee are better. Still have a thumb drive in my belly. Head's throbbing, and no, I can't remember my name." Enough stalling. He tied off the second boot and sat up. "I'm worried about you. Something happened in town."

She sank onto the bed beside him, studying the depths of her coffee a few moments before lifting her gaze to his. "Does the name Luke sound familiar?"

"Luke?" Had someone named Luke sent her that message? Oh. He picked up his key chain from the bedside table. "L.B. Luke… Something… Luke…?" He shook his head and tucked the keys to an unknown home or apartment into his pocket. "Should it?"

"Luke or Lucas Bell, maybe?"

"Bell…" That didn't sound right. Hell, the only name that sounded right to his ears this morning was Larkin. He wasn't forgetting that note or her panic attack, but he'd let her lead the conversation where she needed it to go. "You learned something in town this morning about me?"

"There were two men asking about a missing person named Luke. I spoke to one of them. Roy Hauser?" Nope. That name wasn't clicking anything into place, either.

"He's probably in his forties. Dark hair. Muscular build. He had your picture on his phone. Mr. Hauser mentioned the name Luke. He said he's the security chief of Bell Design Systems, and that you used to work for the company. I wonder if you could be a relative. I didn't want to confirm that I knew you until I ran it past you first."

"Used to work for BDS?" Maybe his automatic use of the acronym wasn't a breakthrough. Bell Design Systems was a big enough company that he'd heard of it. They designed technology that the military used. He remembered the BDS logo on software and scanning equipment he'd used. But he had no recollection of working for the company itself. "You're certain it was me he was asking about?"

"The man in the picture looked a lot like you. At least, a version of you. Less scruffy—more military man than medieval warrior. The shop owner and our local newspaper editor were already talking about my mystery man. Hauser must have overheard them and came up to me."

"*Your* mystery man?" There was already gossip around town about them? If the locals had made the connection, it was only a matter of time before the people who'd tried to kill him did, too.

"From yesterday. Nobody knows you're here now. They think you skipped town."

Larkin pushed to his feet, pacing the length of the room. "I don't like that he singled you out. I don't want anyone associating me with you. It puts you in the line of fire."

"I wasn't singled out," she assured him. "He was talking to everyone. They were on their way to see Dr. Russell when they left. Doc Russell has been asking about you, too."

"I know. I heard the messages from him."

"More than one?"

He nodded.

She ran her finger around the edge of her mug, and he once again felt the kick of a memory of her hands on him. "I lied to Mr. Hauser. I said the picture was different from the man I left at the hospital last night. Should I make up a lie to tell Dr. Russell, too?"

If he was looking for a missing person, he'd be questioning everyone. And he'd be watching for subtle nuances in expression that could give away someone with something to hide. Ava wrote fiction for a living, but was she a convincing liar?

She stood, cradling the warm mug between her hands. "Does any of this sound familiar?"

Larkin was pacing again, fighting to make any bit of this information slide into place. *Option B. Bullet to the head or diving off the edge of a cliff. Lying on the ground, looking up at a gun. And the man holding the gun*…could have been Little Mary Sunshine for all he knew. Larkin swore in frustration. Even if his memory was clear, his vision had been blurred from the head injury.

"Don't try so hard to remember," Ava suggested. "It's like when I'm searching for just the right word to use in a scene, and it won't come to me, no matter how hard I try. Obviously, what you're trying to remember is on a bigger scale, but a lot of times the word that's eluding me comes to me when I stop thinking about it. Like when I'm doing the dishes or walking Maxie."

He grunted a wry laugh. "Got any dishes I can wash?"

That earned a soft smile from Ava. "No. But I will take Maxie for a walk after lunch."

"Do you mind if I tag along?"

"Not at all." The smile vanished and she took another sip of coffee, fortifying herself for her next comment. "I have an Option B in mind for you. In case the cabin is compromised, and you need a place to hide."

"Out in the woods?"

She nodded. "I almost went there this morning instead of coming here."

"Because of the note?"

"There's a place I found when I was a little girl. It's on Grandpa's property, but I never told anyone but him where it was. I've gone there a lot over the years when I needed some quiet time. I wouldn't recommend hanging out there in the winter. But in the summer, it's a pretty sweet hideout."

He could picture her as a little girl, with long pigtails and skinned knees, exploring her grandparents' land. She was probably a bookworm who'd climbed a tree and read for hours. "Sounds pretty special. You sure you want to share it with me?"

"I don't have an Option C for you." The crunch of gravel outside the open windows brought an abrupt end to the conversation. Downstairs, Maxie barked and ran to the front door, her big paws hitting like hoofbeats on the wood floor. Ava crossed to the window to peek through the curtain. "Now what?"

Larkin reached the window half a step behind her. "You expecting visitors?"

"Never." Ava palmed his chest, pushing him away from the window before running past him.

He was tall enough to peer over her head before the curtains closed, spotting the SUV with the circle and badge on its side pulling up to the house. "It's your sheriff friend. Want me to answer it?" Larkin was right behind her, coming down the stairs two at a time.

"You can't." He nearly plowed into her back when she abruptly planted her feet and turned. "You're not here, re-member?" She pushed him back toward the stairs, then curled her fingers into the front of his shirt when they heard a vehicle door slam. She tugged hard and changed direc-

tions, pushing him through the dining area into the kitchen.
"I'll get rid of him, but you need to stay out of sight."

Ava wasn't overpowering him so much as he wasn't
fighting her wishes in any way. "I don't like that guy."

"So I gather."

"He doesn't respect you. He's like Lord Zeville. Willow
wouldn't put up with the way he treats you."

"We can do a literary analysis later." His boots hit the
tile floor of the kitchen and Ava guided him around the
center island. "Right now, you can hide in the pantry." She
pulled her lips to her teeth and whistled at a shrill enough
pitch that Larkin grimaced. "Maxie, come!" Okay, that
should not be such a turn-on, but this woman was completely in control of that dog and as powerful as he'd ever
seen her. The big white dog came loping in at Ava's command and sat beside her. She centered herself by touching
the dog's head before the door closed in Larkin's face. The
door swung open again just as quickly, and she tossed in
the sling he'd left lying on the island. "I'll keep him outside. You stay put."

He couldn't. He couldn't let Ava face the authorities
without any kind of backup. If this was about him, he'd
reveal himself and absolve her of any wrongdoing. And if
this was about whatever relationship Sheriff Touchy-Feely
thought he could force on Ava, then Larkin was going to
do something about that, too.

As soon as he heard the front door open and close behind Ava and Maxie, Larkin crept out of the pantry, assessing his options in case he needed to intervene. His gaze
landed on the butcher block of knives. He palmed the knife
he'd used earlier and edged along the walls. Thank goodness the mountain air was pleasant enough that Ava opened
windows instead of running the air. Although he couldn't
get a clear sight line from the first floor without giving his

presence away, he inched as close as he dared to the dining room window overlooking the porch and listened in.

He heard the clomp of the sheriff's boots on the wood steps. "Ava? I heard you had a freak-out in town. What happened, baby?"

If she'd objected to *honey*, then she was probably seething at *baby*.

Her voice was quiet, but she didn't hesitate to answer. "I figured I'd be hearing from you, Brandon. Did Sue call?"

"Sue and Kris both. They were worried about you. Said you were really upset or having a seizure or something." A third clomp told Larkin that Stout had finally been allowed—or pushed his way—onto the porch. "You never used to be like that, you know, before you came back to town."

This guy didn't know about her PTSD? Did he know how Ava had gotten her scars? Had he ever bothered to ask?

"I guess I overreacted." He heard a pause and figured out the flyer was changing hands. "This was on my truck when I came out of the coffee shop. I don't suppose any of the other flyers in Pole Axe had a personal message like this."

The sheriff took his time reading the note. "Since everybody says you went postal on Main Street, I'm guessing this is a threat and not a love letter."

"It's not a love letter. You know I'm not involved with anyone."

"Not for lack of trying." Did he really think that line would work with her? *Get a clue, pal.* "Somebody been giving you grief? That guy you drove to the hospital yesterday? Doc Russell says he skipped out without leaving a forwarding address. Has he threatened you?"

"Kent Russell? He's called a few times, but he's never threatened me." Wow. Although Larkin couldn't see her face from this position, he had to admire Ava's acting skills. He'd never had the patience to deal with a clueless bimbo who couldn't manage an intelligent conversation.

But Sheriff Touchy-Feely seemed to be eating it up. "Not the doc, baby. That stranger who got you involved in whatever trouble he's in."

"Oh. He's gone?" Could the sheriff not see the intelligence gleaming from the depths of those blue eyes? "I left the hospital right after you and haven't seen him since."

"Sue said you were buying men's clothes."

"I needed new jeans," she answered without missing a beat. "I can't keep wearing Grandpa's things. They're starting to wear out."

"Well, there's something hinky about that guy. Besides stiffing the clinic, I'm wondering if he's involved in something illegal. Running drugs. Hiding out from some other crime. You know, I wonder about that vehicle that was destroyed in Scott Harold's junkyard. First, I thought the old man was being irresponsible. But if Mr. Marine is on the run from someone, he could have torched his SUV to cover his tracks."

"I wouldn't know anything about that."

He nodded. "Of course not. Do you want to come into town? Stay with me for a few days? You could work in my apartment while I'm out huntin' down the bad guys. I could grill dinner on the deck. Give us time to catch up on the old days."

"Thanks for asking, but I'm fine here."

"I want you to be safe."

"I know. Oh." Larkin curled his toes inside his boots at Ava's startled gasp. That lout had grabbed Ava again, and Larkin knew he shouldn't intervene. But if anything Sheriff Stout said or did triggered another panic attack, he'd be out the door right now, turning himself in and doing whatever was necessary to make sure Ava was okay. *One thousand one. One thousand two. Anytime now, buddy, let her go.*

And then Larkin heard a woof. Larkin pressed himself flat against the shiplap as Stout stumbled into view and the Great Pyrenees dropped to her front paws. *Good girl*, Larkin silently praised the dog for pushing the sheriff away from her mistress. The big brute wasn't any kind of killer, but she wasn't letting anybody come between her and her mistress if Ava needed her.

Queen Mother of the Dragons to the rescue.

"I appreciate you looking out for me, Brandon," Ava said. "But I can take care of myself."

"I can see that. Maxie here won't let anybody hurt you." The sheriff petted the dog and then moved out of sight, leaving, he hoped.

"Nope. She won't."

Larkin eased his grip on the knife as he heard heavy boots on the steps.

"Mind if I keep this flyer? Could be one of the high-school kids trying to bully someone else or pull a prank, and they got the wrong truck. I'll double-check your make of truck against others that are registered in the area."

"Let me know if you find out anything, okay? Call," Ava insisted, not encouraging any more visits.

"I'll do that. In the meantime, you take care."

"I will."

The sheriff was back at his SUV, opening the door, when he paused for one last condescending reassurance. "Don't you worry your pretty little head about this, Ave. I'll take care of it for you."

Ava was rubbing her fingers over her unblemished cheek as she locked the door behind her and stalked through the dining room with Maxie at her side. Seriously? Had that guy kissed her? Larkin wasn't so enlightened that his blood didn't boil at the thought of another man touching her in a way he wanted. Ava paused but didn't seem surprised when she saw his position near the window.

"I guess I don't have to repeat anything the sheriff said. The town thinks I'm crazy, and you're a wanted man."

Once he was certain the sheriff had driven away, Larkin followed her into the kitchen. "I really don't like that guy. He's got no respect for the three-second rule." He returned the knife to the block while she opened the fridge and stared inside. "He took the note, didn't he? Not that we can do anything with evidence like that. Maybe he'll get a print off it and tell you who sent it."

"Maybe it was a practical joke like Brandon suggested." He doubted it. He wasn't dismissing any coincidences until he knew who the enemy was, and that the enemy hadn't now targeted Ava. "Hungry? I can throw together something for lunch."

He watched her pull out a loaf of bread and hug it to her chest. "Hungry for answers. *I will always find you.* What does that mean to you? Does Sheriff Stout know? And don't give me that fragile baby flower answer you gave him."

She didn't. "It was a voice from my past."

"I'm right behind you." He pulled her aside and closed the refrigerator door, giving her arm a quick squeeze before he released her, ignoring the urge to pull her against him again and hold her until that haunted look left her expression. "There are no coincidences in my life right now." Her eyes followed his hands as he took the bread from her and set it on the counter. He didn't mind being patient, but they were having this conversation. "Tell me why the note upset you."

She surprised him by pulling his fingers from the countertop. It wasn't the hug he wanted to give, or even the kiss he was longing to try. But it was contact. She'd initiated it. She was still stroking her thumb inside his palm, making him crazy with even that simplest of contact, and he'd already silently counted to seven. He curled his fingers around hers. If she wanted to hold on to him, he wasn't letting go.

He gently asked the question. "*I will always find you* is significant because…?"

"Because that's the last thing my kidnapper said to me before he let me go."

Chapter Eight

"That's the best he can do?"

Ava hung up the phone with Gabriel Charles. Larkin had gone into full-on Marine investigator mode. He'd wanted her to call the detective in charge of her case and ask certain questions. How much of Ava's case was common knowledge? What kind of security protocols did CPD have in place to protect victim anonymity? What specific leads, if any, did Gabriel have on her kidnapper—and were they anywhere close to finding the guy and making an arrest? Was there any way in hell this bastard had made his way to Wyoming to come after Ava again?

The news hadn't been great.

Even though he'd listened to the call via speakerphone, Ava had sensed more than once that Larkin wanted to snatch up her cell to conduct the interrogation himself. Instead, he had to settle for pacing a circle around her kitchen, giving her hand signals she didn't always catch and scribbling follow-up questions on the notepad where she was jotting down Detective Charles's answers.

Ava imagined Captain Mystery Marine had been an intimidating officer and investigator when he had all his faculties and his body was at one hundred percent. He was intimidating enough as is, with his chiseled, battered body, his golden-bronze beard masking half of his face and those deceptively slitted eyes that saw far more than he let on.

Pace to the window, peek through the curtain. Pace to the back door, scrub his hand over Maxie's head. Return to look over Ava's shoulder, decide he was standing too close for her comfort, then back away and resume his circle around the kitchen again.

Pushing to her feet off the stool where she'd sat, Ava tucked her phone in her pocket. "Detective Charles is as angry as you and I are to find that someone sent me that note."

Larkin propped his hands at his waist. "Am I the only one who feels the clock ticking here? You said no one but you and Detective Charles knew what your kidnapper said to you. You're sure you trust this guy?"

"Yes." As much as she could trust anybody. She went to the fridge to pull out two bottles of water. One of them already had too much coffee in his system. "At least he confirmed that Brandon didn't request the police report about my kidnapping."

"Not exactly. He confirmed that Stout didn't request your information through standard channels." He twisted the cap off the bottle she handed him and took a quick drink. "That doesn't mean Sheriff Touchy-Feely didn't access information about you by other means." He reached across the island to take her hand, the way any normal person who wanted to offer comfort might. But at the last second, he pulled back to toy with the bottle's plastic cap. Ava was at once touched by his consideration of her boundaries and disappointed to realize that she'd scared off the one man she didn't seem to mind being close to. "Either your kidnapper has found you here in Wyoming, or the people after me have accessed those files because they think you're the best lead to finding me. I don't like either scenario." He squeezed the innocent plastic in his fist. "I'm torn between wanting to stay here and protect you, and wanting to run as far away from you as I can and take the threat with me. But if this is about you, then I'd be leaving you alone and vulnerable."

Wouldn't be the first time. Though now she was wondering if *alone* was as safe as she'd thought.

"Where would you run?" she asked quietly. "You said I was the only ally you could trust. Plus, you have no vehicle, no driver's license—and no money. I'll float you a loan if you think it would help—"

"No." Apparently, that offer wasn't up for discussion. "With everything else I'm demanding of you, I will not take your money."

"This agreement is mutually beneficial, remember?" It didn't hurt to remind herself of what she was getting out of helping Larkin, too. "I'm proving to myself that I'm strong and normal and capable of being more than a shadow of who I used to be."

"That was before you got that threat from your past." He forced the lid back onto the bottle and exhaled his frustration. "We don't have a lot of options, do we?"

"We'll think of something. Larkin and Willow always do."

He grunted a sound she was learning was his wry laugh. "I thought you wanted to be Ava, not Willow."

She moved to her desk in the living room and brushed her fingers across her unopened laptop. Typically, escaping into her fantasy world was a reprieve for her. But she hadn't written anything substantial for weeks now. Her brain had been too full of fear and self-doubt to do more than write endless narrative descriptions and battle scenes, edit until there was no voice or heart left on the pages, then write the scenes again. She'd been afraid to invest her emotions into the story. Pulling her hand away, she plucked her last book off the shelf behind her desk. "Willow's not such a bad gal. I just haven't felt much like her lately."

"Do we need to have that conversation again? About where Willow's strength and ability to survive come from? You're probably more capable now than you were two years ago." He came to stand beside her, and Ava breathed in the spicy scent that came off the heat of his skin. Had Larkin simply come along at the time when she was ready to notice a man again? Or did this visceral reaction to the look, feel, sound and, apparently, the smell of him mean something more profound? "You may be different. But you're not weaker. You're not *less* than you were before the kidnapping."

"That's what my therapist says."

"Smart woman."

Ava tipped her head up. "How do you know she's a…?" Ah, yes. Narrowed eyes. All-seeing. "You figured I wouldn't be comfortable talking to a man."

He grinned. "I guess I'm the exception. And I don't have to know my own name to remember how to observe the details and piece clues together."

Ava conceded that his skills hadn't diminished, despite the gaps in his memory. "Besides dealing with the hooded man's threat again, I'm concerned about my pseudonym being leaked to the public. Detective Charles never told anyone, not even within his department, that I'm A. L. Baines. I can see it now. Wealthy, World-Famous Author Gets Kidnapped."

"That would cause one hell of a scandal if that headline ever hit the news. Is Detective Charles certain that your kidnapping has nothing to do with you being 'wealthy and world-famous'?"

"He ran that angle into the ground more than once." There hadn't been any disturbing fan letters leading up to the abduction. And during the nearly seventy-two hours she'd been held, her kidnapper had never mentioned the books or characters. "The man who took me wasn't insisting I write a story in a certain way or resurrect a dead character. There was never any ransom demand. It wasn't about the books or the money." There was only the slide of his puckered skin against her own, the acrid, oily smell clinging to his clothes and that gravelly voice rasping against her ear. *"Scream for me, darlin'. Bleed for me. That's it."* And then a blade would pierce her skin like a hot poker. His nose would tease the edge of her blindfold as he lapped up the tears that ran down her cheeks, and his fetid breath would quicken with the throes of his sick rapture. She screamed for him. She screamed.

"Ava?" She heard a crash through the stuffing in her ears. Larkin's bronze beard swam through her vision. There was a shrill whistle and a sharp command. "Maxie!"

For a moment, Ava thought she was falling. She hit a wall at her back and floated gently downward as her knees buckled.

"I've got you." A familiar weight leaned against her, and she was momentarily cocooned between two warm, immovable objects. "Do your thing, girl."

When Ava's senses gradually returned, she was sitting on the floor. Her face was pressed against the warmth of Maxie's fur and someone was holding her arms around the dog's neck, splaying her fingers through the dog's soft coat.

"Good girl, Maxie." Larkin's voice was a deep-pitched vibration that cut through the fog of the flashback. "That's it, Queen Dragon. You take care of our Willow. Do your magic."

"Larkin?" Ava whispered, orienting herself to her surroundings. Home. Maxie. An open book beside her overturned desk chair.

Silvery-green eyes looking down into hers. "You okay? You with me?"

Ava nodded. She petted Maxie around the ears and discovered she wasn't the only one praising the dog. But when her fingers brushed against Larkin's, he sat back on the rug, facing her with the dog between them.

"I'm sorry. I made you go to a place I never meant to. You faded away from me." The lines on his face were harsh with regret. "I'm sorry if touching you made it worse. I set you on the floor—I thought you were fainting."

In a move that seemed as natural as it should have been foreign to her, she reached for Larkin's hand before he retreated beyond her reach. His skin was calloused instead of soft, but as warm as the dog. He folded his fingers lightly around hers. Ava squeezed harder, wanting him to tighten his grasp. When he laced his fingers together with hers, anchoring her grip to his, she exhaled a sigh of relief, and inhaled the strength and comfort that seemed to flow through her with each hand.

"You whistled for Maxie?"

He answered with a sharp nod. But the thumb stroking the back of her hand was infinitely gentle. "I didn't know what else to do, except to make sure you didn't hit your head, and let the dog do what she does best."

Ava rubbed her cheek against Maxie's neck. "For a split second, when you were behind me—I think that's the warmest I've been in two years."

"I wanted to hold you," he confessed, the stroke of his thumb stilling against the pucker of scar tissue on her hand. "But I didn't want to make it worse."

"I'm okay," she reassured him, knowing that, for now at any rate, it was the truth. "I guess it's going to be a rough day. Usually, I don't have my attacks this close together. I'm to the point where I'll go days, weeks, without one."

"And then Larkin Bonecrusher stumbles into your life and sets your recovery back."

Ava continued to hug Maxie, although her gaze was

focused on the self-recrimination in Larkin's expression. "You have nothing to do with what happened to me two years ago. I think you're moving my recovery forward, forcing me to deal with some things." She dropped her gaze to the link of their hands. "This is the second time I've reached for you today. And I'm not afraid." She forced her lips into the semblance of a smile when she realized the truth. "I'm also not counting."

"I am." There was that wry laugh that was husky and deep-pitched and so uniquely male. "Forty-four seconds. I figure those extra forty-one seconds are a gift. Or else you're still in the throes of the attack and don't know what's going on yet."

She squeezed his hand. "I know what's going on." When she didn't immediately protest, he pulled her hand to his lips and brushed a kiss over her knuckles. His beard tickled her skin, and she felt his warmth skitter along her arm and waken things inside her that had been frozen for two years. The pleasurable sensation more than the kiss itself surprised her. But the moment she straightened her fingers to study the sensitive spot, Larkin released her. She hastened to reassure him that it wasn't his touch that had startled her, but the fact she had enjoyed it. "Maybe there is some crossover between fiction and reality that makes me feel like I know you, that I'm safe with you—that... we're meant to be a team."

"I find myself thinking that, too," he admitted. "I feel like I know you better than I should for someone I met just twenty-four hours ago. You are every bit the warrior I am, though in a different way. Maybe reading your books gives me insight into your soul, into the way you think."

Exactly. Only, he'd never written a book that she'd read. How could she be feeling such a strong connection to him? How could she feel like she knew everything about him that mattered? Shared values. Similar histories that offered them a unique understanding of each other. This crazy physical awareness of him.

But twenty-four hours?

Before the kidnapping she wouldn't have questioned her feelings for him. But perhaps she shouldn't be so ready to trust her instincts about this stranger. Helping him was one thing. Working beside him was also an acceptable decision. But falling for him?

With her mind firmly back in the present, Ava focused on the threat they'd been discussing before her panic attack.

"A little help?" When she curled her legs beneath her to stand, he tugged on her hand to pull her to her feet. She kissed Maxie's head before opening the treat jar on her desk and handing the dog a biscuit. "Good girl." The Great Pyrenees trotted over to the rug in front of the fireplace with her prize and Ava picked up the book that had fallen to the floor. "Here's what I wanted to show you." She opened the book to her publicity photo inside the back cover. "What do you think? Even if my alter ego has been leaked to the world, would any of my fans recognize me?"

Larkin studied the photograph of the woman she'd been before the scars and plastic surgery. "You're softer in this picture. Rounder cheeks, less tension beside your mouth. The suit clings to your curves. Your hair is all foo-fooey."

"Foo-fooey?" The stylist had curled and sprayed her hair within an inch of its life before that photo shoot.

Larkin closed the book in one hand and threaded the fingers of his other hand into the simple ponytail hanging over her shoulder. Although she held her breath, she didn't flinch as he sifted her hair through his fingers. "The Ava Wallace I know is a tomboy. Just as accomplished, just as creative, just as smart as this cosmopolitan A. L. Baines lady. Ava Wallace is in fighting shape. She's more streamlined. More practical. She has a sense of humor. She's more approachable to an average Joe like me."

Assuming he meant what he said, the praise made her self-conscious. Especially since she didn't think there was anything *average* about him. She took the book and placed it back on the shelf, reminding him of the truth. "She also has marks all over her body that will never completely go away, and it's hard to prove she's not as weak and fragile as people treat her when she loses it like I have today."

"Having PTSD doesn't mean you're weak. Have you ever known anyone fighting cancer or learning how to use prosthetics after losing their legs to an IED? They're warriors who refuse to give up the fight. Ava Wallace is no different. She's just seen more of life than people should ever have to." With the tip of his forefinger, he brushed aside the tendrils she usually let fall over her damaged cheek. When he tucked the long strands behind her ear, he cupped the side of her jaw and neck, resting the pad of his thumb against her cheek, suffusing her skin with a gentle heat for all of three seconds before pulling away. "Those scars don't diminish her beauty one bit. They prove she's a survivor, and I admire her for it. I can relate to that."

She wondered about the scars she'd seen on his body. Ava hadn't for one second thought they'd diminished how masculine or appealing he was. If anything, they'd made her curious to know more about him. They'd made her ache with compassion for the pain he must have suffered, both physical and emotional, to earn those scars. She supposed what a person found attractive in others changed as their unique experiences changed them. Not that the scars themselves were a turn-on, but they were a part of him. She found *him* attractive. Could she believe he might feel the same way about her? "You give unusual compliments."

Captured between her thoughts and those silvery-green eyes, the air between them charged with a pulsing energy.

The moment felt intimate, magnetic, like some unseen force was pulling her closer to him.

But Larkin was the one to blink and break the spell. He laughed as he took a step back. "Hey, if you want me to fill up your *pretty little head* with cutesy words, I can do that for you, too, *baby*."

Ava swatted the air. "Stop it. Brandon and I were best buds growing up. He isn't that bad."

"You knew who I was talking about, though, didn't you."

She squished her face into an apologetic frown. "I did." Two years ago, she would have swatted the man who was teasing her right on the arm. But somewhere inside she knew that this bantering back and forth was already a huge step forward from where she'd been before this real Bone-crusher had entered her life, and she was grateful. "He believes he's being good to me, taking care of me. And I won't fault him for that. But when he pushes his way into my life to the point of suffocation, I… I feel like I grew up and moved on, while he's stayed as old-school as my grandfather was. He refuses to understand that I need to be in control of my life as much as I can."

"Because you know what it's like to have that control taken from you."

Ava nodded. This man seemed to know her better than the man who'd known her almost her entire life. "Other than the obvious signs of an assault, I haven't told him about what happened to me. He doesn't ask about it, either. I think he still sees me as an innocent teenage girl he once kissed."

"It shouldn't matter that he doesn't know what happened to you in Chicago. I can't respect a man who won't take no for an answer. If you don't want to be crowded and you're not comfortable with the way he talks to you, you have the right to not put up with that."

"Are you feeling rested enough for a little hike?" While spending time with Larkin seemed like a therapeutic catharsis for her, she needed a break to process the emotional changes she was going through. "Exercise and fresh air help clear my head."

"Whatever you need." He followed her into the kitchen where she gathered supplies to take with them. "Hopefully, they'll clear mine, too." When the joke earned him a sympathetic look instead of a laugh, he rinsed off their lunch dishes and loaded them into the dishwasher, helping her prepare to leave. "I wouldn't mind retracing the path I took to get here. If I can track my path back to where I got started, maybe I'll see something that will jog my memory."

After calling Maxie from her lookout post at the back door, Ava put a harness with saddlebags on the dog and packed some water and energy bars along with dog treats in the pockets. "Are you a skilled tracker?"

"I don't know."

Once Ava released her, Maxie bounded to the front door, dancing in anticipation of their outing. "Fortunately, the Queen Mother of the Dragons here is."

The amused smile that matched hers for a moment faded into his beard. "Ava, would you still feel safe with me if I carried my own gun again? With bullets this time? You can say no. I don't want you to be afraid of me."

She considered his request for a moment, then opened the door to the garage and unlocked the climate-controlled storage closet where she kept the gun safe. "I'm less afraid of you having a gun than I am of being blindfolded or locked in a dark room, deprived of my senses. That's probably why that message made me go ballistic and shut down this morning. I didn't see the threat coming. I was blindsided."

"And a few minutes ago? I was pressing too hard, wasn't I. I triggered a flashback with one of my questions."

"We were talking about why I was kidnapped. The hooded man didn't kidnap A. L. Baines. All he needed was a victim. Someone weaker than him who he could control for a few days. Someone who'd be too afraid to fight back." He held the door while she typed in the security code on the safe's electronic lock. "He picked me."

"You did what you had to do to survive. You played his game. You got out of there alive. Detective Charles said not every victim has been so lucky." She opened the heavy steel door and pulled his Hellcat, holster and magazine of bullets from the pockets in the door where she'd secured them while he'd slept last night. "You were smart. Resourceful. You endured. That shows a hell of a lot of strength, not weakness, if you ask me."

"You do give the weirdest compliments. But they have meaning for me. Thank you."

"I don't waste time on words I don't...mean." At his hesitation, she turned to see him looking past her to the display of weaponry she stored inside. He let out a low whistle between his teeth. "You know how to use all these?"

She pointed out the small armory while he knelt to strap on his ankle holster. "That's Grandpa's hunting rifle. His service pistol from Vietnam. Part of gun safety around here was knowing how to use and clean the weapon, how to safely store it and respecting that it was created to kill, not be played with." She pulled out the decorated leather-and-metal sheath hanging behind the Winchester rifle. "This sword is a gift from my publisher. I've used it to research sword fighting, but don't display it for obvious reasons."

"Because of fans like me who might recognize it." He reverently pulled the blade from its sheath and held it up to study the inscription. "This is a reproduction of Larkin's

Bane-Slayer. And you use the bow and arrows to research Willow's character?"

He returned the sword to its sheath, and she hung it back in its place. "Grandpa taught me to hunt with a bow and arrow. I competed in some archery competitions in the summers here. It's what I know best, so that's why it's Willow's weapon of choice." She pulled her own small Glock from another pocket and loosened her belt to strap the gun onto her waist. "I learned to use this and the shotgun after my kidnapping."

Not that either would have saved her from the blitz attack that had rendered her helpless. But the hooded man might have thought twice about singling her out for his sick game if he'd seen the weapons. She felt more confident about defending herself now than she had two years ago, not only with the guns, but with the self-defense classes she'd started as soon as she was physically able after her recovery.

"You could give a guy a complex if he saw how well-armed you are."

She watched him check, load and secure his weapon with a second nature she envied. "Does it bother you?"

"It bothers me that you feel you need an arsenal like this. I wish the man who hurt you could see all this. I wish he could see how much you've done to help me. How brave you are to face the things that frighten you, and you still come back fighting. He'd think twice about coming after you now." Again, the unusual compliment rang like truth inside her and warmed her from the inside out. He stepped back as she closed and reset the lock on the gun safe, then relocked the storage closet door. "But am I afraid of you and all those weapons? No. Willow isn't just the woman Larkin loves. He values her as a comrade in arms. He's not intimidated by her abilities or the crown she's supposed to wear." He held the door back into the kitchen open for her. "Trust me, I get Larkin."

Ava smiled shyly as she moved past him. Larkin loved Willow in her books. He valued her as a friend, companion and would-be lover. But how did this Larkin feel about Ava Wallace? Why did it feel like the lines between fiction and reality were blurring? Like the relationship she'd written on the pages had come to life and already felt deep and familiar?

Why wasn't she more worried about how much of herself she had shared with this man she'd met only yesterday? Did he really understand her in a way that no man ever had? Was she falling in love with the hero from her books? Or was she foolishly setting herself up for a disaster that could break her heart, if not cost her her life?

Too many questions with no good answers. She was beginning to understand the uncertainty and frustration Larkin must be going through with his memory gaps. She needed to get outside and get out of her head. Ava reached for Maxie's leash. "Are you ready to head out?"

"Lead the way."

Chapter Nine

Larkin's quest to retrace his path ended at the base of a forty-foot embankment. Ultimately, he did need Maxie's tracking skills and Ava's familiarity with the area to follow the path he'd left through the woods. In some places, dusty footprints, snapped twigs and swaths of dirt through a carpet of pine needles indicated where he must have rolled or dragged his feet, cutting an erratic path from these rocks to the gravel drive leading to her cabin. But there were other places where it looked like he'd been cognizant enough to erase his footprints and make false trails, sure signs that he'd been in survival mode against the enemy who wanted him dead. Only, as they reached the natural stair steps of craggy granite ledges and skinny trees with exposed roots leading up to a metal guardrail at the very top, he saw almost no evidence of anyone pursuing him.

Why hadn't they chased him through the woods? Had they assumed he was dead? If the man responsible for putting a bullet through his head believed he'd succeeded, or lied to his superiors about completing the job, then why was Roy Hauser in town looking for him? If Larkin was in charge of a task force to take down an enemy, he wouldn't have assumed anything. He'd want the body as proof that the threat had been neutralized—either as his prisoner or in a morgue. And when Ava had driven him to the hospital, it had become evident to someone that he wasn't dead.

Was someone at the hospital in his enemy's pocket? When he'd shown up in the ER at Pole Axe's clinic, had someone called the would-be killer and informed him he had survived the attempt on his life? He still questioned the drugs Dr. Russell had given him. Unless the nurse had incorrectly dosed him. Or had his injuries simply been so severe that he was lucky he'd made it to Ava's place before he'd gone down for the count and slept the grogginess out of his system? Logic told him there was more than one player involved in the threats against him. Once he'd disappeared from the clinic, the hunt for Larkin Bonecrusher—or someone the enemy knew as Luke—had begun anew.

Did they have other means of tracking him? He swung his gaze to the brunette who was having an animated conversation with her big white dog, who was eating up the attention. Ava was every bit the intriguing woman warrior Willow Storm was. Only, fiction couldn't match the warmth, humor and vulnerability of the real thing. Man, he had a bad case of wanting something he probably shouldn't. But there was no denying his physical and emotional response to all things Ava Wallace. There was also no denying the guilt he felt at thrusting her into the middle of all this, despite her claims that challenging her to get involved was therapeutic for her.

He watched her pour water into a collapsible bowl for Maxie to lap up to help the panting dog cool down. After losing the trail a couple of times and doubling back, they'd been hiking at a relatively steady pace for almost two hours, covering several miles through steep terrain and a thick forest. Although he sensed that Ava had slowed her pace for his benefit, he'd been able to keep up, despite the battering his body had taken the day before and his limping stride. He wasn't too proud, though, to give his bum leg and aching shoulder a break and do a few stretches to ease the kinks before finding a relatively flat rock at the base of the cliff to sit on.

He tipped his head up. "Is that where we're headed next?"

When they heard the whoosh of a car passing by on the road above them, Ava confirmed what Larkin already suspected. "That's the highway that circles around the mountain. We were on it last night when we stopped at the scenic overlook. Several miles closer to town than we are now. Do you think this is where you rolled off the edge of the cliff?"

Larkin's gaze settled on a suspiciously dark spot on the rock beside him and he felt his stomach clench with a remembered desperation. He knelt to measure the size of the mark, confirming that the remnants of the bloody handprint matched his own. "Yeah. This is where Option B happened."

When he pushed to his feet, the rocks and trees swayed in front of him. Then he felt a gentle hand at his elbow. Ava guided him back to the rock and put a bottle of water into his hand. "Sit. You're looking a little pale."

He didn't think it was the altitude or the exertion so much as the jumble of memories flashing through his brain with the fuzzy definition of seeing oncoming headlights through the rain at night. "They disabled my car."

"A black SUV?" Ava opened her own water bottle and sat beside him to take a few drinks. She didn't push him to remember everything, yet her questions seemed to help draw out pertinent information.

"Yeah. Company car." He downed nearly half his water in one swallow as he relived the dizzying sensation of whipping around a hairpin turn while his SUV continued to pick up speed. "No brakes. Why didn't I check the status of the vehicle? That's a routine security check."

"You were in a hurry to get away. Maybe there wasn't time," she suggested.

"Or someone I trusted told me it was okay to go."

"Not having any brakes explains why you reacted so strongly when I took a curve too fast driving into town."

He nodded as the empty places inside his head tried to tell him what he'd forgotten. "They were driving the same make of vehicle. When that black SUV passed us yesterday—"

"You ducked." She watched him take another drink before asking, "Who are *they*?"

"The security team I work for," he answered automatically. He nearly spit out his water when he realized what he'd remembered. "My own people were chasing me."

"Roy Hauser was driving a black SUV this morning."

"The guy who was looking for me?"

She nodded. "That must be who you work for. BDS." She glanced up along the rocks before facing him again. "I have a friend who told me BDS uses the Ridgerunner Lodge at the top of the mountain for guests. You said you woke up in a hotel room and went to work. Is there a way to find out if Bell Design had something going on at the lodge this week? If you were there?"

Several pieces of the puzzle were floating around in his head, but they weren't yet falling into place. "Why would BDS be after me if I'm part of their team?"

"Maybe they're trying to help you. Mr. Hauser said he was worried about you."

Put a bullet in his head and make this all go away.

Larkin rose to his feet and studied the precipice above them. "They're the ones trying to kill me." He moved toward the rock face. "It all happened up there. The attempt on my life… Whatever happened before that is why they tried to kill me." He flattened his hand briefly against his belly and the miniature data stick making its way through his system. *That* had happened before losing control of his SUV and Option B. He set down the bottle of water and gripped the nearest outcropping of rock. "I need to get up there. If that's the crime scene, something's bound to jog my memory."

Ava's fingers wound around his forearm, pulling him back. "You can't make that climb. Not with your shoulder and knee. If one of them gives out, you could fall. Besides, if somebody drives past while you're up there, you'd be a sitting duck. If the wrong person sees you, they'll report you to Sheriff Stout or to BDS."

"I don't want you taking that risk."

She was already shrugging out of her backpack and unbuttoning her blouse. "I've climbed rocks before. Steeper than this."

"Without rappelling gear or a helmet? Ava…" She peeled off the long-sleeved shirt and revealed the fitted white tank top she wore underneath. He was at once stunned to see the pale lines of old scars striping her upper arms like hash marks and awed to see the revelation of her true shape. Those baggy clothes disguised a lot of lean, beautiful curves. Ava was athletic and slim, but unmistakably female. He shook off both the flare of anger at seeing she'd been tortured like that, and the smack of desire that flooded the territory behind his zipper with unmistakable interest.

"Talk to me, Bonecrusher. What am I looking for when I get up there?" Hell. She was already on the first ledge, studying the outcropping above her, looking for her next handhold.

She needed him to stop gawking and think like an MP. Like an investigator. She needed him to be her comrade in arms and help her, since she was the one on the front line of this sortie. "Look for anything that seems out of place.

Debris from a car accident. Tire tracks or footprints. Anything that doesn't seem natural to the scene."

She pushed herself up to the next ledge, tested the solidness of a tree root and used it to pull herself up above the level of his head. "There's blood on the rocks here, too." She glanced down at him with a grim expression. "There's a gouge in the bark, as well. Long and narrow, about the size of my finger."

"A bullet strike?"

"That'd be my guess." She pulled her phone from the back pocket of her jeans and snapped a few pictures. She was halfway to the road when she knelt on a wider ledge. "Oh my gosh. How many times did they shoot at you?" Ava held out a casing for him to see. "There are two more up here. We need to get the bullet Dr. Russell took out of your shoulder and compare the caliber. Prove that they all came from the same gun."

"I wasn't counting. And hug the damn rocks." He warned her back from the edge. A fall from this distance wouldn't be fatal, but she could break a bone if she hit something the wrong way. And if he couldn't make that climb, he wasn't sure he'd be able to catch her and break her fall, or get her to the help she might need, either. "Pay attention to your climb. We can talk clues once you're safely back down here."

"Roger that." She took more pictures before tucking the phone and casing into the pockets of her jeans and climbing another few feet to the next outcropping. The rocks were eroded in such a way that there were plenty of places to step onto or grab hold of. But for a man who'd been in free fall, those same protrusions had been blunt objects that had bruised ribs and split skin and pounded his body with an unforgiving assault. He wondered if the ache in his shoulder had more to do with the memories of the pain he'd endured that were trying to surface, or with his fear that Ava would grab the wrong tree or lose her footing and suffer a similar fate.

"Be careful," he called to her as she reached the top. He squeezed his eyes shut at the vivid recollection of rolling off the edge of the road into oblivion. But he opened them again just as quickly. He wasn't sure what he'd do from this distance if she fell, but he wanted to be ready to do something. He hated that she was the one putting herself at risk for him. "Watch for traffic, too. Make sure you're safe."

"I'm good." She grabbed hold of the guardrail and swung her legs over the top. He heard her boots crunch against the gravel, then fall silent as she reached the asphalt.

He wished he could see more than the top of her head and the swish of that long ponytail as she whipped her head from side to side to inspect her surroundings. "What do you see?" he demanded.

Ava leaned back to shout down the mountain. "The cleanest stretch of highway ever."

"What do you mean?"

She turned and leaned over the guardrail so that she didn't have to shout. "Seriously. It's like a road crew has been through here and picked up every scrap of trash and swept the road."

"No skid marks?"

"No." He supposed that made sense. If his brake lines had been cut, there wouldn't be any signs of a sudden stop. "Wait a minute."

"Ava?" When she disappeared from sight, Larkin's stomach clenched with worry. At least two vehicles drove past while she was out of his sight. Hopefully, there was a place to conceal herself up there, and she'd hidden herself from view. When several minutes passed without seeing her again, he damned the pain in his leg and shoulder and climbed onto the first ledge.

"What are you doing?" She reappeared at the top of the cliff and waved him back to the relatively flat slope at the base of the cliff. "I'm on my way down."

He watched her shimmy down the rocks with the confidence of a mountain goat. And though she never uttered one *ouch*, or showed any sign of distress, Larkin couldn't wait for her to be safely on level ground beside him again. When her boots hit the bottom ledge, he reached up to grab her by either side of her waist and lifted her down the last few feet. With her bottom tucked against the vee of his thighs and hips, he pulled her right up against his chest. He circled one arm around her shoulders and the other around her waist, and buried his nose in the fresh, herbal scent of her hair. He treasured the feel of her pressed against him and breathed her in—one, two, three.

He reluctantly loosened his hold, though he didn't push her away. "Why is it scarier to watch you do something dangerous than for me to do it myself?"

Her cheeks were flushed, and she was slightly breathless when she turned to face him, although whether her reaction was from the exertion of her climb or the momentary embrace, he couldn't tell. At least she wasn't lecturing him about this growing need to touch her. Then again, maybe she was just excited about whatever she'd discovered that she was eager to share. "I didn't see anything on this side of the highway." She pulled out her phone and brought up the pictures she'd taken. "There were tire tracks on the far side of the road. The grass in the ditch had been weed-whacked, but only a section of it. The highway department would have mowed everything along the shoulder. If you look closer, you can see the bottom of the stalks have been crushed."

"Like something heavy plowed through the ditch."

She nodded. "And then I saw this."

Ava swiped to a photo of a light-colored patch of unweathered rock that had been gouged out of the granite on the far side of the ditch. He spotted what she must have. "Something hit those rocks pretty hard."

"Like an out of control SUV?"

"They tapped my bumper and I spun out. I glanced off the rocks and flipped the SUV. Came to a stop on this side of the road." He remembered smacking his head against the window, then tumbling and tumbling. "They dragged me to the edge of the road."

"*They?* There was more than one man who attacked you?"

He squeezed his eyes shut, fighting to remember. There were no faces, only words.

It's not on him.

Grab his ID. I don't want anyone to link the body to us.

Nothing personal, Captain. Orders are orders.

Then the bullets and the falling.

Soft fingers brushed against his forearm. "Luke?"

His eyes snapped open. "Yeah. I'm okay." A big, furry weight leaned against his thigh, and he suddenly understood the power of Maxie's healing touch. He gazed down into Ava's deep blue eyes even as he scrubbed his fingers around Maxie's ears. "You called me Luke."

"I called you Larkin first. You didn't answer." She reached over to pet the dog, too. "You went away from us."

"I was remembering yesterday morning. Parts of it. I'm Luke…" Even without the initials on his key chain or any ID, the name finally fell into place. His chest expanded in a deep, unfettered breath as clarity returned. "I'm Luke Broughton. I remember!"

He barely heard her startled gasp as he picked her up and swung her around, celebrating the breakthrough he'd been half-afraid was never going to happen.

"I'm Luke Broughton. I remember now. Lucas How-ard Broughton, Captain, United States Marine Corps, Retired. Honorable discharge due to chronic injury. Howard was my dad's name. I'm Luke..." He stopped when he realized he was staring straight into those cobalt eyes. A gust of warm breath whispered across his cheek as he assessed every inch of body contact between them. Although Ava's left hand was braced against his chest, their hips were cinched tightly enough to feel where hard lines ended and soft curves began. He'd latched on to one of those enticing curves with a possessive grasp of her bottom. Her other hand was still anchored at the back of his neck as he slowly set her on her feet. He held his hands out to either side of her, praying that what had felt so natural for him hadn't felt like confinement to her. "I'm sorry. I forgot the three-second rule."

"It's okay. Recognizing your name again is something worth celebrating." She pulled her hand from behind his neck, stroking it across his beard as she retreated. He looked for signs of panic or fear, but her eyes were following the path of her fingertips through the short hair of his beard. He saw curiosity. No, interest. No. Desire.

She touched a finger to the curve of his lip, but quickly pulled away as if she'd felt that same jolt of electricity arcing between them that he did. Damn, he wanted to kiss her. "Ava..."

She reached out to Maxie, and he grudgingly let the dog offer the grounding comfort she didn't want from him. "What about the men who tried to kill you?"

Luke shook his head. "I don't have faces yet. And I don't know the why." He patted his stomach. "Except they were looking for this. But I've got no clue what's on it."

"Let's focus on what we do know." She polished off her bottle of water and packed supplies back in Maxie's saddlebags, perhaps giving him time to cool his jets so another embrace like that wouldn't happen again. "You're

Luke Broughton. We could look you up online or check military databases. Maybe I could ask Detective Charles to run a background check—if you were in military law enforcement, there's probably some sort of interagency cooperation he can tap into."

"Let's hold off on that. If the person who's after me is the one who hacked into Charles's computer, then a search like that would put him on alert. I don't want them to connect you to me in any other way beyond giving me a ride to the hospital yesterday."

"All right. What else do we know?"

"The chief of security at Bell Design Systems is looking for me. My car was sabotaged and run off the road where someone shot me."

"And to save yourself, you dove over the edge of a cliff and showed up on my doorstep." She pointed to the top of the cliff. "To hide their tracks, someone cleaned up where the accident ended. But they didn't do as good a job cleaning up where it began."

He handed her his water bottle to stow away so that they wouldn't leave any trash or trail. "If I only had the vehicle to match these tire treads to. I could trace the VIN back to BDS…or to Luke Broughton if I'm the owner. I'd be able to get an address at least."

"Want to bet the SUV that was destroyed in Scott Harold's junkyard was the one you were driving?"

He wouldn't take that bet. "Someone went to a lot of effort to clean up any evidence of the crime. Either I'm a big threat to BDS or I did something really bad."

"If my instincts aren't as rusty as I think they are, I'd vote for being a big threat. I'm the one who insisted on getting involved with this. You tried to walk away when you found out about my…history. You've gone out of your way to help me, not hurt me."

"I won't let anyone hurt you, Ava. Not even me," he promised.

She studied him for a moment, then nodded. "I believe you."

Nothing humbling about that. Man, he wanted to be worthy of this woman. He wanted to be her partner, her protector. He wanted to see where a future with her might lead. But first, he had to resolve his past.

"So, we'll assume I'm a good guy. Even if my tactics don't always make that apparent." Although there were still some key gaps in his memory, enough of it was coming back that he remembered how to piece together clues and solve a crime. "I'd like to get that bullet Doc Russell took out of my shoulder and turn it and the casings you collected over to the authorities. Would you be offended if I said I want to give them to the state police and not your buddy Sheriff Stout?"

Her lips curled into a wry half smile. "I get it. Brandon thinks you intend to hurt me or use me, so he wouldn't be very sympathetic." She picked up her discarded blouse and shook off the dirt and pine needles that stuck to the cotton. "In the meantime, you and that secret information in your stomach are the only evidence that BDS or some individual at BDS has left to get rid of." She slipped it on and rolled up the sleeves. "But evidence of what? Any ideas yet about what's on that flash drive you ate?"

"We won't know for a few hours yet. My memory is coming back in bits and pieces, so we're still at a disadvantage. Hopefully, the flash drive will tell us everything else we need to know." He picked up her backpack and held it out to her. "All the more reason to get away from the road and back into the seclusion of the forest for a while longer. You said you had an idea for an escape plan if we need one?"

She thanked him for the pack. "I can show you if you

want. How are you holding up? There's a direct route back to the cabin if you need to get home."

"I've been following that beautiful backside of yours all afternoon. I'm not about to stop now."

Her cheeks turned that adorable shade of pink.

"Not the worst thing a man's ever said to me." He loved that she was clever enough to throw his teasing words back at him. She shrugged into her backpack. Even with all those curves and skin camouflaged, he couldn't look away. "Do you want me to call you Luke now? Or stick with Larkin?"

"As long as you keep talking to me, I'm good."

"So am I." Those were the words he needed to hear. Ava was okay. They—whatever *they* were—were okay. She picked up her walking stick and whistled for Maxie. She nodded toward his injured leg. "Come on, Limpy. I promise this will be an easier hike."

Chapter Ten

A half hour later, they turned away from the creek they'd been following. Although Ava had been true to her word about this being an easier hike, Luke was feeling how hard he'd been pushing himself today.

"Are we there yet?" he teased, pretending his hip and knee weren't throbbing with every step.

She wasn't fooled. "You're really limping now. We need to take a break." Ava pointed to the thick grove of statuesque pine trees. "Fortunately, we're here. The trees camouflage it from the path. But if you climb up onto that first ledge, you'll see it."

"See what?" He followed her off the trail, climbing the easy footholds in the rocks. Once they'd cleared the granite ledge, a shallow, wide-mouthed cave opened up at waist level ahead of them. Luke blew out a long, awestruck whistle behind her. "The fortress at Stormhaven."

Ava smiled and gave Maxie a boost up to reach the next platform of rock that formed the floor of the cave. "You really are a fan of the *Chronicles*."

Although it was only about a five-foot rise, the rock face was steeper here. But Ava had discovered the best roots and safest crevices to grab to climb up into the cave. Luke followed the same path. Maxie was already sniffing around, looking for any little critters she needed to chase out.

"Can you make it okay?" By the time she turned to offer him a hand, he was pulling himself up into the cave beside her. He reached up to touch the roof of the cave and measure the head clearance he had to have to remain standing before turning to take in the view over the tops of the trees. "I see your inspiration. Granite walls. Hidden entrance. A view of the entire kingdom."

She grinned and shook her head. "Or the Hoback River Basin between the Wyoming and Wind River mountain ranges."

"I see rocks and trees and a river when I look out there. You see the Dragon Lands and Larkin's village." He followed her to a dented metal trunk tucked away against the cave wall several feet from the opening. Although the rivets at every joint showed signs of rust, the padlock she slid a key into was shiny and new. He helped her drag it away from the rocks so that the lid would open fully. Inside, he saw a folded camp chair, two blankets in plastic bags, a stash of metal bottles he assumed were filled with water and a faded blue metal tackle box. "The larder is stocked, I see. You could hide out here overnight if you had to."

"If the weather isn't too cold," she agreed. "Grandpa helped me set this up when I was fifteen. He's the only other person who's ever been here."

"Not even Sheriff Touchy-Feely? You said you two were close growing up."

"Nope. Even Grandma never ventured out here. She said a teenager needed her privacy, and as along as Grandpa thought it was safe, she approved."

"I'm honored to make the short list of guests."

Ava pulled out the camp chair and he set it up. Meanwhile, she tossed one of the blankets out, which Maxie immediately scratched at before circling around several times and lying down on it. "I don't keep perishables here because of scavengers. Just some basic supplies in case I misjudge the length of a hike and need to rest, or I need a place to get away." More secluded than her cabin? This woman really did find security in being alone. Next, she opened up the tackle box to reveal her stash. "Flashlight and batteries. Matches. Pocketknife."

He pulled out a weathered journal and box of pencils. "Something to record your inspirations? Or a secret diary?"

Ava snatched it away and tucked it back inside the bottom of the tackle box.

Luke laughed. "Ah. Secret diary. The lovestruck ramblings of a teenage girl?"

She swatted his arm. "There are things in that journal that will never see the light of day. I do write out here sometimes. But I'll put my computer notebook in my backpack and enjoy the fresh air for a few hours." She gestured to the camp chair for Luke, then closed the trunk. "Have a seat. I'm afraid you're overdoing it."

"I'm fine. I'll take an energy bar and one of those bottles of water Maxie is carrying, though, if she'll share."

"Sure." Ava pulled her lips tight against her teeth and let out a shrill whistle. The Great Pyrenees immediately popped up and trotted over to her mistress.

"The dragon summoning that Willow uses. You've whistled for her before."

Ava pulled out snacks and a bottle of water for them both. "Not everything in my life is part of my books." She removed the saddlebags and gave the dog's back and flanks a vigorous petting before urging the dog to curl up on her blanket again. Then Ava sat on the corner of the trunk, and they all took a few minutes to relax and recoup their energy. "How did you become a Bonecrusher fan?"

"A buddy introduced me to the series on a deployment.

When I was in the hospital at Landstuhl, I reread through every one of them. It was a distraction from the pain and the loss. And yeah, I fantasized about gettin' busy with Willow." He hoped the color warming her skin meant she was flattered by his subtle compliments. And yes, now that he'd put a face to the heroine, he'd fantasized about the real thing, too. He washed down a bite of the bar with a drink of water and leaned back in the nylon canvas seat to take in the mountain scenery. He understood how this place could feel like a haven, isolated in some of the most gorgeous country he'd ever seen. "Mostly I related to that sense of having a quest, a mission to fulfill. There was a purpose to what your characters were doing. Just like the Corps. Just like my efforts to heal and make it through rehab. And the team in your books, the bonds they share, it felt like my unit. We weren't dealing with sorcerers and hundred-year-old curses, but the feeling was the same. Hell, I miss those guys." He stuffed the last of the bar into his mouth and took another drink. "So, what's stopping you from finishing the next *Chronicle*? Speaking strictly as a fan, you kind of left us hangin'."

"You, too, huh?" She dabbed at the crumbs clinging to her lips, and he silently warned that most interested part of his anatomy to keep things casual. "I think I took a left turn in the last book by introducing Lord Zeville, and I'm not sure how to come back from it." Nope. Putting her lips around the bottle for another drink wasn't helping his lower half remember to mind its manners. Luke had to shift to a more comfortable position and look away from the temptation. "Plus, there's the whole Larkin/Willow thing. I swear if those two don't get together, I'm going to lose half my readers. The other half can't get enough of the sexual tension, and fear it will go away if those two ever come out and say the three magic words, and—like you said—get busy. It would be such a big moment in the series. I don't know if I could get the details right."

"Are you kidding?" Did she not feel the sexual tension filling up this cave? Whether she believed it or not, the woman got every detail right, as far as he was concerned. "That make-out session in the dungeon in the last book was pretty hot. I was certain they were going to seal the deal then. If the rebels hadn't chosen that moment to rescue them…" Luke could have sworn his own skin was heating beneath his beard. "I have to tell you I got a lot of mileage from that scene. I finished it a dozen different ways in my imagination. That's vivid, compelling writing."

"Thanks." Her smile thanked him for the praise, but the stroke of her knuckles along her scarred cheek revealed the uncertainty within her. "I think because of what happened to me, I'm afraid to let go the way I'd need to in order to create that kind of closeness again. How am I supposed to get Larkin and Willow to kiss or touch, much less make love, when I can't even do it myself?"

"You let me touch you. For three seconds. For more than three seconds a little while ago." She laughed at the reminder, but it was a sad, self-deprecating sound.

He remembered something one of his doctors had said to him when he'd despaired about ever being whole enough to be useful to the Corps again. *"Turn your short-comings into an advantage. If you can't be as physical as you once were, then be more mental."* Although he'd made a joke that being mental was the problem, the doctor hadn't laughed. *"Be smarter, Captain Broughton. Use your brains if your body fails you. A good investigator has to be smarter than the bad guy, not faster."*

Could that philosophy work for Ava, too? "Maybe you shouldn't try to be the same writer you were before your kidnapping. Embrace who you are now. Let those emotions work for you. You've changed. Maybe Willow needs to change, too."

Her blue eyes were dark like midnight in the shadows of the cave. But he knew she was searching his expression, considering his suggestion, wanting to believe it could work. "How do you mean? It's hard enough to talk about the kidnapping. I don't think I could write about it and share it with the world."

"You don't have to. But there are elements of your life now that could enrich a story you couldn't have told two years ago." He left the chair to kneel in front of her. He gently took her hand and clasped it between his. "One one-thousand. Two one-thousand. Three one-thousand." Then he released her and sat back. "Is that something you can work into your story? The three-second rule? Maybe Lord Zeville put a spell on Willow while he had her in his palace chambers, and now Larkin and Willow can only touch for three seconds before her skin burns—"

"Or she turns on him, thinks he's her enemy." Luke had only suggested the germ of an idea, but Ava was turning that idea into a whole story. "They'd have to break the spell by completing a quest."

He splayed his fingers on the flat of his stomach, reminding her of the flash drive. "Deciphering a mysterious text?"

"They'd have to find the text first." She snapped her fingers and stood. "That's brilliant. If they touch too long, it leaves another scar. It brands her."

"You sure you want to add scars to your story? Won't that dredge up—"

"Of course, he won't want to leave a mark on her, so he'll pull away. That push-pull or wanting, but denying it, that's sexual tension. I'll have to work out some kind of action scene where they're forced to hold on to each other, like dangling over the edge of a cliff. She'll turn on him, but he won't let go, no matter how hard she comes at him. The spell will backfire on Zeville. Larkin and Willow will be battling each other—"

"—with Larkin being careful not to actually hurt her because she's bewitched—"

"—and voilà! A pair of sword thrusts and Zeville is dispatched. Destroyed by the very war he tried to create." Ava was pacing circles around the cave, moving her hands in excited gestures, including imaginary sword fighting, as she thought out loud. She shimmered with a kind of creative energy that was as foreign to Luke as it was exciting to watch in her. She shooed Maxie off the blanket and quickly folded it up. "Are we done here? Is Storm-haven enough of a backup plan for you? You think you could find it on your own if you had to? It's not a very well-marked path."

"That's one of the things I like about it." He helped her repack the trunk. "Cabin to creek. Creek to trees. Storm-haven is tucked in behind them."

She locked the trunk and pocketed the key. "I can bring out more supplies tomorrow if you think we need them. Right now, I'd like to get to my computer. Get a couple of hours of writing in yet tonight."

He followed her down the incline and helped her guide Maxie safely down between them. "Is this how being a writer works? You get an inspiration, and you run to your computer?"

"Sometimes. There are days when the words flow out of my fingers and I can't get them down fast enough. And there are others when it's an uphill battle to get a single page written." She hooked Maxie to her leash and headed for the trees. "It's been a while since an idea has really spoken to me like this. I think you're on to something. I need to write who I am now. My characters will be more battle weary. They'll be choosier about who they trust. I have a feeling my voice will be a little grittier. But the ending of the story arc is darker, anyway. And when I reach the resolution and happily-ever-after, it will be a bigger emotional payoff. So, can we go?"

There was not one whit of hesitation to her demeanor now. Luke was pleased to see her so fired up about her work, and he was glad that, in some small way, he'd been able to help—both as a fan of the books, and as a fan of Ava Wallace. "We're good. Stormhaven will do for Option B. Let's get you home to work."

They hadn't yet reached the trees when Luke heard the humming overhead. The familiar buzzing sound was as relentless as a mosquito but reminded him of things far more dangerous. He shaded his eyes and tilted his face to the sky until he pinpointed the black, bug-shaped drone flying back and forth overhead, closer to the creek they'd followed here. Luke got an uneasy feeling in the pit of his stomach. He'd kill for a pair of binoculars right now, to either confirm or negate his suspicions.

He sensed rather than saw Ava move in beside him, her face turned to the clouds, as well. "I saw one of those this morning. People use them to get spectacular video or pictures of the mountains. When they're up that high, there are no trees or rock formations to get in the way."

"That one doesn't belong to a tourist. It's flying in a search grid." He patted his hip, his instincts telling him to radio in the drone's position. Only, there was no radio. There was no team to call. There was only this precious woman and her dog. "Where was the drone you saw this morning?"

"About a mile north of here, higher up the mountain." Closer to where she'd scaled the cliff below the scene of his *accident*.

"This one's a lot closer." Ignoring the twinge in his

shoulder, he spanned her waist and lifted her onto the lower ledge of Stormhaven. "Get back in the cave."

"I doubt they can see us through the tree cover."

"Do you want to take that chance?"

When her blue eyes met his, he silently let her know he wasn't risking their safety on the possibility he could be wrong.

Ava offered a quick nod of understanding and reached for the dog. "Maxie?"

He boosted the dog up. "If it's rigged with infrared, the surrounding rocks and chill of the cave should mask our heat signature."

"Infrared?" Her hand was there to help him over the lip of the opening. "I felt like I was being watched this morning. I thought I was just being me. Paranoid. You think they're searching for you?"

"They're searching for something."

"The forestry department uses drones."

"All right. I won't rule out that it has a benign purpose. But I'm not gambling our lives on it." Luke stood as close to the opening as he dared. Definitely a search grid. The drone had moved half a klick to the south and resumed its linear flight pattern. "BDS has equipment like that."

She tugged him back from the opening of the cave when the relentless drone buzzed toward their position. "Bell Design Systems? How do you know?"

He was glad to see her keeping hold of Maxie's leash. If an infrared-armed drone could pick up something as small as a fox or pika on its scope, it could certainly pick up the dragon queen loping through the woods. "We used one like it for aerial surveillance outside Kandahar." He watched the drone easily from this vantage point, but if the search grid shifted in this direction, they'd be moving deeper into the cave. "My buddy V was obsessed with the things. He was always tinkering with them, extending their range, adding a stronger zoom feature to the lens, more sensitive radar."

"Who's V?" Ava asked.

"Ryan Voltaggio. We came up through MP training together. Our unit…" He glanced over the jut of his shoulder at her, realizing what she'd just done. "I know Ryan Voltaggio."

She squeezed his arm and smiled at yet another breakthrough. "It may be a long shot. But can you call the Marine Corps and ask for his phone number? Maybe he's the friend you remember calling."

The fist of another memory squeezed his heart and he shook his head. "V never made it home."

"Oh, Luke. I'm so sorry." Her fingertips grazed his forearm again. A sympathetic touch.

A touch he needed like his next breath. Luke swore at the pain ripping through him and pulled her into his chest. He wound his arms around her, backpack and all. Her walking stick clattered on the stones at their feet and her arms snuck around his waist. He squeezed his eyes shut against the violent, bloody images bombarding him. The initial flash of an explosion. The helplessness at seeing his men so close to the blast. The betrayal. The loss. The searing pain.

He buried his face against the juncture of her neck and shoulder, breathing in her clean, natural scent. Catching the long strands of silky hair in his beard, tangling the two of them together. He clung to her warmth. Her strength. The mental toughness that was far stronger than his own at the moment.

He locked her in his arms and they rocked together as the nightmarish memories buffeted him. He held on, and she held him right back, well past any three-second mark. "I'm so sorry," she whispered against his ear. "He was your friend."

"Of all the things to remember." He palmed the back of her head, sifting his fingers through her ponytail, needing the reality of thick, soft waves filling his palm. "I lost four people on my team that day. Plus, this kid we knew. We'd taken him under our wing, gotten close to him. He was our friend. At least, we thought he was. It all happened so fast. There wasn't time to save anybody. They were all just…gone."

Her arms tightened around his waist. Her fingers fisted in the back of his shirt. "Is that when you got hurt? I saw the scars." She turned her lips against his ear and nuzzled his neck. "I'm so sorry."

Yes. This was what he needed. Warmth. Reality. Ava.

He brought his other hand up to brush the loose tendrils off her cheek. He cupped her jaw between his hands and tilted her face up to his. Her blue eyes were shiny with unshed tears. She felt pain for *him*. She already had so much pain of her own. He caught the first tear with the pad of his thumb when it spilled onto her cheek.

And then he realized it was his own tear that had dropped onto her skin.

"Luke…" Her lips parted, trembled, and Luke dipped his mouth to capture hers. Soft. Full. Still. He heard her quiet gasp and a moment of sanity returned.

"Oh, God." What was he doing? He lifted his head, but he wasn't a strong enough man to release her entirely. His fingers shook with the effort to pull them from her warm skin. Her eyes were dark with emotion, but he couldn't read them. Ah, hell. He'd probably scared her. "I'm sorry. I overstepped a lot of boundaries. Is it okay if I kiss—"

Ava pushed up onto her toes and sealed her lips to his.

Luke rocked back on his feet as she leaned into him. He might be the startled one this time, but he made a quick recovery. He braced his body to take her weight and tunneled his fingers into her hair to cup the back of her head.

He supped at her mouth, discovering every soft pillow, every agile corner—and then he sampled them all again, drinking in her shy forays and welcoming responses. The feel of Ava's hidden curves flattened against him; the gentle dance of their tongues, and her growing eagerness to touch and taste him, kindled a heat inside Luke that flowed through his veins into every part of him, chasing away the nightmares and grief, filling him with strength and hope and the most perfect sense of rightness he could remember either before or after the amnesia.

Ava skimmed her palms across his beard, smiling against his mouth at what must be a ticklish sensation. Then she slipped her arms around his neck, sliding her hand against his hair, hugging him close. His hands bumped into the backpack she still wore, but it was little deterrent to him finding more of her body to touch, more heat to absorb. His palm wound up on the sweet curve of her bottom. He squeezed her through her jeans and lifted her into his aching response to her healing kiss. Her arms tightened around his neck, holding on as her feet left the cave floor. Her legs parted naturally, falling around his hips and thighs as they traded kiss after kiss. The tips of her breasts beaded and poked him through the layers of cotton between them. So responsive, so proud, so perfect.

He heard a breathless whimper in her throat. Her clutching hands and generous kiss fueled his own groan of frustration. He heard the rasp of denim against denim, and the lazy yawn of the dog stretched out beside them. Maxie's indifference to the embrace was as good as a vote of approval, and Luke's breath gusted against Ava's throat at his sigh of satisfaction while he nibbled on the warm beat of her pulse there.

What he didn't hear was the hum of the drone.

Awareness of another kind washed over him like the splash of a cold mountain stream. Luke ended the kiss, hugging Ava lightly in his arms and turning slightly so that he was between her and the entrance to the cave. He scanned the sky above them and beyond the trees. Either the machine had run out of juice, or whoever was flying it had moved on to a new search grid. "We're alone again. They moved their search elsewhere."

"It's gone? We're safe?" He nodded before resting his chin at the crown of her hair. He took in a deep lungful of air to steady his breathing and regain his senses. Her arms retreated to his waist and he felt her fingers press into the small of his back. "Are you all right now?" she whispered against his collar.

"I haven't been this right since… I don't think anything's ever felt this right," he admitted, then tightened his arms around her, backpack and all, and buried his nose in the intoxicating scent of her hair. "God, woman. You turn me inside out. Especially since I know how uncomfortable you are with intimacy."

"I'm not completely uncomfortable with it. I just need to be in control of it."

He eased his hold on her, not wanting to push his luck. "It sounds naughty, but control me all you want. Any way you need to. Yell at me. Push me away. Sic the dragon on me if I go too far."

"I can't do that. Maxie likes you." She straightened the blouse that had ridden up between their bodies and his roaming hands. "Besides, I'm healing, remember? That was pretty good therapy for me."

He laughed. "It was damn good therapy for me. I'm sorry I dumped on you. The memory of that suicide bomb kind of blindsided me when it all came back to me."

"I know the feeling. I like the way you handle it better. I'll have to remember that next time I have a panic attack—kiss, don't collapse." She reached up and stroked her fingers through his beard again, reawakening all the nerve endings that were just starting to chill. If she was this fascinated with touching a few days' worth of stubble, he was never shaving again. "This tickles when I kiss you. It's…stimulating." She abruptly pulled away as if she was feeling the electricity reigniting between them, too. "I'm attracted to you, Luke. I feel a connection to you. That wasn't just about offering comfort. I wanted to kiss you. I liked…kissing you. I can't remember the last time my blood pumped that hard for any good reason. You needed me, and I wanted to be there for you. It felt freeing. Normal. What normal people do, I mean. Not that you're not normal." Her cheeks turned that healthy shade of pink. "I'm not saying this right. I'm out of practice with any kind of relationship—"

He pressed his thumb to her lips to hush her protests. "I liked kissing you, too. And I intend to do it again. Often, if you let me." He brushed her hair off her face and tucked it behind her ear before leaning in and pressing a gentle kiss right against the scar on her cheek, in case she had any doubts that he wanted to taste every last inch of her. When she was ready. "But we're still not going to rush anything. I'd never forgive myself if I scared you back into your shell. And then there's that whole bad guys trying to kill me thing I should probably take care of." He stepped back, putting an arm's length of distance between them before holding out his hand. "Compromise?"

"You and your Option B. Always got to have a backup plan." She reached out and took his hand. "I can do that."

He checked the sky once more, giving an all clear before climbing down out of the cave. He captured her hand again as soon as all three of them were on ground level, heading back to the cabin. They were well beyond the count of three and still holding hands when he spoke again. "If you trust me in your kitchen, I'll cook dinner so you can write. I can't wait to read the next Bonecrusher book."

She squeezed his hand, assuring him she was okay with the ongoing link between them. It wasn't a sexy come-on or a promise of forever. But to Luke, her ability to trust him with holding her hand meant as much as the smile she gave him. "You know, for the first time in a long time—I can't wait to write it."

Chapter Eleven

Luke should have asked for pajamas when Ava had bought him supplies in town. His new jeans were still a little stiff and itchy, and he really wanted to take off his T-shirt and bandage to let the stitches in his shoulder get some air and dry out after his shower. On his own, he'd sleep in his briefs or nothing at all. But he could hardly prowl around Ava's cabin in the middle of the night in his underwear or his birthday suit. Especially since she was up equally late on the sofa across the living room at the tail end of a marathon writing session that had started almost as soon as they got home from Stormhaven, and resumed right after the grilled burgers and veggies he'd made for dinner.

The cabin was locked up tight, but he'd been cautious about leaving on too many lights that might draw the attention of anyone flying a drone overhead, searching for them. The single lamp he had on at Ava's desk where she'd set him up to work on her computer provided the only illumination in the entire house, save for the light reflecting off their respective computer screens and the patches of moonlight sneaking in through drawn window shades and curtains. After cleaning up the flash drive that had finally made its appearance, and reading the contents, he had no doubt an enemy was still searching for him to complete the task of silencing the veteran Marine who'd blown the whistle on BDS's illegal activities—and the brave woman who had deigned to help him because she needed to be needed, and she wanted to disprove her misguided belief that she was weak or useless.

Not for the first time that night, Luke turned in his chair to glance over at Ava, his dark-haired warrior, to see with his own eyes that she was safe, that he hadn't done anything else to jeopardize her safety despite her willing cooperation with his investigation.

And not for the first time that night, Luke let his gaze linger on the woman who had grown to mean so much to him in such a short time. Who needed a slinky peignoir when that well-worn pair of running shorts hugged her sweet derriere and showed off those long, fit legs as she sat on the couch with her toes tucked beneath a sleeping Maxie? Even the oversize man's T-shirt she wore for a top only served to point out the wonderful differences between a man's blockier shape and the swells and dips that made a woman's figure so irresistibly interesting. Bopping her head to whatever tune was playing inside the noise-canceling headphones she wore, she stared at the screen while her fingers flew over the keyboard as if possessed.

The pillow beneath her laptop couldn't completely mask the faded scars that dotted her thighs and disappeared beneath the hem of her shorts, matching the similar trail he'd seen on her arms earlier. While the marks of torture didn't take one thing away from his body's physical response to her, the visible evidence of some bastard hurting her triggered a primitive, protective anger in him. As strong as Ava was, as much as she wanted to fight her own battles, if there was breath in his body, no one would ever hurt her again.

Perhaps sensing the intensity of his thoughts, Ava looked up from her work to meet his gaze. Although she raised an eyebrow, silently asking if anything was wrong or if he'd found out something new, Luke smiled and waved aside her query. He wasn't sure exactly how the creative process worked, but he was quickly learning that too many interruptions messed with the flow of getting the words down on the page. He'd get an impatient huff followed by a polite smile, which were infinitely worse than a pointed lecture or one of her sarcastic comebacks.

He'd already asked her to stop for dinner and to show her the information in the files he'd taken from BDS—evidence of illegal transactions and moving money around to hide payments into an account marked "JR" from overseas investors for technology BDS was designing for the American military. Ava had asked some smart questions that helped him recall what had put him onto the discrepancies in company records in the first place. And her suggestion that he give himself another night's sleep to allow his battered brain a chance to completely heal and recover other pertinent information, such as what he had done with the evidence on the flash drive *before* the car chase and bullets, if anything—and where he'd been heading when his SUV had spun out of control—made good sense. Although he suspected continuing that conversation would gradually draw out the information he needed, he'd already turned her life upside down this weekend. He wasn't going to let his presence here impact her work, especially now when she claimed to be having some sort of breakthrough. With a sweet little wink, her head resumed its bobbing to the music, and she turned her attention back to the keyboard.

Luke spun back to his own workspace, looking beyond the holstered gun he was keeping within easy reach on the desk beside him to the tiny clock in the corner of the computer screen—1:15 a.m. He wondered how late she'd stay up writing. He wondered if she could understand his need to keep her in his sight, both for her security and for the grounding sense of calm that being with her these past two days had given him. He might not know who his enemies were in the world outside this cabin, but here with Ava he knew peace and trust and—like she'd said up at the cave he'd dubbed Stormhaven—normalcy. He could live this life. Spending time in the outdoors with a great dog, watching Ava write—helping her brainstorm an idea or two. He'd need a job, of course, so he could stay out of her hair while she created her fantasy world on the computer, but he could come home to a brilliant, brave woman and greet her with another one of those kisses that damn near made his body explode. He liked the way she thought. He admired her talent. He appreciated her strength. As inevitably as Larkin Bonecrusher and Willow Storm were destined to be together, he was falling in love with Ava Wallace.

With that sobering thought, he pulled up the internet and focused on his own work, researching the players at Bell Design Systems, wondering which of them—or if all of them—wanted him dead.

The reason why BDS had put a hit on him was obvious. Some very powerful people were doing some very illegal things. Selling plans for US military tech to a subversive Chinese faction was a threat to national security. Maybe the insurgents intended to build the tech and start a revolution in their own part of the world, or maybe they were paying to have the inside scoop on what America and her allies might be using in a war zone or on border patrol duty.

Either way, this sort of industrial espionage and infiltration had been part of what he'd been up against when he'd been promoted to investigative duties as an MP. He'd recognized the money laundering in accounts and the encrypted emails that included both schematics and negotiations. Although he suspected these files didn't tell the whole story, along with his testimony, they would certainly give a federal prosecutor, or even the IRS, plenty of material to obtain a search warrant to go through all of BDS's files to find more evidence and pinpoint all the players involved in the illegal transactions. If he'd been as smart as he thought he was, he'd made more than one copy of the files and had hidden them somewhere, or he had sent the originals on to someone else. But maybe the perp at BDS had blocked his messages or rerouted his voice mails. Maybe that's what had led to the desperate act of fleeing from the people he worked for and swallowing the flash drive. He'd be a fool to risk his life for one little data stick, knowing that destroying it and killing him would eliminate the threat to BDS. He must have had a backup plan in mind that he'd forgotten, a contact he'd been trying to reach in case things went south for him.

They had gone way south, and he still had no idea who he was up against, and how much anyone in the outside world knew about the secrets he'd uncovered.

Take a deep breath. Do your job. You got this.

Luke pulled up a recent magazine interview and stared into the eyes of the main man himself—Gregory Bell. The founder and CEO of Bell Design Systems was a brilliant engineer in his own right. More than that, he was an adept businessman who'd built BDS from the ground up. Bell knew how to hire the right people, and when to buy out the competition or sell off a division, to turn his company into a billion-dollar empire. So why would a guy like that resort to under-the-table dealings? Was someone else in his company dealing with the Chinese faction? Or did the white-haired man in the tailored suit have a secret to hide? Blackmail to pay? A lover he was keeping in diamonds and a penthouse? Good old-fashioned greed? Did he have a personal vendetta against someone that made him willing to risk the expensive contracts he had with the government and military? The article included a picture of Bell with his wife and three daughters. But while the information sounded familiar because of his job, any spark of recognition about the CEO himself did not.

The next player he pulled up was Roy Hauser, the chief of security. Hauser had hired him earlier this year, fresh after his Marine Corps discharge, to work as a military consultant and do background research on potential hires, and to help provide security for BDS executives and visiting guests, including the Chinese dignitaries he remembered from the hotel at the top of the mountain. What had Ava called it? Ridgerunner Lodge. He'd mistakenly thought he'd uncovered some hacking activities from their guests or from someone in IT who'd been working with them. There'd been a late-night meeting with Hauser where he presented his suspicions about someone in the company leaking information to the Chinese.

The next morning he'd been racing down the mountain highway in a car with no brakes and a contingency of BDS security hot on his trail.

He had no idea how many people at BDS were involved in the treasonous business activities. He had no idea if Hauser or Bell were involved, or if Hauser had reported Luke's findings and had inadvertently alerted the wrong person in the company. The men pursuing him could simply be taking orders. Whoever was behind this had probably labeled Luke as the traitor so that they could use him as a scapegoat, eliminate him and his evidence and go on their merry way, making illegal millions and endangering his fellow military men and women.

He had to have told someone outside of BDS what he'd found. Or at least been on his way to do so. But who? Who would he have trusted enough to share the secret with? A military contact? An attorney? State police? The FBI? He'd told Ava he'd called a friend in the Corps the day before all this started. Was that the connection he'd shared his suspicions with?

He needed to make phone calls.

He needed to find numbers first. They'd probably been programmed into the phone that was taken from him. BDS had that, too. They could know his contacts before he did.

Step one was to recapture those last elusive bits of his memory. Who did he think was responsible for these crimes? Who would he have called for backup?

Then he heard a soft snore from behind him and smiled.

Who would he call besides his very own Willow Storm?

Time to give his battered brain a break. With the clock ticking past two in the morning, Luke strapped the Hellcat around his ankle and powered down the computer. It was nice to be able to stuff the data stick into his pocket instead of feeling the need to hide it down his gullet again.

Now that Ava was clearly ready to turn in, Luke got up and went to the sofa. When Maxie sat up in curiosity, he put a finger to his lips, as though the dog would understand the warning not to wake up her mistress.

Ava's lashes were long and dark against her pale skin, and they barely fluttered as he saved the story on her laptop and removed the headphones.

When she didn't stir, Luke stretched his shoulder to test its tenderness and strength. Confident that he was the man for this job, he slipped his arms beneath Ava's knees and back and picked her up, laptop and all. He held her for a few seconds, waiting to see if she'd wake or panic at being confined to his arms. But when she snuggled her cheek against his chest with a sleepy sigh, he turned toward the stairs.

"Come on, girl," he whispered to Maxie, and the dog followed as he carried Ava upstairs to her bedroom and laid her on the bed.

He pulled the sheet and quilt over her and set the laptop on the bedside table. But when he spotted his name on the middle of the screen, he picked up the laptop and read the page she'd written there. The voice of the A. L. Baines he knew leaped off the page and he scrolled back to the beginning of the scene.

Although the chapter took place between Larkin and Willow in a cave where they'd been stranded after a rescue from Lord Zeville's castle, he found at least two instances where she'd slipped and typed in his name instead of Larkin's. Luke stood there beside the bed in the shadows, completely engaged in the newest chapter of the *Chronicles*. Son of a gun. It turned into a love scene. Luke felt a punch of desire in his gut. It wasn't a technical love scene with a bunch of bells and whistles. It was a tender, slow and sensual, okay, a freakin' hot love scene between Larkin and Willow.

A drowsy voice interrupted him before he reached the last paragraph. "Nosy. You better not plagiarize my book or leak that onto the internet."

Luke sank onto the edge of the bed beside her. "Is this what you want to have happen between us?"

Her eyes opened wide. "What?"

"You used my name a couple of times. Slip of the imagination?" he teased.

Suddenly wide awake, Ava sat up and snatched the computer off his lap. She closed the program and shut the laptop completely, stuffing it under the pillow next to her. "That's a rough draft. Not even my editor gets to read that version. I spew out all my ideas, and then I go back and make it pretty."

"It gets better than that?" He didn't have a creative bone in his body, and her talent was oozing out her pores. "Don't tell me you can't write a love scene. That was... really good."

"It's fiction."

Fortunately, Luke Broughton had other talents. "It doesn't have to be."

And there was that beautiful blush he loved. "How did I get upstairs?" Unexpectedly shy about a man sitting on her bed flirting with her, or maybe realizing too late that she'd been vulnerable to him while she'd dozed, she pulled the covers up and hugged them to her chest. "What about your shoulder?"

"Loved every second of carrying you."

"You know what I mean. Did I hurt you?"

"I loved having you in my arms. Figured if you were sleeping, I didn't have to count." Her hair hung loose and wavy around her face and shoulders. Luke brushed the long waves back behind her ear, wanting to let her know there was nothing she needed to hide from him. "You're a snuggler, by the way, when you lower your guard. I loved every second of that, too."

She briefly turned her cheek into his palm before scooting away and changing the subject. "Did you find out everything you needed from the data stick? Is BDS selling their tech to someone besides our military?"

He nodded, knowing he shouldn't push her to admit she wanted the same thing he did. That love scene could have been an extension of her subconscious mind, not a conscious wish. And he wanted her fully with him when he made love to her, whether it was an hour from now or a year from now. Providing, of course, he survived this mess at all. "I still don't know who the players are. But I uncovered something big. When I alerted Hauser to what I found, I set a chain of events in motion."

"You think he's behind the attempt on your life? Did he shoot you?"

"I don't know." With his mind focused back on where it needed to be, Luke got up, allowing her to slide farther under the covers. "I do know that as long as I'm alive and the information I found can destroy BDS, someone will be coming after me. I hope I called for backup before everything went FUBAR. That someone I trust is out there looking for me."

"I hope so, too."

"I'd better let you get your sleep. Looks like you're mentally all played out."

"Thanks for the inspiration."

So that chapter *was* about the two of them. At least, a little bit.

"Anytime." He patted the bed, urging the dog to jump up and curl up beside her. "Maximillia Madrona Draconella Reine will keep you safe tonight."

"Good night, Larkin."

"Good night, Willow."

Chapter Twelve

Luke woke to the sound of muffled screams. What the hell?

He rolled over in bed, orienting himself to the darkness. Not screams, but whimpering, muffled words that didn't make sense. He glanced over at the clock on the table beside him—4 a.m. Then he heard a thump, panting. A big dog scratching at a door.

Luke swung his legs over the side of the bed. Although the doors were closed between them, he recognized the sounds from the morning before.

Ava.

"I'm coming, sweetheart." He grabbed his jeans from the foot of the bed and slipped them on. He thought about retrieving his gun from the drawer of the bedside table, but he left it behind and ran to the door. He'd be scary enough charging into Ava's bedroom.

He pushed her door open and was instantly greeted by Maxie. The big dog glowed with the light from the moon seeping in around the curtains, the only illumination in the room. The dog seemed to be in distress, possibly because she wasn't able to wake her mistress. Ava was thrashing in the bed and crying out, in the full throes of a nightmare. He scrubbed his hand around Maxie's ears, soothing the beast. "I'm here. We'll help her. Don't you worry, girl."

Although he didn't want to alert anyone who might be

watching the house, Luke didn't hesitate to turn on the lamp beside the bed. Ava's skin was flushed, her forehead dotted with perspiration. Her long hair clung to the dampness on her skin, masking her expression. But her moans were full of pain, and he couldn't stand by while she muttered pleas to be let go. Looking at the sheet and quilt twisted around her legs and the hair covering her face, he had a pretty good idea about where her mind was right now. He prayed that what he was about to do wouldn't make it worse.

He touched her.

"Ava." He grabbed the covers and pulled them from beneath her, unrolling her from her cloth prison. She screamed into her pillow. Luke pulled her hair away from her face and saw she was still in the grips of the scene that was haunting her. "I'm sorry, sweetheart." He grasped her by the shoulders and gave her a slight shake. "Ava, wake up." He tapped her cool cheek. "Ava!"

She came awake, knocking his hand from her face, screaming.

He retreated several inches away from her on the bed. Her eyes were wide, frightened, unfocused in the moonlight. She blinked. They darkened as she looked at him. Luke nodded to the furry caretaker sitting beside her, and Ava reached for Maxie, burying her face in the dog's neck and breathing deeply.

Luke watched for several minutes, making sure she was all right. Gradually, she eased her grip on the dog and Maxie licked Ava's face and neck, earning a soft laugh and making Luke smile. Content that she could finish recovering without his help, Luke pushed to his feet. "I'll leave the light on for you, okay?"

Then she surprised him by reaching for his hand. She lifted her beautiful eyes to his. "Thank you."

When her grip tightened around his, he moved a step closer. "Way to scare the team, Wallace."

She nodded. "Instead of trying to hash any of this out, would you…?"

Luke sat on the edge of the bed again. He switched hands and tucked a tendril of coffee-colored hair behind her ear. "Anything. Just ask."

"Would you hold me? I'm so cold."

Whatever the woman needed. He didn't have the power to say no. After folding the quilt and sheet at the bottom of the bed so that nothing could tangle between them or around her again, Luke stretched out beside her, propping up the pillows beneath his head and gathering her to his side. She rested her head on his shoulder and her hand in the middle of his chest where he threaded his fingers with hers and held them against the beat of his heart. Maxie curled up on the other side of her. Cocooned between their body heat, he doubted she needed any covers. "Better?"

She slipped her toes between his ankles, draping herself more fully against his side. "I'm such a mess."

He stroked his fingers through her hair with his free hand, lightly massaging her neck and back. "No, you're not. I'm afraid I've aggravated everything you're dealing with."

"But I'm *dealing* with it," she emphasized. "I might be online with my counselor every day this week as all these emotions surface again, but I'm not hiding from it anymore. Thank you for that."

"For giving you nightmares?"

She chuckled against his skin, and the brush of her lips felt like a kiss. "For waking me up. I don't mean tonight, although I appreciate that, too. Figuratively. You forced me to change the status quo. I realize I've been hiding away, not because of how others see me. But because of how I saw myself." Although their hands were still linked, she freed her index finger to trace gentle circles on his chest. Her touch left a trail of goose bumps in its wake and stoked a lambent desire deep inside him. "I thought of myself as a victim for two years, so that's how others treat me. But you don't."

"The people around here have known you since you were a kid. They watched you grow up. They've seen the changes in you. People aren't always sure how to deal with it." Luke turned his head to press a kiss to her forehead. "I only know the woman who greeted me with a shotgun and then saved my life. She's pretty tough. Pretty resourceful. Doesn't give up. I know the woman in your books. She's talented. Speaks an important message about purpose and loyalty, never giving up hope, and fighting to do the right thing. I know the woman in my arms right now. She's beautiful. Tempting. Caring. I can't associate any of that with you being a victim."

"Absolutely the best compliments ever." This time, there was no mistaking the kiss she pressed beside the stitches on his shoulder. Then she rose up on her elbow beside him, her hair falling around him like a sable waterfall. "Thank you."

Luke raised his head to meet her halfway as she bent over to kiss him. Her lips were soft and pliant as they sampled each other with a leisurely thoroughness. Then her tongue swept across his lips and snuck inside to deepen the kiss. Luke was more than happy to oblige. He palmed the back of her head and took over. The other hand reached for her bottom and pulled her more fully on top of him. Her breasts pillowed against his chest and her hands roamed across his skin, stoking the fire she kindled inside him. There was no hiding how much he wanted her as her thigh slipped between his.

But when a cold nose butted his shoulder, then sniffed into Ava's hair, she laughed against his mouth and ended the kiss. Although parts of his body demanded they continue, the other, more important parts were thrilled that Ava settled back against his side with a heavy sigh.

"Better?" Ava nodded. "Do you want me to leave?"

She was still hugging him with her arms and body. "I want you to stay. Is that okay?"

"I'm very okay with that." Several minutes passed with them simply holding each other, and the fire inside him eased to a less urgent level. He caught her hand and stilled it when she started tracing those mindless circles across his chest again. "Do you need to talk about it?"

Her answer was a quick no. "Not my first nightmare. I'm guessing it won't be my last."

Luke was beginning to wonder if she'd let him hold her for a couple more hours of sleep, or if she'd ask him to leave so that she could completely relax. Until she said the words, however, he wasn't going anywhere. Holding Ava like this was a gift. Her touch felt as much a part of him as each and every memory he was slowly regaining. Her trust felt like he'd finally come home to the place where he belonged. But if all she needed from him was a few pushes out of her comfort zone and some tactile therapy, he wasn't going to ask for anything more.

Ignoring his body's demands for another kiss, Luke reached over Ava's back to stroke the dog, who had settled on the other side of her again. "Maxie's the real champion. She sounded the alarm."

"She's a natural. I got her to be a guard dog, but she's adapted these natural protective behaviors. She's the best thing ever to bring me out of an episode." Ava's fingers stopped their circles, and he felt her gaze snap up to the bottom of his chin. "Is that a turnoff? That I have a third party in bed with us?"

Luke was still petting Maxie. "You know I'm no stranger to PTSD. Dogs can be trained to do any number of things with repetitive practice and us understanding what a meaningful reward is to them. I'm guessing this one is all about the affection?"

Gradually, Ava relaxed again, as he accepted the Queen Mother of the Dragons on their team. "She won't turn her nose up at a treat, trust me. But yeah, she's a sucker for a belly rub or a scratch beneath her chin. Have you worked with dogs before?"

"Oh, yeah. Used them all the time with MP work. Can't beat a canine nose or ears when it comes to finding trouble or alerting to danger. Or comfort." Memories of a black-and-tan Belgian Malinois ran through his mind. "My last K-9 partner was Axel. When I got promoted to a desk job, he was transferred to a new handler. But when it came time to retire him, I got him back as a pet for a couple of years. I miss that boy. Smartest dog I ever knew. Buried his ashes on the base where we served together after he passed."

"What base is that?"

"Fort Leonard Wood." They both stopped their petting at his automatic reply. Ava pushed herself to a sitting position and Luke met her knowing gaze. "I served at Fort Leonard Wood. That's where I ended my career. Earlier this year."

"That's in Missouri, right?"

"Yeah. It's an Army base. But different branches of the service and even civilians do police training there." Luke sat up beside her. The memories were flooding in now, all as clear as if they'd just happened. So much for relaxing and helping Ava fall back to sleep. He was breathing hard with excitement. Sitting still was no longer an option. He climbed out of bed and paced the room. "My buddy Joe Soldati works there. He took my place when I left. Are all my memories finally coming back?"

"Don't push it. Let's think about this one memory." Maxie

woofed as Ava crawled to the edge of the bed and stood. "Is Soldati the friend you called before all this started?"

"I think so."

She picked up her cell phone from the bedside table and held it out to Luke. "Call him."

"It's four in the morning."

"Our time. It's 5 a.m. in Missouri, and you military guys like to rise early. Besides, if you called him three days ago with what you uncovered, and haven't checked in since then, he's worried about you. I would be."

He was a veteran Marine who had survived a car crash, dived off a cliff and taken a bullet. Why was he afraid to make this phone call?

Ava pushed the phone into his hand. "Call him. I'll be right here with you." She grinned. "In case you forget anything."

The tension in him broke and he laughed out loud as he took the phone. "Wiseacre."

Since he couldn't recall a phone number, he called the information operator instead. "I need a number for Fort Leonard Wood Army base near Waynesville, Missouri." After she dialed a general office on the base for him, Luke identified himself. "Captain Luke Broughton, USMC, Retired." He rattled off his serial number as if he was still active duty. "Captain Joe Soldati, military police. I know it's early, but does he happen to be on base?"

The corporal manning the communication center wrote down Ava's phone number and took Luke's message. Thirty minutes later, a plan was in place and the backup Luke needed was on its way to Wyoming. Joe had given him plenty of grief about waking him from a good night's sleep, but not as much grief as he'd given Luke for missing the flight he'd promised to be on Saturday morning. Apparently, Luke had given his friend an abridged version of what he'd uncovered, and arranged a rendezvous to turn over the evidence he had on BDS.

"When you didn't get off that plane, I thought the worst," Joe confessed. "If what you say is true, you're damn lucky to be alive."

Luke looked across the room to Ava, who was settling Maxie into her bed with a rawhide chew and eavesdropping on every word. "I couldn't have done it on my own. You'll take care of things from your end?"

"I've got all the phone calls made. All I need is my star witness to come out of hiding and debrief my superiors and the JAG office."

"I'll owe you one, buddy."

"Damn straight you will." Joe Soldati had served under Luke for several years before getting the promotion. He knew the guy was a lot of guff and wiseassery, but as solid and dependable as they came. "This is at least a three-beer and an introduce-me-to-your-sister favor, Broughton."

"I don't have a sister."

"Then I'll settle for the beer."

"You're on."

Then Joe got back to business. "My go bag is packed. I'll contact the JAG office while I'm in the air to see if they want to get the feds involved at this point. My contacts at the Wyoming state police have been waiting for a follow-up call from me. I'll get on the horn with them. The cavalry's coming. Keep your head down until we get there."

"Roger that." Ava crawled back into the bed and patted the mattress beside her, telling him he was welcome to rejoin her when the conversation ended. Every cell in Luke's body leaped at the invitation. "And Joe? You know those *Bonecrusher Chronicles* books you got me into?"

"Yeah?"

"The woman I told you about who's been helping me?" Ava's momentary frown was probably her worrying that he was going to give away her secret identity. She had to know him better than that by now. "She reminds me of Willow Storm."

Joe laughed. "Lucky dog. See you in a few hours."

After disconnecting the call, Luke set the phone beside her laptop and crawled onto the bed to sit beside her. Although he knew they wouldn't be completely safe until Joe and his team arrived, criminals were identified and arrests were made, Luke felt his guard dropping, knowing the authorities were on their way to give him and Ava true sanctuary. He felt like they'd done this a hundred times when he draped his arm around her shoulders and she snuggled against his side; it felt so natural.

He pressed a kiss to her temple. "Once again, you've helped me find the truth. Ever think about a career in law enforcement? You'd make a hell of an interrogator."

"I've already got a pretty good gig."

"Writing books?"

"Being with you." Her fingers were doing that lazy circle thing on his skin again. This time farther down the flat of his stomach, sending tiny electric pulses straight down to his groin. "Do male readers really think Willow is hot?"

"Oh, yeah." His voice came out as a throaty growl.

Her fingers stopped their magic spell and she sat up on her knees to face him. "Luke, I want to try... I want...you."

"Ava, I don't deserve—"

"Don't you go all noble on me now. Larkin Bonecrusher is a rogue. And I know... I mean, earlier at the cave, and a while ago when we kissed... I could feel... I think you want me, too."

He glanced down at the tightness pushing against his zipper. "I'm not hiding the fact I do." He cupped her face between his hands, reading the certainty in her eyes. "Are you sure? You don't owe me anything."

"No." She smiled. "You owe me."

Well, hell's bells. He could add seductress to the list of things this woman did well. "Luke Broughton reporting for duty."

He pulled her into his lap and covered her mouth with his. When he pushed his tongue between her lips, she opened for him, welcoming his claim. While he feasted on her mouth, her hands mimicked his, framing his face, sliding into his hair, learning all the places that liked to be touched. She tore her lips from his, clamping her teeth gently on the point of his chin, eliciting a feral growl.

"Whatever you want, Ava," he promised. "However you want it." He blazed his own trail down the side of her neck, paying special attention to the bundle of nerves at the base of her throat that made her squirm each time he teased it with his beard or soothed it with his tongue.

"I can't guarantee how good—"

"Don't go there." He lifted his head to press a hard kiss to her swollen lips before pulling back and settling his hands at the relatively neutral position at her waist. "We're in this together, remember? If there's anything you don't like—if you need to stop, I will. Scaring you in any way would be worse than not being with you."

Although he was breathing hard from the things this woman did to him, Luke held himself as still as humanly possible.

But his warrior princess was having none of that. She grasped his wrists and pulled his hands around to cup her bottom. "But I'm brave." She leaned in and kissed him.

"You are." He squeezed her bottom, holding her close as she came in for another kiss.

"I'm tough." Their lips got intimately acquainted while she unsnapped his jeans and slowly pulled down the zipper.

Luke groaned into her mouth. "The toughest."

"I'm tempting." Her eyes locked onto his as she slid her hand inside his pants.

He hissed at the way his body jumped to her touch. "Yes."

Luke couldn't hold back anymore. If she asked him to stop or give her space, he would. But until she gave any hint of panic setting in, he was going after what he wanted so desperately. He tugged the T-shirt over Ava's head and snapped her to him, needing the feel of skin to skin. He claimed her mouth with a deep, drugging kiss, hinting at his intent, assuring her of his desire. He licked and nipped and kissed his way down to that bundle of nerves and lower still until he sucked the pebbled tip of one pretty breast into his mouth.

One moment she was arching into him with a breathy moan, the next she was sitting back, covering herself with her hands. "Should we turn the light off?"

Luke eased himself up to a sitting position beside her. This was the hesitation he'd been worried about, the changing of her mind that he would respect. "I thought you'd be more comfortable with it on."

"But you'll see all my scars."

Luke bit down on his cry of relief. This wasn't about stopping. This was about reassurance, and the healing they seemed to give each other. "I'll show you mine if you show me yours."

Ava's mouth opened in a startled O, then quickly closed. "It's not a competition."

"Wanna bet?" He gingerly shucked off his jeans and tossed them to the floor. He pointed to the wound on his shoulder. "Bullet hole, obviously." Then he tapped the stitches on his knee. "Split this open on a rock." He pulled down the waistband of his shorts and brushed his fingers over his hip. "Bomb fragments. Hip surgery."

She was laughing by the time he got to the three dots on the back of his hand he'd gotten holding a sparkler one Fourth of July as a boy. "Enough. You're a stunning man. I watched you yesterday morning while you were sleeping." Her cheeks turned rosy with an embarrassed blush. "I guess I'm a bit of a voyeur."

"So, you can treat me like a piece of meat, but I can't enjoy ogling you?" Luke traced his finger along the mark on her chest. He leaned in and brushed the gentlest of kisses against her injured cheek. "I know the scars are here. I know everything they symbolize. But I don't see them when I look at you. I see *you*."

"You're sure?"

"Sweetheart, I'm a man. At the moment, I only have one thing on my mind." He feathered his fingers into her glorious hair. "Are *you* sure?"

"I have only one thing on my mind, too," she confessed. She dropped her hands, baring herself to him.

Luke thanked her for her trust by pulling her into his lap and loving her mouth with his. Then he rolled her onto her back and kissed her all the way down to the line of her shorts before removing them. He kissed her between her legs, and she bucked against his mouth. "Luke…"

He reached for his jeans to retrieve a condom and swore. "No billfold. You?"

She pushed herself up onto her elbows, looking as bereft as he felt. "No boyfriend." Then her face lit up and she scrambled off the bed. "Wait. Don't move."

She tugged the sheet around her naked body and ran downstairs.

"Ava?" He hurried after her in his briefs to find her digging through the bottom drawer of her desk, tossing out letters and printouts. "What are you doing? We can finish like that. I'm fine. What's wrong?"

"Nothing." She held up an envelope in a weird sort of victory dance before grabbing his hand and leading him back up the stairs. She lost the sheet somewhere between the door and the bed as she pushed him onto the edge of the mattress and tore open the envelope.

"What's that?"

"A fan letter." She pulled out a familiar, sealed foil package. "Someone sent me a condom, saying maybe if I got laid, I'd be able to write that love scene for Larkin and Willow."

His blood simmered at the audacity of some stranger thinking he had the right to overstep the lines of privacy. "You mean someone got that personal with you? Some idiot accused you of not being sexy?"

"Shh." She pressed her finger to his lips and climbed onto his lap. "They were talking to A. L. Baines, not to me. Right now, I'm just glad to have this."

He had to admit that he was, too. Her hands shook as she tried to roll it onto him. Luke took over and sheathed himself before falling back onto the bed and pulling her on top of him. "However it happens. Whatever happens. You and me—we've got this. We're a team, remember?"

She brushed her fingers over his lips. "I will never forget."

Then he was inside her, thrusting up to meet her tight heat, loving every touch, every gasp of pleasure she gave.

When they were on the brink, she braced her hand against his chest. "This is where you say, 'I love you, Willow.'"

He shook his head. "I love you, Ava."

He pulled her down on top of him, claiming her mouth in a kiss. He slipped his thumb in between them where they were linked and pressed the sensitive bud that took her to the top of the mountain. And as Ava gasped his name— *his* name, "Luke…"—beside his ear, the tension in him released. He thrust into her one more time, topping the crest and following her down the other side.

Chapter Thirteen

Ava slept soundly, free from nightmares, claimed by the most beautiful kind of exhaustion. After waking with the sunrise to put Maxie out for her morning constitutional and feed her beloved pet, she went back upstairs to return to Luke's arms and discover other sorts of pleasure that didn't require the protection they lacked.

She'd learned that the numbers beneath the tattoo were a tribute to the men and women he'd lost in his unit, marking the date of their ultimate sacrifice. Ava had kissed each number, then kissed the man bearing the tribute, before he'd pulled the quilt over them both and she'd drifted off with her lips smiling against the eagle, globe and anchor.

The morning sun was shining brightly through the gaps around the window when she awoke to the suffocating sensation of being pressed down onto the bed. She came awake, gasping for air, shoving at the weight that pinned her down.

"It's okay, Ava. It's me."

Even as Luke moved the arm and leg that he'd thrown over her while they slept, she was rolling off the edge of the bed. She tumbled onto her knees, then quickly stood up, orienting herself to her surroundings and the sound of Luke's voice. By the time she focused in on him standing on the opposite side of the bed in his boxer-briefs, she knew she'd ruined the beautiful night they'd shared.

"I'm sorry," she apologized. "For a minute, I forgot you were with me. If I had opened my eyes first—"

"Stop it," he ordered, his slitted eyes raking over her from head to toe. Ava hugged her arms around herself, knowing that she'd hurt him, but not knowing the words to say to make it right. But then Luke was striding around the bed, pulling her into his arms and giving her the kind of hug she really needed. "I'm not angry at you. I'm mad because you think you need to apologize. Neither one of us is going to be fixed overnight. There are going to be setbacks, but as long as we're working through them together, I can handle it. I'm in this for the long haul with you, sweetheart. I just need to know that you're in the fight with me."

Sighing with relief, Ava snaked her arms around his waist. What she and Luke had shared this weekend had been more than therapeutic. He hadn't just reawakened her courage. He'd awakened her heart. Her feelings for this man were new and tender and strong, and she didn't want to jeopardize this precious gift before she had the chance to explore where a relationship between them might lead once they got past the obstacles of her PTSD, his amnesia and people who wanted him dead.

How could she not love a man who wasn't scared of her mood swings, and who kissed like a man on a mission. Wait. Love? Was that where her thoughts had gone? Was that what her heart wanted?

Clearly needing to start this morning over again, Ava opted for humor. "'I just need to know that you're in the fight with me.' That's good. Can I use that line in the book?"

He laughed. "As long as you understand that my promise to you is real, not fiction."

Luke stiffened a split second before she heard the crunch of gravel in the distance and Maxie woofed a warning downstairs as a vehicle approached the cabin.

Luke didn't bother to ask if she was expecting visitors. "This conversation isn't over." He released her to pull on his jeans and dashed across the hallway to grab a T-shirt, boots and his gun.

Ava pulled underwear and a tank top from her dresser. "You need to get to Stormhaven. Now. Take the back door straight out to the trees. You'll run into the creek. Turn north and follow it about fifteen, twenty minutes to the cave, depending on how fast you move. They'll never see you."

He reappeared in the doorway, tucking his gun into the back of his jeans. "You're coming with me."

"No. I can distract them while you get away. Nobody's after me. I need you to be safe. Until your friend gets here, we're still on our own." She gestured to the rumpled bed. "I want to do this again. I want to do it better."

He took two steps, palmed the back of her neck and pulled her onto her toes for a hard, quick kiss. "Sweetheart, it doesn't get any better than last night." Her cheeks were on fire at that blunt reassurance. "But I'm more than willing to practice if that's what you want." She laughed and they traded another quick kiss. "Now wipe that blush off your face and throw some pants on so you can answer the door."

Ava pulled on her socks and jeans while Luke peeked out the window to see the approaching vehicles. "Looks like the sheriff's car and a black SUV." He let the curtain fall shut again. "I don't like this." He picked up her cell phone and tucked it into the back pocket of her jeans while she zipped the front. "You're coming with me."

"No." She grabbed her boots and pushed him into the hallway, hurrying him down the stairs in front of her.

"Brandon won't hurt me. He's still trying to get me to go out with him again. You, on the other hand, he'll probably slap in jail."

"Ava—"

"Luke. You're not supposed to be here. Don't be here." She picked up the backpack of supplies they'd prepped the night before, in case they'd needed to make an escape like this, and handed it to him. "If whoever is in that black SUV is the man who tried to kill you, what's to stop him if he finds you here. And what's to stop him from killing Brandon and me, too, so there are no witnesses."

"Damn, I hate that you're right."

She laid her hand against his jaw, stroking her fingers through his beard. "Sometimes, the only way to win a battle is to avoid it until you're ready to fight."

"Larkin Bonecrusher, Book Two."

"You do read my books."

"You've got my new cell number?" Ava nodded. "Call as soon as you can and let me know what's going on. If I don't see your face in an hour, I will come back for you."

"It might not be safe."

"If anything happens to you, none of this matters."

"Hang on." She ran back to the living room and retrieved a key from her desk. She looped the lanyard attached to it around his neck. "The key to the closet where my gun safe is. The combination is JMW-7334. In case you and your Marine buddies need some backup and I'm not here."

"JMW-7334," he repeated back to her. "I will come back for you." He brushed his fingers into her hair and tucked it behind her ear before turning to the dog, who watched them curiously. "You. Keep her safe."

The crunch of gravel stopped, and they both knew their unwanted guests had pulled into the driveway.

"Go." Ava closed the door behind Luke and watched him run to the tree line and disappear.

Maxie barked and got up as the first car door closed out front. Ava took the time to tie her boots and button her blouse before answering the repeated knocking at her front door.

She plaited her hair into a loose braid and pulled it over her shoulder to mask her damaged cheek before unlocking the door and opening it to greet Sheriff Stout. Brandon wore mirrored sunglasses beneath the bill of his hat, making it impossible to read his expression. All she could see was her own pale reflection. She needed to do better than cringe and chase people away if she was going to help Luke.

You're smart. You've got skills now. You're a survivor. You've got this, Ava.

"Hi." Brandon pushed her inside and closed the door before she could see who was in the second vehicle. "What are you doing here?"

"A guy can't come see his best girl?"

"With company?" She moved around him to peek through the sidelight and realized the SUV's windows were tinted. She couldn't see the driver or if anyone was with him. "Can I get you some coffee or iced tea? Do your friends want anything?"

When had Ava Wallace ever invited anyone inside her remote home for tea and cookies? But Brandon didn't seem to notice her unusual politeness. Maybe she was finally acting the way he expected her to.

"Nah." He took off his hat and worked the brim between his hands. "Sorry to bug you. I guess you were working?"

Not exactly. But out loud, she answered, "Yes."

"Well, this won't take too long." Was the man in the other vehicle not coming in? Or worse, was he walking around her property, searching for Luke? "I understand you talked to a man named Hauser in town yesterday. I'm helping him look for an employee of his who's gone missing."

"Missing?" It was too easy to play dumb with a man who expected her to be clueless about the dangers of the world. Maxie leaned into Ava's thigh and she gladly ran her fingers over the dog's head. She needed to stay calm to keep up this friendly facade. "That sounds terrible. His family must be so worried about him."

"According to Hauser, he doesn't have a family. No wife or kids. Dead parents. Only child."

She wondered if Luke had remembered that. That was probably one reason why he'd formed such tight bonds with his fellow Marines. They were his family. It was also probably why he'd taken the deaths of Ryan Voltaggio and the rest of his unit so hard. "Well, I'm sure someone's missing him."

"The people he works for would sure like to find him. Hauser wants to come in and ask you some questions. See if you've remembered anything helpful about the man you brought in. Doc Russell is looking for him, too. He's worried your John Doe could be a danger to himself. With that head injury, if he passes out and can't get help, he could die." Brandon took off his sunglasses and tucked them into his shirt pocket, finally letting her see the concern lining his eyes. "And since he took off before I got a chance to interview him, I wanted to know if he'd contacted you. Maybe to thank you."

Maxie circled around Ava's legs, perhaps sensing something that Ava couldn't. Had she missed the other man getting out of his SUV? "Like I told Mr. Hauser yesterday, I couldn't tell if the picture he showed me matches the man I met or not. I haven't seen him since."

When the dog trotted to the front door and woofed, Brandon rolled his eyes with an impatient huff. "Would you mind putting Maxie in her crate?"

"Yeah, as a matter of fact, I—"

"Hauser's waiting outside, and you know how Maxie is with strangers. The sooner we can have this conversation, the sooner we can get out of your hair."

The sharpness of his tone was a little unexpected. "Couldn't I talk to him out on the front porch? You know I don't like company at the house."

Brandon caught her hand and squeezed it. "Please, Ave. I need your help." Maybe Hauser had already threatened Brandon. *Get the weird recluse to talk or your brakes might go out, too.*

If she'd really been playing her part, she would have pulled free of his grasp. But his plea was her Achilles' heel. The last time she'd stopped to help a man…had been Luke Broughton. And her time with him had changed her life. He'd changed her self-perception and he'd changed her heart. The least she could do was help a friend she'd known since she was eight years old.

"Okay. I'll talk to him. For you."

"Thanks, babe." It wasn't an act when Brandon hugged her. Her pulse pounded in her ears and her breath locked in her chest. She couldn't stop herself from pushing away.

"The Rule of Three, Brandon. Let go." As soon as he released her, she whistled for Maxie and led her to her crate in the kitchen. She paused for a few seconds to pet the dog, centering herself. "Sorry, girl. Not everybody knows what a love bug you are."

She'd just clicked the latch shut when Maxie let out a warning bark.

In the next second, a scarf looped over her head, settling in front of her eyes and pulling her back. Ava screamed and scratched at the silky material as a knot tightened at the back of her head, catching strands of hair and pinching her scalp.

She scratched at the hands that were tying the blindfold on. The same hands cinched her arms and lifted her off her feet. "Stop! Why are you doing this?" Something else looped around her eyes, tighter, elasticized, blocking out even the light. Ava twisted, breaking one hand free, and clawed at the nightmare against her skin. "You don't understand. Please don't do this! Brandon!"

The arms that carried her tightened their grip. "It's for your own safety, babe. If you don't see faces, you can't identify anyone, and there's no reason to hurt you. I asked them if we could handle it this way."

"Them?"

"I don't want you to get hurt. I love you. I want a future with you."

Ava was screaming, thrashing against the restraint of his arms and chest. She kicked at his shins, tried to throw him off balance. She was sinking into the darkness, helpless again. "Do you know what a panic attack is? Did you ever wonder why I have them?"

"This is the only way. These people don't like witnesses."

Think, Ava! Stay in the moment. With Luke fleeing for his life and Maxie caged, no one could help her if she got trapped in the past. She had to be strong. She had to be smart.

There was a flaw in Brandon's logic. She might not know who he was talking about, but she knew *him*. And if he was involved with Bell Design Systems, then she was a witness to that involvement. She wasn't safe. Brandon might not even realize that he wasn't safe.

The front door opened. She felt the warmth of the sun on her skin, but she couldn't see anything. "Brandon, please!"

"It's all right." Brandon was shouting past her to someone else. "The dog is secured, and she can't see anything."

"Let go of me!"

She heard footsteps on the wood porch. More than one

set of footsteps. At least one person was heavy enough to make the steps creak.

"Why is she flailing around like that?" an unfamiliar voice asked. "Tie her up. If she raises her voice again, put a gag in her mouth."

She felt light-headed when the first metal bracelet locked around her wrist. She took a wild swing at her captor, but Brandon caught her arm and pulled it behind her with a painful wrench to her shoulder. "Come on, Ave. I'm trying to save you here. Cooperate."

With the handcuffs locked around her wrists, Brandon dragged her back into the living room and pushed her down onto the sofa. As he warned her to stay put, she heard the other men moving through her house. Opening doors, clinking dishes in the kitchen. Rifling through her desk.

"What are they doing? Please take off the blindfold. I have a phobia—"

"There are no BDS flash drives here." That voice she knew, didn't she? But it was hard to place it with the terror swirling around inside her head.

"Brandon, I can't see."

"That's the whole idea. Come on, baby. Stop acting crazy. These men need to ask you a few questions."

"And I have to be blindfolded and handcuffed to answer?" And poor Maxie, growling and barking, desperate to get to her. Someone banged on her cage and she stopped for a second, then barked again, sounding a lot less like a big, friendly galoot and a lot more like a beast who wanted to take someone's head off. "You're a fool, Brandon. No wonder I couldn't confide in you."

"Confide in me about what?"

"Didn't you ever wonder why I'd changed when I moved back here?" She rocked back and forth, willing the past to stay in the past, knowing she needed to focus on the present to survive.

"It's okay, Ave. I'm taking care of everything."

"I don't need to be taken care of."

"Do you know who I am, Ms. Baines?" A new voice spoke. An older voice. One she didn't recognize.

Brandon squeezed her shoulder and she nearly jumped off the couch. "I told you this is Ava Wallace."

"He doesn't know?"

Ava forced herself to stop rocking and shrugged. "I don't know what you're talking about."

"Don't be stupid. I dislike stupid people." Then this man must despise Brandon.

She heard footsteps on the stairs. One man. She wondered how many were still here with her.

The older man's voice continued. "I know you're A. L. Baines, Miss Wallace. My daughters are huge fans of yours. They have a crush on some knight named Larkin Bonecrusher."

Play dumb. "*The Bonecrusher Chronicles.* I've read those, too. Pretty entertaining books."

"I also know what happened to you in Chicago two years ago." Everything in Ava went still. "I know that Detective Gabriel Charles has made an arrest based on a recent murder, and he will be calling you later today about identifying the man and giving a sworn deposition."

"You hacked into my case file at CPD?"

"I'm pretty good with technology. What I don't know personally, I can hire people from all over the world to do for me." This man thought he had the upper hand. Right now, he probably did. But this fight wasn't over. She needed to assess her enemy and gather evidence until the moment came to fight this battle. "I needed to know who I was working with and the best way to get what I wanted from you."

"Which is?"

"I believe you know more about Luke Broughton than you let on to Sheriff Stout."

"And you thought inciting a panic attack by sending me a message from my kidnapper would ensure my co-operation?"

"I figured—correctly—that reminding you of that trauma would throw you off whatever game you've been playing with my men." The man sank onto the cushion beside her, and she instinctively shifted away from the invisible threat. "You see, I'm very good at reading people, Ms. Baines—"

"It's Wallace."

"—and I believe you've been lying."

No more pretense. No more playing dumb. "Is there something I could help you with, Mr. Bell? It is Mr. Bell, isn't it?"

Brandon swore beside her. "Damn it, Ave. I can't protect you if you know too much."

"Don't you need a warrant to search my house?" she challenged.

Brandon might be on edge, but Gregory Bell wasn't fazed. "I'm looking for Luke Broughton."

"I don't know anyone by that name."

"Perhaps not. You took him to the hospital with amnesia, but he escaped. Vanished from existence, it would seem. Now, whatever name he might be using, I think you do know him."

"Intimately, from the look of things." The man who'd gone upstairs returned. "There are men's toiletries in the bathroom. The bed in her room has seen some action."

"You slept with him?" Brandon raged above her. "You won't give me the time of day, and you slept with that stranger?"

"Better him than you."

She never saw the hand that slapped her across the face.

208 A Stranger on Her Doorstep

Tears soaked into the cloth covering her eyes and burned
along her cheek as she cowered in the corner of the sofa.
But it wasn't pain that finally made her cry. It was the
memories. Her skin crawled with the imprint of knives cutting into her. She anticipated the next touch, the next cut,
never knowing if she would bleed or gag at the mockery
of tenderness. Her fingers ached to latch on to Maxie's familiar warmth. Her heart needed Luke to remind her that
she could handle this. She could handle anything.

She turned her head toward Brandon's heavy steps pacing beside her. "How long have you been part of this?"

"On and off over the years," he answered. "They paid
me a lot of money to look the other way when they con-
ducted certain business up at the Ridgerunner. I got rid of
your boyfriend's car for them."

"You started that fire? What if it had spread to Mr.
Harold's trailer?"

"What if you stop talking." Gregory Bell didn't care
about a dishonored badge or a friendship betrayed. "Where
is Broughton?"

Ava understood that the weakest link here was Brandon. "I know him better after seventy-two hours than I
know you after twenty-seven years. You're working with
these people?"

"I'm looking for a fugitive. He's a danger to you, Ave.
Can't you see that?"

"You're the danger because you won't stand up and do
the right thing. They're a danger to our military. To our
country."

Metal screeched against the kitchen's tile floor as Maxie
threw her weight against the side of her crate.

"Damn it, Maxie, shut up!"

When she heard the snap of Brandon's holster, Ava
lurched to her feet and charged at him. "Don't you dare!"

Another pair of hands clamped down on her arms and

pulled her against a solid chest. She screamed at the startling touch. There was another grab and she screamed again.

"Quiet," Brandon warned, his grip cutting off the circulation above her elbow. "You keep your hands off her," he warned the other man. Although she hadn't heard his voice enough to be certain it was Roy Hauser, the bulk of his build and the slab of protective armor she'd slammed into made her doubt it could be anybody else. Brandon stroked her hair, no doubt trying to placate her, but simply reminding her of the blindfold knotted at the back of her head. "I'm sorry I hit you, baby. Cooperate with me now, and I'll protect you. Can we get her out of here now?"

"I'm not the only one who's changed, Brandon." As much as she had once treasured their friendship, any loyalty she'd felt to this man was done.

"Patience, Sheriff," Gregory Bell spoke again. "We can assume Captain Broughton is hiding nearby. A gunshot will bring him running. We'd be at the disadvantage. He has to bring me the flash drive. And I need to know anyone he's shared that information with over the last seventy-two hours before we kill him. With your temper, I'm afraid you'll shoot him before I get everything I need from him."

The door opened and Brandon dragged her outside. "You said you wouldn't hurt Ava. That she would still be mine."

"Yours?" But no one was listening to her.

Maxie was barking to raise the dead. The men had to shout to be heard.

"What are you going to do with her?" Brandon asked.

"Take her with us, of course. Put her in my car. I have a feeling she'll make fine bait."

A vehicle door opened, and she was shoved into a back seat. "Brandon, don't do this," she pleaded. "I won't come back from this trip. Neither of us will."

She heard a blam from somewhere in the distance and a hard thump on the ground at her feet.

She didn't need to see to recognize that sound. That was a blast from a Browning double-barrel shotgun. Brandon Stout was dead.

Chapter Fourteen

"What the hell is going on here?" Gregory Bell shouted. "Who fired those shots?"

She heard another vehicle door opening, feet scrabbling through the gravel.

"Ava! Stay down!" *Luke.*

Her heart surged in her chest. Luke was here.

That brave, wonderful man hadn't gone to Stormhaven to save himself. He'd doubled back to the cabin to save her. He'd raided her gun safe and was going to battle against the men whom she was sure intended to kill her once she'd served her purpose.

"Side of the garage, boss."

Ava heard an exchange of gunfire. Smaller caliber weaponry this time. Handguns.

She huddled down in the seat.

"Call off your goon, Bell!" Luke shouted once the bullets stopped flying. "I've got what you came for. I'm putting down my gun and coming out. Let Ava go."

Ava stiffened. This wasn't the plan. This was so not the plan. What happened to Option B?

"Luke! Don't do it!" she yelled. "They'll kill you!"

"Hands where I can see them, Captain." Roy Hauser gave the order she prayed Luke wouldn't obey. "Show me the flash drive."

Luke chuckled. "Do you want me to reach into my pocket or hold my hands up?"

Gregory Bell wasn't waiting to see who won this duel of wills. "On the ground, Broughton. Hands on your head. Roy, you search his pockets."

"He has a gun hidden on him, sir. I know how he thinks."

"I gave you an order."

Hauser capitulated to his CEO's command. "On the ground, Captain. And don't try anything funny."

"What? Like pretend to be my friend? Act all concerned when I bring you evidence that someone inside BDS is selling company technology to Chinese insurgents? That kind of funny?"

"He's baiting you, Roy. Search him!"

Then he heard Hauser curse. Something heavy hit the ground and there was a scuffle. The horrid thud of fist hitting bone. A moan of pain.

"Luke!"

Gravel flying. A breathless curse.

Then the fighting stopped. Ava held her breath until she heard Luke's stern voice. "Don't do it, Roy. Things look a little different when you're staring down the barrel end of a gun, don't they?"

"You and what army are going to take us down?" Hauser taunted.

Something small hit the rocks. "Put those on," Luke ordered. "Chain yourself to the bumper. By order of the United States Marine Corps, I'm placing you under arrest for attempted murder and a whole bunch of other treasonous crimes that my buddies at JAG and the state police are putting together right now."

Hauser muttered a curse, but judging by the clank of metal on metal, he was securing himself to the bumper of one of the SUVs. "I was carrying out orders. You understand that. You weren't the first problem I was told to eliminate, and you won't be the last. It wasn't anything personal."

"Funny how getting run off the road, shot and being forced to dive over the edge of a cliff feel personal."

She heard someone breathing erratically and feared that Luke had taken a blow to the head or reopened the wound on his shoulder.

"Luke? Are you all right?"

But Luke Broughton was a Marine on a mission. "You're next, Bell. You've got nobody left to do your dirty work for you. It's you and me."

"Stop all this pointless prattle." Bell's voice was right beside Ava. She curled up her legs and pushed across the seat. How had she missed his approach? She jumped at the hand that clamped around her ankle and dragged her from the SUV. The moment her feet hit the ground, she stumbled over Brandon's inert body. But an arm locked around her neck and shoulder and pulled her upright. She felt Gregory Bell's hot breath against her ear and the cold steel of a gun press into her temple. "I still have the upper hand, Broughton. Hand over the flash drive. Now!"

Luke cursed. For the first time in this whole showdown, he sounded like he was losing it. "You put a blindfold on her? You're lucky I don't shoot you like I did Stout. You want this flash drive? You let her go first."

She felt Bell shake his head as the tip of the gun ground against her skull. "The flash drive first. Then your girlfriend and I are driving out of here. I'll drop her off at one of the scenic overlooks and you can pick her up there."

"And trust that you're not going to push her off the side of the mountain so she can't testify against you, either? You hired me to be smarter than that."

"Fine. You've got no shot, Marine. Keep your evidence against me. I'm keeping her."

"No! I'm not your victim!" Ava stomped on Bell's foot, and threw her hips back against him.

"Don't struggle, Ava."

"I'm not going with him. If he doesn't care whether you live or die, he certainly doesn't care about me."

"Summon the dragon, Ava."

She froze at the odd request. "What?"

"Summon the dragon."

And then she understood. *Sometimes, the only way to win a battle is to avoid it until you're ready to fight.*

Larkin and Willow were ready to fight.

Ava pulled her teeth to her lips and gave a shrill whistle. "Maxie! Come!"

"What the...?"

Gregory Bell must have seen the pony-size dog charging toward him a second too late. Maxie leaped and her great, muscular paws hit Bell, knocking the gun from his hand, loosing his grip on Ava and sending all three of them tumbling to the ground.

Luke was there before Ava got to her feet. "It's me, sweetheart," he announced a split second before he unknotted the blindfold and whisked it off. "I'm so sorry they did that to you."

She blinked against the overly bright sunshine. "I'm okay. I kept it together." It took a moment to bring Luke into focus. Oh, no. He *was* bleeding. A spot of red stained the front of his T-shirt. "You're hurt. Your wound opened up."

"The stitches split when Hauser punched me there. I'll live." She could also see that his stance was strong and unwavering, just like the Hellcat he had trained on Gregory Bell. The CEO looked a lot less powerful lying in his dusty suit on the ground with an unhappy guard dog standing over him. "Where is the key to the cuffs?" he asked.

"On Brandon."

Keeping his gun trained on his former boss, Luke knelt beside Brandon's still body and checked his pockets until he found the key to unlock Ava. Then he handed her the cuffs. "Put them on him."

Ava handcuffed Gregory Bell's wrists behind his back and came back to stand at Luke's side. She brought Maxie with her, smoothing her fingers on the dog's head and praising her as she leaned against Ava's thigh.

"I'm a good man, Mr. Bell." Luke kept glancing down the road, as if he expected to see more company on her doorstep. "I did the right thing. And you tried to kill me and the woman I love for it. This time, the good guys win."

The woman he loved? Ava glanced up at Luke's rugged profile. Earlier, when he'd said he loved her, she thought he'd been caught up in the heat of the moment, riding the emotional catharsis of their lovemaking. But now he was telling the bad guy that he loved her? Oh, man, did they have a lot to talk about. And she needed to get back to her computer. She'd conquered the love scene. She'd just figured out that Larkin and Willow would exchange those three little words on the battlefield.

"Uh-oh. I know that look." Luke reached over to capture her hand in his, startling her from her thoughts. "Sorry."

Ava squeezed his hand and held on tight when he would have pulled away. "Before anything else happens, I love you, too."

Luke leaned in and claimed her lips in a hard kiss that spoke volumes about all that had passed between them, and all that might yet come to pass. By the time he pulled away, there was a trio of state police cars racing up the gravel road.

A cloud of dust settled over them as the cars pulled to a sudden stop and several armed men and women streamed out, splitting up and going to each of the three men Luke and Maxie had taken down. A stocky, black-haired man in a tan uniform emblazoned with several ribbons and captain's bars headed straight to them.

Luke returned his weapon to his ankle holster and reached out to shake the Marine's hand. "Joe Soldati. I never thought I'd be this happy to see your ugly face." Joe pulled Luke in for a back-slapping hug that made him wince before pulling away. "This is Ava Wallace."

"Ma'am." Joe touched the brim of his cap in a polite greeting before turning his attention back to Luke. "You do understand the concept of civilian life, don't you, Cap? You're supposed to take it easy. Not risk life and limb for your country anymore."

"Old habits die hard, I guess."

"Leave it to you, Cap. Having all the fun without us. I would have been here sooner except we took a wrong turn at some Podunk town about twenty miles down the road."

Ava and Luke answered the uniformed MP at the same time. "Pole Axe."

"When you said you wanted a change of scenery, I had no idea. You okay, ma'am?"

Luke slipped his arm around her waist, pulling her to his side. "I've got her, Joe."

"Would you at least let me arrest some of these people?"

"Gladly."

Several hours later, the sun was a red-orange fireball sinking behind the western ridge of the mountains when Ava and Maxie strolled onto the porch to join Luke where he'd stretched out in a rocking chair to reread her first book. He slipped a bookmark between the pages and set the book on the bench beside him. "Did you get your chapter written?"

Ava nodded. She was glad to see he'd changed into a clean shirt after another trip to the clinic to get his stitches resewn, fill out the forms with his proper name and take care of his bill. "Did Joe get all the bad guys off my property?"

"Uh-huh." Luke spread his knees apart and invited her to take a seat on his lap. "Joe's got a ton of paperwork that will keep him in Cheyenne for a few days. When he's done with that, he'd like to come back and spend some time here. Get to know you. See if I'm good enough for you."

"A true friend of yours would always be welcome here. Did I hear you say he was the one who got you interested in *The Bonecrusher Chronicles*?"

Luke nodded. "I'm afraid if he finds out you're A. L. Baines, we'll never get rid of him."

"We? Are you staying?"

"I'd like to. You said I could stay until I got the flash drive or regained my memory. I handed the flash drive over to Joe so, technically, I don't have it. And... I can't seem to remember where I put my car keys."

"They're in your pocket. Neither excuse holds water." She stroked her fingers across his lips and watched his eyes narrow to silvery-green slits as she ran her palms across all the interesting textures of his face. "Is there any other reason you want to stay? I'm grateful for everything you've done for me, but now that your quest has ended, what's to keep you here?"

His hands settled at her waist and he pulled her closer, tucking the crown of her hair beneath his chin. "I'm the one who's grateful. You saved my life. You love me. I'm finally getting to read a new Bonecrusher novel." She swatted him on the arm for that last one and he laughed. "You and I make an even better team than Larkin and Willow, and I'd like to stay. Besides, our quest to get all the bad guys isn't over yet. I intend to go with you to Chicago to confront your attacker and help the police nail that guy."

"You'd do that for me?"

"I'll move to Chicago to be with you if that's what you want once everything is settled."

Ava tilted her face to his. "What if I want to stay in Wyoming?"

He lowered his lips to hers. "Well, Pole Axe is going to need a new sheriff."

* * * * *

SEARCHING FOR EVIDENCE

TYLER ANNE SNELL

This book is for my father and the shed he built from scratch. Both are in this book and both make me insanely proud.

Prologue

If Bella Greene had met the newest hire at the Dawn County Sheriff's Department six months ago, things would have been much different.

She would have seen the man getting out of his fast-looking car, wearing jeans that were a grace from God and a smile that would have been a knee-wobbler and started the conversation out on a good note. One that might have included some light flirting and mild self-consciousness, considering she wasn't wearing her usual work clothes but instead a party dress and heels that brought her that much closer to Heaven.

Under different circumstances, she would have been Southern-belle polite, laughed a little at her own misfortune and tried to make a new friend, something she'd been lacking since she'd come back home to Kelby Creek, Alabama.

Under different circumstances.

But the note clutched in her hand, so tightly that her nails bit into her palm around it, had taken whatever her normal reaction might have been and flung it away into the darkening skies above them.

Bella didn't care that the man looked good—olive complexion with complementary dark eyes, heavy brows, jet-black hair that was styled back and a sharp nose and jawline, all which made her instinctively think of her childhood crush of A.C. Slater from *Saved by the Bell*— the fact was she didn't know him.

He was a stranger.

A tall, dark and handsome stranger, but a stranger all the same.

And out beside the county road with the town-limits sign in the distance and a broken-down truck behind her, Bella didn't want a stranger.

Not after the note she'd found in her tool bag just before he'd pulled over and not after the hang-up calls, anonymous emails and *the box* from the last few months.

Bella Greene was only for trusting two people right now and she'd been on the way to meet them in the city for a small-business award ceremony before her truck had decided it wanted to strand her just as night was falling with a storm rumbling in the distance.

"Hey there."

The man's voice was deep and low. Strong, smooth. He moved across the two-lane with purpose. When he made it to the dirt shoulder she was standing on, his gaze flitted across her.

She might have thought he was checking her out— she *was* wearing her party best after all—but then she zoomed her focus out from him and remembered that, while in one hand she had the note, in the other she had a wrench.

A wrench she was holding like a bat, ready to swing.

"I'm assuming you're having some car trouble?" His gaze swung behind her to the propped-open hood of the old Tacoma she'd purchased after the family business had started making decent money. It was rusted and worn but was a miracle when it came to transporting building materials from the store to a jobsite. Even now it held a truck-bed toolbox filled with nails, screws and plastic shams.

None of which she could use as a good weapon on the fly.

Hence her trusty wrench.

"I'm okay. I'm waiting on my brother to show up," she lied.

The man didn't seem convinced. He motioned up and over to the thundercloud, which was getting dangerously close. That and night was not a great combination for a broken-down vehicle in the country.

"Is he getting here soon?"

Bella tightened her grip on the wrench.

She was doing fast math now.

If he came at her, how long would she have to counterattack? How hard and fast could she get the wrench against him to give her the lead?

Bella slid her foot back a little on reflex, trying to strengthen her stance like a little kid readying for someone to come her way during red rover.

The man didn't miss the move.

His eyes widened a little.

He held out his hand and surprised her with a laugh.

"I'm only asking because the radio just said the storm is moving fast and I know it's fall but I've heard enough tornado talk in the South to be afraid of the possibility of them year-round." He put his hand into his back pocket and nearly gave her a heart attack as he pulled something out.

Then the object he'd reached for was out in the waning daylight and the logical part of Bella's brain forced that fear to pause.

It was a badge.

He held it so she could see it.

"It's also my sworn duty to make sure everyone in the county is as safe as can be."

"You're a deputy?"

He nodded.

"The newest at the Dawn County Sheriff's Department. My first official day is tomorrow but—" he nodded again to the approaching storm "—I thought I'd stop to help."

This time Bella took a moment to eye the same cloud.

Her brother, Val, and their father, Grant, were nowhere near her. Her mother was far away with her aunt in Huntsville and, as Bella had been keenly aware of recently, her own friend circle had shrunk to acquaintances from growing up. And even those few acquaintances she'd grown apart from since she'd fled town. Then there was Bob Sanders's tow company half an hour out. And, last she checked, he had prices that were more problematic than his pickup time.

"My name's Marco. Marco Rossi."

Bella snapped back to the present and away from her list of people she hadn't yet called.

Deputy Rossi returned his badge to his back pocket but didn't make any move to come toward her. In fact he held up his hands in defense before she could respond.

"And, listen, I get it. Creepy guy you don't know approaching you on the side of the road when your truck is disabled is a bad look. That said, I can't in good conscience just leave you stranded out here. So I'm going to go back to my car and wait until your ride gets here.

But if they can't or the storm is too quick, I wouldn't mind at all giving you a ride into town. I mean, Kelby Creek is so small, it's not like anything is out of the way. Sound good?"

Bella hadn't expected that. Still, she nodded.

It was all Marco needed.

He said, "All right," and went back to his car. Instead of getting in it, he leaned against the opposite side and faced the field.

Bella loosened her grip on the wrench.

But not the note.

She was still clutching it when she spoke to her father and Val on the phone, also saying she was going to have to miss the event, and still had it pinned against her palm when the rain started.

It was only after she locked up her truck and approached the deputy that she moved the note to her bag.

"Could you take me to Crisp's? It's a restaurant off Main Street."

Marco was quick to nod. He was also quick to open the passenger-side door for her. Bella caught a scent of cologne that reminded her of the woods as she hesitated in front of him.

"I took a picture of your car, your license plate, and sent it to my dad and brother. I also described you to them and told them your name. I'm supposed to call them in ten minutes, which is how long it should take to get there."

Marco surprised her again and laughed.

"I can appreciate the caution."

Bella took a breath and slid into the passenger's seat.

She settled her bag on the floorboard.

She might not have been holding it in her hand anymore but Bella still felt the weight from it.

And even though she was watching as the rain picked up and hit the windshield, three words written in red ink were as clear in her mind as when she'd first read them.

Hello there, friend.

HE WATCHED AS she got into the car and drove off with the stranger. If the storm hadn't been approaching, she would have stayed.

He was sure of it.

Bad timing.

That's what it was.

Or fate.

He stood up, the field of grass around him so tall she hadn't noticed him running toward her after she'd first pulled over.

Then he packed up his bag.

Maybe this was fate's way of letting him know he'd been reckless. That he shouldn't have abandoned his plan just because a tempting opportunity had come up.

Maybe it was time to go back to the drawing board altogether.

He sighed into the rain.

No matter the reason, there was no denying the eventual outcome.

Bella Greene was going to be his and nothing, and no one, was going to stop that.

Chapter One

Two weeks later and Marco Rossi was ending a hell of a day.

"Does this town ever have predictable weather?" he asked, peeling his rain-soaked boots off his feet while water collected on his desk chair beneath him.

His partner and desk mate opposite him, Carlos Park, wasn't faring much better. He mumbled when he spoke, trying his Boy Scout best to dry himself off with some paper towels the sheriff had tossed them on his way out.

"Don't act like your weather was miles different than ours. You came here from North Carolina, not Switzerland."

Marco couldn't fault that truth. Though he was, as his sister often said, a hothead. Which meant when everyone else was trying to stay cool, he was always at an even spicy. He was, after all, Italian. Born in New York to a family who could be traced back all the way to Sicily. If they were still around, Marco was sure he'd be sitting somewhere near them now, still being just as spicy.

But a lot had changed since he was five, in New York and as part of that family.

A lot.

"Our wild-card weather was more light showers and

the occasional ice storm," he returned. "Not chilly one second, monsoon the next."

Carlos shook out a sigh.

While Marco had been having a day of it, Carlos seemed to be having a week of it. They might have been partners but the Dawn County Sheriff's Department had been understaffed since The Flood, the name locals had given to a series of events that had shaken everyone's faith in the community.

It sounded dramatic because it was.

The extraordinary tale of corruption and crime within town leadership that led to murders and more, making state and national news and leaving a whole lot of mess in its wake.

A by-product of the mess?

Locals still not trusting anyone they didn't know.

Which was why Marco was having a bad day.

Carlos's bad luck, however, ran more personal.

"I just don't get it, man," he said, all exasperation. "She told me she had a great time and to give her a call if I wanted to do it again and *I did* and now she's a phantom."

That got Marco. He laughed.

"She *ghosted* you. She's not a phantom."

Carlos threw the wad of paper towels he'd collected onto his desk. It landed next to his tray of paperwork. Most of it was old. The interim sheriff and lead detective were trying their best to comb through old cases for one reason or the other. That meant that every deputy in the bullpen had a tray full of files, no matter how uneventful the month had been so far.

"Whatever it is, I'm not a fan," Carlos said. "I'm going

to have to see what Millie thinks. Get a woman's opinion on what to do next."

Millie Dean was a name that had made the news less than a year before, along with that of her brother's. They'd gotten caught in the fallout of The Flood and, thanks in part to Dawn County's lead detective, Foster Lovett, they'd all survived it. Now Millie had an engagement ring on her finger and the total and utter appreciation and respect of Carlos. Something that, according to Libby at the front desk, wasn't easily earned.

Carlos pulled his phone out and tried to wipe it down with the already-wet paper towels. It made him grumble again.

"How about we go out for a drink instead?" Marco looked up at the clock on the wall. Their shift had technically ended half an hour ago but helping Mrs. Finnigan get her car looked at had taken longer than either expected, no thanks to the rain.

It had been an odd déjà vu for Marco to find another truck broken down on the side of the road. This time, instead of encountering a woman he still couldn't get out of his head with a wrench in one hand and deep mistrust in her eyes, they'd been met with a deflated tire and a woman hell-bent on letting them know just how much she hated the Auburn football team.

"You can give me some more fun facts about the town and I can pay you for it in free drinks," Marco added.

That seemed to do the trick. Carlos perked up.

"You had me at *free*."

Marco reached into his gym bag next to his desk and pulled out his tennis shoes. He laughed.

"That's the second to last thing I said," he pointed out.

Carlos waved him off.

"And it was the magic word. Now let's get out of here before another call about car trouble or weird power outages comes in." He started to stand but paused. "Let's also make sure I don't text Janice again. Not until after I talk to Millie first."

Marco gave him a thumbs-up. He liked Carlos but didn't know him all that well yet. Which meant he wasn't about to point out that his experience with the ladies only ever earned him the status of a short-lived Casanova. He knew how to do the one-night stands and serial-dating moves; he didn't have the experience in anything that was supposed to last.

Once again his sister, Amy, had an opinion on that too.

I think all kids who were given up for adoption have trust issues, Marco. That doesn't mean you have to drag them into your romantic life too.

It was an old piece of sisterly advice but she'd been doling it out more frequently since her marriage to her high school sweetheart. She'd found love and she wanted the same for him.

Instead she'd watched him transfer out of his job, their hometown and to a place in dire need of a second chance.

No one was perfect.

Marco changed into his gym clothes and met Carlos out at the only bar in Kelby Creek.

Once a motel, then renovated into a bed-and-breakfast and then split into a bar, storage and office spaces for rent, the Rosewater Bar was as eclectic as some of its regulars.

Marco had been there twice already and gave a polite nod to the local psychic as he went in. She was at a table with the neon pink–haired coroner, Amanda Alvarez.

Carlos made a beeline for the group while Marco went to the bar to order two beers.

It was almost six at night and his stomach growled as he waited. He started to wonder if Carlos wouldn't mind grabbing a bite to eat instead of a second beer when the front door to the bar opened and a new set of patrons walked in.

Bella Greene was nothing but magnificent.

Even in overalls.

Her hair was twisted up in a messy bun, though half of the light brown locks had escaped and rested against the denim straps across each shoulder like she'd meant to do it that way. However, Marco got the feeling it wasn't a deliberate style. Instead he picked up more of a Belle vibe from the woman, the heroine from *Beauty and the Beast*, a movie that Amy had had on repeat when she was in middle school. It was like Bella had been wandering around in her overalls, patches of dirt across the pants, and had only come into the bar because she was guided by someone.

Her eyes, ice blue, were still on her companion as he let the door shut behind them.

They were laughing.

Marco didn't like the man, though he knew how irrational that was.

Bella followed him to a booth against the wall and they settled just as Carlos made his way over to the bar. Marco averted his gaze from the woman he'd barely had a conversation with and looked at the defeat on his partner's face.

Marco snorted.

"Listen, I said I'd keep you from texting Janice. You

never said anything about keeping you from talking to a psychic or medical examiner."

Carlos rolled his eyes and it was their turn to find a seat.

Marco still had a sightline to Bella but tried to keep his attention off her. Though he'd already failed that in the last two weeks. The ride from her truck to the restaurant had indeed been almost ten minutes on the dot. During that time their conversation had been limited to a few throwaway facts about their route into town, the mention that she worked with her brother and father, and that she'd been to North Carolina on vacation but hadn't been to where he'd moved from.

Then Marco had waited in the parking lot until two men, dressed as fancy as she had been, had picked her up.

Because, while he fully understood how she could have thought his watchfulness was creepy, there had been something about the way she held herself that made his gut stand at attention.

Bella Greene hadn't just been wary of strangers, she'd been afraid.

Afraid and clutching a piece of paper.

Marco would have asked her about that detail had she still had it in her hand when she'd first gotten into the car, but she hadn't.

Still, it was enough to worry him.

Even after she'd left with, he assumed, her brother and father, Marco had wondered about the paper.

About her.

And now there she was across the bar from him. No fear, no note, no broken-down truck in the background while she held a wrench like a bat.

No—

Marco felt his brows push together seconds before the thought that troubled him was staring him in the face.

Carlos, who had been talking about how the attic above them had been part of some case, stopped mid-sentence.

"What is it?" he asked.

It might have been nothing but it might be something. Either way it wedged into Marco's mind like a popcorn kernel between teeth and he had to pick at it.

"How long have you been working at the sheriff's department?"

Carlos was fast with his math.

"Seven years and a few months. Why?"

"In that time, how many calls have you gotten for people with broken-down vehicles?"

This time he wasn't as fast.

"Uh, I mean, I can't really remember every one but I'd guess…twenty times? Maybe? Why? What are you thinking?"

Marco tapped his thumb against the beer bottle. He looked back over at Bella.

"I've been to four since I got here."

Carlos shrugged.

"Half of the town works outside Kelby Creek. Stands to reason that breakdowns would happen. Maybe since it's been colder than normal for us, people have been moving around more."

Marco nodded but that kernel was still there.

He decided not to mention that, of the four he'd responded to—Bella included and the first—every one of them had been a woman. Brunettes, to be specific.

Coincidence, Marco told himself.

He took a swig of his beer and forced himself back into the conversation Carlos had been trying to have.

Yet his mind and gaze kept wandering to the booth against the wall.

Bella.

And the paper that had been in her hand.

What exactly had it said?

BELLA HAD HAD an off day the first time she'd met Marco. She had known it then, knew it after when she replayed the meeting and knew it again when she finally realized he was in the same bar she was.

Not even the same bar, but standing at the edge of the booth and grinning.

She also had known and now knew again that Marco Rossi was a man whose image belonged on a poster in a teen girl's bedroom. Or a model in an ad that you saved to your phone and then sent it to your friends with fire emoji or GIFs of women fanning themselves.

Bottom line and with the bottom dollar, Marco was as good-looking as he had been weeks ago.

She, on the other hand, was no longer the woman who had threatened him with a rusted wrench while wearing her party heels.

Now Bella was in a familiar place, with a friend, and had already looked into Marco's tale of being a new deputy at the sheriff's department and deemed it true.

She was also now in, what her brother had dubbed, her yeehaw overalls. Something she wore on workdays when rain was predicted so she had enough pockets to store materials if it came down before she could find cover. Something that often happened despite all three Greenes having a radar app on their cell phones.

It wasn't a cute look, even without the dirt and mud splotches. At least now she wasn't terrified and ready to defend herself with whatever was around her.

It was the little things.

"Deputy Rossi!"

Marco laughed while she cringed. She'd overcompensated for her self-consciousness and applied her enthusiasm a little too hard. He was kind enough not to mention it.

"Miss Greene, nice to see you again."

The way his voice rumbled over her one-syllable name took the low heat from her drink and fanned it a little.

Justin, her current drinking buddy, wasn't as coy about it. His eyebrow rose in question. She hurried to answer it.

"Justin, this is the deputy I was telling you about. The one who gave me a ride when my truck broke down. Marco Rossi. And, Marco, this is my friend Justin Hastings."

Justin was his own kind of handsome, though it was more of a classic Hollywood type. He was tall, very tall, and wore suits that were custom, fitted and expensive. He had brown hair that was, as long as she'd known him, always cut short and impeccably groomed. Though she'd never thought it was polite to ask, she estimated his age to be midthirties. He'd become a local after Bella left town, and since she'd been back, he had been one of Greene Thumb and Hammer's biggest supporters. Like Bella he was good at networking *at* work but not the best at socializing outside of a small subset of people. Val and her father belonged to that group but were running behind because of the last rain.

"Nice to meet you," Justin said. "And thanks for helping Bella here out. I know her dad appreciated it since all of us were out of town."

They shook hands.

"It was no problem," Marco replied. "Just doing my job." He turned and addressed Bella directly. "Actually, if you don't mind, could I talk to you really quick? It'll take two seconds."

Color her surprised, Bella hadn't expected that. Justin, however, was the first to respond. He stood.

"I was just about to head to the restroom really quick so feel free to take my seat."

"Thanks, man."

Bella watched, confused and equally intrigued, as the deputy switched places with Justin.

"Sorry, I didn't mean to interrupt your date. I was just going to ask you something about your truck."

"It's not a date." Marco's brow rose, most likely at the quickness of the answer. It wasn't the first time someone had mistaken her occasional outing with Justin as more than platonic. "We're just friends. Justin and me, I mean. He's actually a client too."

For some reason, Bella felt she had to prove herself. She pulled out her phone and went to the second to last picture in her camera roll that she'd taken.

"See, we built a small shed for his mom when we first started the family business and he liked it so much that we're doing one for him now. It's bigger though, a six-teen-by-sixteen. We had to tarp what we had of it today because of the rain. Which is why I'm—well, wearing these."

Bella motioned to her outfit with one hand and used the other to hold the phone for him. He looked between the picture of the partially built shed and her overalls.

It was around then that she realized she'd talked faster than normal.

She was self-conscious again.

Bella blamed it on the heat that was steadily crawling up her neck at his closeness. She had been caught wholly off guard by the man being in the bar. Never mind actually sitting across from her.

Her gaze went to his left hand. No ring and no tan line from one.

Did that mean he was single?

What if he was?

Bella could have kept entertaining those thoughts but then the man in question went and did it.

Deputy Rossi went and put his foot in it big-time.

Whether he meant it to be offensive or not, his next words threw whatever attraction she was feeling for the man out into the night.

"You actually did that? That's really impressive."

Maybe, just maybe, if he'd asked her father or brother that question instead, Bella wouldn't feel the anger pop up. But she'd already heard it and variations from several men throughout the last three years. None of them had been as good-looking as the deputy, but when it came to defending herself, nothing—including whether or not she wanted to run her hands through a man's hair—stopped her from standing tall.

Even if she was sitting down in a booth in a bar.

"Did I actually help build the shed I told you that I helped build?" she deadpanned. "Yeah. I did *actually* do that. You know, because it's my job."

She took her phone back with speed and went to her purse for a business card. She had it out and was handing it to him before he could find an appropriate response.

"See that name? Greene Thumb and Hammer, emphasis on the Greene part," she said, face going hot. "Not the Greene Men or Greene and Son. *All* of the Greene family." She decided it wasn't pertinent to amend her statement with the fact that her mother didn't help in any way with the business because she was happily and joyfully retired after years of working administration in a high school. Instead her arms went over her chest like armor.

Then the deputy finally rebutted.

"I didn't mean any disrespect." He also sat up taller. Going stiff like a football player ready to protect his quarterback. She'd offended him with her being offended. "I was just trying to say that it was impressive. I once tried to build a table for a girl I was dating and it fell apart."

Bella could feel part of herself cooling into regret. A part of her letting her know that she was, in fact, being a bit unreasonable. Yet she'd spent the last three years being questioned by enough sexist men to go for the throat before pulling back on the throttle.

"Oh, so because you can't do woodworking, then the fact that I, a woman, can do it is really impressive?"

"No. That's not what I meant either. I just didn't know what your job was. If you did the business or social media side or—"

Bella's eyebrow rose high.

He held up his hand to stop her.

"Wait. That sounded like I was proving your point, and I'm not," he interrupted. "You're taking this out of context. If you could just listen to me for a second and—"

"Oh, I *am* listening, *deputy*," she shot back. "I'm listening to every word."

Marco surprised her by making a strangled kind of grunting noise.

"What is it with this town and how much everyone talks?" he asked. "You're all so frustrating."

If she had mistaken his intent earlier, she knew she wasn't now.

"Frustrating? You just need to learn how to choose your words more carefully. We're living in the twenty-first century, Deputy. Not some kind of '80s cop movie where the short skirt with car trouble is only there for eye candy and a reason for the hero to want to save the day." Like Bella knew her anger was unreasonable, she knew part of it was from another place too. One of fear and worry.

One tied to a note she'd put in her bedroom safe.

But anger was unruly and it flailed around without hesitation and with no empathy for the man it was striking.

Bella went for her purse and pulled it up, readying to leave the table, the conversation and maybe the bar entirely.

Another man, however, changed her course.

Carlos Park, a longtime sheriff's deputy, which was a rare claim, considering what had happened to the department with The Flood, hustled up to the table, phone in hand.

He nodded to Bella, seemingly unaware that she was seething, but spoke to Marco.

"Sorry to interrupt but a call just came in that I'd like to check out. Mind if we go? I already paid the tab."

Marco's brows knitted together but he stood all the same. He glanced at Bella, nostrils flared.

There was that heat, that not entirely angry heat, again. Sizzling beneath the surface.

Bella doubled down on resisting it long enough to make sure she didn't do the polite Southern thing and smile.

"That's no problem for me," Marco answered.

"No problem at all," Bella added. "It was good to see you again."

Just like that, Marco followed Carlos out into the night, leaving Bella to cool down from everything while Justin settled back into his original seat with a raised eyebrow.

It was only later that night, deep beneath her covers as she was trying to fall asleep, that Bella wondered what Marco had wanted to know about her truck.

And what situation he'd just run off to that had kept him from asking it.

Chapter Two

Sheriff Chamblin wasn't outside the local grocery store but Detective Lovett was. And boy, Marco hadn't spent a lot of time with him but could see he was spitting mad.

"A prank call," he grumbled, pocketing his phone into his off-duty clothes. He, Marco and Carlos were the only law who'd responded to Main Street and all three were in their street wear. The uniformed deputies had gone to the two other locations that had called in suspicious activities around town.

Apparently they hadn't found anything either.

Or, at least, not more than the two words spray-painted somewhere at their location.

Got you was small, in black spray paint and extremely annoying, staring Marco in the face from the brick wall on the grocery store's facade.

Detective Lovett ran a hand through his surprisingly long blond hair and stared at the words a moment. Then he blew out a breath.

"I get that this town has issues with us but I wish they'd funnel that into something else," he said. "Like running for local government and applying for the empty spots we have. Help us be the change we all want, not pull us in all different directions for a lousy prank."

"Small towns also breed boredom," Marco had to point out. "Doesn't mean whoever did this was trying to prove anything."

The detective agreed to that with a few small nods.

Then he was smiling apologetically at the men.

"Thanks for coming out. I know it wasn't a normal call but I had to reach out just in case."

It seemed Carlos, who had led the charge to Main Street, had lost the tension that had also wound Marco up without knowing why. They'd taken both of their cars and sped to Main Street with purpose and determination. Now those feelings ebbed into a tiredness for Marco. A low after an adrenaline high. He thought Carlos might be feeling the same. The deputy let out his own low, long breath, deflating his once-uptight stance.

He nodded toward the grocery store.

"The last time you came out to this place with no plans on shopping, a lot went down," Carlos said. "I wanted to make sure that didn't happen again. At least not alone."

"And I'll be sure to let Millie know you two came to the rescue. Even if there was no rescue that was needed."

Marco knew what they were referring to—Millie and the detective had nearly died in the store when going up against a very angry and trigger-happy man—but neither man spoke to the story further.

Instead Lovett shook out his shoulders and cracked a grin.

"Since this isn't life or death and, since my lady is out with her ladies, what do y'all say about getting something to eat?" he asked. "Fallon and I usually eat together when Millie has a girls' night but he's out of town with his boyfriend and I really am not feeling the Hot Pockets I was eyeing in the freezer before the sheriff called me." The detective looked to Marco and added on, "Fallon is Millie's little brother. Really funny but can't cook to save his life."

"I'll take you up on that," Carlos was quick to say. "I've had half a beer and that only made me hungrier. Rossi?"

They both turned to Marco.

He wasn't a shy man by any means. In fact his sister, Amy, once likened him to a bottle rocket that kept going off. Hotheaded, loud and sometimes a spectacle.

But under the gaze of both men, Marco felt a wariness that often settled against his chest since his time at his last department in North Carolina.

Marco grinned but shook his head.

"Thanks for the offer but I think I'm going to head home," he said. "It's been a while since I got to bed early. I might try it tonight."

Both men accepted the answer and soon all were in their cars and off.

Marco's stomach growled as he drove and he didn't get into bed until one o'clock in the morning. He did, however, pull out the business card Bella had given him.

He'd met her twice now and both times she'd been different. The first she'd seemed worried, scared, ready to attack. The second? Ready to defend, quick to talk and wholeheartedly frustrating.

Marco had been told by his sister that he was quick to get under people's skin but he'd seemed to have broken a record with Bella Greene.

MONDAY WASN'T AS exciting as Friday had been but it did take a quick turn for interesting right after lunch. Of all people, Bella appeared next to his chair, brought in by their front desk clerk, Libby. He hadn't expected to see Bella again but that didn't stop his body from reacting to her.

"Miss Greene," he greeted, trying his damnedest not to look her up and down. Still, it wasn't hard to notice she had gone from overalls to a worn set of blue jeans and a somewhat tight T-shirt that said Support Local on its front that looked just as good as the outfit from the night before. Her hair was partially down, the top framed by a red flannel hair band, and her lips were rimmed with gloss, the color of a peach, making her mouth as distracting as the freckles running across her nose and cheeks that he hadn't noticed in the darkness of an approaching storm or the low light of the bar.

"Deputy Rossi." Her tone was clipped. "I hope it's okay that I came by to see you."

Marco nodded to Libby that it was. He motioned to the chair butted up against his desk. He'd be a lying fool if he denied how aware he was of the lack of space between their knees when she sat.

"It's no problem. Though if we're about to go round two, I'd like to at least go make another cup of coffee first."

Bella snorted. A small smile tugged up the corner of her lips.

"That's actually one of the reasons I came by," she started. "I wanted to apologize for jumping the gun and somewhat accusing you of being sexist. See, when you work in a job like I do and hear some of the things I have, well, it makes you a little more defensive than normal. Hence the me-jumping-the-gun part."

That intrigued Marco. He felt his eyebrow rise in question.

"Jumping the gun implies that you jumped to a conclusion before you found out the facts. Which almost sounds like you still think I'm sexist, you just haven't found the proof yet."

That smile turned into a smirk fast.

"To be fair, I don't know you all that well," she countered. "Who's to say you aren't sexist and just waiting for someone like me to figure it out?"

Marco laughed.

"I guess I can't argue that airtight logic, now can I?"

"It must be *extremely* frustrating."

They kept each other's gaze as they stared in a silence.

Marco knew he should probably apologize but he'd never been too great at that. Instead he chose a different path.

He leaned back in his chair and let his smile melt down into a more professional expression.

"You said *one* of the reasons you came here? What was the other?"

Bella's sarcasm also changed. It turned into quick curiosity.

"I realized that I never got to answer your question the other night. The one about my truck? You never really got to ask it. So, I thought I'd try to see if I could answer it."

Marco hadn't forgotten but he had prioritized, their fight only making it easier. Work had shifted his wayward thought again and again until he'd apparently put it on a shelf. Now he got it back down.

"It's probably nothing but I was wondering what exactly ended up being wrong with your truck. I had a buddy in North Carolina who had a Tacoma and even the older ones tend to be more reliable than not."

It happened quick.

One second he was asking a simple question and the next everything went dark.

BELLA WAS THINKING about her truck. She was about to tell the deputy that, according to her former mechanic brother, it had been a problem with her fuel. That Val had cussed about the poor quality, suspecting it was watered-down gas.

She also started to feel the building sensation that she was going to have to pull her expression tight when she answered the question to keep it from slipping an inch and showing the man that what had happened that day had scared her. That the note written in its pristine handwriting and its three little words had put a wobble in her knees and a coldness in her gut.

That, even though weeks had passed and nothing else had happened, Bella still felt like the worst was yet to come.

And she'd been right.

Though she hadn't imagined it all would start at the sheriff's department.

Not when she was there.

Not when a part of her had started to relax on reflex being with the deputy.

The lights went out all at once, followed immediately by a pop sound.

Chatter kicked up around them. Someone close was asking about the backup generators when the darkness stayed thick. Bella's eyes were drawn to the light in the distance from the hallway's end that she'd just come through. There were no windows in the large room she was in now, since it was at the heart of the building, which only made every part of her go on the alert.

Bella's hands fisted into the thighs of her jeans. Adrenaline toggled her body between her fight-or-flight responses while her mind stuck to one sentence.

Hello there, friend.

Movement from her side jolted her to stand.

"It's probably another damn prank," someone on the other side of the room called out.

There were some answering grumbles while a flashlight app on a cell phone turned on near her. It illuminated enough of their area to show that Deputy Rossi's chair was empty.

Bella opened her mouth to say something but the lights came back on like they'd never had the audacity to go out.

Bella turned around to face the direction of the hallway she'd come through. She was startled by a figure looming between it and her.

Or perhaps protecting.

Marco was a wall of defense. Muscles visibly tensed, ready to strike. That tension lessened only as he faced her after a moment.

His brows slammed together but she couldn't place the emotion behind his new expression.

That made her uneasy.

Just like the memory of the note…and the box.

Bella had tried not to think of either but it was a rock rolling down a hill. Hard to stop once it started.

"I think that's probably all of the excitement I can take for my lunch break," she tried, adding on a smile she hoped wasn't strained. "I should get out of here while y'all see to whatever happened."

Marco searched her face but nodded.

"I'll walk you out."

Bella accepted the escort and soon they were out in

the somewhat cold air. October in South Alabama was always a mixed bag when it came to weather.

Even more so when it came to surprises.

Bella found another one as they stopped next to her truck.

This time, thankfully, it wasn't bad.

"You still don't know if you jumped the gun." Marco's words were strong and low. He had his hand on the opened driver's-side door of the truck.

"Beg your pardon?"

He half shrugged.

"About me," he clarified. "You drew some pretty harsh conclusions the other day—"

"Which I admitted I did without any real evidence," she added.

"Which you admitted but you still don't have enough now to know if you were right or not, do you?"

Bella moved her hand side to side to show she was on the fence. That heat, that slow burning that felt like they were doing more than just having an innocent conversation, started to move through her again.

Marco smiled. It was all polite.

"Then let me take you out to dinner tonight and redo my, I guess, second impression. Help you see if you jumped the gun about me."

Bella hadn't expected that. This time there was no hiding her thoughts.

Marco laughed, she assumed at her wary expression.

"Listen, I grew up in a small town and know that if you offend one local, you offend them all. Help me right that awkward wrong."

This time it was Bella who laughed.

"Fine," she agreed, hopping into the truck. When the

door was shut, she rolled down the window. Marco hadn't moved an inch. He knew he had her attention. "But, let it be known, I'm paying for myself. Or will that be a problem, Deputy Rossi?"

Marco raised his hands in defense. His casual smile went into a smirk in a split second.

"Whatever rocks your boat, Miss Greene."

Chapter Three

"It's not a date."

Bella was at the top of a ladder, holding up one side of a rafter, and in a fight with her father and brother.

"This deputy man asked you out to dinner," her father repeated. "That sounds like a date to me."

It had been two hours since she'd come back from the sheriff's department. Bella should have kept her mouth shut about the experience but, when they were doing repetitive work like hanging rafters, chatting among themselves became a necessary habit to stay sane. That or listen to her father's alternative rock Pandora station for eight hours straight and, today, Bella wasn't feeling that.

"He's just trying to make up for putting his foot in his mouth and *I'm* trying to make up for getting so defensive way too quickly. It's not like there's another venue or activity to do those things. I'm not about to take him to the creek to fish and talk out our problems."

The scraping of a ladder's legs against the floor sounded as her dad moved to the rafter Val was holding, making sure it didn't fall out of the spot it had been wedged into. Their father was the most comfortable with heights and used the tallest ladder they had to move between each frame and temporarily screw it against the two-by-fours that ran along the top of each. It was the last thing they'd do as far as framing went before starting on building the walls.

It was also an extra pain for Bella but that was more from the fact that she was so short compared to the other two. The extra effort to reach the rafter she was supposed to be watching made her arms wobble even more.

It didn't help that, despite her experience doing what they were currently doing, she was still somewhat afraid of heights. That included their larger-scaled stepladders like the one she was currently on.

"I'm not even sure you should have dinner with him. You know nothing about him," her father went on.

Bella blew out a breath. The nip of cold she'd enjoyed earlier had melted into sweat at working.

"That's what the dinner is for, Dad. Getting to know him."

Her dad grumbled. It finally keyed in her brother, who had, weirdly, been quiet during most of the conversation. Though Bella expected that had more to do with the texts he was receiving and sending when he wasn't actively holding the rafter. If her father had seen his phone, Val would have received a talking to, she had no doubt.

"Wait, who is this guy again?" Val asked. "A deputy?"

She sighed.

"Like I said when I started the conversation, he's the sheriff's department's newest hire. He transferred from some small town in North Carolina."

"*To* Kelby Creek? Why would anyone want to do that?"

No one immediately responded but Bella knew it was expected of her.

"I don't know but, like I said, I don't know much about him. Which is why we're going to dinner."

Like all locals, their opinions about Kelby Creek had changed after what had happened with Annie McHale, who had been caught up in The Flood awfulness and the fallout from it. That went double for the sheriff's department.

Bella's father finished up with Val's rafter and moved on to hers. He didn't speak again until the first screw was in.

"Maybe it's a good idea if you don't go to the department anymore, at least. There are still a lot of people angry in this town about how they failed us and, just because it starts with pranks, doesn't mean it will end with them."

Bella didn't know if Val or her father did it too, but she took a moment to glance up the hill to Justin's house. He wouldn't be back until his work ended at four o'clock.

His wife would never be back.

"At some point we had to expect the department to start rebuilding," she finally said. "Maybe Marco just wants to help do that."

"Or maybe it's the only place that will take him."

Bella found her brother's gaze. He shrugged.

"I'm just saying, you need to be careful, Bells. Not only with strangers but strangers with power in this town." He shook his head. "Especially since we've seen what our friends do with it."

No one, not even Bella, could dispute that. Though the urge to defend Deputy Rossi tickled the back of her throat.

She knew, logically, that not everyone should be held

accountable for what had happened during The Flood but it was a hard feeling to shake.

The confusion, disbelief and betrayal.

Bella glanced back at the house in the distance.

She was grateful.

There were much worse things someone could feel.

SINCE MOVING BACK to Kelby Creek, Bella had lived in three different places. The first was in her old bedroom turned workroom at her parents' house. She'd had to rent a storage unit to hold her belongings and had spent three months sleeping on a daybed that her mother had bought to hang out with her dad while he worked. It hadn't been awful but it had been cramped. Especially when her dad continued working in there and her mother continued to hang out with him as he did it.

After being woken up at dawn on a Saturday by both, Bella had decided she needed a change.

That led to an alternative that wasn't that great but was a bit better. Bella had moved into her brother's guest bedroom in a house he'd bought to renovate with his ex-wife. Since the divorce happened two months into the process, most of the house was a total mess. The deal was that Bella could stay there rent-free as long as she helped him try to complete it.

That's where the idea of Greene Thumb and Hammer had been born. She, Val and their dad framing walls and talking about how it wasn't all that bad to work together.

By the time the business got off the ground and they were getting good press, Bella had fallen in love with another house in need of attention. It was ten minutes from her parents' house and a mere ten houses down from her brother's house.

Two stories, two bedrooms and in desperate need of upgrading from its early '90s roots. Which included a hot water heater that was in desperate need of being replaced. It gave out more cold showers than warm and was wholly responsible for Bella being late to dinner, and it was why she was frowning when she took the seat opposite the deputy.

"I'm so sorry," she greeted. "I was holding out hope that my cold water would somehow go and stay hot and then somehow it was twenty minutes later and, well, it went all downhill from there."

Marco, who was giving absolute life to a black T-shirt, leather jacket and jeans, stood while she sat down. They were at Crisp's, where down-home cooking was the norm but fancy table settings were not. The only thing between them on the table was his drink and two plastic-covered menus.

"I hope you haven't been here too long," she added.

Marco waved her off.

"Don't worry. I was a little late myself because of work."

Bella pushed past Southern decency and instead was all curious.

"Did y'all find out what happened to the power? I heard someone when the lights were out say it was a prank."

Marco's jaw tightened, then unclenched. A flash of anger followed by calm.

Despite knowing her father and Val were overprotective of her, Bella decided then and there she needed to know why Deputy Rossi had come to Kelby Creek.

To help, to coast or a place to run away to?

"Someone messed with the building's outdoor breaker

box and, prank or not, tampering with a state building like that is no small thing to do." It was a diplomatic answer. When he continued, his words, however, lost that official flare. "It's not the first *prank* I've dealt with since being in town. I knew the sheriff's department wasn't well-liked but I thought almost two years since all the trouble that's gone on before would have helped soften people's opinions, especially since it's a mostly new staff."

"You should know that small towns have long memories. That goes doubly for something like The Flood."

Marco's brow rose but he held off on whatever it was he was going to say. Their waitress, one of the actual owners of Crisp's, came up and took their orders. Bella didn't even have to look at the menu. She'd been getting Crisp's famous potato chip turkey sandwich since she was a teen. Not exactly gourmet, but absolutely delicious.

When the waitress was off with promises of a sweet tea showing up within the minute, Marco readjusted his focus.

His stare was as intense as it was stimulating.

Bella realized that while her mind wanted to answer the questions she had about the man across from her, her body didn't care.

It just liked being with the deputy.

THE FOOD WAS GOOD, the company was intriguing.

Marco finished off his burger and Bella finished telling her story about the time she and her father had dropped a bucket of paint down Val's house stairs and then tried to blame it on each other.

"What people don't get about dads is that they can get really sassy when they want to," she said, breaking a moment for another long pull of sweet tea. "Mine loves us, would take a bullet for us and won't hesitate to say he's proud of us and the business. *But* he'll also throw us under the bus to save his own skin." She snorted. There were no bad feelings in her tone. It was clear that the Greenes were a close bunch.

"What about you?" she added. "Any family back in North Carolina?"

Marco nodded.

"My parents moved to Chimney Rock, a small town outside Asheville, right after my sister, Amy, went with her husband back to New York. Though the way she talks about traffic and her commute to work, I'm thinking she'll come back to the South sooner rather than later."

A thoughtful expression crossed Bella's face. Marco had to give it to her, she definitely paid attention.

"*Back* to New York?" she asked. "Are you from there?"

Marco readjusted in his seat, putting his back a bit straighter in the chair. Though he felt fine with the subject, he'd come to dislike the reactions of pity or several questions that usually followed him talking about his family's past.

"My bio mother was." He dived in. "She died after Amy was born but my grandmother raised us in Queens until we had to go into foster care when we were five and six. We moved to North Carolina after our parents adopted us. They wanted to slow down and my mom is from there."

To her credit, Bella took the information in stride.

"I get the slowing-down thing," she said, skating over the parts that usually made people stumble. "I was working at a software company in Atlanta before I was laid off and came here. I missed the city rhythm at first but

I find myself continuing to settle in more here. Though the pace hasn't exactly been slow in Kelby Creek since I got back."

She looked uncomfortable. Physically uncomfortable at the thought.

One that seemed to be easy for all the residents of Kelby Creek to get to without much prodding.

Marco didn't like the change. Just as he hadn't liked the look on Bella's face in the department after the power went out or in the parking lot.

It was one reason he'd been prompted to ask her to dinner.

One of several reasons.

Now he wanted to focus on the uncomfortable expression. The memory of something bad that had happened.

The Flood as told by a local outside of law enforcement.

"Feel free to not answer but, I'm sorry, I have to ask—" Marco made sure his voice was low enough so the patrons around them didn't hear but Bella still could "—The Flood… Was it as bad as the news said it was?"

Bella took her time answering, as if she were trying to find the perfect response.

"My brother, Val, used to be married to a woman named Darla," she started. "They were in love kind of like what you'd see in a romantic comedy. Goofy meet-cute at the grocery store, first date on the golf course with a late-night picnic that ended after the sprinklers came on, and that almost ridiculous kind of happiness that others can feel just by being in the same room with them." She'd smiled at the beginning and now that smile fell the more she spoke. "Everyone was surprised when Darla up and left Val, saying that she wasn't happy with him anymore and instead wanted to start a life with a guy she'd met in Mobile. But not as surprised as Val was. He told me that he didn't understand how someone he thought he'd known and loved for years turned out to be someone he didn't really know at all. But, even more than being upset at her for leaving, he'd been furious at himself for not seeing the signs. For not figuring out she'd been lying to him."

Bella's expression softened, as did her tone.

"When The Flood happened, we all became Vals. The people we'd grown up with, learned to trust and respect, hurt us, and worse, made a lot of us angry with ourselves. Angry that we never saw it coming."

"And I guess to make an entire town feel that way, it had to be bad."

Bella nodded and laughed, despite the topic.

"Yeah, I guess I could have just said that instead." She moved her straw around her glass, an idle motion that matched a faraway look that took over. "I think it'll be a long time before anyone around here lets go of what happened. Some people got far worse than being angry."

The waitress brought their check and pulled them out of their darkening conversation. Marco wanted to ask more specific questions but decided against keeping the dark topic going. True to her word, Bella paid for her meal and soon they were out standing between her truck and his Charger.

"You know, my dad also wanted me to find out why *you* came to Kelby Creek," she said around a smile. "He and my brother are really protective of me like that, which can be annoying." She took a step closer to him, leaving a foot or so of space between them. Marco got a better scent of the perfume he'd been smelling all throughout the meal. It smelled like cookies and Christmas.

"But, you know what? I don't think you're the kind of man who wants to admit that kind of truth." She tapped her chest with her index finger. "You're one of those guarded type of people, aren't you? The ones who wear invisible armor around their hearts."

Marco laughed.

"What are you, a mystical figure from an '80s fantasy movie?"

Bella rolled her eyes. It was in good humor.

"That would probably be a yes," she said with a nod. "I bet you have just as many secrets as charming smiles."

The lack of distance between them became charged. Somehow Bella had dipped, dodged and woven through his past, his present and now was throwing him off his game for the future.

Disarming was the word.

Bella Greene was distracting.

Marco took a small step forward. His gaze went to her lips before he had to drag it up to her eyes. Their height difference forced her head back, drawing attention to how bare and perfect the curve of her neck was.

He smiled and lowered his voice when he spoke.

"Miss Greene, does that mean you think I'm charming?"

Bella's cheeks became flushed. For a second he wasn't sure she was going to respond but then she was the one with the smile.

"I said your smiles are. As for you, I haven't decided yet."

She took several steps back and only broke eye contact when unlocking her truck's doors.

Marco had to take a quick breath to steady himself. Or, rather, his body. He'd thought he had been quick to get underneath Bella's skin but, now, he realized it might have been the other way around.

"Thank you for dinner, Deputy," Bella said as she climbed into the cab of her truck. "Maybe we can do this again."

Marco opened his mouth with every intention of pointing out they didn't have to let the current night end, but what he actually said was much less obvious.

"Maybe next time I'll leave my armor off," he teased.

Bella took the comment and threw it right back.

"I don't think you're the kind of person that leaves his armor at home."

Another quick smile and Bella was off.

Marco got into his car but paused, his hand and the key hovering over the ignition.

He was so wrapped up in Bella, wondering if he was running from something, that he didn't notice the power go off in the restaurant behind him.

Chapter Four

The call came in on Tuesday night, just after Marco's shift ended. He was on his way to the parking lot when Carlos swooped in and asked if he'd give him a ride since his car was in the shop.

Marco obliged but didn't understand why Carlos wanted to respond to a call when two other deputies already had. It wasn't until he saw the way Carlos was staring at the woman who had made the call that Marco started to understand.

Deputy Park might have been trying his hand at dating but it was clear that Jennifer Parkridge had a special place in his heart. A place that had woken up at the news that her house had been broken into. Off duty or not, that was enough to get the man over to the scene.

If the responding deputies minded the second set of questions, they didn't say so. Once they had confirmed no one was still in the house or in the area, they'd separated and spread out, along with Detective Lovett, who *was* on shift.

Jennifer was clearly shaken but, thankfully, okay. She hadn't been home when the break-in happened.

"I was out with Madeline going over some figures on a work project and only came by to grab a few files before heading back out," Jennifer explained to them once everyone had left. "I didn't notice the broken planter or the back door being busted until I was about to leave again."

She walked them into the house and to the back door. Sure enough, it looked like it had taken a powerful hit. The wood around the lock was splintered, all the way down the doorframe too.

"How do I even fix this this late?" Jennifer asked, palpable fear thumping against every syllable. "I can't just leave it like this."

Carlos was quick to answer.

"You don't worry about it. We can fix this tonight," he offered, slapping back at Marco, "Right?"

Marco was still focusing on the house. He heard their conversation but his attention was splitting. He nodded, then immediately regretted it.

"See? Don't worry, Jen. We can get this all squared away. You just worry about work."

Jennifer let out a sigh that held more stress than any one person should. Her smile was tired but seemed genuine enough.

"Thanks, Carlos," she said. "I'll be attached to my phone all night. Call me with anything."

Carlos saw her out, helping with the boxes she'd come home for, and then was back looking as close to sheepish as Marco had seen his new partner.

"She works at a lawyer's office in the city."

"And she left you and a stranger in her house while she went back to it?" That seemed a little more friendly than stereotypical small-town community trust. Especially considering Kelby Creek was a small town that had lost that trust, doubly so for the sheriff's department.

"We, uh, go way back." Carlos cleared his throat and

then seemed to decide against a more diplomatic answer. "She was engaged to my older brother for a while during college. It didn't work out because he's a horndog. But if you ask me, he never deserved her."

Carlos's gaze trailed to the front window where the headlights of Jennifer's car flashed by as she pulled out into the street.

Marco liked Carlos but, when it came to personal lives, he had already decided not to make the same mistake he'd made in his old department. Friendships there had only created problems when the incident happened.

The same one that had caused him to transfer to Kelby Creek in the first place.

He wasn't ready to chance something like that happening again, so Marco steered clear of any personal talk and motioned to where Jennifer had found the shattered planter just inside her living room archway.

"So the door and the planter were the only things that were damaged?"

Carlos zipped back to attention.

"Yeah. I'm guessing whoever broke in was keeping the lights out or just using a flashlight. Probably accidentally hit it since it was kind of tucked out of the way."

Marco went through the motions of walking through the hallway and living room. He passed the flat-screen TV, a computer in the corner on a desk beneath the window and went in the open bedroom door, right up to a vanity covered in loosely strewn jewelry. Carlos followed.

"And Jennifer said nothing seemed to be missing."

Carlos nodded an extra affirmation.

"She did a walk-through with Foster to make sure."

"But why? Why go through the trouble of breaking

into someone's house, only to leave without doing anything? I can get not wanting to steal the bulkier items but
why not grab the easier stuff?"

Carlos shrugged.

"Maybe they chickened out? Got spooked by a car
driving past or a neighbor moving around. Decided to
cut their losses just in case."

Marco had that feeling again. That there was more,
that something was off, but sidestepped them to the present.

"Regardless of the reasoning, there's a door we need
to fix and I don't exactly know how to do that. Do you?"

Carlos stood tall.

"Nope, but I know how to search tutorials on You-
Tube!"

But right after they watched a few minutes of a tu-
torial online on how to repair a busted door and doorframe, Marco realized there was only one path to fixing
both that night.

"Let me make a call," he told Carlos after they both
admitted neither had the right tools for the job.

But Marco knew who might.

He dialed the number and stood on the front porch, already grinning when a woman's hurried voice answered
the call.

"Greene Thumb and Hammer, this is Bella Greene,
how may I help you?"

SHE HADN'T EXPECTED to talk to Marco so soon. In fact,
Bella had been convinced that her talk of armor around
his heart had been enough to squash whatever interest
he might have had in her.

Not that she'd blame him. Bella hadn't known where

that kind of talk had come from, yet there she had been with a man she barely knew, teasing him about not opening up.

To her.

To someone he barely knew.

Bella had sank into her couch when she'd gotten home from Crisp's. A full stomach and a full-body cringe.

She'd tried to keep her expectations low for the dinner and yet, there she had been, enjoying herself.

It was only after the meal had ended that Bella realized while she'd talked about herself and the town, somehow the topic of Marco's life had gone unchecked.

Well, until he'd told her he was adopted and had a sister.

Bella had rolled over on the couch, trying not to wonder about the life Marco had been living that had led him to Kelby Creek. She had grumbled into the throw pillow and found that not one part of her wanted to think about anything other than the man. It had been frustrating because, while she regretted telling Marco that he had armor, she stood by the observation.

It was one thing to drop the ball socially like Bella had since coming home; it was another to outright keep out all attempts at connection.

So when the call came the next night and Marco was on the other end of it, Bella had to ask him twice to repeat his name. Though it wasn't like he had called her for a second outing.

He'd called her because of a broken door.

"This is just a shame," Bella's dad said from the passenger seat. He'd been tsking off and on since Bella had relayed the call to him and Val. Her brother only a few grumbles off.

"You know, I think this is an eye-opener for us," he said from the back seat. "We need a security camera at the office. One of those fancy ones that we can record and open on our phones."

Bella pulled up behind the red Charger, and her stomach started to flutter in anticipation. That flutter only became more aggressive as Marco himself stepped out onto the front porch.

Bella made sure not to give an inch to her family and stayed on the topic at hand.

"Our offices include a room in Dad's house, your truck bed when the weather permits and a square of my kitchen counter," she pointed out. "Plus, it's not like we have anything valuable just lying around. I'm still not convinced that you don't sleep in the same room with your favorite electric saw."

Val made a noise like a snort.

"For how much we paid for that thing, you'd sleep with it too," he mocked.

"All right, let's focus," their dad said as Bella cut the engine. "I want this to be right so Jennifer doesn't have to add a busted door to her list of worries. Val, grab the tools. Bells, since you know these guys, you're stuck with being the nice person."

Bella groaned and Val laughed. Being the nice person was code for being a buffer between a client and the work they were currently doing. Depending on the site, the job and the client, it switched between the three of them. Though, as Bella had been sure to point out regularly, that hardly ever included their father.

They jumped out into the night air and started to pull materials from the truck bed. Marco began to walk down the driveway to them.

"Wait, I thought it was Carlos Park that called," Val whispered. "Who's this guy?"

Her father, ever the well-humored, was less quiet with his answer.

"That's the guy Bella went on a non-date date with."

"What?" Val returned.

"Dad, stop it," Bella said at the same time.

Marco, unaware, made it to the truck.

"Hey, guys, thanks for coming out."

Just like the call had been a surprise, the way he greeted them was different from what she had expected. It wasn't matter-of-fact or brooding. He was all smiles and extended handshakes. Something she knew was a slam dunk when it came to meeting her father for the first time.

"No problem," she said. "We're more than happy to help."

They did a quick round of introductions and then got down to business. Carlos showed them to the door and planted himself next to it, arms crossed and clearly determined to watch. Bella's dad gave her a nod that let her know it was okay not to try and nice-person him away. After she helped set up the tools, she moved back to the living room, where Marco had stationed himself.

At first he didn't seem to notice her presence. Even in profile, he looked like he was mulling something over. She probably could have assisted the repair and Marco would have been fine.

Bella cleared her throat.

"So, I talked it over with Dad and Val, and we're not going to charge anything for this job."

Marco turned to her but he still seemed far away.

"You might have to fight Carlos on that. He seemed really determined to pay for it."

Bella shrugged.

"It's not that big of a job. It would actually be preferable to doing any extra paperwork. Val usually does that and he complains the entire way through. Not getting paid would *be* payment enough."

Marco nodded to that. His gaze listed over to a wooden stand next to the doorway.

"Why would you break into someone's house but not take anything?"

His voice had hardened. Gone colder. Like it had detached from knowing the person it was with. Bella followed his gaze back to the wooden stand.

"Uh, did I do something instead?"

"Do something?"

"Yeah, I mean, if I didn't take anything, do I do something to something? Like rearrange the furniture or shred important documents?"

"Shred important documents?" Marco's eyebrow slid up. He grinned.

"Hey, I've seen enough TV shows and movies to know that sometimes people break into places with the sole purpose of shredding sensitive papers," she said. "Or scan them! I forgot about scanning them."

Marco turned his head away from her, looking in the direction of where the bedrooms must be. He shook his head and returned to the conversation.

"I'm pretty sure she doesn't have a scanner here and that nothing else happened." Marco let out a breath.

"And it wasn't another prank?"

He crossed his arms over his chest. That tone came back.

"If this was a prank, then whoever is behind them is escalating," he said. "And following a weird trajectory.

Flipping the breaker at a sheriff's department and then breaking into a house only to do nothing and leave."

"Maybe it's who's getting targeted that's important? Law enforcement and then a lawyer? Doesn't Jennifer still practice law? I know she did when she helped with Val's divorce."

He didn't light up but Marco did seem intrigued.

"Could be."

They stood in silence for a moment, both looking at the room. Bella felt the urge to talk about armor again but decided to think of something else.

"To see if I could." The words came out before she could structure them correctly.

Marco's eyebrow slid up again in question.

"Bella? Come here a sec!" Val's voice broke in before she could answer. "Or, actually, go to the truck and grab my flashlight. Dad's is out."

"On it," she yelled back. Then, to clarify her thought, Bella turned to the deputy. "Even if you break in to someone's house and don't take anything, you've already done something by breaking in in the first place. That's the only other reason I think I'd do it."

"Break in just to see if you could," he added.

Bella nodded.

Then she was back out in the night air.

Marco didn't follow. She tried not to be disappointed.

Chapter Five

The house was quiet and cold. Bella dropped her keys on the entry table and didn't even care that she missed the flamingo dish they always went in that her mother had given her for Christmas. She was distracted and there was no point in pretending that it was by anyone other than a tall, dark and handsome deputy.

She knew Kelby Creek was a small town but that didn't keep her from noting how she seemed to be drawn to the man. That, whether intentionally or not, they kept bumping into each other.

Bella sighed into the mostly dark house. A month ago, her thoughts hadn't been this frustrating.

She went to her bathroom at the back of the home and decided that her plan of watching late-night HGTV to unwind would have to wait. Greene Thumb and Hammer had had a long workday. The chance of rain for the next three days waffled between 60 and 80 percent. That meant that the big sheets of plastic she detested had to come out. She and Val had rotated between three different ladders to cover Justin's custom shed-in-progress while her father had used clamps to hold it in place.

Because perfect first attempts were seldom, they'd had to readjust a few times.

Then there had been the trek up the sloped backyard to Justin's house. It was a large plantation-style home with two-story columns along the front porch and balcony, white siding and black shutters framing windows he'd had to replace, considering the age. It was one of a kind in Kelby Creek and had been a purchase he'd made with his wife with the intention of renovating, modernizing and then selling it.

But then The Flood had happened and Justin's plans had seemingly died along with his wife.

Now, almost two years later, he was paying them good money to make a custom shed for all the things he didn't want to keep in his garage.

Which, if Bella were being honest, never made much sense to her. He had plenty of space in his garage as it was. He was even letting them store their tools there overnight for safety. Why did he need another place for tools?

"It's a guy thing," Val had said once when she asked him and their father the same question. "When it comes to storage, more is better."

Either way it was a pain to pull their cart up the slope and that had been before one of the tires had popped and they'd had to transfer each tool individually by hand.

Honestly, it was nothing too bad in the grand scale of things but each task had really rubbed her the wrong way today. Bella had been thoroughly annoyed as she went home and was still feeling it when someone had called the work landline.

When that person turned out to be Marco, well, that had changed her minor stress to a different kind of tension. One that she needed to unwind from now.

She turned the shower faucet to hot and went into her bedroom to undress. Since she was no longer living with her brother, Bella had reverted to blasting music while she showered. Tonight she put on an '80s station from her Pandora app and made sure to grab a fresh towel from the pile on the chair in her bedroom that she'd been meaning to fold and put away for a week.

"Hungry like the Wolf" filled the bathroom, mingling with the building steam. She thanked God for the hot water and stepped in. Bella sang the lyrics to the song, only one of four she knew by heart, while she showered. It was a nice way to forget about everything else for a while. An easy way.

She was almost sad she had to get out and go to bed, knowing that if she didn't instantly fall asleep, her thoughts would revolve around a man she barely knew, but if it didn't rain the next day, then work would be tiring. She needed her rest, and kept that mini pep talk on repeat in her head as she got out and wrapped the towel around her.

It was a good talk with a good reminder.

But then she looked at the mirror and every part of her froze in place.

The music faded around her, the invading cold from no longer being wrapped in heat hitting her wet skin dulled. Her breathing caught and shallowed.

The only thing that sped up was the beating of her heart.

Bella's eyes were locked on the mirror.

Or, rather, the words written in condensation across its surface.

She saw the fear in her own eyes as she reread the three words.

Hello there, friend.

MARCO DECIDED TO take a run that night. Jennifer Parkridge's back door was shut and locked, Greene Thumb and Hammer had left their card behind if she had any questions and Carlos had given Jennifer the all clear.

Detective Lovett had called him around the time they were getting ready to leave Jennifer's and Marco hadn't stayed long enough to eavesdrop.

He was restless when he got to his apartment and that restlessness had turned into the decision to run.

Though that decision wasn't exactly a fruitful one.

Each step against the asphalt, each kick up of rock and dirt, each pulse of endorphins only pushed him deeper into a sense of urgency. Of concern.

An itch he couldn't scratch.

Instead of continuing to try to figure it out, he decided around the third mile, according to his smartwatch, to redirect his focus on his surroundings. Without wanting to or meaning to, he compared them to North Carolina.

Which led him right to thinking about the sheriff's department he had once sworn he'd never leave.

You don't have to go, Rossi. You're blowing this entire thing out of proportion.

No matter how many days passed since he'd heard those words and no matter how far away he got, Marco still felt a deep anger well up inside him.

Trying to do the right thing wasn't always easy but he couldn't help resenting how hard it had been all the same.

Kelby Creek wasn't the only one with trust issues.

The chill in the air from the day had dropped down into actual cold. Marco wasn't a marathoner when it came to running but he did enough work that he made sure to never be caught in the South outside in anything more than a tank top and shorts. Now both were starting to retain sweat. He decided to slow down and turn back so he wouldn't be miserable on the way home if he kept up with what was turning out to be a long, long run.

Marco's apartment was just outside a neighborhood that looked like a mini suburb in the city. Houses were close together and bathed in the light from occasional streetlamps. Front lawns held lawn ornaments, kids' toys or some variation of the two. There were a few houses that needed a face-lift but most seemed well-kept and loved.

He ran by one that had an industrial dumpster in the driveway, most likely for ongoing construction on the inside, and wondered what kind of home Bella lived in. During their dinner, the most he'd said about where he lived was the name of the apartment complex, if she knew it, and then complained slightly about his second-floor neighbors who were a little too in love. Since she worked in construction, did she prefer a ready-to-move-in home or had she gone with a fixer-upper because she didn't mind the hassle of making a house her own?

Marco could have asked her those questions, or any for that matter, while they waited for her father and brother to do the repair. Instead they'd stayed relatively quiet. Maybe the armor comment wasn't too far off.

Or maybe it was that urgency, that restlessness, that had him off his game.

How could he focus when he was sure there was *something* going on and he was all but missing it?

You need to get out of your own head, he mentally chided himself. *Not everything ends up being a case.*

He nodded into the night to reaffirm the belief and took a right turn out of the neighborhood. Most of Kelby

Creek had some kind of view of woods and the road that led from this neighborhood to the apartments was no exception. There were tree lines on either side of the street and very little light that carried in between them. It was why Marco had a pocket flashlight hanging by a cord on a wrist and his phone tucked into the waistband of his shorts.

It was also why he should have seen the car coming sooner.

Much sooner.

But he didn't. The best Marco could do was lunge to the side as the car appeared.

He yelled out in pain as something struck his hip. The force of it pushed his center of gravity off. Marco hit the dirt shoulder hard.

There was no time to assess the damage.

He whipped his head up to see the car slam on its brakes a few yards away.

Marco couldn't make out too many details but he could see enough to make his gut worry that it wasn't an accident. There was no license plate, for one.

For two? When the driver stepped out of the car, he made no move to run over and check on the man he'd just struck.

Instead he turned around slowly, just inside the driver's-side door.

It turned out that Marco's gut had been right to worry.

The driver was wearing an oversize black coat, dark pants and gloves.

But the most concerning part was the mask, and not just any mask.

It was the Ghostface mask from the movie franchise *Scream*. A white face stretched to have wide black eyes and a mouth that sagged while black cloth wrapped around and behind the head, hiding any distinguishable features.

Marco held on to the hope that it was someone getting ready for Halloween a few weeks away.

"Hey," Marco called out. "Dawn County Sheriff's Department! Step away from the vehicle!"

The man didn't move.

Marco struggled to stand. The pain at his hip was radiating. The full car itself couldn't have struck him or he'd have been much worse off. He bet it was the passenger-side mirror that had clipped him.

Even though he was pretty sure the driver had meant to collide with him head-on.

"I'm a deputy with the sheriff's department and I'm telling you to step away from your vehicle," Marco yelled out again. He went for his phone but it wasn't there. He didn't want to take his eyes off the man to look for it either.

Since he was on a run, he hadn't thought to bring his service weapon or his badge.

He regretted both decisions.

The man shook his head.

Adrenaline was already moving through him, now the floodgates had opened.

Everything happened too fast.

The man got back into the car. Marco started to run at it, hoping to stop him before he could drive away. It was a fool's errand. His hip was killing him. It made for a labored limping gait.

There was still several feet between them when the reverse taillights came on.

Marco knew he only had two choices.

Stand his ground and hope the driver was bluffing, or try his best to make it into the trees before he found out the man wasn't.

Though, in hindsight, that wasn't much of a choice at all.

HE SHOULDN'T HAVE done it. He knew that. He *knew* that.

But he had. He'd done it anyway. He'd left his plan and become impulsive. Become reckless.

Become angry.

Which was bad.

So bad it could ruin everything.

"You're smarter than this," he told the basement. "You shouldn't have done that."

The basement didn't answer. There was no one in it besides him, but that wouldn't be the case for long. He looked at the suitcases, empty but ready, in the corner. His eyes lifted over to the chair, the ropes and the syringes he was hoping he wouldn't have to use.

Then it was Bella.

The pictures of her pinned to the corkboard didn't do her justice. Nothing did. Only her. Only *being* with her.

He walked up to his favorite picture and traced her lips with his thumb.

She was lovely.

They would miss her.

They would try to stop him—try to stop fate—to keep her.

"But I'm not going to let them," he said.

Anger pulsed through his resolve. Anger at an obstacle he hadn't foreseen.

Deputy Marco Rossi.

He growled at just thinking the name.

He wasn't good for the plan. For her.

Which was why the plan was changing yet again.

Instead of taking his time, things were about to get a lot more chaotic.

In fact they already had.

He looked down at the mask in his other hand.

Then he smiled.

Chapter Six

"This is ridiculous."

Marco opened the to-go box in the small hospital room. Carlos shook his head, pointed to its contents and decided he was funny.

"No. That's pancakes." He sat in the chair by the bed.

Marco rolled his eyes and caught the plastic cutlery that came along with his surprise meal. He knew he looked rough without seeing the quick frown on his partner's face. He'd gotten painkillers for the worst of it, despite trying to persuade the doctor that he was fine. Marco was glad now that he hadn't listened.

"I meant having to wait to be discharged," Marco clarified. "I'm good now and just want to get home and change and get back out there. Not stay holed up here."

He motioned to the hospital room around them.

Haven Hospital was Kelby Creek's only health-care facility of any size. Privately funded, it was small, clean and surprisingly modern. That still didn't make Marco feel good about being there though. He'd only agreed to be admitted in the first place because the amount of blood along his side had been alarming.

Well, and the fact that the sheriff himself had ordered him to go.

Now, hours after escaping into the woods and walking back to his apartment, he *was* fine. Bruised, stiff and sore, but fine. No broken bones, no internal bleeding, no concussion.

Carlos, however, wasn't as convinced. He moved to Marco's side.

"Even if you were discharged, you wouldn't be back out there today. You were hit by a car and then had to anger your injury by walking a few miles before you got help. And, unless you've squeezed in a quick nap since, I don't think you've slept yet. If the doctor didn't make sure you were good before clearing you, he wouldn't be doing his job. Wouldn't you do the same in his place?"

Marco grumbled. Carlos wasn't wrong.

It still didn't mean he liked being told to stay in a hospital bed. And in a hospital gown to boot. He'd already been eyeing his bag of clothes that he'd grabbed before coming to Haven, sitting on the love seat along the wall. If he thought he could get away with changing into them, he definitely would have already.

"Now, since I think your rumbling means you know I'm right, why don't you eat your breakfast? Not eating delicious pancakes won't change the fact that you have to wait it out. It's just you punishing yourself."

"Fine," Marco relented. "I'll eat the pancakes. But if I'm not out of here in an hour, I'm leaving. Even if that means escaping through the window."

Carlos eyed the third-story window but didn't point out the pitfalls to that plan. Instead he stood and readjusted his holster. He was on duty, just like Marco was supposed to be.

"We're going to find whoever did this," Carlos said

after a moment, all humor gone. "It's one thing for this town to have trust issues. It's another to do this."

He didn't stay long after that, but he did make sure that Marco had his number written down since his contacts list was now gone. After he'd borrowed a neighbor's phone in the apartment complex, deputies and the sheriff alike had swarmed the area where he'd been struck. No one had found his cell.

Which was extremely annoying.

No one wanted to deal with replacement phones when they were trying to find the son of a bitch who tried to kill them. At least, not Marco Rossi.

He leaned back against the bed for a few minutes and wallowed in frustration until his stomach growled. The smell of the pancakes lured out his practical side. If he couldn't control anything else, he'd at least control filling his belly.

He was two bites into his new plan when a knock sounded on the door. Other than Carlos, only the sheriff had visited when he'd first come in. Maybe he'd returned because they found something? Or maybe Carlos had a change of heart and was going to help him break out.

"Come in."

Ice blue.

Marco found her eyes first and then the rest of the details filtered in. Her hair, almost the color of honey, was pulled up in another messy bun, strands hanging down to frame a face where freckles danced cheek to cheek and lips that he'd seen colored peach the night before were turned down in a severe line.

Bella was only timid for a moment. Long enough to look him up and down. How he wished he wasn't sitting up in a hospital bed, wearing a gown partially covered by a blanket and eating pancakes over a tray.

For whatever reason, he didn't want her to see him like that. To be down and out. It was bad enough Carlos and the sheriff had seen that.

"I heard you got hurt," she started, leaving her spot by the door and stopping next to the bed. Marco noted her eyes were also a little bloodshot, like she was tired. Or maybe had been crying? Surely not about him. "Libby said it was a hit-and-run?"

"I forgot how fast news travels in a small town." He smirked, trying to lighten the mood, but Bella didn't seem to accept the change. He sighed. "I was out on a night run because I couldn't sleep and the next thing I know some guy hits me." He motioned to his side, hidden under the blanket. "I was lucky he wasn't going that fast when it happened. I'm bruised and the cuts were only superficial wounds. I'm fine."

Those cold blues seemed to scan him again, as if the quick pass could prove him true or false. He expected more questions or maybe even a quick verbal barrage telling him of the dangers of running so late, but as usual Bella Greene caught him off guard.

"I only know what happened because I came to the department this morning, hoping to catch you when your shift started." Her voice hollowed a bit toward the end. Like she was walking on eggshells over her own words. Marco moved to sit up straighter, finally feeling the tension in the woman, but winced.

It was a move that Bella didn't miss.

Worry contorted her expression.

"I—I shouldn't be here," she hurried. "I thought about waiting? Or calling up here? But then I started thinking about how you're new to town and you might not have anyone to check on you yet or that maybe your family was still in transit so you might need a friend. And *then* I thought I could tell you in person because surely I'd sound crazy on the phone but—"

She had her keys between her hands, fiddling with them. Marco grabbed all three to steady her.

"I appreciate you coming," he interrupted, though he left out the part where he hadn't told his parents or sister what had happened. That would be a call he'd make after he got a phone again and not one he made through the hospital. "It was really thoughtful of you, and nice."

Bella nodded but she didn't return his smile.

Something was off with her.

And he didn't like it.

Marco let go of her hands and leveled his gaze.

"Now, what did you want to tell me?"

"MY ROOMMATE IN COLLEGE, Darcy, had a really bad breakup right before spring break our sophomore year." Marco didn't stop her seemingly odd jump in topic. Instead he listened, focused. "She went to one of her sorority's parties to try to distract herself but, instead, found a lot of hunch punch. A sorority sister called me because Darcy ended up locking herself in a closet and talking about how she wasn't ever coming out. *So* I walked into this room filled with mostly tipsy ladies all trying to coax Darcy out and did the first thing that came to mind to try to help. I bent down, put my face against the door and said, *Hello there, friend.*" Bella would have smiled at the story had the purpose of it not chilled her to the bones now. Still, she paused where the smile would have gone. Marco was patient and waited through it.

"It was just the first thing that popped into my mind but it weirdly did the trick," she continued. "Darcy came out and her sisters thought it was so funny that they started greeting me like that. All over campus, at every event, until eventually I even started saying it after college, at my old job and when I moved back. It just became my thing."

Bella's palms were sweating. Not because she was nervous to tell Marco what she was about to tell him, but because she couldn't help but see the words in her head, written in an email, a note, a box and now a mirror in her home.

It wasn't just terrifying.

It was violating.

She sat down on the edge of the bed, so close she would have been distracted by that closeness otherwise, but instead she went to her purse. The paper felt worn in her hand as she pulled it out. Bella handed it over and let him unfold it.

"Hello there, friend," he read.

Bella shifted in her spot.

"The day I met you, when my truck was broken down, I found that in my tool bag."

Marco flipped the paper over, ran his hand across it and flipped it back over.

Then he was all eyes on her again.

Bella knew by his look that he'd already figured out that part that made her feel like she needed to take another shower.

"And this isn't the first time you've gotten something like this," he guessed.

Bella shook her head.

"No. It's not." She took a deep breath and tapped the

paper. "About six months before I found this, I got an email from some spam-looking address that said *Hello there, friend*. And then nothing else. I figured it was someone from college, trying to be funny. They kept sending the message until finally I replied a few days later. It bounced back. The email had been deleted. That happened some more off and on for about a month or two. Work was starting to really boom so it was just like this annoying little thing that happened, so I wasn't exactly focused on it." She sighed. The sound wobbled. She kept on.

"Then the hang-up calls on the landline in my house that I use for Greene Thumb and Hammer started. It went to my cell phone from there. I called one of the numbers back and it was disabled. Then, just like the emails, it stopped."

The box came next.

Bella was embarrassed to admit she'd never told anyone about it, even more so now, but the way Marco was homed in on her every word, the way his brow was drawn in concentration, seemed like a man who wasn't judging.

Just listening.

If sighing would have lessened the stress, she would have done it again.

But it wouldn't help.

It wouldn't fix what she should have done, just like it wouldn't stop what was happening now.

"A few months later, we had finished up a landscaping job for a client just outside Kelby Creek," Bella continued. "I was getting pictures of the finished project for our portfolio when I found a box with my name on it next to a portion of the fence we had installed. It was small and white, had one of those thin ribbons that people attach to helium balloons around it and a little stick-on tag with my name typed on it." She had a picture of it on her phone but Bella didn't stop. She needed to get it off her chest. All of it. "I thought it might be from the client but it was a napkin."

This time, Marco did speak up.

"A napkin? Was there anything on it?"

Bella nodded. She took one of the napkins from his tray, folded it in half, and put it between her lips. She pressed down and then released it.

She hadn't slept a wink since finding the message on the mirror. Something she'd tried to hide as she put makeup on before going to the department.

Now they were both looking at the dark peach lip print.

"It's something my mom always taught me to do after I put my lipstick on, after a meal, sometimes before getting a drink so I don't stain the glass more than needed," she explained.

"The napkin had a lip print," he spelled out.

"Not just any lip print. *Mine.* I *compared* mine to it when I got home."

"And they were the same?"

Bella nodded. "Like it was a mass-produced stamp."

"Was there anything else? In the box?"

She pointed to the note in his hand.

"A piece of paper with the same message. That was it."

Bella saw it then. A hint of emotion breaking through across the deputy's face. Tension. Anger.

And she hadn't even gotten to the worst part.

He opened his mouth to, she assumed, point out the obvious conclusion to jump to in her situation. Bella cut him off before he could. Even more, she reached out and touched his hand.

It was to still her nerves more than it was to make him realize she wasn't done.

He closed his mouth.

Back to impassive.

He wouldn't be for long.

"I thought maybe it was all someone messing with me. Or maybe that Kelby Creek is just becoming a place where people play awful pranks on each other. *But* then last night after we left Jennifer's house, well, I saw this." Bella went to the picture she'd taken on her phone. She gave it to the deputy with her free hand. He took it, not moving the other hand she was holding an inch.

"Where was this exactly?" Marco's voice was clipped. Tight.

"The bathroom mirror," she answered.

"But where?"

This time Bella let out another shaky breath.

"In my bathroom. *In* my house."

Marco tensed. His nostrils flared. He clenched the jawline that would make most women's knees weak.

His eyes widened but only for a second.

It was his voice that changed the most though.

No longer clipped. No longer impassive.

It was all emotion that he was no longer hiding.

He looked up from the phone and locked in on her.

Bella didn't know the man well but she swore she knew what he was going to say before he even uttered the words.

"Bella, you have a stalker."

Chapter Seven

There was no doctor, nurse or anyone else around to tell Marco he couldn't leave the hospital.

And he said as much to Carlos on the phone.

"I'm bringing her to the department and then we're going to her house," he told his partner as he pulled on the jeans he'd packed. When he went for his shirt, he cussed. "Scratch that, we're swinging by my place first so I can grab a shirt that's not destroyed. *Then* we're getting all of this sorted."

Carlos didn't try to tell him to stay put. He agreed to meet at the department and would call ahead to see if Detective Lovett was still there. Dawn County, Kelby Creek specifically, had a trove of cold cases. The number had only become higher after what had happened with Annie McHale during what locals, honest to God, all called The Flood. Marco thought that maybe what was happening to Bella could be connected to an older complaint of suspicious activity or stalking. Carlos had agreed.

Marco ended the call wearing his jeans, boots and the hospital gown. He'd been lucky that instead of forgetting a new shirt, he'd at least remembered to bring a jacket. His shoulder holster and service weapon went beneath it while he slipped his badge into his back pocket.

When he met Bella outside the door, she looked him up and down with a fleeting smile.

"I didn't know you were allowed to take the gowns with you."

Marco's sense of urgency had been climbing on top of itself the moment after Bella finished her recounting of someone stalking her. It was getting worse every second she was somewhere that he couldn't control, at least in some part. The hospital might have been considered small but right now it felt too big. Too open.

Too vulnerable.

It made Marco's skin crawl.

It also made him feel more protective.

Like he had on the hospital bed when his body reacted to hers on reflex.

Marco reached back and took her hand.

"They're just going to have to make an exception for this one," he said, already leading them to the elevator. "Worst-case, I'll pay them back."

Bella didn't say much but she also didn't complain about the contact. Her hand was warm and small, and how did it fit so perfectly in his? He didn't move at all as they waited in the elevator and, when she spoke, it had nothing to do with the fact that she was squeezing his hand back.

"What happens now? I mean, once we get to the department."

The elevator beeped off their passing of the second floor. Marco used his free hand to pull his jacket closed so it kept his gun out of sight. When they'd come in, the hospital had been all but dead. A few staff mulling around but, thankfully, no emergencies that had the building filled.

He hoped it was still just as dead.

Again, the feeling of being too vulnerable was eating at him.

"You'll do an official statement and timeline if you can and we'll go from there to see if we can find anything."

"And you'll go to my house? To make sure no one's there or there isn't some kind of hole in the wall where someone's secretly been living, right?" She was trying to use humor to undercut the fear. The same fear he now understood from the first day they'd met.

She'd thought it was him. The person leaving her the same message, over and over again.

Hello there, friend.

Marco had to admit that its creep factor rated high when used the way it had been.

"Yeah," he answered as the doors opened. "Carlos and I will make sure there's nothing going on there and see if we can't find some kind of clue."

She nodded and together they walked out into the parking lot with no one talking to or stopping them.

"My truck is over here," Bella said, pulling him gently in the opposite direction. They finally broke their contact but only after Marco held open the vehicle's door for her. He shut it and scanned the parking lot as he went to the passenger's side.

The lot was empty. The sky above them was not. It had darkened considerably since earlier that morning. Rain was coming. Marco could smell it in the air.

It only added to the ominous feeling starting to tangle with the urgency telling him that he wasn't waiting for the second shoe to drop—he was still waiting for the first real one to hit the floor. The boot to come crashing down.

And he didn't want Bella anywhere near it when that happened.

They drove in silence out of the parking lot. It didn't hold long.

"Aren't you going to ask me why I didn't tell anyone?"

Bella's voice was small. She kept her eyes focused on the road ahead.

Marco made sure to choose his words carefully.

"I think there are times when something happens that you don't expect, something that isn't *right*, and that *not* talking about it can help keep it from feeling real. I get it. I really do." He paused, then decided to go ahead and ask the first thought he'd had when she'd opened up to him. "What I don't really understand is, out of everyone—your family, friends and a department full of people—when you did speak up, you did it to me. Why?"

In profile Marco could see Bella tense. Just as he could see that tension leave in a sag of defeat. If she had planned to keep the answer to herself, it was a plan that didn't last long.

"Honestly? I think it's easier to open up to people who don't know you. Better to tell your innermost fears and anxieties to someone who has no comparison to your former self, I guess. *But*—" Bella sighed "—truth be told, I… Well, I trust you. I don't know why, I don't know *you*, but I can't seem to get around the feeling."

Marco was stunned into silence.

For many, many reasons.

It was only after he saw her in his periphery turn to him that he shook out a response.

"I guess you jumped the gun again, huh?"

Bella actually laughed.

"I guess I—"

The truck started to choke, shuddering and cutting Bella off.

"Not again!"

She put on her flashers and pulled off to the shoulder.

Marco was already on high alert when she flipped off the ignition. He had his hand hovering over the butt of his gun when she tried to restart it but nothing caught.

"Bella, is this what happened last time? The day we met?"

Marco was scanning their surroundings. They were on a street that had a storage-unit complex boasting air-conditioned units in the back, buildings on one side and a stretch of trees on the other. There were no cars on the road and only one car in the parking lot next to them at the storage-unit facility.

Again, like the hospital, it made him feel exposed. Vulnerable.

Unable to fully protect Bella if something went wrong.

Judging by her answer, Marco knew that something wrong was closer than further away.

"Yeah. I guess I never actually told you but the problem was—"

"Water or sugar mixed in the gas tank?" he interrupted.

Bella's eyes widened.

"How did you know?"

Marco unbuckled his seat belt, and he reached for his gun.

"I think I know what's happening," he hurried. "But I need to use your phone and let Carlos know—"

Marco didn't get a chance to pull out his gun.

Whatever slammed into the back of the truck crumpled any and all plans he was forming.

All Marco heard was Bella scream, then everything went dark.

"Marco? Oh, my God, Marco!"

Bella's seat belt was digging into her side. She couldn't figure out why at first.

Why was it digging into her right side so much? Why did she feel so weird?

And why wasn't Marco answering?

The details came in all at once.

They weren't kind.

The windshield was shattered but intact. She could see through it still, yet it wasn't the scene she'd last been looking at. There was no street ahead, only trees.

Trees facing the wrong way.

Then Bella put together why the seat belt was unforgiving against her chest and side. Also why she felt so weird.

The truck wasn't on four wheels anymore. It was on its side, the passenger's door against the ground and her door facing the darkening sky. The wrongness and pain was from gravity trying to pull Bella toward the ground.

Toward Marco.

"Marco?" she tried again. "Are you okay?"

Bella finally looked to her side and down.

She sucked in a breath just as her heart plummeted.

Marco had taken his seat belt off and because of that he was lying against the door pinned to the ground.

He wasn't moving.

"Marco?" Her voice was broken. Just like her truck around them. "Hang on. I'm coming."

He didn't stir.

Was he breathing?

She couldn't tell and she wouldn't find out if she stayed where she was.

Bella reached for the buckle at her hip and winced as pain scattered through her. She couldn't focus on it. She wouldn't. Not until she got to Marco. Adrenaline, and she was sure shock, helped her along. The second time she pushed the button, it released.

Gravity got its way and she dropped in an instant. It was a bad idea, which she should have realized before unbuckling. If Marco had been wearing his seat belt she would have smacked against him. Instead she managed to grab the seat to keep her full weight from hitting him.

Bella was even less graceful trying to move around him to stand. She ignored the blood that was on her arm, not knowing if it was his, hers or both.

Then she heard it.

A car door shutting.

Bella froze.

In her haste to help Marco, she'd glazed over one terrifying detail.

Someone had hit them. Hard. While they were parked on the shoulder of the street with their flashers on.

That couldn't be an accident, could it?

The message on the bathroom mirror blared to life in Bella's mind. Just as Marco's words in the hospital gave them sound.

Bella, you have a stalker.

Was it him?

Was he after her?

Bella reached on reflex for her cell phone in her pocket. It wasn't there. She'd put it in her cup holder when they'd gotten into the truck. The sound of footsteps echoed outside from near the back of the vehicle.

If adrenaline hadn't already been pulsing through her system, it would have been a new flood now.

Bella kept looking for her phone.

She could have cried in relief when she saw the time readout glowing near her feet. That meant it was still working. It was next to Marco's chest, next to the broken glass and dirt.

Bella was quick.

She didn't stop to check to see if Marco's chest was rising or falling, she didn't pause to think about calling her family first. All she was able to do was dial 9-1-1 and slip the phone into Marco's jacket pocket before she heard the footsteps turn into the noise of someone climbing.

Bella didn't know what else to do other than brace herself the best she could. She used her body to cover as much as Marco from view as she could and hoped against all hope that she was just being paranoid.

That it had been an accident and whoever had caused it was coming to help them.

That her stalker was terrifying but not the cause of this.

That it was just an awful coincidence.

But her hope shattered quite quickly.

A face came into view and she knew it wasn't about to get any better for them.

The man was wearing a mask. One she recognized from the movie *Scream*, only because her brother had bought the same one to wear almost every Halloween. White and twisted. Black eyes, black mouth.

Not something you wear to help someone crashed on the side of the road.

It wasn't fair.

It wasn't right.

And Bella had no options to fix any of it.

She liked to think she was a brave woman but she also believed that there were some situations that broke even the bravest.

Like being in a violent accident only to be greeted by a mask worn by a cult classic killer.

"Who—who are you?"

The masked man moved his head side to side, hanging down into the truck.

Bella wished the windshield had blown out from the impact or flip. She didn't know if she could drag Marco through it and into the trees if it had but she damn sure would have tried. There was no way to defend Marco or herself from her position.

"What do you want?"

The man disappeared for what only seemed like a second. His hand, gloved, came into view long enough to drop something.

Bella caught the paper on reflex.

Handwriting she was all too familiar with spelled out one statement.

Come with me or he dies.

Chapter Eight

There must have been a patrol car nearby. Bella heard a siren before the mechanical gate to the storage-unit area closed behind them. The gate did nothing to block the sound, but the street, the wrecked car and Marco felt a world away.

Now it was just them. Bella and the masked man.

And he didn't seem bothered by the sound of the law coming closer.

In fact his body language was nothing but casual.

Minus the gun he was still holding.

Bella didn't know much about guns but knew shooting a moving target was often harder than one that willingly followed your every request.

Bella also knew what her father would tell her to do in her current situation. Mainly because he'd been coaching her for it most of her life.

If you're ever in a parking lot and someone tries to grab you, run around the car and yell, he'd told her during his first sit-down with her about safety tips. *If you can't do that, then yell your head off while you crawl under a car. You make yourself too much trouble for anyone to want to take you.*

Bella didn't have the chance to listen to either piece

of advice, just as she couldn't use them now, but her father had spent years having this conversation off and on. So much so that she didn't actually need him there to have it again.

His voice came in as clear as the masked man's intent to have them go inside the air-conditioned storage building at the back of the property. The giant warehouse with enough places to stuff her if he had the urge to do so.

If you can't keep someone from catching you, then you don't let them take you, Bella, her dad had told her, the epitome of paternal severity. *Never ever let them put you in a vehicle. Once that happens, statistically, your chances of survival plummet.* He'd shaken his head. Then, during the first time he'd ever told her what to do just in case, he'd taken her hands in his and given her a smile that hurt. *And if they ever do take you, you make sure they don't keep you. Even if they have a weapon, even if they're bigger and meaner, you fight or you run as hard as you can. No matter how scary it might be, you make them regret ever thinking they had a shot of keeping Bella Greene.*

The walk up to the storage-unit building was a straight line from the main gate. On either side were two rows of the outdoor units, all orange-and-blue doors closed and locked. The main office was next to the main gate but on the opposite side of it. If anyone was inside, if anyone had seen what happened, no one made a peep.

Bella had hoped for a longer walk from the gate to the building but it felt like only seconds.

She stopped next to the main door inside. Her father's voice rang through her mind as she spoke to the masked man.

"It needs a code to open." She pointed to the keypad

next to the door. It was one of the main reasons the storage facility was open at all times. No one could get in unless they were clients.

Bella glanced down at the gun. It was still in his hand but not aimed at her. She made sure to keep her eyes on it as he moved to the keypad. To add to the list of surprises that were making up her day, the masked man typed in a code.

And it worked.

The door beeped, unlocked, and the man opened it.

He turned back toward her and motioned her past him.

Bella could feel the wave of cool air come out of the building. She could smell the staleness of a building rarely frequented. The fluorescent lights came on because of the motion sensors and showed a clean, shiny painted concrete floor.

It was a nice building. Not a terrible place to be under normal circumstances.

But Bella loved her dad a whole, whole lot, which meant there was no way in the world she was going to go inside of it.

With what her brother had once called sneaky speed, Bella kicked out at the man.

He hadn't expected that.

Her foot connected with his groin and, mask or not, he was like every other man who'd been kicked there. He let out a groan and all reflexes went to him trying to process the pain while attempting to protect himself so it wouldn't happen again. He bent over, gun still in his hand but now pointed away, and staggered back past the door.

Bella didn't waste her small opening.

She turned on her heel so fast that she kicked up dirt. Then she was running toward the gate with everything she had, already planning to hang the first right she could around a row of units so she could hide.

But then something odd happened.

Something that slammed the brakes on her fight-or-flight response.

The masked man yelled out but not in pain. It was for her.

"Bella!"

His voice echoed around her.

His voice.

It stopped her in her tracks, like a slap to the face.

She turned around, chest heaving up and down as she tried to breathe.

She knew that voice.

She *knew* it, right?

The man was in the doorway still. Mask on, gun at his side. With his other hand, he went to the bottom of his mask.

Was he about to take it off?

"Bella!"

This time, Bella recognized the voice instantly.

And it was coming from behind her at the gate.

"Get down!" And then to the man: "Drop the gun! Now!"

Bella hit the dirt and covered her head. She closed her eyes tight as the sound of gunshots exploded around her.

It only took a second or two.

Then the world was quiet again.

Bella lifted her head only enough to look at the second man to call her name.

Her heart squeezed.

It was Marco and what a sight he was to see.

Standing a few feet from her, he had his legs braced

apart, and his gun aimed ahead without any part of him wavering. His jaw was hard, his eyes were focused, and even though he looked like he had seen better days, thanks to cuts and blood across his body, Bella only felt strength from him now.

Even as he spoke, it was all steel and gunpowder.

"Bella, come to me now."

She didn't have to be told twice.

Bella was off the ground and running to him like she'd been practicing for this her whole life. The moment she was near him, he took her hand and spun them both around.

The gate wasn't all the way open but there was a new gap that hadn't been there before.

Marco pushed her through it, then pulled her to the other side of the concrete beam it attached to. There they were, facing the street, her truck in the distance, with the main office to their side.

"Are you hurt?" Marco asked, pushing her gently against the concrete.

Bella shook her head.

"Are you? Did you get shot?"

The strength she'd seen only seconds before had done a one-eighty. Now Bella could read the pain in his expression as clearly as she could see the blood.

"No. He's a poor shot but I think I could have gotten him. He ran inside that building. Which is why—" Marco stumbled to the side. Bella had to throw her arms out to steady him. He kept on like it hadn't happened. "Which is why you're going to take my gun."

"Why don't you keep your gun?" she asked, alarmed.

Marco didn't look happy with the answer he was about to give.

"Because I think I'm about to pass out."

True to his word, the second she took the gun from him, Marco started to go slack. It was all Bella could do to slide down to the ground with him, trying desperately to keep her hand and legs between him and the ground.

"Marco? Marco?"

The deputy didn't answer. All she could hear now was a siren getting louder.

It was only after the sheriff's deputy patrol car came to a screeching halt on the street between them and her truck did Bella realize a heart-squeezing detail.

With his back to her chest, Marco had positioned himself in between her and anyone coming their way.

Even unconscious he was still trying to protect her.

THE RAIN CAME. A thunderstorm rode into town and turned severe just after everyone showed up at the hospital. At least, that was the best Marco could figure how it played out.

After falling unconscious, he'd woken up in the back of an ambulance, a whole two minutes away from Haven. When Bella wasn't next to him, he'd pitched a fit. Then Carlos had met him when they'd gotten to their destination and assured Marco she was safe with the sheriff and would be there soon.

The rain started pouring then. It beat against the roof and walls while the thunder shook the windows and showed him a day that had turned dark. Even though that had already happened before the storm.

"We have everyone looking for him," Carlos said, trying to assure Marco before the doctor came in. He was talking about the masked man. The one who had sent Marco to the hospital. Twice. "We'll get him," Carlos added. "Until then, we're going to make sure you and Bella are safe."

His definition of safe was a deputy and a hospital security officer positioned in the hallway of the third floor. But only after Marco had a CAT scan done and that was only after he'd gotten stitches. Ten along his chest.

It was those stitches he was looking down at when he got his first visitor since being moved.

Though it wasn't whom he had hoped it would be.

And it definitely wasn't even someone on his top-five list of possibilities.

"Can I come in?"

Grantham Greene, called Grant as Marco knew, was already walking in before he could be invited. Marco didn't mind.

He said as much and motioned to one of the chairs next to the bed. Unlike his daughter, Grant decided to sit in one of them instead of next to Marco on the bed.

"Bella wanted me to let you know that she'll be in here as soon as she's done," he started. "The sheriff was talking to her and a detective is with her now. Detective Love or whatever his name is. The new guy before you showed up."

"Detective Lovett. He's good. I like him." Marco couldn't deny he was disappointed that Bella wasn't there but he was also relieved. Before Foster had come to Kelby Creek, he'd been a hotshot detective in Seattle. When he'd come back to his hometown, his fame had only grown after he'd put to bed a town-wide investigation. Having him on the case would only strengthen their chances of finding the masked man.

And Marco was going to find him, all right.

"Is she okay?" Marco asked, hoping he didn't betray

every inch of concern he had. "Deputy Park said she was but, well, I haven't seen her yet."

Grant gave a nod that became a shrug.

"She's worried about you and still a bit scared but, physically she's okay. A nasty cut on her arm but she managed to not need stitches." His gaze went to Marco's bare chest and the bandage over the stitches he definitely had needed. "That's probably going to scar. How about the rest of you? Bella said you had to get a CT?"

Marco felt oddly at ease with Grant Greene so he answered honestly instead of deciding not to share.

"I have a concussion from the wreck—that's why they think I passed out. Twice." He sighed. "It's also why I'm in observation here until I'm told otherwise."

Grant nodded again.

It was a slow, thoughtful movement that turned into silence.

He'd come to say something. Marco waited.

After a moment, Grant was ready.

"Do you know the story of what happened to Annie McHale? What everyone around here refers to as The Flood?"

Marco nodded.

"I know what most of the country knows after the story went viral. And the details the sheriff filled me in on when I got the job here. But, to be fair, I haven't heard it from a true local. Someone who was outside of law enforcement or the media."

Grant seemed to approve of that answer.

"Then let me be the first local who lived through it to tell you." He leaned forward so his elbows were on his knees and his hands were domed between them. "And when I'm done, then you're going to tell me exactly why *you* came to Kelby Creek. Or else you, Mr. Rossi, will never see my daughter again."

Chapter Nine

"My wife and I were born in Kelby Creek and decided to stay in it when we found out we were pregnant with Bella."

Grant hadn't skipped a beat since issuing his threat. Marco hadn't stopped him to talk about that same threat either. Instead both were focused on the story. Marco more so than Bella's father. The Flood had become a national story and, in its wake, had nearly destroyed an entire town.

Hearing the details that hadn't been in the newspapers or weren't part of some conspiracy theory posted online was a welcome change for Marco.

"We were also extremely broke," Grant continued. "I was taking care of my mother at the time and my wife had no living family left so there was no one to help us, or to reach out to, but us. I worked two jobs and she worked long shifts and, still, some days it felt like we weren't living, just surviving. That kind of stress was grinding. Even though I didn't want it, that kind of stress turned into resentment, for me, really quick. Especially for people who had a lot of money they did almost nothing to get. Then, one day, I met Arthur McHale and my resentment at the rich in this town went away." Grant sighed. Then smiled for the briefest of seconds.

"See, Arthur was a nice guy. So was his wife. They could have lived out their days not doing a thing and still with enough money to support them and theirs for another generation or two, but instead they invested back into Kelby Creek. They put money in the town and community and were active in seeing that they helped it grow. The McHales could have been one of those rich families you see on TV or movies who don't care about the poor around them, but that wasn't their style at all. They were kind and smart and never missed an opportunity to help and everyone loved them for it. Even their kid was like them in all of the best ways."

There was no hint of a smile now. Not even for the briefest of seconds.

"That's why when Annie went missing, it became a town full of people trying their best to find her. And, when the ransom call came in, even though it wasn't our kid, we all wanted a piece of whoever had had the audacity to take her. We took it personally." He moved his hands from being domed to resting on top of his knees. A tell for someone who was trying to seem like he wasn't angry. That he was in control. His hands fisted once and then relaxed. He continued with a bit more heaviness to his words. "You know what happens next."

"The ransom call asking for money to be exchanged at a park," Marco supplied. "The sheriff and some undercover deputies went with Mr. McHale to deliver it. The sheriff was Annie's godfather, right?" Grant nodded. "Then it was a bloodbath," Marco added. "Five people died and several were injured."

"Bloodbath is a phrasing that's more accurate than

some I've read," he said. "A Georgia paper called it a small trap, but there was nothing small about it. Bella said you met Justin? Our current client."

"Briefly."

Grant's frown deepened, becoming more severe.

"Him and his wife were there. In the park. No one was supposed to be but, according to the sheriff, there wasn't enough time to clear everyone and, even if they did, it would raise suspicions. So when the kidnappers opened fire on the deputies, they also opened fire on Justin and Carla."

Marco didn't need him to spell the outcome out based on his body language but Grant did all the same.

"She died in his arms at that park and Annie McHale was still nowhere to be found."

"The video was next, right?" Marco recalled the grainy footage he'd seen on the internet once the story had gone viral. "Of Annie somewhere, tied up."

"Yeah. Uploaded to our town's official website. The mayor, also the best of friends with the McHales, tried to get it removed but it took a while. By then Annie had grabbed the FBI's attention. They sent a set of partners here to get to the bottom of it."

Grant sighed again. In just retelling the story, he seemed to have grown more tired. Marco wanted to help him get to where he was going without doing it all on his own.

"I was told that one of the FBI agents, Ortega I think was her name, told her partner she found a lead but then disappeared. He looked for her but a storm came and he found the mayor instead," Marco said, trying to remember the details.

Grant swore under his breath.

"We call it The Flood because a flash flood warning had been issued and the mayor was such a bad driver when the sun was shining that he didn't stand a chance on the roads during it," he said. "He ran off the road and the FBI agent just happened to come up on him. He was trying to help him when the agent saw something that had flown loose during the wreck. A necklace. Annie's necklace."

"That's when he figured it out," Marco guessed. "That's when the agent realized the mayor was connected."

"Yep. He opened his own investigation in secret and, well, you know the rest."

"The sheriff and mayor were the ones who came up with the abduction and ransom—"

"—and when a new FBI task force showed up to figure out how far their corruption led, they were able to nearly shut down every law enforcement and government position in town. The guilty were either caught, killed while trying to flee or managed to leave town and hide. Annie was never found. Neither was Ms. Ortega."

Grant shook his head.

"The people with the most power in this town, with the most respect, used all of us for one selfish reason or another," he said, anger etched into every word. "They used our trust to their advantage and, at the end of the day, we paid the price."

His eyes moved to the table next to the bed and found Marco's badge. It was resting on top of his holster.

"They did good things, the people who broke our trust," he continued, looking back at him. "But good deeds don't cancel out bad apples. And just because you saved my daughter, something I will always be grateful

for, doesn't mean you're not one of those bad apples."
Grant was finally at the reason why he'd given Marco a
history lesson. He squared up his shoulders and his gaze
never wavered once he continued.

"So I need you to tell me why you came to Kelby
Creek and why any of us should trust you."

THE MASKED MAN hadn't been caught. Once he'd gone
into the storage building, he'd all but disappeared. It
had seemed to weigh on Detective Lovett when he went
through every detail of their terrifying adventure and
then backtracked to Bella's escalating messages.

It was there in the hospital, talking with a relative
stranger—something that was becoming all too common—that Bella found out the truth behind Marco's earlier accident. The reason why they'd been in the hospital
only that morning.

She'd been under the impression the hit-and-run had
been an accident, but Detective Lovett wondered if it
wasn't her close proximity with Marco that had put him
on the masked man's radar for the first attack.

Bella had been unable to hide her surprise, though the
detective had taken it as offense instead.

"I didn't mean this happened because of you," he'd
tacked on. "I'm just saying that from my experience with
stalkers, sometimes obsession can turn into trying to get
rid of threats. Romantic threats."

He'd swept his gaze down to his notes on the last
part. Bella was thankful for the quick privacy. Mainly
because she didn't know which emotion had sprung up
across her face.

From there they didn't talk too much more. He got
all of her information and Bella was becoming more

and more restless. Detective Lovett did, however, leave her with something that eased a mind already becoming afraid again.

"Until we find him, and we will find him, we're going to station a car outside your house for surveillance. But, if you want to stay with your family, we'll also station a car at whatever house you end up going to."

Bella sighed. More from being tired at how stressed she knew she was going to be that night.

"You saw my family come into the hospital when you first got here, right?" she asked. "The big loud blob that turned into a massive hug? There's no way my father lets me stay anywhere other than my parents' house. That or everyone is going to come to mine."

Detective Lovett chuckled.

"To be honest, if I were a father, I'd do the same. Just call me with where you decide to stay and we can have someone go there."

Bella agreed and, seconds after the detective was out of the room, she was up and hurrying to the third floor. She hadn't seen Marco since he'd come in and it was bothering her. *Really* bothering her.

Recounting everything that had happened had only watered a seed of worry and urgency within her. Seeing Marco in the truck, not knowing if he was dead, and then having him save her only to pass out in her arms?

It was too much.

Too much without seeing him.

Without making sure he was okay.

So Bella didn't stop to check herself in the mirror or make nice, polite chitchat with the deputy in the hall, the nurse in the elevator she'd gone to high school with or even her father, who was leaving Marco's room right as she got there. Though she did pause long enough to listen to what her father reached out to her to say.

"He's doing good," he said with a smile. "A little bandage on his chest but good. I think all he'll need is a little rest after this. A good home-cooked meal too. But he's going to be fine. He's tough."

But tough wasn't the same as indestructible.

And Bella needed to see him.

To hear it from Marco himself that he was okay.

Yet it wasn't until she was in the room with the deputy that something shifted. That the way she felt about the man changed.

It only helped matters that the moment he saw her, he was smirking.

"I think your dad just—" But Marco didn't get a chance to finish.

Bella had been cleared by the doctor and deemed lucky to only have a few cuts across her from the accident. She had some bandages but that was it. No leg injuries. No impaired movement. Not even a reason to take pain meds.

Which made it all the easier to get to the bed in record time. It was even easier to reach out to him, take his face in her hands and pull him into a kiss.

One she hadn't meant to do.

One she hadn't even *thought* to do when she'd come in.

Yet one she absolutely needed.

Bella reveled in the warmth of his lips and how forgiving they were despite the surprise. They melted against hers without resistance. But this kiss wasn't about pleasure.

It was about relief.

Relief and being grateful.

Bella ended it as quickly as she started it and stepped

back, somehow breathless despite how brief the whole interaction had been.

Marco's lips were still parted. His eyebrow rose.

"I'm glad you're okay," Bella said, simply.

Marco leaned back again. He was smiling.

"Not only am I okay, I'm very awake now."

Bella felt the relief and gratefulness burn away in a blush that heated the whole of her. She stood by the kiss but now the awkwardness was making its way in too.

"I—I'm sorry," she said in a rush. "It's just, uh, in my defense you saved my life and, well, it's very hard not to kiss someone who's saved your life."

Marco actually laughed. It made the blush running amok through her body heat up even more.

He waved his hand through the air.

"Listen, I'm just glad your dad took a different approach."

Bella tilted her head to the side in question.

"What exactly did he say when he was in here?"

Marco's smile transformed into a grin.

"Well, apparently, since I passed his trust test, that means he's allowed to threaten me."

Bella felt her eyes narrow.

What had her father done?

"Threaten you with what?"

Marco chuckled. He sat up, adopted what she could only assume was his impression of her father and pointed at her with a sternness that *definitely* was her dad.

"Southern hospitality."

Chapter Ten

Carlos dropped him off at the curb like Marco was going to a sleepover and Deputy Park was his father. The deputy must have thought the same thing, as he rolled the passenger-side window down and called through it.

"Don't stay up too late or you'll be cranky tomorrow." Carlos said it with a smile. It made Marco chuckle.

He was careful as he moved his duffel bag from one hand to the other. His stitches wouldn't pull from such a small task but he wanted to make absolutely sure he didn't have a reason to go back to the hospital.

Not again.

At least, not for the third time in twenty-four hours.

He didn't think his sanity or his insurance could handle it.

"Sure thing, Dad," Marco returned. "Just make sure you leave your phone on in case we need to talk."

Carlos laughed. Then he sobered. It was no longer a joking matter. He nodded toward the patrol car parked out front against the curb. Dawn County Sheriff's Deputy was printed along the side. There was one man behind the wheel, his badge no doubt pinned to his uniform.

"That's Cooper," Carlos said. "He's night shift and one heck of a determined guy. Good at the details too.

I put his number in that new phone of yours if you need him for whatever reason. He'll change out with me in the morning and I can update you then on what's happening. That good?"

Marco didn't think any of this was good but he appreciated the concern and consideration Carlos kept giving him.

If he were being honest, it was something he sorely had missed since the incident at his last department.

"That works. Just shoot me a text when you're out here and I'll come meet you."

"Ten-four."

They said their goodbyes and Marco made eye contact with Cooper through his windshield. They exchanged nods and then Marco was walking up to a front porch covered in ceramic gnomes of varying colors, shapes and themes. It was a far cry from his nondescript apartment, that was for sure.

The front door flew open before Marco could knock.

Bella Greene smiled back at him, a bit rosy-cheeked and breathless.

"I still can't believe you agreed to do this." She waved her arms around to include the general house behind them. "I *had* to be here but you definitely didn't. If you thought me being awkward and intrusive during our dinner at the restaurant the other day was bad, then you're in for a treat. A really unsettling, loud treat."

Marco laughed.

"It's not like your dad gave me much of a choice," he said. "He didn't right out threaten me with what he'd do if I turned down the offer but I'm good at reading between the lines. And between his lines told me to accept staying here for the night with grace instead of trying to get out of it."

Whether it was his imagination or the poor lighting from the rustic lantern fixed to the wall or the darkness of night around them, Marco almost thought he saw a look of disappointment cross Bella's face. He didn't get a chance to clear the air to let her know that he was grateful. That had Grant not asked him in, he would have been alone. And while he'd grown accustomed to that, after the day he'd had, Marco found he didn't want to be alone just yet.

The man himself popped up behind Bella, beer in one hand and the only other Greene family member that Marco hadn't yet met holding the other.

Valerie Greene was an older version of her daughter in beauty *and* volume. She beamed as she greeted him.

"You made it just in time, Deputy Rossi! I hope you like lasagna!"

THE GREENE FAMILY home was an interesting collection of rooms, colors and architecture. Marco could tell the house was older and yet some parts of it seemed absolutely brand-new. It was something that Bella must have realized he'd picked up on because she smiled and motioned to the stairs that were tucked just inside the entryway.

"My dad's been renovating this house since my parents got it from his mother after she passed." Bella ran her hand along the stair railing. "It's why Val and I didn't realize in school that not everyone spent their weekends and some nights renovating different rooms of their house. For us it was always normal to be installing new flooring, replumbing and learning the hard way that we're really bad at grouting things." She nodded up the stairs. Her hair was loose and managed to shimmer beneath the LED lights in the entryway. "My parents like their privacy and have a suite behind the kitchen. All other rooms are up here. Follow me."

Bella led him upstairs to the second-floor landing, which was as nice as the downstairs. The walls were soothing in color, the floors were hardwood and shone, and weird little knickknacks that oddly worked in the space dotted shelves and nooks along the way. But what Marco liked more than the nice furnishings and surroundings were all the pictures.

Photographs of the Greene family stretched across every available inch of wall. Like wallpaper that could easily be rearranged when the desire struck them. Marco recognized younger versions of everyone he'd met; most notable, though, was Bella. Marco had to stop and press his finger against a small frame next to the first closed door in the hallway.

"Is this you wearing a tutu and holding on to a jackhammer?"

Bella laughed. Her cheeks tinted again.

"If it's not, then I have several questions for my family." That laugh had turned into a smile that was sitting pretty across those lips. He was starting to see that Bella had a knack for dealing with stress. Or at least compartmentalizing it. That didn't mean the fear, the worry and the stress weren't still there though. While he was enjoying seeing a smiling, happy Bella, a part of him wanted to see the other side. The one she hid, whether it was for pride or self-preservation or simply because she thought she had to. He wanted to see it and to help her through it.

He wanted her to be happy, more and more with each passing exchange between them.

Once again Marco found himself wondering who Bella had been before he'd come to town. Before she started getting the messages from the masked man. Before she'd come back to Kelby Creek. He even wondered what she'd been like as a teen.

He wondered so much about Bella that he realized that in itself was significant. Yet, standing in the upstairs hallway of her parents' house after such an intense day, Marco knew now wasn't the time to deep dive into who Bella Greene had been and was currently.

So he stayed with his jokes. He tried to be charming and smile and laugh and pretend like he was on a normal tour of her family's house and that he was staying in their guest bedroom only because he had nowhere else to go. Even though he did. It just happened to be a long lonely way across town. Again, something that normally wouldn't bother him but was now pricking at his skin.

Bella added on to her sarcastic answer with the real one, never the wiser to his ongoing internal battle between staying a loner and wanting to get closer to her.

"Despite not really getting into construction as a job until after I came back to Kelby Creek, I actually had always really wanted to use a jackhammer." She shrugged. "Some girls dream of doing dance or following boy bands and going to concerts where they have really nice hair and somewhat provocative PG-13 dance moves, but me? I had seen the movie *Tremors* with Kevin Bacon, and at the very beginning, you have two construction workers who are using a jackhammer to break up the road. For some reason, I couldn't get over how cool it was to watch that little thing break up something as hard and sturdy as a road, and I became obsessed. Every birthday after that I told my dad all I wanted was to use a jackhammer."

"Well, it looks like dreams come true. Though I have to ask, did the tutu come with it or was that your own personal touch?"

Bella laughed again.

"I was on the way to a birthday party that had a theme," she said. "I don't remember exactly what the theme was or who even threw it because right before the party Dad brought me to the garage and there was this beaut. He had to rent it for the week to do work on the kitchen floor." Bella grinned. "I'd like to say that I took that picture and then went to my party like any normal kid would but…"

"Please tell me you skipped the kid's birthday party just to use a jackhammer."

Bella shrugged and walked through the door.

"I'll let you use your imagination on that one."

They were standing in the guest bedroom that Grant had all but pushed on Marco at the hospital. It was quaint, clean and more room than he had expected to be given. The bed was a queen, there was a love seat at its foot and a door that he believed led to a bathroom.

"This is nicer than my apartment," he said. "Can I get Greene Thumb and Hammer to come to my apartment and do some renovations? I'm sure my landlord won't mind the upgrade."

Bella took his bag from his hand and placed it on the dresser against the wall. Marco noted she was just as careful to take it as he had been to move it from one hand to the other.

"You're all for praising us now but just wait until we actually sit down to eat." Bella did an overdramatic sigh.

"Remember when I accused you of having armor around your heart? I only had the audacity to say such a corny thing because I grew up with this bunch. You just entered the house of cheesy '80s lines and fortune-cookie jargon. And football talk. Alabama football, to be exact."

The smile and humor Bella had been projecting wavered as her eyes glanced out the window. Marco followed her gaze, adrenaline dangerously close to rising, but all he saw was a backyard. Fenced in, barely lit and void of anyone or anything. When he turned back around, he could tell she realized she'd been caught. That an emotion had broken through her courtesy and curiosity. If only for a second.

This time Marco decided not to let the moment go without probing. Not after everything they'd been through just within the last twenty-four hours.

"This seems like a really obvious question, but I have to ask, what's wrong?" Marco moved so his body was between her and the window. He kept his eyes firmly on hers, hoping that she saw he was as invested in the answer as he was in asking the question.

Bella didn't immediately respond. At least, not with her words. She did, however, point down to the floor.

When she spoke, it was soft, quiet.

"Everyone I love is in this house," she said, simply. "If someone really wants me, if that masked man is obsessed with me, isn't my being with all of you putting you in danger? More danger than we were in earlier? Am I just putting the largest of targets on my family's back?"

Marco had actually waited for this exact conversation. When he told her in the hospital that he'd accepted her father's invitation to stay that night, Marco had seen that Bella wasn't a fan of the idea. But not because of him. She hadn't like it because of her staying there too. Marco understood her reservations and knew he couldn't completely remove them but that didn't mean he didn't want to squash them. If only a little.

"*You* are not doing anything."

Marco took her hands in his, hoping the contact fastened her to him.

"None of this, none of what has happened, is or ever will be your fault," he continued. "Someone else's obsession has become dangerous and that's my job. That's the department's job. We do our best to stop the danger and keep those who are in it safe. While no one should or can tell you how to feel, I think it's best if you try really hard to let go of that guilt, that worry, and give it to me for now." He smiled, dropped one of her hands and pointed down at the floor like she had. "Because all I know is that beneath our feet is a family who would do anything to protect you and each other—" Marco pointed to the wall that faced the front of the house "—a sheriff's department that is personally and completely invested in keeping you, us and your family safe—" then Marco pointed to himself "—and a deputy who is also personally and completely invested in not only keeping everyone safe but has proved that he cannot be easily sidelined when it comes to protecting you."

He shrugged, trying to show he was nonchalant when in fact his heartbeat had started to speed up. Marco wanted, needed, to prove that Bella was safe with him even though they'd been attacked.

"I don't think that masked man will be coming here tonight," he added. "In fact I can't imagine he's even still in town after what happened. But, on the off chance that he has the gall to try something, I don't think he'll even make it past the front door. I'll make sure of that."

Bella's eyes flitted down to his lips but she nodded. "Okay."

It was such a small and simple and quiet answer that his heartbeat went from picking up speed to a gallop. Because there was one detail they had both skipped over during their limited conversation at the hospital. One that he now fully felt standing in Bella's childhood home, staring into her icy blues and holding her hand.

"Did you hear why the department and ambulance got to us so quickly after the wreck? Why the first patrol car got there within five minutes?"

Bella shook her head.

"No. I just assumed they were close."

"They weren't actually. Instead they were flooring it to us because the dispatcher heard you." Marco felt the smile but had no idea if he was hiding the emotion behind it. "She heard you say that a deputy was down and needed immediate medical attention or he could die. She *also* heard you tell the man that you would come along with him so he wouldn't shoot me." He let out a small breath. Marco didn't know if Bella knew enough about him by now to hear how he was equally in awe and proud.

So he made sure he showed her after he explained.

"You must've only had a minute, maybe less, to react after he hit us and you used every second of that and made them count. You could've also found a way to protect yourself but, instead, you protected me."

Marco put his hand up to Bella's cheek. Her skin was warm against the palm of his hand. Their second kiss was just as soft, sweet and brief as their first. Yet this time it was Marco who started and then ended it.

And he was more than aware of how little he wanted to end it.

Bella's eyelashes fluttered up, dark against her rosy cheeks. Her lips were still parted when he recalled back to the first time they had touched like this.

"You're right," he said. "It *is* hard not to kiss someone who's saved your life."

Chapter Eleven

Dinner wasn't that bad. At least it wasn't what Bella had expected it to be. Which, she realized, was starting to be the constant in her current life. Things she didn't expect and everything else that happened after.

When she was a teenager, Bella had had a boy over to meet her family. His name was Rodney and he was as shy as the day was long. He'd done everything a boy trying to impress her parents was supposed to do. He'd shaken her father's hand, complimented her mother's cooking and made harmless jokes at her expense to try to win over Val. Yet, nothing had really clicked. Her father had been suspicious and openly wondered what his intentions were, her mother hadn't liked Rodney making jokes at her expense just to score points with Val, and her brother had never really told her why he wasn't a fan of Rodney other than he wasn't.

"You just get a feeling sometimes, Bella," he'd said. "And the feeling I got with him was that he's a high school mistake you should avoid making."

Since then Bella had always been a bit concerned with bringing people over to the house. Her parents thought it was because she was embarrassed by them, of how they had a hard time keeping their thoughts to themselves, but the truth was Bella often found herself persuaded to her family's point of view, negative or not. She knew if her family didn't like someone that, even though she was her own woman with her own opinions and thoughts and experiences, having the people she cared about the most decide to not be in someone's corner meant that she too would eventually decide the same thing. So instead of chancing that, she decided not to bring over anyone else since Rodney—at least, no potential boyfriends or romantic interests.

But now there was Marco.

They were in a completely different situation than when she was a teenager and bringing a boy over, yet here Bella was, stomach tight with nerves, as they settled around the dining room table she'd grown up eating at. Next to a man she was starting to get to know through a terrifying crash course that was a football field's length away from normal.

A man who had kissed her and then managed to walk away like his heart wasn't about to beat through his chest.

Bella had been afraid that any goodwill or feelings her family had had for the deputy would change over the course of one very delicious lasagna.

Thankfully, nothing of the sort happened.

"Wait, wait, wait a minute," Val said, hand holding a fork out, and pointed at Marco across the table from him. "You got there and this guy had no pants on but was wearing whipped cream instead?"

Marco laughed, something he was doing a lot more of since devouring two chunks of Valerie Greene's infamous homemade lasagna.

"No joke," he said. "Apparently he was trying to be funny and romantic for his ex-girlfriend, who, also apparently, wasn't a fan of the gesture. I had to bring him into the department and then spent the next few hours cleaning my patrol car. You'll never believe such a small guy could make such a big mess."

Val howled with laughter. Bella took a sip of her wine. While Marco talked, she occasionally studied her parents' expressions to see if they were unimpressed with the deputy. Everyone was all smiles though, even Justin, who had made the trip to the house at the request of her father.

As he'd gotten Bella's call from the hospital, her father had managed to lose his keys in his haste to leave the site of Justin's shed. It was only luck that Justin had been working from home that day and had been kind enough to drive him and Val. He'd also been kind enough to offer a handful of security cameras that ran off an application now on her father's phone. Something to give them a temporary peace of mind while they all ordered their own security systems for each of their houses.

Marco, Val and Justin had set up the cameras on loan right after Bella and the deputy's quick kiss. It had been weirdly cute to see the three of them palling around. When Justin went home for the night, they even hung out on the front porch, talking about who knew what before parting ways.

It made Bella wonder if Marco wasn't as much of a loner as she'd once thought.

"All right, I don't know about y'all but I'm exhausted and I didn't even do anything today except worry," her mother announced once the table was cleared and the dishes were done. Valerie Greene was all about creating order in the chaos as a way to keep herself sane. They could be in the middle of a tornado warning and she'd be folding laundry to keep her nerves in check. It was also why they'd had her lasagna instead of something easier like a pizza or ordering in. Bella's mom deep dived into domestic distraction when things got bumpy. She was almost sure that the kitchen would be spotless by the morning. "So, I know you two need some sleep."

She made a whooshing motion with a hand towel toward the stairs but not before pulling Bella into a hug that she felt all the way into her bones.

"I'm so glad you're okay, my sweet Bells," she said to Bella's hair. "I don't know what I would do if something happened to you. To any of you."

Bella patted her mother's back.

"I know. I'm okay though, Mom. I promise."

They ended the embrace and then Marco was in her sights. She was more careful at putting her arms around him. While he'd been cleared by the doctor to leave the hospital, there was no getting around the fact that he had seen better days. There was also no denying that he was tired. Even his speech was starting to thicken. Bella had no idea when the last time was that he'd slept.

"And you," her mother said as she stepped back again. "If there's anything you need, anything you *ever* need, you don't hesitate to come get us. You understand?"

Marco nodded.

"Yes, ma'am, I understand."

Bella's father expressed his feelings with a handshake to Marco and a quick hug to her. Then he turned to Val and pointed toward the stairs too.

"You're gonna stay the whole night and not sneak out to go back to your house," he scolded. "I don't care if you think you're some big bad adult, tonight all of my children are under my roof. You got it?"

Bella stifled a laugh. Their father was using his I'mraising-two-teenagers voice. She had to admit it was still effective, even as an adult.

Val rolled his eyes. He agreed.

"I already said I was going to stay," he added. "I'm not going to skip the chance to get homemade pancakes from Mom tomorrow. And, for future reference, you can just lead with that instead of trying to act tough."

He laughed all the way up the stairs as their father tried to chase him. Her mother caught their father by the belt loop and pulled him in the direction of their bedroom, chuckling as she went.

Marco walked Bella to the room across from his. The same one that she'd grown up in. He stopped just inside the door and looked around, his eyebrow raised.

"This room used to be a lot more chaotic," she offered before he could ask why it was obviously not a bedroom anymore. "Or at least chaotic in the way of how many stuffed animals and posters of the Backstreet Boys it used to have. It's Dad's office now but the daybed sleeps like a dream. Which was nice when I stayed here for a while after I was laid off and came back to town. If I'm not mistaken, there are plans to make Val's old room into a gym next. Even though we have our own homes in town, this piece of news still offends him. He tried to have a vote last family supper to change their minds. I haven't had the heart to tell him yet that Mom already said it's been decided and the treadmill comes in at the end of the month."

Marco grinned at that.

"My parents would fight me and my sister tooth and nail if we ever told them they needed to pack up our childhood things. They moved once Amy and I left the nest and they still set up bedrooms for us in the new house, just in case we ever wanted them."

Bella softened and let out an *aww.*

"That's kind of really sweet."

He shrugged.

"Occasionally they overcompensate to make sure that we know they love us. Amy calls it a great hazard of being adopted from foster care. They're always trying to be our family, even though they're already there."

It was only the second time that Marco had spoken about his family. This time, however, Bella wanted more. She wanted to ask questions that would define him, that would make her understand him better, and that would show him that he was becoming more than just someone who was interesting to her. More than some shiny new object in town. But the timing, like so many other instances in their short acquaintanceship, was off.

She let the comment stay just as a series of rhythmic beeps and buzzes came from his pocket. Marco pulled out his phone.

"Speaking of my family, this is Amy," he said. "And knowing her, this will take a while."

"Oh, that's no problem," Bella hurried. "I'm just about to turn in anyway. I'll see you in the morning."

Marco answered the phone and was in the guest bedroom before Bella could think of something else to better end the night with. There was a restlessness in her. She wanted to say more, to do more, but there were only so many hours in the day. Plus, they all really did need to rest, Marco more than any of them.

Still, Bella was slower than usual getting ready for bed. Like she were a teenager again, she fought the immature urge to listen really hard as she walked by his bedroom door to the hall bathroom, trying to see if he was still awake.

Leave the man alone, she mentally chided herself after the third pass by. *Just because you kissed him and he kissed you, doesn't mean you need to keep thinking about kissing now.*

It was a ridiculous little pep talk but it did the trick. Bella finally laid down as ten o'clock rolled around.

But then eleven o'clock came.

And then midnight.

Bella could no more sleep than she could stop thinking about everything that had happened. About Marco. About the masked man.

Who was he?

She'd thought she recognized his voice earlier but every time she'd thought of it since, Bella doubted herself.

Was it someone she knew or was it a stranger who had become obsessed?

What had she done to even warrant that kind of obsession? Her day-to-day life since coming back to Kelby Creek had been utterly boring. When she wasn't working with her dad and Val, she was at home. When she wasn't at home, she was at a worksite. It was rare to be at neither place. Like the few times she'd gone to the bar with either Val or Justin, the one or two times she grabbed dinner with a friend from high school, or like the day she met Marco when she was supposed to be heading to accept a small business award.

If the masked man had been the one sending messages to her for more than six months, then why had he waited? Why had he waited to grab her, to attack, when for the first time in a long while, her life had actually become interesting?

Like a shot of lightning coming down from the heavens and striking her bed, adrenaline went through Bella so hard she sat up. The covers came off next as she kicked her feet over the edge of the bed. She skipped putting on her slippers, completely forgot to grab her robe and hurried out to the hallway as quickly and quietly as she could. This time she didn't feel like a teenager spying on a boy she might or might not like. This time she was a woman, afraid yet thinking about the details for what felt like the first time.

Bella put her ear to the door and tapped it lightly.

Marco's deep voice managed to be quiet yet fill her at the same time as he said, "Come in."

A look of alarm passed over his face at the sight of her. He was sitting up in the bed, a notebook and pen on his lap, and nothing but a bare chest with the bandage above the covers. She was glad she hadn't woken him.

Instead of being cute or clever, Bella got straight to the point.

"The day I met you, when I was broken down on the side of the road, he was trying to take me then, wasn't he? The man with the mask. That's why there was water in my gas tank and that's why I broke down in the middle of nowhere. He was trying to take me then."

Marco didn't try to sugarcoat it. He didn't try to give her a pep talk or even one of reassurance. Instead he nodded.

"I think so," he said. "But the thing that concerns me more is I think since then he's been practicing to do it again."

Chapter Twelve

Marco laid the notebook down on the quilt top. Bella joined him, sitting just on the other side of it so she could face him. A part of him was still hyperfocused on the case, the masked man and trying to figure out who exactly he was. Yet Marco might've gone through a lot that day but he sure wasn't dead. Which meant there was no way he wasn't going to take a moment to marvel at how beautiful the woman now in bed with him looked.

Bella's hair was soft and hung against her bare shoulders, skimming the tops of the very small straps keeping her nightshirt up. Her shorts didn't match but they did show off legs that had curve, freckles and smoothness. Since the car accident, her makeup had been washed off but that didn't subtract anything from the woman. In fact it almost added a warmth, a feeling of being comfortable that made him feel like he in a way had earned enough of her trust to be shown a version of her with her guard down.

And then there were her lips.

Ones he now knew felt every bit as great as he'd thought they would feel.

Now those lips were downturned. Her crystal blue eyes, magnetic in nature to him, scanning the paper he'd been jotting his notes on. When they traveled back up to his own, he knew that his attraction for Bella Greene was going to have to take a back seat if he was going to help keep her safe.

"After we met that first day and up until the night we ran into each other at the bar, the department had responded to several calls about cars breaking down and people being stranded," Marco started. "When I was thinking about it in the bar before I saw you, I realized that I hadn't actually asked what was wrong with the truck. I thought it was kind of strange that all of these vehicles were having problems so close together."

"Water in the gas tank," Bella guessed.

He nodded.

"One car couldn't even start and was blocking a parking lot entrance. That one had too much water in the tank. When you get over a certain amount, it basically kills the engine. There was another car that made it a little bit before it shut down. The tow truck operator who showed up used to be a mechanic and gave the car a once-over before hooking it up. His best guess without really getting into it was that there was sugar in the gas lines and tank. But I didn't pick up on the pattern right away because in between those two were two other vehicles that had broken down for unrelated reasons. One had a transmission that went kaput. The other had a hole on the inside of their tire that took us way too long to actually find. For us, it really just seemed like a series of bad luck and random people until I saw you. Then it started to bother me."

"You think that the masked man was behind all of these?" Bella readjusted where she was sitting, clearly becoming uncomfortable at the thought.

"If he's been sending you messages for almost seven

months and only tried to take you this past month, then that means there's a reason he hasn't come for you before." He tried to choose his words carefully. There were only so many delicate ways he could talk about an obsessive stalker with devious intentions. Still, he didn't like what he was about to say. "I think he's trying to come up with a plan that gets you without getting him caught. I think the reason why your truck had water in its gas tank twice was because he was looking for a way to delay you from going wherever you were going. He wanted you to be able to leave your house or work or wherever you were and get caught out by yourself so he could approach you. So he could take you. I think the water in the gas tank worked but not how he wanted it to. Maybe it took too long to go into effect, maybe it happened too fast, but I think after that, after I interrupted and potentially messed up his plans, I think he played around with different methods to make it fit what he wanted."

"But there was water in my gas tank again," she pointed out. "He went back to the first thing he tried."

"That's the other thing," Marco said. "I don't think he planned on doing any of what he did today. I don't think it was his intention to put you in danger, attack me and then try to take you."

"Why do you think that?"

Marco shifted, lifted the covers enough to where she could see the very top part of the bruise that ran along his side.

"Because he would've killed me the night before when I was out running had I not heard the car and jumped out of the way at the last second. I think he would've run me down again if I hadn't managed to make it to the woods."

"He wants you out of the way. Because of me. He's targeting you."

It was something that they hadn't directly talked about since the accident but Marco knew others had discussed it. It was one of the first things Detective Lovett had pointed out when he'd come in to check on Marco at the hospital.

"I think that whoever this is doesn't like you spending time with me and when he put that message in your house, on your bathroom mirror, I don't think he imagined you'd come to me for help. Especially not to the hospital."

"So you're thinking that he acted on—what?—emotion? That he decided to move up his original plan because he was mad?"

"Jealous," Marco corrected. "You're the object of his obsession so to him my presence might be his biggest threat in his mind. Which made him impulsive. It made him sloppy." It wasn't the time but it was absolutely the emotion. Marco smirked.

Instead of getting upset at it, Bella's eyebrows went up and she mirrored the look.

"It's when people like this get sloppy that people like me get them." He put his finger down on the words that he had circled right before she'd come in. Marco waited for her to read them out loud.

"Hospital parking lot security camera."

"Hospital parking lot security camera," he repeated with a flare.

"He had to put water in my tank in the hospital parking lot," she realized.

"And since he was impulsive with how he tried to take

you, then maybe he was impulsive with how he tried to sabotage your truck."

"He could have gotten sloppy there too."

Marco nodded.

"Which means we might know by tomorrow morning exactly who this guy really is."

WHEN BELLA WOKE up the next morning, she was a little confused and a lot disoriented. It took her a moment to realize that she wasn't in her own bed, in her own house. Then, slowly, she remembered whose house she was in and where in that house she had fallen asleep. It was *not* her old childhood room, that was for sure.

Instead Bella woke up in the bed meant for Marco, sans the deputy himself.

Once that memory unblurred from sleep, Bella sat up like she been shocked again by that same lightning from the night before.

With a haze over her eyes, she quickly looked at the space next to her. That part of the bed was still made from the night before. There was no Marco there, above or below the sheets.

"He slept on the couch, by the way." Bella yelped and turned toward the bedroom doorway. Val had a coffee cup in his hand and a smug look on his face. He nodded to the love seat at the end of the bed. "I caught him coming out earlier and he told me y'all had been talking about the case and you'd fallen asleep when he had to take a call. Even though your room is four steps that way."

Val gave her a cheeky smile.

Bella rolled her eyes.

"Next time you get a crazy stalker trying to take you, then we'll see how badly you want to sleep alone."

Val's smugness wiped away. Then it was the protective brother.

"I overheard Marco and his friend the deputy talking earlier," he said. "Apparently they're looking at a lot of different leads, which I think is good, but so far haven't found anything new. They haven't found him."

That was and wasn't what Bella had wanted to hear. The idea of someone practicing for her abduction had added a new layer of fear. It was why she'd asked Marco if she could stay in the room while he mulled over some things and took a quick call from Deputy Park. The masked man had managed to make the one place in all the world where she felt the safest into somewhere she was now afraid to be alone.

She hated it.

Just like she hated that the man hadn't been caught despite being impulsive.

"Where is he now? Marco, I mean."

"Downstairs on the phone the last I saw. I think he's talking to his sister. Or at least someone he's very comfortable rolling his eyes at." Val gave her a knowing look. "I know personally I'm very comfortable with showing my sister just how much she annoys me. Which is quite frequent."

Bella grabbed the pillow next to her and threw it at the door. Val dodged it, laughing, and left.

By the time she got ready and made it downstairs, her family and Marco were together in the dining room, talking. Her mother squeezed her shoulder, her very own form of good-morning, and handed her a cup of coffee. Bella took a seat next to Marco, who remained in conversation with her father. It took her a few sips before she realized that they were talking about her stalker.

"Wait, I thought you said no one had been caught?" she asked, directing her question to Val.

He shook his head but it was Marco who answered. Being so close to him, she could smell his aftershave and noted that the stubble along his jaw was gone.

"They haven't been. Detective Lovett is still manning the search but your dad pointed out that we haven't had a chance to see how your house was broken into." He passed her the plate of muffins her mother had no doubt stress-cooked earlier that morning. "After we were attacked, no one went over there to see if they could figure out how he got in to leave the message. So, since the department is short-staffed and currently on a manhunt for this guy and, according to the sheriff, I'm not coming back in today to work, I thought I could check it out. Maybe find a clue that could help."

A feeling of equal parts excitement and nerves pulsed through Bella.

"I would personally love to figure out how he got in too," she said. "The only people who have keys to my house are in this room. I don't even have a spare one hidden outside just in case I get locked out."

Marco nodded like he was mentally taking notes. Bella knew that part of being a deputy was thinking on your feet and problem-solving but the more she looked at him, she was starting to see the makings of a detective. She decided later on, maybe when life calmed down, she would ask if he had any aspirations to try to become one. Until then she was thankful for every inclination he had and acted on to help her get to the bottom of what was happening.

"Okay, well, you give me your key and I'll head out in a few minutes once Carlos is here and I can have a chance to talk to him and see if we can get someone else out here."

Bella didn't realize that she was shaking her head until her father made a noise at her.

"You're not going alone," she interjected.

"And you're not coming," Marco was fast to reply.

"It's my house. You can't tell me I can't come. Plus, I know it better than anyone. If there's something out of place, if there's something wrong, I'm the only one here who has the best chance of seeing that."

"If this masked man has come after you in the daylight and in the company of a law enforcement officer and in such a brazen attack, then going home to a place where we know he's been inside isn't the best idea," Marco said.

He was getting feisty. That was the only word Bella could think of for it. It was as if he were as excited as a child jumping up and down because he was next in line to see Santa.

Marco wanted to help. He wanted to solve this and he wanted to do it now.

Still, she shook her head. This time her father spoke up but before he could make his own argument Bella firmly planted hers.

"I am no more safe here than I would be there," she stated. "But at least there I have a chance to find something that might be able to help us stop this guy from ever coming for me again and hurting any of y'all who get in his way. I'm going." She looked Marco square in the face. "The only choice you get to make now is if *you* want to come with *me*."

Marco chewed on that for a moment. Her family remained quiet. She thought she was about to have to make a second argument, maybe throw in a few minutes of her raised I'm-serious voice that she used on suppliers who tried to overcharge Greene Thumb and Hammer, but finally Marco caved.

And he did so with a smile that put heat into her veins. "Yes, ma'am."

Chapter Thirteen

Watching Bella convince her family that they couldn't come with her, Marco and Carlos was like watching a master class in persuasion. She managed to shift paternal and maternal worry enough so that they now believed they'd help more by staying away. Though maybe it did help that her father seemed to genuinely trust Marco.

Grant had pulled him aside before they left with Carlos and had quietly told him in no uncertain terms that he protected her the first time and he expected even better results the second time around. If there was a second time. He was of the same thought with Marco that the masked man, if he had any sense, was long gone from Kelby Creek. Or at least in such deep hiding that he wasn't going to chance another attempt at getting her.

"You told me your story," Grant had added. "I know your résumé from your last job now. Which means I know you're good. I need you to stay good. You hear me?"

"I hear you."

Now Bella was standing on the front porch of her own home, peeking in through the windows, trying to figure out if it was safe for her to come in. At all times Marco kept his eyes on her while moving from room to room at the front part of the house while Carlos swept everything else.

It was then, standing on a rug that had more personality than most people Marco had met, that he started to suspect not only did he like Deputy Park but he was also starting to trust him.

"Unless you have some kind of hidden compartment or underground bunker, there's no one in this house but us," Carlos concluded when they all converged on the front porch again.

The tension that had been building in Bella's shoulders on the ride over lessened but didn't entirely drop.

"All right," she said, turning to Marco with nothing but focus. "Let's see if I can't super-sleuth us a clue."

Marco trailed behind Bella while Carlos stayed outside. They went from room to room, as she inspected everything in silence. Marco was almost ashamed to say his attention kept splitting from the woman to what the woman had built around her.

Before then Marco had formed an opinion about Bella Greene. If he'd been asked about what she was like before entering her home, he would've said that the one word he would use to describe her was *surprising*. Then he would have probably followed that up with *loud*, but not loud in a bad way. She knew what she wanted, she said what she wanted and she wouldn't stand by and let someone else tell her what she wanted. After spending time at her family's home the night before, Marco would've added that he believed that Bella fiercely loved her family, just as they fiercely loved her back. But going through her home? Marco found a new word to describe the woman.

Warm.

It wasn't a poetic description, and it certainly wasn't

original, but the more he saw of her private life, the more he felt warm just by being there.

The house was older, tidy, but also messy exactly where it counted. There were magazines on the coffee table, straightened and obviously for guests, but then there was an empty coffee cup with lipstick on the brim and different colors of nail polish resting on a coupon for takeout. Marco could almost imagine Bella sitting on the couch, watching TV and trying to do her nails at the same time. He even spotted a smear of purple paint with glitter against the table. He bet she'd missed with the applicator and had left it, admitting defeat about ever getting it off the wood without hurting the finish.

From there Marco fell into unintentionally comparing Bella to his last girlfriend. She'd been obsessed with plants. She had potted everything you could think of, sitting on or hanging from almost every available space in her apartment. Bella was in no way the same. There wasn't a living plant in any room of the house. But fake succulents and cacti? She had those in spades. The thought of her getting fake plants instead of real ones almost made Marco chuckle to himself. Green Thumb and Hammer worked on landscaping as well as building structures and yet Bella was 100 percent fake plants. He could just imagine her complaining about how she didn't want to take her work home.

There were other details throughout the house too. Subtle and not-so-subtle. Details that told a story about the woman who lived there. Framed photos across all the walls, just like at her parents'. Family and friends and adventures between them all. There were books strewn around on how to knit tiny gnomes and how to cook quiche in tiny iron skillets. A small closet filled with costumes presumably for Halloween and a small office that was still being renovated but housed a small plastic trophy that said World's Best Daughter.

There was personality in the house.

And it was warm.

For a moment, after seeing the colorful quilt on her bed, the empty wineglass on her nightstand and one stuffed bear wearing a construction hat sitting on the chair in the corner, Marco forgot why they were there.

All he knew was that he wanted to stay.

"I have no idea how he got in," Bella said, throwing her arms up in defeat. "I know this place inch for inch and yet I'm not seeing anything that sends up red flags."

She motioned to the windows.

"Every window is locked and can only be opened from the inside," she continued. "There's no broken glass or broken doors anywhere. I unlock and lock every door I walk through that leads from the outside to inside and—"

Marco went from feeling warm to startled by his own interrupting thought. He reached out and grabbed her elbow, stopping her midsentence.

"That's it. Jennifer Parkridge."

Bella's eyebrow slid up.

"Jennifer Parkridge?" she repeated. Before he could explain, that look of excitement of something clicking into place came over her. "Her house... But that could be a coincidence, surely."

Marco felt like he was onto something he should have seen already.

"She had a broken door and nothing taken. You don't have any broken doors and a message was left behind. If the masked man has been making a plan to take you at a specific time and in a specific place, who's to say that it's not just cars he's been practicing with?"

"I don't know. That's kind of a stretch, don't you think? All the bad that's been happening in Kelby Creek the last six to seven months can't be because of him. Can it?"

Marco could feel it in his gut, just like the night at the bar when he had first seen Bella and Justin. He knew something was up about the cars and yet he had pushed it to the back burner. That error in judgment, that lack of hustle to get to the bottom of his feeling, had almost cost Bella and him their lives.

He wasn't going to make the same mistake now.

"I think it's time we head back to the sheriff's department."

BELLA WAS SURPRISED at how big the file was. Or really how thick. Its pages nearly covered the meeting room's tabletop after Marco spread them all out.

"This is just in the last six months?" she asked. "These are all transcripts of people calling in?"

"They're calls that we responded to," he corrected, eyes down and scanning the current paper he was standing over. "The department, I mean. I physically didn't go to all these."

Bella whistled and she side-eyed the door. It was closed.

"And you're sure it's okay for us to be doing this?"

Marco wasn't as quick to answer that one. When he did, he added in a shrug.

"We're trying to help stop a stalker, which can only help the town, which can only help the department. So *really* we're not actually looking at papers we're not supposed to, we are just helping in a way that we need to be discreet about. Besides, most of these are public records, and since I'm guarding you, it's just more efficient to do this together."

Bella couldn't help it. She chuckled.

"*Wow*, if that wasn't some fancy footwork around a good ole *no, we shouldn't be doing this*."

Marco shrugged.

"If you'd rather me say we're being fluid with the law to get to where we need to be to *help* the law, would that be better?"

Bella returned her gaze to her own stack of papers.

"You know it wouldn't, but, hey, you were cute when you said it so I'll let it slide."

She hadn't meant to say *cute* out loud, but just like she let his stepping around the truth go, he let her schoolgirl description of him lie. The meeting room became quiet again just as it had been off and on for almost half an hour since they'd gotten there. A few minutes later and that silence was broken.

"There have been three break-ins in the past six months including Jennifer Parkridge's house," Marco said, putting his hands on his hips. "While each happened differently, aside from Jennifer, the intruders were caught and both are currently in prison for previous offenses. As for anything else that might be suspicious or look like someone acting out parts of a plan to abduct someone, I'm not finding anything that jumps out at me."

Bella didn't want to but she said the same for her section of papers.

"The only thing I really found is that there are still a few people in Kelby Creek who aren't exactly fans of the department." She tapped a paper that was near her.

"Like someone continuously messing with the department's breaker."

Bella dropped back into the chair that was next to her. She let out a hefty sigh. This search was starting to wear away at her will to live, buried among the complaints and police reports from the residents of Kelby Creek. Marco followed suit. He took the chair opposite her and shook his head.

"Whoever the masked man is, he knows you," he started. "Which means there's a good possibility you *actually* know him. You said he sounded familiar when he called for you at the storage facility, right?"

Bella nodded.

"Familiar but I couldn't place it. Just that I *know* it. And, believe me, I've been trying."

"So maybe it's someone that you had contact with in the past six to seven months. When it first started." He leaned forward on the table and made a temple with his hands on its top. His eyes latched on to hers and Bella knew she couldn't look away even if she wanted to. And she didn't. "I know we've already been over this, but can you think of anyone who might have shown that strong of interest in you? Maybe an ex-boyfriend or someone you dated?"

Bella didn't look away but she did squirm a little. It was slightly embarrassing. Like her social life since coming back to Kelby Creek, her dating life hadn't been that great. Her last ex had called her too intimidating. The one before that had called her annoying. He'd been easy to break up with.

"The last guy I was serious with lives in Florida now with his wife and newborn baby. And before you ask if I'm sure, let me just tell you that I stalked his social media profiles last night to make sure. There were a ton of tagged pictures of him and his family at some little kid's birthday party at a Chuck E. Cheese around the time we were attacked. My ex *before* that was someone I dated two years ago. The last I heard he was in Germany as a contractor with *his* family." She shook her head. "Neither one of them showed that much interest in me when we were dating, so I can't imagine they'd be coming for me after the fact. I doubt they'd even have the time."

Thankfully Marco didn't seem to focus on the news that Bella had only dated two men in the last few years. Not that that was particularly a bad thing, but for her it wasn't something that she liked to lead with in a conversation.

"Okay, so let's guess that it's not someone that you've been in a relationship with, but is there anyone you dated in the last year? Someone you weren't exactly serious about but went out with?"

Bella started to laugh, mostly because once again, she was about to point out that her social life and her romantic life hadn't been that impressive in the past. But then she remembered something.

Marco must have realized it.

"What?" He leaned forward with rapt attention.

"I *did* go out with a guy, about maybe seven or eight months ago. I don't really count him since I didn't actually stay the entire dinner."

"What's his name?" Marco reached for a piece of paper and pen.

"If you believe it, Conrad Abernethy."

Marco looked up at that.

"And you're sure he wasn't using a fake name?"

She laughed.

"Yeah, his name was Conrad Abernethy. From what I was told, he almost became a Conrad Abernethy the Third but his mother took pity on him."

"He lives in Kelby Creek?"

Bella nodded.

"I don't know where exactly but I met him at the Rosewater Bar. He was nice, cute and made pleasant conversation when we first met so when he asked me out I said yes. We went for dinner, I think two nights later, but I didn't stay all the way through it."

"Why not?"

"From the moment I sat down, he talked about himself nonstop and then the one time I tried to add something to the conversation, he did not respond in the way that I thought he should have. I texted a friend to come get me, which I have never done before, and made an excuse to leave before we'd even finished our meal."

Marco's eyebrow had slid up in question.

"What did he say that you didn't like?"

Bella felt the heat lift from the embarrassment whirling in her stomach and pool in her cheeks. She cleared her throat.

"Conrad told me during his one-man soliloquy that he was a taste entrepreneur. And, before you ask if you heard me right, just know that you did. Conrad was a self-proclaimed taster of all things alcohol. He was telling me a story about how he traveled the world tasting all these different drinks one summer in between his freshman and sophomore years of college. He told me that before he had gone off on this trip that he'd had a six-pack of abs. But when he came back, he'd had so much to drink that those six-pack abs had become more of a keg. So, me trying to be funny, I said that before *I* went to college I also had a six-pack but now all I had were two jugs." She motioned to her chest, now fully immersed in embarrassment.

Thankfully Marco burst out laughing.

"See?" she exclaimed. "That's the reaction I was hoping to get! It was a joke after all! But no. He stared at me like I'd just insulted his very soul. Not only did he not laugh, he didn't say anything and let us fall into this really weird tension-filled silence. I had to break it myself and I think what I said was something along the lines of *man I really hope they come by with breadsticks soon!*"

Marco was still laughing.

"That's when you texted your friend to come get you?"

Bella nodded, relieved that the story was over.

"He even told me he had better things to do when I made an excuse about Dad having an emergency," she added. "He didn't try to reschedule and he never texted or called. I haven't seen him since then. I'm not even sure he lives in Kelby Creek now."

Marco's laughter had died away. He was back to workmode.

"You can never tell what someone is capable of until they do it." He took the paper and stood up. "This Conrad may be full of himself and he may not be able to take a good joke but that doesn't mean he couldn't be the one who has been after you. For all—"

Bella sat up, ramrod straight.

"I'm an idiot," she interrupted. Adrenaline had burst through her as a memory dislodged. She found Marco's gaze again and shook her head. "You remember how I said that *hello there, friend* was kind of like my catchphrase during and after college?"

"Yeah?"

"Well, it also kind of became how I greeted people when I was nervous."

Marco caught on quick. She could tell by how the muscle in his jaw twitched and his eyes narrowed. A bloodhound catching on to a scent.

"And did you greet Conrad like that when you first met him at the bar?"

Bella's mind was flashing through the memories of the first night she met him. She wasn't sure if she would have remembered it otherwise but now she did.

"Yes. I was so awkward with it. After he introduced himself, I said, *Hello there, friend. I'm Bella Greene.*"

Chapter Fourteen

Conrad Abernethy was technically a local yet no one could agree on the last time anyone had seen him.

His employer at a production factory in the city hadn't seen him in weeks. His neighbor hadn't seen him in days. The bartender at the Rosewater Bar hadn't seen him in months. When Marco called his last-known number, it went straight to voice mail.

It was more than enough to pique his interest, if only to rule out the young man.

"I don't know how you are at reading women, but she was really mad at you back there." Carlos came around the side of his patrol car and kept his voice low. "I mean, for a second there, I thought she was about to go for my gun and make us take her with us."

Carlos was joking but, then again, they both realized that wasn't exactly true. Telling Bella that she couldn't come with them to talk to Conrad had been a harder fight than Marco had imagined.

"I'm in this more than you," she had said, frustration punctuating every word. "And didn't you also say you think the masked man would be long gone by now?"

"Or in hiding," he'd pointed out. "And if it is Conrad,

and he is in hiding, then what better place to hunker down than his own home?"

After that it was a volley of back-and-forths until Detective Lovett and his fiancée came in. Millie must have sensed that Bella needed to vent and to someone preferably not in law enforcement. They went into the detective's office while Marco updated Foster on their small-but-still-there lead.

"Let me know if you find anything. I'm about to finish off a few of my own from yesterday."

Carlos had been more than eager to get to the bottom of who the stalker was and, surprisingly, not just because it was the right thing to do. He'd been candid during the car ride to Conrad's house.

"I don't think it's right that you go through what you did at your old department only to come here to ours and be nearly killed by a guy with a Halloween-mask fetish," he'd said. "I know things that aren't fair happen to a lot of people and that in itself is not fair but still, definitely not cool."

Marco had stiffened at the mention of his last job. Not that he had been in denial about everyone else in the department not knowing about his past. Civilians being oblivious made sense. What had happened had nothing to do with anyone other than the cop Marco had taken down.

That didn't mean he wanted to hash it out with his new partner. Though Carlos did manage to get a few more words in before they arrived at their destination.

"I know some people don't get why you did it but I just have to say I do, and I would have done the same. It's crazy you had to leave because of it."

He hadn't corrected the man.

Marco hadn't had to leave—he'd chosen to do it.

"Thanks," was all Marco had said in response.

The focus shifted off the past and onto Conrad and his future. If he was the masked man, everything was about to change.

Since Marco was technically off duty, Carlos went around back to check the perimeter while Marco went right up to the front door. Conrad lived in a house that had the creek butted up against his backyard. There was a dock in the distance and a boat anchored there but it and the house were more run-down than well-kept. The one-story was small and splintered, a shutter hung on for dear life beneath one of the front windows, and if it hadn't been a little cold, Marco was sure he'd see a lot more overgrowth and weeds around the yard. There was a detached garage to the left of the house but the metal door was closed and locked by a padlock against the concrete.

Marco couldn't tell if anyone was home but he was getting the impression that, if they were, it hadn't been for long. The home seemed largely unlived in.

Marco made sure his jacket was hiding his holstered gun so he wouldn't potentially spook the man. His badge was in his back pocket, also ready to go if needed.

He knocked on the door and realized he was holding his breath.

Nothing.

Nothing sounded on the other side of the door and no one called out.

Marco knocked again, moving to the closest window when done. The curtain was drawn. Just like all of the windows facing the road. He couldn't see in and he still couldn't hear anything.

Was Conrad not there or was he hiding?

Movement made Marco turn to the side of the house. It was Carlos and he had his gun out.

"I think you should come see this."

Marco followed his partner around the side and up to the back porch. He slowed down considerably as he moved up the stairs. Marco pulled his gun out.

"There." Carlos pointed to the back door. It was ajar, its wood splintered around where it should have been locked.

Carlos shared a look with him. They nodded, a wordless understanding of what to do next. One stood in the doorway while the other pushed it open. Marco called out but it was Carlos who went in first.

"This is Deputy Rossi with the Dawn County Sherriff's Department. If anyone is inside, identify yourself now!" Carlos was already inside but Marco kept on. "We're coming in. If anyone is inside, let us know now!"

No one called back and nothing made a sound. Only their boots against the tile that led from the back door and into the kitchen.

But what it lacked in sound, it more than made up for with smell.

"Oh, my God."

Carlos put his freehand over his nose and pinched. Marco threw his nose into the crook of his arm.

They didn't say it then but they'd been in law enforcement long enough to know exactly what they'd find around the corner. Or at least Marco did. He'd once done a wellness check that had turned into him calling in the coroner when he was a rookie. That smell was bad. This one was too. Marco guessed he was about to have to make a similar call to their dispatcher.

Carlos rounded the corner first. He lowered his gun just as Marco stopped at his side.

For a moment, neither one of them spoke.

"Well, I think it's safe to say we found our guy," Carlos said. "But I don't think he's going to hurt anyone anymore."

Marco lowered his own gun.

Conrad Abernethy was lying on the ground, surrounded by dried blood and eyes open and staring at the ceiling. That would have been bad enough but it was the mask on the couch behind him that had all of Marco's attention.

"THEY THINK ONE of Marco's shots landed on Conrad at the storage facility and instead of going to the hospital and chance getting caught, he went home to hide."

Bella's father shook his head. Justin did too. They made various tsking noises. Disappointed at the unnecessary loss of life and the violence that had led up to it. Bella didn't know how she felt. Was she disappointed that the man had thrown away his life for no reason? Was she relieved that it was over? Was she angry that it had started in the first place?

Bella couldn't stick to one feeling. Mainly because she hadn't had the time to process Conrad's death herself.

Or, really, with the person she wanted to process it with.

"I still can't believe any of this happened," Justin decided on after a moment. "I feel sorry for everyone involved."

They were all at her parents' house, ruminating on the news. Since Marco and Carlos had made the discovery, the threat level over Bella had ceased to exist. Which meant standing around the sheriff's department, waiting, didn't make much sense. So Justin had picked up Bella and her father, who'd not yet found his keys, and taken them both to the house. Now everyone had coffee. Everyone but Val, who was still at the site of Justin's shed-in-progress. Bella bet dollars to donuts that the gossip mill would reach him before they even headed back.

"But this means it's over, right?" Justin added. "For you, I mean."

Bella nodded, then she cringed. Caught between several emotions still.

Conrad's body wasn't the only thing Marco had found. In his brief phone conversation with her, he'd listed the other concerning items within the house. Chief among them was the Halloween mask their attacker had worn, next to Conrad's body.

That would have been enough for her to believe Conrad was her stalker but, if it hadn't been there, the trash can full of notes that read *Hello there, friend* would have done the trick.

"I'll feel better once I get all the details from Marco." She looked to her father, who, in any other instance, might chastise her for trying to skip out on work. "I was wondering if I could wait here until he's done?"

She didn't say it but Bella knew her father picked up on the reason she didn't want to stay at her house to wait.

Bella didn't want to be alone yet.

"I'm sure your mother would love the company."

He smiled and ruffled her hair as they left. Bella slid into that familial warmth and safety, and stayed there with her mother until afternoon turned to night. Then the anxiousness set in, especially when she called Marco and it went straight to voice mail.

Instead of waiting for the man to reach out to her, Bella decided their last few days warranted her reaching out to his partner.

Deputy Park was surprisingly forthcoming with information.

One minute she was wrapping banana nut bread with her mother and several minutes later, she was sitting in her mother's car outside an apartment complex, staring at number 12B.

According to Deputy Park, Marco should have just gotten inside after a long day. His emphasis on long was probably a not-so-subtle point that Marco needed rest.

Bella agreed with that sentiment; in fact she believed he deserved it more than anyone, and yet there she was, holding banana bread on a Halloween-themed plate, wearing perfume and hoping that the deputy wasn't so tired that he couldn't see her.

"Just go knock on the door, you dingbat," Bella told herself with mounting annoyance riding along with her nerves. "Worst-case, you just say thank-you, drop off the bread and go back to your parents' place to have leftover lasagna. So, just get out of the car."

Bella finally listened to herself but nearly chickened out halfway up the stairs to the second floor. Apartment 12B was a corner unit and that meant extra steps to get to it. Those extra steps were filled with an anxiety that Bella was struggling to tamp down.

She didn't like it or understand it.

She'd been around the deputy time and time again. Heck, she'd even kissed and been kissed by the man!

And that's the problem, her brain spit out just as she knocked on the door. *You want to kiss him again but this time you don't want to stop.*

Bella didn't get the chance to give a rebuttal to herself before the door opened.

If his eyes weren't so quick to lock on to her, Bella might have taken a second to let out a breath.

She'd seen the man shirtless before at the hospital and in the guest bedroom. She knew that his upper body was well-toned and was no doubt an exciting prequel to what lay below, but just because you know that water with ice in it is cold, doesn't mean you're always prepared for when it's thrown into your face. It didn't help that Marco's pants were gone, a towel in its place hanging low. It did nothing for the water droplets across his chest or the slickness of his wet hair.

"Bella." His eyes widened in surprise but he stepped back quickly and motioned her in. "Hey. Come in."

Bella felt the heat of a blush rising but went past him with a smile.

"Sorry to just drop by like this," she said in a hurry. "I was worried about you and your phone was off so I called Deputy Park and he told me where you lived and—" Bella cut herself off and whirled around to face him once the door was closed. She held out the banana bread like the racing baton at a track meet. "Mom and I made you some dessert since you, you know, saved my life and—"

This time it was Marco who interrupted.

He closed the space between them in two long strides. Bella didn't have time to move as he caught her face in his hands, leaned down and pressed his lips against hers with force.

Not that Bella would have wanted to move if she'd had the time.

Though the dessert on the plate between them couldn't

take the heat. It made a loud crack as it hit the wood floor and broke.

Marco was startled at the sound.

He jumped back like she'd bitten him.

His eyes went down to the plate, then right back to hers. Bella could read his apology before he put it into words. So she thought it prudent to stop him and set him straight first.

"It's okay. I promise I've always hated that plate."

That was all it took. Marco closed the space between them again and pulled Bella into an embrace that made her tingle from head to toe.

Had she known those were the magic words to get Marco Rossi to kiss her again, she would have broken the plate herself.

Chapter Fifteen

The road to hell is paved with good intentions. The path to Marco's bed was paved with desire, surprise and the faint smell of banana lingering between them.

Marco's hands were tangling in Bella's hair, pulling her lips against his without much breathing in between. She'd already made a noise against his lips, a moan. It was enough to make the voice inside his head, telling Marco to calm down, go absolutely quiet.

He'd spent the entire day dealing with the aftermath of finding Conrad Abernethy's body. The sheriff started off the official aspects of it when he showed up at Conrad's house and reminded Marco that he wasn't supposed to be there. That he was off duty and supposed to be resting. But just as Marco was about to rally up a response that would keep him firmly tied to the case, Sheriff Chamblin relented with a grin.

"This was good work," he'd said. "Another reason why I'm really glad you decided to come to Dawn County."

Marco had good reason to not be a fan of authority despite actually being a part of authority. Yet he became a fan of the sheriff that day. Not only had he allowed Marco to stay at the scene, he'd okayed him and Carlos to stick around Detective Lovett as he did his investigation. To-

gether the three of them had been painfully thorough
going through Conrad's house. The only break Marco
had taken was to call Bella and let her know that Conrad
would no longer be stalking her. That he would no longer
be a threat to her or her family ever again.

What happened after that became a blur of cataloging
evidence, talking to several people that Conrad's death
would directly affect and, his least favorite, paperwork.

In between that paperwork and coming home, his
phone had died just as his thoughts became consumed
with everything that had happened. He needed to let go,
he knew that, but during his shower he couldn't focus
on anything else.

Not calling his sister or parents to let them know that
the threat was gone. Not notifying Carlos to let him know
that he was no longer at work but would be coming in
the next day. Not even reaching out to Bella, who was
starting to become an almost every-moment thought in
his head.

Something felt unfinished to Marco but he didn't know
what or why and that something had been bothering him
when he'd heard the knock at his front door.

Seeing Bella had been a shock to his system that had
quickly turned to fire in his veins. Seeing her standing
there, face deepening into the shade of crimson, and with
a Halloween platter holding dessert, something inside
Marco changed.

All at once and yet, not.

He hadn't planned on kissing her and he decided
against planning to stop. And, unless he was missing
the mark, Bella seemed to be on the same page.

While his hands ran through her hair and then down
to the small of her back, hers roamed the space across his

bare chest and up over his shoulders. They explored the back of his neck, then up into his hair. Then they went rogue, traveling everywhere.

Her lips were hot against his, her body too. He could feel the heat through her blouse.

It made him want her more.

They seemed again to be on the same page.

At the edge of his bed, she took her own shirt off and threw it across the room like she was playing a carnival game and gunning for the top prize. It was such an abrupt movement that Marco actually paused to laugh.

"What?" Bella's voice was low and smoldering. The towel around his waist was becoming tighter by the second.

"Nothing. Nothing at all."

Even to his ears, his voice had dropped to gravel and a growl.

After that, there was no space between them until both were on top of his bed. Somewhere between the floor and the covers, Bella had lost another article of clothing.

Marco ran his hand down the curve of her breast before hooking his thumb around her nipple. She let out a little gasp as he replaced his hand with his tongue.

"Holy macaroni," she breathed.

Marco hadn't heard that one before but he found it oddly endearing.

He moved his mouth up to her collarbone before dancing the line of her neck to her jaw. There he kissed up to her ear and whispered once more with the voice that let her know exactly what it was that he wanted even if he didn't say the exact words.

"I never got to ask, if you decided that you'd jumped the gun with me or not."

Bella's lips were parted. She was breathing heavily, not a pant but definitely not steady.

"If you're asking if I've decided if I like you, Deputy Rossi, I can assure you I don't make banana bread for just anyone."

Those lips, those perfect lips, curved up at the corners.

Bella Greene was being cheeky.

And Marco was loving every second of it.

THE TOWEL CAME off with unsurprising speed. Mostly because Bella was the one who freed the deputy from it. After that, there was no more banter or teasing. It was just two people who had been fighting an attraction finally giving in. Finally being free.

At least, that's what it felt like to Bella. Logically she knew that she and Marco hadn't known each other long. That she didn't know his middle name or even his mother's name and if you asked her what his favorite color or his favorite movie was, she'd have had to shrug. But life was weird and timing was even stranger. Because, even though she knew she didn't really know the man, Bella couldn't help but feel like he was it.

He was the reason why she hadn't been that interested in her dating life since coming to Kelby Creek.

It felt like a part of her had been waiting.

Waiting for Marco to come to town.

It was a significant thought that popped into Bella's head as the two of them collided beneath the sheets, but it was one that was still there two hours later as they tucked back into bed after their shower. Something that was also very stimulating.

Bella's head was resting against Marco's bare chest, her arm carefully thrown over his stomach, and she was vaguely aware of the sound of the heat turning on and blowing through the vents above. She'd helped rebandage his stitches and had finally been able to take a closer look at the bruising and now-healing cuts he'd gotten from the attacks. Even though she was looking at the ceiling, she knew she was near a particularly nasty cut that had very narrowly missed needing stitches.

It was all the reminder needed to pull a sigh from her.

The arm Marco had around her shifted, and his thumb rubbed her back.

"What's wrong?" His voice brushed against the darkness around them. Moonlight, streaming through a crack in the blinds over the window across from the bed, provided the only illumination in the room. Instead of being afraid as she had been at her parents' house at the thought of being in the darkness alone, now she felt oddly content. No doubt because of the man wrapped around her.

Still, all the good in the world couldn't chip away the idea of Conrad Abernethy and his obsession that had led to his own death.

"What's right?" The question slipped out of her mouth before she could stop it.

Marco continued to rub her back.

"I happen to think this feels pretty right," he said, tone light. "And I *really* enjoyed how right it felt to do what we did earlier in this very bed and then in the shower." She felt him shrug. "But that could just be me."

Bella let out a small but true laugh.

Then it all went away. She could no longer keep herself from talking about the one thing she had told herself she wouldn't when she had been headed to Marco's in the first place.

"I'm sorry you had to shoot him," she said. "I can't

imagine how hard that is and, I just wanted to let you know that I'm here if you want to talk about it. Anytime."

Bella thought she had messed up. Marco stiffened. But then, slowly, that tension let out. His voice was soft as he responded, though he caught her off guard with what he said.

"Can I ask you a question? One that might sound a bit pointless now?"

Bella nodded against him.

"Sure. Anything."

"Do you know why your dad decided to trust me? I mean, did he tell you why, because I got the impression he doesn't do that with everyone."

"He doesn't," she said, sure in her words. "For my dad, trust can only ever be earned. It's never something that's given. So, I guess in the hospital you must've earned that trust. Though, I have to point out, you did also save his favorite child."

She meant for him to laugh or do that quick chuckle that she was becoming accustomed to. The one that felt like a bad boy still trying to be bad despite being humored by a woman a full foot shorter than him.

He didn't.

He was sticking to her father and the trust he'd earned.

"I told him something," he went on to say. "In the hospital. I told him the story of why I came to Kelby Creek, of all places, and I don't understand why that was enough to earn anything, especially trust."

Bella switched her focus to avoiding tensing. She wondered why her father had been so quick to get on Team Rossi but hadn't asked him. Just like she hadn't asked Marco what had happened that made him decide to become the law in a town that couldn't help but look down on those in charge.

But now that he was on the cusp of potentially telling her, Bella hoped he would shed the rest of his armor and trust her with the answer.

To her utter surprise, he continued talking.

And he gave her more than she could've hoped for.

"What I didn't tell your dad was something that I've already touched on with you a little bit," he started. "See, my biological parents were really young when they got pregnant with me and then they were still young when they got pregnant with Amy. That in itself wouldn't have been necessarily an issue but my mother was killed in a mugging shortly after Amy was born, and my father couldn't handle that. He took us to his mother's house and then left and never came back. My grandmother tried to take care of us but had never really wanted to be a mom in the first place. That went double for a grandmother taking care of her two small grandchildren. That's how we entered foster care two years after we were dropped off."

Marco didn't pause or hesitate. It was like he was reading a teleprompter or saying something that he'd rehearsed. It made Bella's heart ache even more at how detached he sounded from it.

She couldn't help but hold him a little bit tighter as he continued.

"We got lucky and were adopted pretty quickly. They're very loving parents and since they got us so young, they're really all we know. A lot of the time, I know 'specially for Amy, we forget that we aren't biologically theirs. But, sometimes, there are these moments where all I can see are the cracks that had to be created for us to fall through to get to them."

He sighed. Bella waited.

"Originally I thought I joined law enforcement because I had always felt protective of my sister and wanted to keep her safe, even when we were little. I felt an almost peace in that. But then I realized that the real reason I wanted to be an officer or deputy was because of what happened to my biological mom. In my head, I knew there was nothing I could have done to save her, not even the remote possibility, considering I was a toddler. But I guess in my heart, I always felt that if I couldn't save her, then the least I could do was save someone else."

He let out another breath. It was long and low. Bella doubted even if the lights were on that she would have been able to read whatever emotion was currently resting in his expression. The best thing she could do for him in that moment was to stay still and listen.

So she did, her own heart in a vise.

"Because we were lucky enough to have such great adoptive parents and, honestly, a great childhood, Amy and I became big believers in the idea of choosing your family, instead of just being born into it," he continued. "When I became a deputy at the sheriff's department at my last job, I didn't mean to do it but I chose everyone there as my family."

This time tension ringed Marco's body. No hint of relaxing came with it.

"There was one guy in particular that, in hindsight, I realize I might have looked up to as a father figure. He was my mentor when I first got there and, because of staffing issues, actually became my partner for a while." Bella felt him shake his head, as if disapproving of his past self's actions. "I didn't see it at first. I should have, but I just didn't. You know how they say you can only ever be betrayed by your friends? Well, it was a hard truth that I learned very quickly when I caught him planting evidence on one of the town's repeat offenders."

The way he said it, the clear pain and anger in it, made Bella shift so she could stare up at his profile. He was looking up at the ceiling but she knew all he was seeing was the past.

"He was quick to remind me that this guy was a nobody and that this way we could get him out of our hair for good. But that didn't work for me and so the guy who was supposed to have my back tried to use that friendship as a reason not to turn him in. I *owed* him. But I didn't listen. Instead I marched right up to the sheriff's office and told him everything." That anger came out again, moving through the end of his sentence like a snake hiding in the tall grass and waiting to pounce. "I'd been there for three years, *three* years of hard work, dedication and absolute loyalty. And not just with any one person but with the entire department. They were family. I trusted them. But they didn't trust me."

Bella had to say something then, partly because she herself was starting to get angry too. Marco had already done so much for her and it had only been a few weeks since they met. Having him around for three years? She couldn't imagine not believing in him completely.

"What do you mean they didn't trust you?" she asked, hotly. "They thought you were lying?"

Marco shrugged.

"My partner managed to convince them that I was trying to pit cop against cop in some weird power trip and everyone jumped on the bandwagon. Then, when I brought up the hard evidence I had against him, no one said a word until the sheriff offered me a deal to save face for the department. He would make my partner retire early, I would get a promotion and no one would have to know outside of the department what had happened if I just dropped everything."

"I can assume by you being here that you didn't take that deal."

Marco shook his head.

"I made it public so it would warrant an investigation. The sheriff took heat, lost his reelection, and all the people who were so quick to not trust me decided that I was still in the wrong. I even had one guy tell me that you don't stab family in the back, to which I replied they weren't my family after all. A week later, I decided to apply for a job here, in Kelby Creek. In my mind, if I was going to have to work for redemption, then I should at least do it somewhere people worthy of that redemption were. That's why I'm here. And *that* is what I told your father."

Bella's body was sore. From a myriad of things that went from pain to pleasure, but she wasted no time sitting up to look at the man still holding her.

Even in the darkness, his eyes were easy to see.

They locked on to her gaze and waited.

Bella smiled.

"If you're asking, without asking, why my father decided to trust you based on that story, I can tell you exactly why and even use an example I've heard him use before." She placed her hand gently on his chest, his heart beat thumping against her palm. She hoped he heard her, *really* heard her, and the pride that went behind her words. "You walked into someone's house that was on fire and you tried to help them and you got burned. Then instead of never ever risking that pain again, you walked into another burning building, trying to help those who might be inside."

She shrugged, knowing it was not a pretty or completely accurate analogy but she still brought it home, just as she'd heard her father do before when talking about trust.

"The people who earn trust are those who deserve trust. And those who try to help people by being selfless and asking for nothing in return but the common courtesy of being decent? Well, that's a slam dunk in my father's book. Just as it is in mine. I trust you because you're worth trusting."

Bella lowered her head to his and kissed Marco for all she was worth. When she pulled away, her lips were still tingling. Had someone not started banging on the apartment's front door, Bella was sure that kiss would've continued.

But someone did and that was all Marco needed to become her protector all over again.

Chapter Sixteen

When danger struck and the woman you were falling for was with you, there wasn't any time for a wardrobe change.

Marco was out of bed in nothing but his boxers and to his gun in a flash.

"Stay here."

Bella wrapped the covers around her and didn't listen. Marco made sure he was at the door first, Bella securely behind him. His weapon was low, his shirt and pants were back in his room, and he sounded ready to fight when he called out.

"Who is it?"

There was an immediate answer back.

"Marco?" It was a woman's voice. "Let me in! It's cold out here."

Bella made a quick plea to hold on but he was acting on reflex. Marco couldn't believe what he was hearing. Out of a protectiveness that was wholly different than what he felt for Bella, Marco didn't try to make himself decent. He lowered his gun and opened the door.

The cold from outside rushed in and hit his chest and legs. Marco didn't mind it. He was caught between smiling, laughing and being absolutely concerned.

"Amy?"

Amy Rossi-Johnson had a suitcase at her side, a hand on her hip and was nothing but stern.

"First of all, how dare you not call me back *or* answer your phone when I call," she nearly yelled. "Secondly—"

Amy stopped herself. Her eyebrow rose and she did a quick scan of the scene in front of her.

Marco in his boxers.

Bella wrapped in the blanket from his bed.

Clearly past normal visiting hours for just friends.

Definitely not what she had expected.

"Oh, well, if I had known I was interrupting..."

Marco groaned, realizing there was no way to spin what he was seeing. Not that he wanted to but he doubted this was how Bella had wanted to meet his sister for the first time.

"If you'd known, you'd still do it. Now get inside." Marco grabbed her suitcase. "I don't need the neighbors seeing me in my underwear too."

Amy went from maternal worry to sisterly curiosity in a flash. She moved past him like water around rocks in a persistent stream and was on Bella in a second.

"Hi, I'm Amy. Marco's sister."

Bella, to her credit, went with the flow. Despite how red her face had turned, she held out her hand and was all polite.

"Nice to meet you! I'm Bella. Bella Greene."

Marco took the suitcase and set it down next to the couch. In any other circumstance, he knew Amy would've been ravenous for more details, but in the moment she put her hand on her chest.

"You're the one who saved him," she exclaimed. "You went with the bad guy so he wouldn't get hurt."

None of it was a question. Still, Bella nodded.

"Though, to play devil's advocate, I was the reason he was in danger in the first place."

Amy shook her head.

"I don't think so, lady. You deserve the praise I gave you and more."

Unlike Marco, his little sister was a very openly affectionate person. She believed in pats on the back, hands on cheeks and hugs that were too tight and went on for far too long. Bella being her target warranted no exception. Amy pulled her into a hug while saying thank-you.

Again, to Bella's credit, she was nothing but grace as she accepted it.

"Where's Matthew?" Marco asked, trying to distract Amy from squeezing the life out of his guest. "And why are *you* here?"

It was like she'd been slapped. His sister turned around so fast even her short hair moved at the speed.

"Matthew is at a work conference that I assured him he didn't have to leave unless I needed him to. I won't dignify your second question with an answer other than I am your sister and you were in the hospital two times in one day. Not to mention you were there because someone was trying to kill you. If that doesn't warrant your sister-bestie coming down to check on you, then I don't know what does."

Marco snorted.

"I thought you weren't going to dignify my question with an answer."

"And you're just lucky that I convinced Mom and Dad to wait to come out here next weekend and not with me instead." That annoyed sisterly affection turned quickly into a smirk. "Can you imagine if Mom and Dad walked into this? You'd never live it down."

Marco rolled his eyes, mainly because he knew that since Amy had interrupted them, he still wasn't going to live it down. She was going to tell this story at all holiday functions for the rest of their lives. Because that's what the Rossi siblings did. They loved each other wholeheartedly and they loved to tease each other wholeheartedly too.

"Can I just say that I personally am thankful that you showed up and not your parents?" Bella chimed in. "As far as first impressions go, I was kind of hoping with your parents I'd be a little more charming and a lot more clothed."

Amy laughed out loud. Marco caught himself pausing.

He'd told Bella more than he'd ever told anyone else. Not only about what happened at his past job but why exactly it hurt him so deeply. That meant a lot and he wasn't sure if she even realized how much. But he also knew that the kind of situation that they had been in the past few days, one that was high stress and danger and fear, could incite an emotional and physical connection that could go away just as quickly as it had come on.

Now that Conrad was no longer a part of the picture, how would Bella feel the next day about him? Without emotions running high. How would she feel the next week or month?

Would she really want to meet his parents or did she just feel that way because of the connection they'd shared earlier?

Marco didn't know the answers and, as Bella searched his face, he wished he did. Instead he excused himself.

"Speaking of clothes, I think I'm going to go grab some more."

"I think I'll join you," Bella tacked on, jumping ahead of him to hurry down the hall.

Amy laughed and called after them.

"And I'm going to make some coffee, because there's no way we're not talking about *everything* that's happened, Big Brother!"

FRIDAY MORNING CAME like nothing out of the ordinary had gone on the week before. Bella returned to her house and walked through it alone, trying to shake off the fear that had settled in her chest when she had first seen the message written on the mirror.

The sky darkened outside, promising eventual rain, but slowly Bella started to melt back into the warmth that her house had always made her feel. Then she took out a page from her mother's book and worked the rest of her anxiety off by doing the one thing that she could absolutely control.

She cleaned.

To the normal chores of laundry and dishes, she added a deep clean of the bathrooms and kitchen. After that, she took to her bedsheets and quilt. All the while trying not to think about Conrad Abernethy or, even, Deputy Marco Rossi.

Bella failed on both accounts but none more so than the man she'd almost spent the night with.

Bella caught her reflection in the hallway mirror and smiled. That smile brought on a blush and a giggle only meant for her. There she had been taking banana nut bread to a man who'd saved her life only to fall into his bed, then into his shower, then right back into bed again.

It had felt so right, especially after a week that had felt so wrong.

But then Amy had shown up and brought Bella and Marco back down to reality.

Then Bella had seen the look.

The look Marco had given her while standing there with his sister.

Bella's reflection frowned.

Had they moved too fast? Had danger fused them together and now without it they'd fall apart?

Bella looked away from the mirror. She gathered up the rest of her linens and marched to the laundry room.

After getting dressed, she'd excused herself from Marco's apartment, insisting that the brother and sister spend time together, considering Amy had come all the way from New York out of worry.

Marco hadn't fought her on it and only asked that she text him when she returned to her parents' house for the night. She had and his response had been a simple Good.

And then when she stopped feeling like some schoolgirl with a crush, Bella thought about Conrad.

It didn't make sense to her. His obsession? He barely paid attention to her during their date. In fact she'd even made the joke to her mother that she could have put a mirror in her chair and left and Conrad would have been perfectly happy still talking to himself *about* himself.

Was that how obsession worked?

Someone who paid you no attention suddenly couldn't do anything but?

It put another chill down Bella's spine. She was almost thankful for the distraction of someone ringing the doorbell.

Bella hurried down the hall, phone in the front pocket

of her overalls, and felt the nerves tighten her stomach when she realized it was none other than Amy standing on her front porch.

"Two days in a row that I've caught you unaware," Amy greeted, laughing as she did so. "I hope you don't mind. Marco went to work and I don't want to stay all day in his depressing apartment." She motioned around herself to the house. "I'll be honest, I'm a much bigger fan of this beauty."

Bella laughed, stepped to the side and waved her in.

"Anyone who compliments my house is surely allowed inside of it."

Amy was a study in contrasts to her brother. She was petite, wide-eyed and didn't seem to hold back when it came to talking. She graciously took a seat on the couch in the living room and got down to brass tacks without any provocation.

"I honestly thought I'd be more tired since I felt like I was in airports and flying all of yesterday but after Marco left for work I couldn't go back to sleep. I also kind of wanted to see what Kelby Creek was like on my own."

Bella took the seat opposite her on an old, worn chair that had once belonged to her grandmother. It felt as comfortable as she was starting to feel with Amy, a feat considering she still felt embarrassment from being caught in just a sheet the night before.

"I'm sure our town's past and what's happened with me the last few weeks probably hasn't given you the best impression," Bella said. "Not that any of that has been sitting well with any of us locals."

Amy surprised her with a shake of her head.

"Not to sound blunt but I didn't actually care about what happened here in town. With the corruption." She raised her hands in defense. "Not that I'm saying it doesn't matter, just that I already understood why Marco wanted to move here in the first place. He wanted to help and, from what I can tell, this town might need that. And as for you and this whole creepy stalker business, I'm not about to blame you for something a guy with issues decided to do. Plus, find me a place in this world that doesn't have at least one guy doing something absolutely creepy."

Her laugh undercut the seriousness of the topic, though Bella could see that she wasn't happy with any of it.

"What I really wanted to figure out, to really understand on my own, is what about this place has made Marco want to stay."

Bella's cheeks became hot. She wasn't exactly sure why. She tried to cover the quick change with a little laugh of her own.

"I didn't even know that he was thinking about leaving but he definitely wouldn't be the first to skip town given our history."

Amy waved her hands through the air, dismissing the thought.

"He isn't talking about leaving or anything like that but I feel like he is thinking about staying. For a while." Even though Amy didn't really know Bella and vice versa, she dropped all pretenses and became serious. "Normally I wouldn't do this to my brother, pry into his personal life. At least, not so directly. I also am not going to pretend that his job can't be dangerous, and there's not anything that would stop him from doing it. But when he called me at the hospital and then when we talked later that night, I could tell something was different about Kelby Creek. Something that was important."

Bella found herself leaning in, completely enraptured by the insights of someone so close to Marco. It was like a mirror effect—Amy leaned in a little as she continued to talk.

"I asked him last night if he had told you about our past, our family and what happened to him and his last job." She smiled. It was brief but poignant. "To say I was absolutely surprised that he had opened up to someone about that is the understatement of the century in my book. In fact I don't think he's ever told anyone the specifics of how we ended up where we are now, and that goes double for how he was completely let down by those he considered his close friends in North Carolina. But, given the fact that he did open up to you, I'm going to take that on good faith and do the same."

Amy hesitated but Bella didn't think it was because she wasn't ready to talk about whatever it was she was about talk about. Instead it was like she was trying to choose her words carefully. When she finally found them, Amy didn't break eye contact once.

"Marco thinks the reason why my husband and I moved to New York was because I was feeling nostalgic for our biological family. I wasn't. The truth was that I realized early on that Marco would spend the rest of his life just as he had up until then trying to take care of me. To protect me. I realized that he would most likely always go where I went to keep that up and, let me just say, I am so grateful to have such a great brother and I truly love him with all of my heart, but I didn't want him to do that. I didn't want him to mold his life around mine just because he felt he had to because of everything we had been through. So, my husband and I moved to the one place in the entire world that I knew Marco would never willingly live because of our past."

"New York."

Amy nodded.

"I know that kind of sounds harsh, but honestly my husband and I don't plan to live in New York for the rest of our lives. The fact of the matter is I've been waiting for *Marco* to find the place he wants to live. Somewhere that he himself chooses without any thought or feeling of responsibility for me. And then, and only then, will Matthew and I try to find a place there too."

"You'd move to Kelby Creek if Marco decided to stay?"

Amy didn't skip a beat.

"I know it probably doesn't make sense to a lot of people to uproot their lives just to try to make a new one around a sibling, but I've seen the world be cruel to my brother and entirely undeserving of him. I have seen foster parents, biological family members that have come out of the woodwork and people who were supposed to have Marco's back let him down. And still he worries about them. About everyone, even if he won't admit it. In my opinion Marco deserves, at the very least, to be surrounded by people who care about him and want to be there because of their feelings for him."

Amy stopped, like she was ending the conversation, but Bella felt like it was just getting started.

"So, you came to Kelby Creek to check on Marco but also to scope out the town?"

Amy was smiling again, her dark eyes almost a match for her brother's.

"I came to check on him, yes. I also came to figure out what about this place made him talk like he was already growing roots." That smile turned into a grin. "And let's just say, I don't think it has anything to do with the weather."

That blush that had been turning up throughout her conversation with Amy had now moved down into Bella's stomach and become a different kind of warmth. She didn't push for any more specifics about Marco or what his sister thought about him. Instead Bella did what she felt in the moment to be right.

She laughed, smiled and stood up, raring to go.

"Speaking of the weather, would you be interested in seeing the reason why I'm wearing overalls before the rain sets in? It's only a quick drive across town."

Amy matched her energy. She jumped up, keys already in hand.

"A lady's day while Marco freaks out about what we're doing while he's stuck at work? Count me in!"

Bella got a few things, grabbed her bag and locked up the house. They were sitting in Amy's rental and heading in the direction of Justin's house within minutes.

Neither woman saw him standing outside, watching them. Neither woman had any clue that, even though he no longer had his mask, that wouldn't stop what he had planned next.

Nothing would.

Chapter Seventeen

It was a piece of paper. Harmless and plain. The words written across it? Also harmless and relatively plain.

Hello there, friend.

Marco looked up from the note Bella had given him from the tool bag that had been in her truck. Carlos was in his desk chair and looked about ready to fall asleep.

"Sorry," he said. "Probably not the best thing to greet you with. I just can't get over this case."

Carlos tapped the notebook beneath the piece of paper Marco had been staring at. They were his notes, beneath them the official paperwork he was supposed to be doing instead.

In any other case, Marco still would have procrastinated on that paperwork. Crossing the *t*'s and dotting the *i*'s. It felt like he was back in grade school with an assignment he was wondering how to make his sister do instead or, another old pain, taking a standardized test. This time around though, he was avoiding it *because* of what was across each paper.

This case.

Conrad Abernethy's documented stalking, undeniable attacks and eventual death.

Marco wasn't sure about that. About any of it.

"Did you know Conrad?"

Marco leaned back in his own office chair. They were in the bullpen at the department and two of three who were strapped to desks doing the more technical side of being a deputy. Detective Lovett was still out and about while Sheriff Chamblin was dealing with a press conference on Conrad's death. Thankfully the sheriff had agreed to leave Bella's name out of his speech and comments. Something Marco was grateful for.

"I knew *of* him but I can't remember actually meeting him." Carlos's brows furrowed in thought. "I might have seen him at a Super Bowl party once, but that could be said about the whole dang town."

Marco ran his thumb along his jaw. He was frustrated and couldn't pinpoint one reason why.

He felt the weight of his service weapon in his holster against his hip. His thoughts went back to the night before. He shook his head at himself.

"Listen, I'm not going to pretend to know you all that well yet," Carlos said. "But I think I can swing and hit something based on how you're all scrunched up in the face. Something isn't sitting right with you. What is it?"

Marco debated on saying anything, but then he heard Bella and her claim of him having armor. Marco knew it was there and, for the first time in his life, he'd told someone who wasn't his family why it was there.

He hadn't meant to open up like that to Bella and yet, once he had, he felt no regret. Instead there was a calmness to him after. With just a look of encouragement or a soft touch to remind him that he wasn't alone, Bella had made him feel…safe.

Which was why his concern now bothered him so much. He should have felt relief at Conrad's death.

He didn't.

Instead he was bothered by it.

Ignoring that wouldn't do anyone any good, so for the second time in two days, Marco opened up to someone he hadn't planned on.

"I guess I don't feel like this thing is over." It was the first time Marco had said it out loud. Carlos took that concern and mirrored it.

"What do you mean?"

Marco motioned to the paperwork on his desk.

"There are holes," he said, simply.

"Holes."

Marco touched his own notes on top. There was a descending list of events that had happened in chronological order.

"This whole thing is like a rotted-out tree. All we did was cut off the branches but the roots are still there. The problem *seems* solved but I have a feeling that we haven't dealt with one damn root."

Carlos didn't laugh or question the clumsy analogy. Instead he jumped in.

"We found Conrad with the mask and letters that matched the handwriting on the messages Bella had been getting. Plus Conrad and Bella had a connection right before she started getting those messages."

Marco conceded to that but he still couldn't get over the feeling.

"All the leads we followed or got during the last month came to a dead end. The only reason we're saying Conrad is guilty is because of what we found in his house."

"The very damning evidence that we found in his house," Carlos interjected. "Not to mention a bullet that did him in."

Marco snapped his fingers.

"It seems like that happened—that I shot him at the storage facility—but if I had, wouldn't there have been blood?" It was something he'd already brought up right after finding Conrad. "Escaping from that building before backup arrived was his number one goal. Not cleaning up any and all traces of blood. I mean, you saw his wound. There's no way he didn't bleed somewhere after being hit."

Carlos moved his head side to side, accepting the less than concrete story they'd had to put together.

"He could have gotten lucky. You said it yourself that neither you nor Bella got a really great look at what he was wearing. He could have been layered up and that caught the blood."

Marco didn't like that answer. Just as he hadn't the first time they'd come up with it. He didn't like the unsettling feeling still there either. It's what had weighed on his gut around the time his former partner had planted evidence. Marco had picked up on something being wrong; he just hadn't figured it out until it was too late.

He didn't want to make that same mistake now. Not with Bella.

"Okay," Carlos kept on. "Let's step through the rest and see what's hanging you up. Starting with Bella and her truck breaking down and you stopping to see if you could help. You think Conrad was going to try to take her then, right?"

Marco sat straighter in his chair.

He nodded.

"There was water in her gas tank, not enough to keep her engine from starting but enough to make her break down away from her house. She also found the note in her tool bag, though she admits she hadn't opened it in a while so there's a chance it had been there longer."

"So you potentially interrupt the attempt and take her to Crisp's to wait for her dad and brother to get there. Then you don't see her until we're at the bar two weeks later."

"In between that time, we run into an unusual amount of car trouble where the gas tank and lines had been tampered with, along with a slashed tire. So I approached Bella at the bar to ask her about her truck but don't get the chance because we were called away."

"Almost everyone was that night," Carlos added. "Thank you, prank calls."

"The next day Bella comes by to finish our conversation but we're interrupted again. This time by the power going out. So we decide to get dinner instead." Marco left out the part where most of their conversation had been personal and that he hadn't actually gotten around to talking about her truck then either. "Then the next night we get the call about Jennifer Parkridge's break-in and see that only her door was broken and a plant inside along with it. We call in Bella and her family to fix it."

"And later that night you go for a run and—" Carlos clapped his hands together and made a splat sound effect.

"A guy in a Halloween mask tries to run me down, just as Bella finds the message on her bathroom mirror." Marco paused, only because he hated that part. Just like he wasn't a fan at all of the next. "Bella comes to the hospital to tell me and, during that time, someone puts water in her gas tank. Someone who wore a mask to do the deed, so getting him on camera at the hospital parking lot did nothing for us. The same *no luck* with the truck that rammed us after we left."

That truck had been turned inside out but no clue, piece of evidence or record of who owned it and where it had come from was found. There were no vehicle identification number or prints either.

And, once again, no blood.

"Then there's the fact that he had a code to the storage facility," Marco continued. "The list of people renting the units that Lovett got from the building manager didn't have Conrad's name on it. In fact he had no record of Conrad ever using any of their outside units either."

"But then we loop back to the small-town thing," Carlos pointed out. "Who's to say he didn't get it from a friend he was helping move to speed up the process? There were a lot of people on that list and just because we didn't find a connection to Conrad, doesn't mean there wasn't one."

Marco, again, had accepted that earlier. Like Carlos said, it wasn't outside the realm of possibility in a small town like Kelby Creek.

"And then we go to see if Conrad is around and find his body, the mask and the notes with the same phrase and handwriting that Bella had gotten in his room," Marco concluded. "The back door cracked open, just like it was waiting for us to come in."

Carlos rolled his chair closer to his desk. He lowered his voice.

"You seemed okay with all of this yesterday. What changed?"

Marco had been struggling with that all night. Ever since his sister had shown up. Just like he hadn't planned on sharing with the deputy, he hadn't expected to explain in detail what he did next.

"Bella was at my apartment last night, late," he started.

Carlos remained impassive but Marco bet it was a topic he'd bring up later when they weren't in such a serious conversation. "While we were talking, someone started banging on my front door. We weren't expecting anyone so I got my gun, made Bella stay back and then called through to the door to see who it was."

"Who was it?"

"My sister, Amy. She came into town because she was worried about me, but I had no idea it was her—none at all—until she said something." Marco lowered his voice and glanced down at his gun. Finally he hit the moment that had shaken his confidence in the case. "When I first heard the banging against the door, I was on my gun in seconds. Every part of me was ready, but not to defend us. I was ready to use it because I was sure it was him."

That, Carlos took seriously. His expression darkened.

"The masked man?"

Marco nodded.

"My gut yelled and told me that there was still a chance that he was coming for Bella and I needed to fight first, reason it out later."

"But it was your sister."

Marco nodded, slow.

"And I calmed down after that," he said. "I went through the facts and told myself it was over."

He looked down at his notes again.

"But it doesn't feel like it's over anymore," Carlos finished.

Marco shook his head.

"No. It doesn't."

They lapsed into a small silence. It wasn't like his feelings could compete with actual evidence.

Carlos seemed to pick up on the thought.

"Why don't we head to see Amanda?" he asked. "She'll probably be done with the autopsy by now and can give you a little more peace of mind. Plus, I wouldn't mind stopping for some food on the way back. I've already eaten half of the vending machine today."

Marco decided that was better than sitting around, brooding.

They took their lunch break and Carlos's car and headed to Haven Hospital. There were a few people bustling around the waiting room but Carlos led Marco to the elevator and down to the basement. It wasn't the first time Marco had gone to a hospital's morgue for work but it was the first time he'd had the displeasure of doing it in Kelby Creek. Though, if he were being honest, all morgues to him looked the same.

The coroner, however, did not.

Amanda Alvarez had neon pink–tipped hair and scrubs, and didn't notice them at first. When she looked up from her desk, she made a *yip* noise and put her hand to her chest.

"Geez Louise, Park," Amanda exclaimed. "Give me a one-way ticket to my own metal slab, why don't you."

Park laughed.

"Sorry, Amanda. I should have called ahead."

Amanda's surprise shifted when she looked at Marco. He wasn't sure if she remembered meeting him during his first week but she made it clear that she meant the pointed stare.

"I was about to call you."

Marco and Carlos shared a quick look.

"You were going to call me?" Marco repeated.

She nodded.

"I called Foster right before you came in. He told me to call you because of your friendship with Bella Greene."

Marco's gut was yelling. Still, he kept his voice calm. "Why?"

Amanda stood up, came around her desk and took Carlos's hand. The deputy raised his eyebrow but let her lead him a few steps back from Marco.

"Pretend this is Conrad Abernethy," she started, focused on Marco. "The bullet that killed him landed here." She pressed her finger to a spot below Carlos's rib cage. It made him jump but she continued, unperturbed. "Now, the assumption was that he was hit from several yards away and then bled out at home after not getting seen about it."

"But you don't think that happened," Marco guessed.

She shook her head.

"He *was* shot here but it was at a closer range. And I don't think it was a through-and-through."

"I thought you said you couldn't find the bullet?" Carlos interjected. "If it wasn't in him, then it had to have gone through."

"But you didn't find it either," she returned. "Same with an impact area that would have been made after it went through him. Which got me really thinking about where this missing bullet went."

If Marco had been sitting down, he would have been on the edge of his seat.

"What conclusion did you come to?" he asked, muscles tightening in anticipation. His earlier feeling that something was off was slowly becoming worse.

Amanda put her finger back on Carlos's stomach.

"When I went to take a closer look, I noticed trauma halfway through Mr. Abernethy and then more trauma on the way out." She turned Carlos so his side was facing Marco. He made a noise but she shushed him. "I think he was shot at a much closer range, the bullet lodged inside him as he bled out and *then*—" she ran her finger from Carlos's stomach, over his side and then to a spot on his back that would have made a straight line "—someone extracted the bullet postmortem."

Marco felt his own eyes widen.

Carlos no longer cared that he was being used as a live dummy.

"Wait," Carlos started. "You think someone shot him and then took the bullet out. Why?"

Marco took a step forward, as if closer proximity would make a new truth materialize. Yet it wasn't happening. That bad feeling had expanded into an ever-growing balloon. Adrenaline was already starting to flood through him.

Because he knew.

He knew right then that he'd messed up.

That he never should have left Bella alone.

Not when he had doubt.

Not until he was 100 percent sure.

"He did it so we wouldn't find out that the bullet that killed Conrad didn't come from my gun. So that we'd think that Conrad was the one I shot at and not him. He did it so we'd leave Bella alone."

Even to Marco's ears, his voice had gone cold. Dark. Unforgiving. When he bottom-lined the terrifying reality, he knew that everything was about to get worse.

"He did it so he could try and take her again."

Chapter Eighteen

"Well, not to be that person, but I don't know why he'd want a shed." Amy was staring at Justin's house in absolute awe. "No offense to you or your business."

Bella laughed, mostly because she'd heard it before. She said as much.

"My brother, Val, can't believe it either. He said if he had *Justin money*, he'd build a pool instead. He meant to say an infinity pool but he said X-finity. You know, like the cable service." Bella snorted. "Which is why I'm pretty sure Val will never have *Justin money*."

Amy laughed and followed Bella around the house to a seldom-used worn path she and her family had made during the construction process. They didn't always use it since they were now storing their tools in his garage, but since she had no idea if Justin was home or not, she didn't think it wise to try to walk through his house with a stranger just to get to his backyard.

"And this guy won't care that we're just walking around his place during the weekend?"

Bella nodded, though she wasn't entirely confident.

"I probably should have asked but when we started building the shed, he gave us free-range of the yard. I don't think he'll mind me just popping by to show it off."

Bella felt her own smile turn into a beam. "We're very proud of what we've made so far."

They cleared the house and the path curved, going downhill for a few yards before finally stopping.

Bella knew not everyone was impressed at their structures, especially when compared to the almost-mansion behind them, but she side-eyed Amy, hoping for a positive reaction. Since meeting Marco, the shed had gotten siding, a custom-built door and a roof. Plus, it had passed a few inspections. Even though they had windows, trim, the small porch and landscaping left, Bella was immensely proud of how it had turned out. More so because Justin had let them design the entire thing themselves, saying he trusted their vision.

Now Amy was smiling at the vision.

A warmth of pride spread through Bella, especially when Amy clapped.

"Holy guacamole, Bella! Did you really *build* this? Like with your own hands?"

Bella laughed again.

"Yes, but also with my dad and brother," she said. "It's a team effort when it comes to Greene Thumb and Hammer."

Amy shook her head, still smiling.

"Has Marco seen this? Surely he knows how much of a bad butt you are."

A blush, hot and true, scorched up Bella's neck and filled her cheeks. She might not have reacted so strongly to just the man's name but his sister catching her in a blanket the night before was still a fresh embarrassment.

Not only because they'd been caught, but because Bella hoped it was something that they could repeat.

That could become normal.

The two of them.

Did Marco feel the same?

She had no idea.

Bella decided not to hover around the uncertainty and instead enjoy Amy's company. One thing had been clear the night before and that was how much Marco loved his sister and vice versa. It made her want the youngest Rossi to like her as much as Bella was starting to like her.

"I've barely been here lately," Bella hedged.

Amy was persistent.

"Well, when we all have supper tonight, I'll make sure I tell him to get on that ASAP. This is seriously impressive."

Bella hadn't been aware they were doing supper but didn't question it. Instead she unlocked the padlock on the front door and gave a more in-depth tour of the structure. Amy asked questions about several things and how they were built, what came next and the vision of how it was supposed to turn out. It was exciting to have someone, especially a woman, paying such close attention. So much so that she didn't even notice at first when Justin walked up.

He cleared his throat and gave a small wave.

"Didn't mean to interrupt but I saw you out here and thought I'd see how you were doing," he greeted. Then he turned to Amy with a smile. "And introduce myself so you didn't think I was being inhospitable."

That blush came back full burn. Bella laughed through it.

"I'm so sorry, Justin. I wanted to show it off. I should have asked first."

He waved her off.

"Hey, I'm proud of this thing too. It's no sweat off my back."

"I'd be proud of it too," Amy said. "My husband and I couldn't even put together our IKEA bed frame!"

They all shared in another round of polite laughter and then Bella did the introductions. Justin, as always, was polite and engaging, the hallmarks of the businessman.

"We've been really lucky to have your brother here," he said after they'd shaken hands. "I don't know what we would do if something had happened to Bella. This town has already had too much bad in it. We don't need any more."

An expression she couldn't nail down went across Justin's face. He'd often had moments like that during the span of their friendship. Bella imagined she too would have those moments if the love of her life had died from such senseless violence like what had happened during The Flood to his wife.

Amy must have sensed that he had fallen back into a less than ideal emotion. She motioned to the shed as a whole.

"Well, I can't wait to see a picture of the finished product," she said. "I'm really bad at imagining finished products, hence my and my husband's lack of IKEA-building skills."

"I think I might be able to help with that." Justin thumbed back toward his house. "I have the sketch inside if you want to see it."

"Sketch?" Amy asked.

"We actually designed the structure ourselves and my mom sketched what the finished product is going to look like. We gave it to Justin for his okay." Bella smiled. "I didn't think you still had it."

"I wanted to hang it inside when it's all done." He shrugged. "I thought Grant would get a kick out of that."

Bella agreed her dad would.

"Well, if it's all right with everyone, I'd like to see it," Amy said. "I don't have anywhere else to be either."

"I wouldn't mind seeing it again," Bella admitted.

Justin led them up the slope of the backyard and to the patio. There were two doors. One going left to the garage and the other going into the eat-in kitchen area to the right. They followed him through into the kitchen.

"I have it downstairs in my workroom or either upstairs in my office." Justin chuckled. "I was never the most organized when it came to this house."

"You've seen the state of our tools," Bella pointed out. "Clearly you're a lot more put together than us Greenes."

They followed him through the kitchen, into the main entryway and up to a door tucked beneath one of the staircases.

"You go low and I'll go high?" he asked.

Bella's reaction was immediate. She cringed.

"Is there any way we can switch? Basements freak me out." It was the main reason she'd never gone down there before. And why she was glad that most houses in the Deep South didn't have them.

"I agree with that," Amy chimed in.

Justin smiled but hesitated enough to show that he felt something. Something that wasn't his polite, normal self.

"My wife was the same way." He seemed to shake himself and the feeling off. Then he pointed up the stairs. "First door on the left. It should be open already and either on my desk or on the cabinet behind it."

They split up and Bella and Amy made their way to

the designated room. Along the way, Amy commented on how well done the inside was.

"Does he live here alone?" she asked as they walked into the office. It, like the rest of the house, was pristine and grand. Bella imagined her own cluttered and small workspace at home. Before she could stop it, she wondered what Marco had thought of her home. Had he liked it? Had he wanted a tour that didn't involve her looking for clues?

Would he like to spend time there with her?

Bella pushed all those thoughts to the side and answered Amy, hoping she hadn't noticed the pause.

"Yeah, he has since his wife passed."

Bella smiled when Amy went to snooping around Justin's built-in bookcases and the picture frames and knickknacks it housed along with the hundred or so books on its shelves.

"I don't think I could stand being in a place this big by myself," she ventured. "Though I don't think I could stand being alone anywhere to be honest. I've been with Matthew since I was fifteen. I don't think I could even function without him."

Bella felt an odd ache. For Justin and his loss and for never having a loss at all. It was a weird feeling but somehow it pointed out the emptiness she'd had for the last few years.

This time she couldn't quite shake it off. So she focused on Justin and went to the desk at the back of the room. It was cluttered. She made sure to glance at the door before she spoke.

"When I first met him, he actually wasn't all that great," she said, quietly. "He was three-whiskeys deep at our local bar and looked like he was ready to just melt into the floor. I knew what had happened to his wife and I just felt so bad for him that I had to say something. After that, my family and I became friends with him and his mother. He's seemed a lot happier lately, which is nice."

After moving the papers and work debris around on the desk to find the large sketch, Bella came up empty.

But she did find something.

They was a set of keys, hidden beneath a pile of mail. She wouldn't have thought anything of them but the keychain caught her eye. It was bright pink instead of silver, a keepsake from a breast cancer awareness fundraiser. Bella knew this because she'd gone with her dad to it to show support for one of his friends.

"You found some keys?" Amy asked, losing interest in the contents of the bookcase.

Bella nodded.

"They're my dad's. He lost them the other day when he was rushing to come see me at the hospital. Justin ended up giving him a ride."

"Why are they up here?"

It was an innocent question. One that could have had an innocent answer.

Yet Bella froze as she looked at the keys. Or, rather, the old check signed beneath it.

Then, all at once, it clicked. Just like that.

Bella went from happy, content and safe to feeling sick.

Amy was no fool.

She noticed the change right away.

"Hey, what's wrong?"

Bella put the keys down and reached for her phone. She came up short. Her cell phone was in the car.

"Call your brother," she hurried, her voice wavering

and breaking. She was drowning in adrenaline, her heart-beat going from carefree and steady to terrified and panicked all at once.

Amy followed her instruction but asked why as she pulled her phone from her pocket.

"We need to get out of here," Bella hurried.

She started to move but something blocked the door. Someone.

Amy hadn't seen him yet. She repeated her question of why.

Justin, at the very least, was polite enough to respond, despite the gun he was holding in his hand.

"Because she just realized something, didn't you?"

Amy turned and froze. Her still-locked cell phone in her hand.

"What—what's going on?"

Bella wished she could close her eyes and make it all go away, but Justin kept on, never leaving the doorway or lowering his gun. He had it trained between them but he could change his aim in an instant, if he wanted.

"Go on, Bella. We don't have to keep any secrets from each other anymore," he said, all smiles. "Tell us what you've just figured out."

Bella shook her head. Justin wasn't a fan.

He moved his aim to Amy. She didn't move an inch. But Bella did.

She took the woman's hand in hers and held the other one up in a Stop motion.

"Don't! Please!" Bella pointed down at the desk. "It—it was the check right here. It's—it's the same handwriting as the notes."

Justin shook his head.

"I know you, Bella," he said, almost like a coo. "I

know your every expression. That face you're doing now?
It's the same one you do when you're trying to figure
out the dimensions on something when you're working.
You're calculating something and you can't calculate
without more than one figure. So what's the rest? Because I know there's more than just that."

He took a step inside.

Bella lowered her hand but didn't let go of Amy's. If
they weren't on the second floor, she would already have
pulled the woman to and through the window if possible.

But this wasn't a movie, and they'd probably never
even make it to the window without being shot first.

Bella didn't want that for Amy or herself.

She didn't want it for Marco either.

"The—the keys," she stumbled. "We figured that the
only way someone broke into my house was with a key.
Only—only my family has that."

She glanced down at her father's keys.

Justin seemed humored.

"But your father didn't realize they were gone until
the day after you found the message. So that could have
been nothing more than me finding them and holding
them here until he came back." He shrugged. "There has
to be something else."

There was.

Amy squeezed her hand. She was surprisingly calm.

Bella was barely keeping it together, but she answered,
not knowing what it would accomplish.

"I remembered the bar. When I first met you," she
managed. "I remembered that Conrad wasn't the only
person I said hello to when I was nervous."

"And, can you tell Ms. Amy here how you greet people when you're nervous?"

That sick feeling in Bella's stomach only spread. Justin's smile deepened. He was proud of her and that somehow made it all worse.

Bella let out a low, shaky breath, but she answered the man all the same.

"Hello there, friend."

Chapter Nineteen

No one answered their phones.

Not Bella. Not Amy.

Neither were in his apartment and neither were at Bella's house.

Marco met Grant and Val there while Bella's mom stayed at home, hoping they'd show up there.

"Mom's car is still here," Val greeted, face darkened with worry. He pointed to the car in the driveway.

"She's been borrowing it since her truck got totaled," Grant added, huffing up to them on the front porch.

"I think she might be with my sister. Her rental is gone and she's not answering either." Marco had to move past the anger and panic at both women missing and stay on their current course of action. He pointed to the door. "No one answered but I don't have a key."

Val nodded emphatically, bringing out his personal house key. He lived down the road from Bella and had gotten there within what felt like a minute. His father being with him had been a well-timed coincidence. It was lucky for Bella's house that they were quick. Marco had been about to break down the door when he called.

"I would have brought mine but my keys are still missing." Grant cussed low. After Marco had told Val that he needed to get inside Bella's house because she was missing, he'd underlined the urgency by saying that Conrad most likely wasn't the stalker.

Now they were all on high alert.

Val opened the door and all three spread out while calling Bella's and Amy's names. If his heart weren't beating out of his chest and his senses all sharpened to figure out what had happened to them, Marco would have taken a moment to feel something at the fact that the Greenes were calling out for his sister with just as much concern for her safety as Bella's.

But neither woman answered their calls.

The house was empty.

"The house is still locked up and her purse is gone," Marco summed up when they all made it back to the living room. Grant looked like he'd aged a decade just since the last time they'd seen each other a minute or so ago.

"So we think she left on her own?" Val asked.

"If she was taken," Marco said. "She most likely wouldn't have grabbed her purse unless her abductor needed it."

Grant shook his head.

"Her boots are gone. I think she left here without duress."

Marco gave the man a questioning look.

"Her boots?"

Val whirled around to the entryway. Marco followed. He pointed to a line of shoes against the wall. Between a pair of flats and a pair of tennis shoes was an empty space.

"She hates wearing them but said they're the only things that don't make her overalls look dorky," Val and

Grant started at the same time. Her father beat Val to the punch.

"Which means she's probably wearing her overalls!"

Marco didn't get it.

"Why does that matter?"

Grant grabbed Marco's wrist and pulled him to the front door.

"Bella only wears her overalls to do chores in or to work in. Never to leave the house in—not since some old classmate of hers said she looked like a strung-out farmer in them."

Val followed, unlocking his car over their shoulders with the remote. It honked twice, like it was picking up on their mounting urgency.

"The only reason she'd wear her boots was if she had on her overalls and the only reason she'd leave the house with both was because she was going to a jobsite," Val added on. "And the only site we have now is at Justin's."

"Bella might have wanted to show Amy the shed," Marco realized. He could work with that. He hurried along to his car. "Call Justin on the way. I'll follow."

Marco relayed where they were going to Carlos, who was meeting with Detective Lovett over at Conrad's house.

"Maybe their phones are just off and they're just fine," Carlos tried. But even as he said it, Marco heard the uncertainty in his partner's words. Especially since they'd already pointed out something that had sent chills down Marco's spine.

"Whoever did this had to know there was a possibility that we'd catch on once an autopsy was completed," Marco had said in the hospital. "Which means they had to know they had a shrinking window of opportunity until we realized we had the wrong guy."

Which meant he had a shrinking window of opportunity to take Bella.

Marco growled at his steering wheel once he was off the phone.

He should have been with her.

Now the two women he cared about most were missing.

Care about the most?

Marco didn't have time to focus on that thought.

He put pedal to the floor just to keep up with Val until they were whipping into Justin's long driveway. There was only one car there, and Val called out that it was Justin's as they all parked.

"Doesn't mean they weren't here," Marco pointed out. "Val, get Justin. Grant, show me the worksite."

The Greenes didn't waste any time. Val hustled to the front door while Grant led Marco around the house and down a path to the shed they were currently building.

If the situation had been different, Marco would have marveled at the structure. Instead he was all about the details. And one blaringly obvious detail was that Bella and Amy were nowhere to be found.

Grant paused at the door to the shed and then pushed it the rest of the way open. Aside from some work tools and ladders, nothing of interest was inside. Still, Grant looked around in silence while Marco looped around the structure to make sure he didn't find anything.

"He said—he said he hasn't seen them." Val ran up to them a few moments later. Justin was right behind in a jog.

He skipped any introductions.

"I've been on the back patio doing work since the weather's good," Justin added. "I haven't seen Bella or Amy all morning. I'm sorry," Justin said. "Is there anything I can do?"

Marco cussed this time. It was loud. The adrenaline that had been pouring in and out of him all day came back in. The urgency that was with it already had Marco moving again.

"Just call if they show up," he yelled over his shoulder. "We have to keep looking."

Justin nodded while the three of them rushed back to the cars.

Marco was cycling through everything that had happened in the last month, through everything Bella had told him that had happened over the last seven months to her, and trying to find something that might give him a lead. A place or a person or—

Marco slowed down by the hood of his car. He turned on his heel, looking for Val but finding Grant. His face was pinched, his brow drawn. His eyes focused but not on what to do now.

No. He had thought of something too.

"What?" Marco wasn't polite with the question. He was on Grant within a second, towering.

Bella's father didn't seem to mind. Instead he shook his head.

"He lied," Grant said, simply.

"Who lied?" Val asked, closing in their three-person half circle.

Grant was looking at Marco while he answered, his face severe.

"Only Val, Bella and I have the code to the lock on the door to the shed. We have never given it out to anyone. It's one of our main rules. We also always make sure it's always locked—we check it twice before we leave every time we're here." Grant shook his head. "It wasn't locked. It wasn't even closed. Bella was here today and Justin lied about it."

Marco didn't skip a beat. He turned to Val.

"Did you tell Justin that my sister was missing too?" he asked.

"Yeah. I said we were looking for her and Bella."

Marco lowered his voice, as if the massive house behind them could hear.

"But did you say her name? Did you call her Amy?"

Realization dawned across Val's face. Even before he shook his head.

"No. I just said it was your sister."

Marco's adrenaline was now a thundering weapon of destruction in his veins.

How could he have been so stupid?

"No one look at the house. Act like we're talking about our next steps." Marco followed his own instructions. He didn't even glance around at the large home. There were too many windows. Justin could be watching them for any hint that they'd caught on. If he really did have Bella and Amy, then tipping him off could make him panic.

And panic was never a good thing when hostages were involved.

"What's going on?" Val asked.

Marco pulled out his phone but kept it low. He finally figured out what his gut had been trying to get him to look at. One of the holes he hadn't even thought to fill.

"When Bella went on the date with Conrad, she said she had to get a friend to come pick her up while in the middle of it," he hurried. "I never asked, but do you know who that friend was?"

Grant was becoming red in the face.

He was angry.

"Justin."

"And since Bella never told anyone else about that, then Justin is one of the only people who knew about the connection between her and Conrad," Marco said. "And, if I had to guess, he was one of the few who knew Bella would be going to the city the first day I met her."

Grant nodded. "He even knew we were taking separate cars because we talked about it in front of him the day before."

Val seemed to finally get on board. His voice was flat as he added another nail in the coffin.

"He has a storage unit. Or had one for his wife's things after she died." His eyes were wide. "Which means he had the code to get into the building."

Marco had already been ready to act, but now?

Now he was ready to bulldoze the man who had played them all.

But he had to be smart about it.

He couldn't misstep. Not with Bella and his sister on the line.

"We need to leave."

"What?" Val said. "They're probably inside."

Marco got his phone out. He was ready to call everyone in, but not until he was sure Justin wasn't watching.

"That's why we have to leave," he said. "We can't let him know we're on to him. He could do something in a panic that we'll all regret. So we're going to drive down the road and pull off and try to hide our cars."

"What happens after that?" Grant's voice was low. A father angry and worried all at once.

Marco wished he could spell out exactly what would happen next. He wished he could tell him that they'd hide their cars, wait for backup, and then enter the house to find Bella and Amy safe and sound. That everyone would leave the house happy and healthy.

But Marco couldn't do that.

He couldn't predict what Justin might do or, maybe worse, what he'd already done. There was always the chance that if Justin was obsessed with Bella that that obsession could turn deadly.

For both her and Amy.

Marco couldn't think about that though.

Not now.

Grant and Val stared at him in nothing but acute worry for their family.

Marco might not be able to give them an exact plan and outcome but he could assure them of one thing.

"Then I get them back."

JUSTIN STEPPED AWAY from the window. He smiled.

The satisfied smirk spread wide across his face, from one side to the other, and remained in place all the way down into the basement.

"Well, that was Deputy Rossi and the Greene family and now it looks like they're on their way to try to find you two again," he said. "I *was* hoping that I'd have more time but I guess if I've learned anything living in this town, it's that you have to work with the hand you've been given."

He went over to the middle of the room and the chair now bolted to the ground. Using the Greenes' tools over the past few weeks had sped up his reinforcement of several items in the basement. The chair, though, was his favorite accomplishment. He'd seen enough movies to know how a simple chair tipping over could ruin any plan.

That wasn't going to be him.

He wasn't going to let anything happen.

Not to her.

"I'm sure they'll be back but we'll be long gone by then," he added with some cheer.

The women didn't respond.

It annoyed him but, at the same time, he was happy for it.

They were struggling. Or, really, Bella was.

He crouched down next to her.

There was that face again.

That look of pure calculation and concentration.

She didn't even look away as he continued talking.

"This is good, Bella. This is good for you." He reached out and tucked a strand of hair behind her ear. It had come loose from her hair tie during the unfortunate fall down the stairs. "Now you get to see how this town causes nothing but pain."

He stood up and stretched, checking his watch as he did so. Justin had already done some quick math based on the women's sizes and assumed strength. They wouldn't last much longer.

Then he and Bella could start a new life away from the damned Kelby Creek.

He took another long look at the women and smiled once more.

"And, once you let go, you can feel the relief of leaving it all behind."

Chapter Twenty

Ten minutes earlier

It wasn't real.

It couldn't be.

The pain in Bella's fingers, hands and arms begged to differ.

Still, she couldn't wrap her head around what she was currently seeing.

And doing.

Amy was pale and bloody and the first thing that made sense. Their attempt to fight Justin and get the gun away from him in the office hadn't worked. Instead they'd wound up at the stairs to the basement, where Amy fell down after being grazed by a bullet. In Bella's attempt to stop Amy's fall, she'd gone down the basement stairs with her.

Bella had lost consciousness in an instant.

Amy hadn't.

Her cheeks had been tear-stained when Bella came to, and her voice was hoarse. She'd been yelling at Justin. Then, when she saw Bella was lucid, had spoken quickly to her.

"Hold on, Bella!"

Her first thought had been that Amy's words were a rallying cry. One of emotional support. Maybe even one to take her mind off the pain and injuries she'd no doubt sustained falling down the stairs.

But then the tug had happened and Amy repeated herself with a cry.

Bella on instinct tightened her hold on whatever was in her hands. She cried out in pain. Then the details came in and she understood Amy's words weren't metaphorical. They were instructions.

That's when fear and panic had become so intense that Bella went numb.

Both she and Amy were tied up, but in very different ways. Bella's legs were bound by thick rope to a metal chair that wasn't budging despite the pull she was fighting against. Her upper body wasn't bound but her hands had been wrapped around a length of rope.

Rope that led up to the ceiling, wrapped around a pulley and then attached to Amy, wrapping around her body. Most notably her neck.

"Now, let me explain this," Justin said with nonchalance.

Bella yelled as Justin moved at her side. She realized he must have been the one to give her the rope as soon as she became conscious. One hand was still on hers. He squeezed that one and used the other to point up at the pulley above Amy.

"See, after we met, I started learning about construction as a way to impress you," he continued, as if it were a causal conversation. "Along the way, I learned how to make my own pulley systems and learned a bit about physics. That's how I made this little contraption and how I'm going to prove my point with it."

He stood up and touched the part of the rope that traveled up from Bella's hands to the ceiling.

"I've rigged this to follow a simple rule," he said. "If you don't hold up Ms. Amy's body weight, then the second she gets too much slack, the rope at the top will tighten around her neck. So tight that, I might add, she'll suffocate even if her feet make it to the floor."

Bella looked at the rope all around Amy. The rope at her wrists had already pulled out blood. The rope at her neck and upper body hadn't.

Yet.

Justin shook out his hands, flexing them when he was done.

"I'll be honest, I've been holding her up while we waited for you to wake and, it's not an easy task. Especially since your hands were, well, hurt from your accident down the stairs."

Bella's hands were in front of her face, holding on to the rope as best she could, given Amy's bodyweight. There was blood dripping down the rope and across Bella's hands.

That's why it hurt more than it would have, she realized.

Her palms were open wounds trying to hold slipping rope with the weight of a body at its end.

"I don't understand," Bella said, voice breaking. "Why are you doing this?"

Justin pointed to Amy. She glared.

"Because she's a lesson. One I'm proving to you. One—"

He cut himself off and pulled his phone out. He wasn't been happy with whatever he saw.

"I'll be right back and we can discuss this further."

He bent down next to Bella and smiled. "Don't worry. I'm doing this for us. For you. Once this lesson is done, we can go and never come back. Just remember, if you let go of that, even a little, it's lights-out for our guest."

Justin left them in the basement alone with that. Amy spoke first, angry.

"*He* cut your hands."

"What?"

Amy let out a frustrated, shaky breath.

"He said you hurt them in the fall but after he strung me up, he got a knife from his pocket and cut your hands open. He did it so it would be harder for you to hold on."

The mention of the cuts seemed to make the pain that much worse. Bella winced as the rope slipped a little. Amy in turn dropped just that much.

"Oh, God. I—I'm sorry," Bella said, tightening her grip through the burn. "It—it's also slippery."

Amy shook her head, slowly.

"None of this is your fault. It's all his. Don't you let him make you forget that."

Bella didn't say so then but she was already struggling to keep Amy up. Every part of her was pounding in pain, including her head. It swam, never mind the weight on the other side of the rope. Bella was a small woman and being completely tied to a chair, unable to get a better stance at least, made everything worse.

"I just don't understand why he's doing this," Bella let out, tears threatening to push through. "If he's obsessed with me, then why is he torturing us?"

"I don't know but—but he definitely wants you to be the one to kill me." Amy didn't mince her words. "He said he wanted you to learn now and not later like Carla had? Who's Carla?"

That confused Bella even more.

"His late wife," she said, trying to piece together what lesson she needed to learn and why Carla had learned hers later. "Some corrupt law enforcement staged a shoot-out and she got caught in the cross fire. But—but I don't get how that has anything to do with me or this nightmare scene."

Amy didn't have the answer either.

So they tried to do what they could before Justin came back.

It wasn't a lot.

Amy was a good foot off the ground and, based on the small slip and how the rope had tightened, Bella knew she couldn't slowly lower the woman down. She also couldn't get free from her chair to grab her or help. Even if she could support the woman's weight with one hand and use her other to try to untie herself, it wouldn't work. Justin had knotted the rope holding Bella beneath the chair. She couldn't reach it without getting up. As for anything around her in reach, there was nothing.

The basement wasn't opulent or large like the rest of the house above it, but there was enough space around them to keep both women isolated.

"The only thing I can use is him," Bella decided once they'd listed off all the things they couldn't do in quick succession. "If he gets close enough, maybe I can grab him with one hand and try to get something off him to get myself free."

Amy seemed to like that idea but there was no disguising the anger there. Behind those eyes that matched her brother's to a T. She didn't have to say his name for Bella to know whom she was talking about next.

"This will destroy him," she said, quiet but filled with

rage. "If I die and you're taken, he'll burn the whole world down until it's done. And I don't know if he'll be able to come back from that." Amy's eyes widened and that anger quickly turned to determination. "Bella, if this doesn't work out, you have to fight and then when Marco comes, you have to make sure this all doesn't consume him. Okay?"

"You're not going to die," Bella promised.

Amy wasn't willing to hear that.

"But if I do—"

But Bella was just as stubborn.

"You're *not* going to die," she said. "We're going to get out of this somehow. You'll see."

"Bella, look up at this thing I'm attached to," Amy said. "This guy learned how to and then built a pulley system just for this purpose. He's been planning this for a long time. And he's clearly good at it."

Bella shook her head. She heard Marco's words in her head and added on to them.

"We weren't supposed to be here today," she said. "Which means he acted on impulse. And when you act on impulse, you get sloppy. And when you get sloppy, you're just asking for a man like Marco to figure out that plan and ruin it."

At that, Amy smiled.

But then footsteps sounded on the stairs and Justin came in, cheerful.

Bella ignored him the best she could while he spoke. Focusing instead on two things: holding on to the rope no matter how much it was hurting her hands and starting to make her arms shake, and any opening she could use to try to grab Justin and save Amy.

After tucking a piece of hair behind her ear, though,

he moved out of range. Then he spoke about the relief of letting go and Bella couldn't keep quiet anymore.

"What are you talking about, Justin?" She heard her own struggle to hold the rope come through her voice. She pushed on, finding his gaze and hoping it would keep her pain on the back burner long enough to buy them more time. Or just enough conversation to get him closer to her again. "I don't understand why you're doing this or whatever lesson you're trying to teach me. How can it work if I don't understand it?"

Justin, who she'd always thought was a good guy dealt a bad hand, now looked like a crazed man who was unaware of just how far he'd thrown the deck of cards out the window. But, at the very least, he seemed to care about what she had to say. He even considered a moment before he answered. Bella was surprised at how lucid he was.

"Did I ever tell you I drowned here? In this town and in that awful creek?" He didn't pause for a response. "I was in high school and had gone out with some friends for a late-night round of truth or dare and the next thing I know I'm gulping for air and sinking to the bottom of that disgusting water." His face contorted into anger. "I was saved but after that, not only did I hate the creek, I hated the town."

Justin took a step closer, maybe four feet from her. Bella tightened her grip on the rope. She held in a wince from the pain the best she could. Justin kept talking, unaware of it or he simply didn't care.

"I was ready to leave but then I met Carla," he continued. "Now, she—*she* loved this town. Loved it so much that she said she knew she wouldn't be happier anywhere else in the entire world. Made me buy this house when

I could have given her a castle anywhere else. But no. It was Kelby Creek or die for her."

This time, he caught Bella off guard and laughed. It was unkind.

"If she had only known that would end up becoming the choice for her, then I'm sure we could have been happy anywhere else. But she dug in her heels and won every fight we ever had about leaving."

Justin took a step closer. Instead of moving his gaze around the room, now he focused on Bella only. Her arms started to shake at the strain of holding Amy up.

Now she was trying not to cry.

She didn't want to give him the satisfaction.

"Then she got caught in this town's muck and, with her last words, admitted that I was right. That we should have left." Every emotion drained from him. It was such an alarming change in tone that Bella became afraid to look away. His voice was hard. Steel against the road. "And she didn't even know why she died. She didn't know that this town killed her for money of all things. Money I had. Money I could have given them instead of them taking her. But no. That's not how this godforsaken town works, is it?"

He moved to Amy with such speed that Amy yelled out. Justin jabbed his finger into the blood on her side where the bullet had grazed her. She cried out again.

"Everything this town did and I have to sit back and watch them walk around like nothing ever happened? I have to watch more people like her brother come in and try to redeem this place?" He laughed. Goose bumps spread across Bella's body as a violent chill went through her at the sound of just how far gone he was. "This town doesn't *deserve* redemption."

He shoved Amy. Not hard enough to hurt her but enough to make holding her still impossible. The rope slipped over an inch. Bella yelled as she tried to stop it from falling farther. The pain and blood all over her hands was a nightmare, but not as much as seeing the rope around Amy's neck tighten. She started to cough.

"Then why me? Why take me? What lesson are you trying to teach?" Bella cried out. She needed him to focus on her. She needed him to get closer.

The question, at the very least, distracted him.

Justin stepped away from Amy. She could still breathe but there were tears in her eyes.

"Because, Bella, the moment I made the decision to *finally* leave this awful place, you showed up. On the barstool next to me. Smiling." At that, his rage switched back to unsettling cheer. *"Hello there, friend."*

He finally walked to her, crouching down between both women. He put his hands on her knees and smiled.

"That's when I knew. That's when I knew I had to save you from it all. But not before showing you how much this place can hurt. How much bad it can bring. I had to give you pain so you could see how good life can be without it. Without this town."

He was so close now. Leaning in, almost like he was going to kiss her.

Bella wanted nothing more than to get far, far away from him. But she needed that closeness.

She needed him near.

So she goaded him.

She wanted him to get sloppy again.

"But then Marco showed up and confused me, didn't he?" Bella tilted her head to the side. Justin mimicked the motion. His eyes were glazed over, lost in his own obsession and anger. She nodded slowly. He did that too.

"I had a better plan. Poetic too. I was going to take you and make a statement and show you pain through your father. Not like this but I had a way."

Bella swallowed her own rage. She needed him just a little closer.

"But Marco messed that up and you had to improvise," she spelled out.

He nodded.

"He even messed up my plan B." Justin's eyes dropped to her lips. Bella held in every urge she had to gag. "But now look at us. You're about to learn your lesson and then we can finally leave this place together."

Bella didn't want to but she looked away from the man. Only for a moment and only for one reason.

Amy met her stare with an absolute calm. Without saying a word, the youngest Rossi knew exactly what Bella was asking.

And she was ready for it.

Her voice was a rasp but it was clear.

"Do it."

Justin never saw it coming.

Bella knew she couldn't hold the rope with one hand, just like she knew she couldn't do that much damage to him with just one either.

So she channeled the extremely familiar motion of coiling up an extension cord. Something she did every workday when they were done using the saws and cleaning up.

This time though, instead of wrapping up a cord to keep it neat, Bella used the last of her strength to try and wrap the rope around his neck.

Justin was too close to escape the move. Bella yelled as she jerked the rope down. A new wave of adrenaline was the only reason she got the rope around his neck once. She pulled down as hard as she could.

It wasn't enough.

Justin's hands went to his neck, putting his fingers beneath the rope with ease. Once there he one-handedly pulled it away while using his other hand to hit Bella across the face.

It hurt but she stayed focused through the pain.

She still was holding the rope. If she didn't keep that hold, then Amy was done.

Though her good intentions weren't enough.

Not compared to Justin's rage-filled strength.

He tore the rope from her hands and stood.

"I guess I'll have to teach you the lesson myself."

Everything happened in an instant.

Bella screamed as Justin let go of the rope.

Amy made an awful sound.

A gunshot went off, so loud that Bella felt it in her bones.

Justin fell back, away from Bella.

She didn't have time to look to see who had done it. Though she knew in her heart who was there.

Instead she scrambled for the rope and caught it as Amy went red in the face.

"Marco, the rope!"

He was fast. He was between them as quickly as he had appeared.

Marco grabbed the rope and pulled it down like it was the easiest thing he'd ever done. Amy let out a gasp as the move allowed her slack.

Bella wanted to cry in relief but then she heard her father.

"Gun!"

Bella turned in time to see that Justin hadn't hit the ground. Even though blood was coming out of his shirt at the chest, he was still standing. And he was still moving, right toward the cabinets along the far wall.

And the gun he'd used on them earlier that was on top of those same cabinets.

Bella watched in muted horror as Justin grabbed the weapon and spun around to face them.

She had no way to protect herself. No way to protect Marco or the sister he loved with all of his heart. No way to keep her father, who was somewhere behind them, out of harm's way.

Bella couldn't do anything except watch as he took aim at her.

But what a sight it ended up being.

Marco let go of the rope with one of his hands. Instead of Amy dropping, he pulled the rope with him as he took one giant step to the side, and she lifted all the way to the ceiling. The sheer strength seemed to ripple out and across the man as he used his new position to do the unthinkable.

Marco used his body as a shield for Bella just as Justin took his shot.

Bella and Amy yelled out as the shot hit.

Marco's body folded in as the bullet struck somewhere in his upper body. Bella couldn't see.

When the second shot sounded, she was sure that it was all over for the three of them.

It took her far too long to realize that the third shot had come from behind her.

"He's down!" It was her father's voice. He came into view behind Amy, gun raised and aimed still on Justin. "Val, grab the rope!"

Bella felt that numbness again. Her family's voices became background noise. All she could focus on was the man still standing in front of her.

Marco didn't speak.

He also didn't let go of the rope.

He just continued to stand there, being his sister's savior and Bella's shield.

Her very own set of armor.

Chapter Twenty-One

"Well, I hate to say it, but I think that's going to scar a little worse than the last thing I saw when I was in here."

Marco rubbed the sleep from his eyes and, for a moment, forgot where he was.

Then the dull ache of pain meds wearing off hit him, along with the fluorescent lights above, the hardness of the bed below and the man beside the bed in a chair next to him.

Grant motioned to the second bandage just below his collarbone. Getting shot had hurt like hell but he'd thanked his lucky stars the second it had happened that it had happened.

The fact that it wasn't a through-and-through only made the news better.

If either hadn't happened, then Bella might have been in his place. Or worse.

And Marco definitely wouldn't be looking at a smiling Grant Greene right now.

"I heard chicks dig scars," he said with a chuckle. "Though I'm hoping two will be enough. Not a fan of being a frequent flyer at this hospital."

Grant laughed.

"I'm sure I'm not the Greene you were hoping to see when you woke up either," he teased.

Marco shook his head.

"No offense," he joked back.

Grant laughed again and waved him off.

"None taken."

Marco glanced at the love seat next to his chair. There was a sheet on it with a folded blanket and a pillow on one cushion but no woman who had spent the last two days there. Grant let him take a moment before speaking again. His tone shifted into the more serious.

"Last time it was just me and you in here, I wasn't sure what kind of man you were," he started. "But after what you told me, I thought I had a good sense of who you were. A good man with good intentions. Someone I didn't mind hanging around with my only daughter." Grant cleared his throat. Marco heard the break in his voice but didn't address it. He let the man say his peace. He would *always* let the man say his piece. Not only had Grant Greene shot Justin, in doing so he'd saved Marco's, Amy's and his daughter's lives. Marco could try to pay the older man back for the rest of his life and still never come close.

"But then—then I saw you make a decision without time to even think about it," he continued. "And then I really saw you. A great man. And, for what it's worth, a great man who I'm extremely proud of."

Marco hadn't expected that, especially since Grant, Valerie and Val had spent the first half hour of his recovery time going over and over how grateful they were for what he'd done to save Bella.

Marco also hadn't expected how much he felt at the words now.

"It's worth a lot," he said, simply. "Thank you."

Grant cleared his throat again and nodded. The older man had managed to avoid any injuries but the stress at what had happened, the anger at Justin, it had made him tired. It had made them all tired.

But time would help with that.

Time and the fact that Justin Hastings was, and forever would be, gone.

He'd bled out before Carlos and his backup could arrive. Both Marco's bullet and Grant's had managed to do equal damage. Amanda had already stopped by to tell Marco that there was no way to know which one had killed him first. That, in a weird way, felt poetic. The two men who would take a bullet for Bella had given one each to the man who had tried to take her away from them.

Now those men were tired and ready for everything to settle back down.

Grant stood and was back to smiling.

"Bella should be here soon," he said. "She and your sister should be back from the airport any minute now with your parents."

"Ah, so you got stuck with babysitting duty?"

Grant chuckled.

"Better to watch you audition for *Sleeping Beauty* than be stuck in another conversation about renovating your home versus buying it new between Val and your brother-in-law. They haven't quit since Matthew came into town the other day. I've watched paint dry as a part of my job and found more joy in that."

Marco couldn't help but laugh at that.

"But now that you're up, want to watch the game with me?" Grant grabbed for the remote, already turning the TV in the corner on. "It's a rerun of Auburn's dang Kick

Six but it's better than another round of *Family Feud*. You and Bella smoked me on that last night."

Marco assured him that he didn't mind and thought that maybe one day he'd tell Grant just how much such a simple request meant to someone like him.

Someone who had always wanted a big family.

Someone who had always wanted to feel love without the worry of it going away.

But, for now, Marco decided to save that detail for his speech when he asked Grant for his daughter's hand in marriage.

Because, as Marco had already figured out, that's exactly what he was going to do. Just not until he asked his mother for his grandmother's ring.

"Hey, you better pay attention to this game," Grant piped in when Marco got lost in his thoughts about the future. "This game is a big topic at Thanksgiving *and* Christmas every year."

Marco laughed.

"Yes, sir."

IT WAS BEAUTIFUL. Despite everything, it really was beautiful.

"Are you sure you made this?"

Bella rolled her eyes and turned to Marco with a smirk already up.

"You keep talking like that and I'll take back my *third* impression of you," she warned. It made the man laugh.

"You've already admitted you like me, and you can't take that back. So—" Marco wrapped his arm around her and gently pulled her against his side so they were both still facing the whole reason they'd made the trip. He bent down and placed a kiss against her hair "—you're stuck with me."

A month ago Bella would have worried that the movement was too much for his bullet wound but in the time between then and now, he had recovered fully.

"As long as being stuck with you means we can grab some food tonight at Crisp's, I'm in."

Marco agreed that could definitely happen, then they both quieted again.

The shed behind Justin's house was finally done.

Some people didn't understand why Bella, Val and her father had wanted to finish it but Marco had never been one of them. One late night, in the dark and beneath the sheets, Bella had told him why it meant something to her despite what Justin had done.

"He wasn't wrong," she'd said, though she'd been quick to continue. "Justin, I mean. He wasn't wrong about Kelby Creek in part. It's hard not to remember what happened to Annie McHale, just as it's easy to forget that the damage and pain didn't stop with her and her family. She was just the first. After her, it all just spread." Bella had shaken her head within Marco's embrace. "I never even thought to wonder what it must have felt like for Justin to walk around this town—to see you or anyone with a badge—and just be expected to be okay."

She'd sighed. Marco had stroked her hair.

"I guess, no matter how it turned out, I feel like finishing the shed is the smallest of ways to honor the part of him that was there before Carla died. Have something that was made with love there for the next person who moves in to enjoy at least."

"That sounds like a good plan to me," Marco had said.

"I can even help if you want me to. Though I stand by being awful with building things."

Bella had been learning that Marco surprising her was just par for the course with the man. Just as he'd supported the idea of her finishing the shed with her family, he'd helped her pull some strings to get Justin's body buried in a cemetery just outside the town limits since, it turned out, Carla was buried alongside her parents in the local one and there was no room left for him. At the very least, they'd helped Justin finally make it out of Kelby Creek.

"Okay, Dad and Val already got all the pictures for us earlier," Bella said after a while. "I think I'm ready to go now."

Marco took her hand and together they used the old, worn path to go back to Bella's new old truck. It wasn't the same as the one she'd had before but she was starting to fall for it all the same.

The man who held the door open for her when they got up to it?

Well, she had a sneaking suspicion that she'd fallen for him the moment he'd offered her a ride in the rain.

"Okay, so we're doing Crisp's tonight, but what about until then?" he asked, pulling her against him before she could get inside the truck. "As a reminder, Amy and Matthew will be back in town tomorrow to look at that house Val wants them to buy and, as your dad says, listening to Matthew and Val talk shop is going to drain us of our life force. *So* is there anything you want to do this afternoon with just the two of us?"

It had been an innocent question.

Bella knew that because she'd heard many a not-so-innocent question from the man.

Yet she couldn't help but grin up at him.

"I can think of a few things."

Marco threw his head back in laughter. When he was done, she knew she'd gotten him.

"Give me the keys and I can get us back to the house in two minutes flat," he said. "I can even call ahead so no one stops us. Carlos owes me anyway since he enjoyed the date I set up for him and Amanda. He'll look the other way if he sees us speeding home for a good cause."

Bella didn't say it but hearing Marco call her house their home felt better than any tumble beneath the sheets would.

Though she wasn't about to turn down one of those either.

She tossed him the keys, pulled him in for a deep kiss and broke it with a laugh.

"Then why are we sitting around here wasting time, Deputy?"

Marco pulled her back to him. This time the kiss was longer, deeper. One that Bella melted against.

When they parted, she sighed.

Marco ran a thumb along her cheek and smiled.

"It's never wasted time when I'm with you."

Bella could have lived in that moment for a long while, but life wasn't about staying in one moment. It was about living through all the good, bad and in-between moments.

If you were lucky, living those with someone good by your side.

And, as Bella felt the warmth of Marco's hands on her waist, lips still warm where his had pressed against hers, she knew she sure was lucky.

* * * * *

COMING SOON!

We really hope you enjoyed reading this book.
If you're looking for more romance, be sure to
head to the shops when new books are
available on

Thursday 5th August

To see which titles are coming soon, please visit

millsandboon.co.uk/nextmonth

MILLS & BOON

THE HEART OF ROMANCE

A ROMANCE FOR EVERY READER

MODERN

Prepare to be swept off your feet by sophisticated, sexy and seductive heroes, in some of the world's most glamourous and romantic locations, where power and passion collide.

HISTORICAL

Escape with historical heroes from time gone by. Whether your passion is for wicked Regency Rakes, muscled Vikings or rugged Highlanders, awaken the romance of the past.

MEDICAL

Set your pulse racing with dedicated, delectable doctors in the high-pressure world of medicine, where emotions run high and passion, comfort and love are the best medicine.

True Love

Celebrate true love with tender stories of heartfelt romance, from the rush of falling in love to the joy a new baby can bring, and a focus on the emotional heart of a relationship.

Desire

Indulge in secrets and scandal, intense drama and plenty of sizzling hot action with powerful and passionate heroes who have it all: wealth, status, good looks…everything but the right woman.

HEROES

Experience all the excitement of a gripping thriller, with an intense romance at its heart. Resourceful, true-to-life women and strong, fearless men face danger and desire - a killer combination!

To see which titles are coming soon, please visit

millsandboon.co.uk/nextmonth

LET'S TALK

Romance

For exclusive extracts, competitions
and special offers, find us online:

- ⓕ facebook.com/millsandboon
- 🐦 @MillsandBoon
- 📷 @MillsandBoonUK

Get in touch on 01413 063232

For all the latest titles coming soon, visit
millsandboon.co.uk/nextmonth

MILLS & BOON
A ROMANCE FOR EVERY READER

- **FREE** delivery direct to your door

- **EXCLUSIVE** offers every month

- **SAVE** up to 25% on pre-paid subscriptions

SUBSCRIBE AND SAVE

millsandboon.co.uk/Subscribe

JOIN US ON SOCIAL MEDIA!

Stay up to date with our latest releases, author
news and gossip, special offers and discounts, and
all the behind-the-scenes action
from Mills & Boon...

 millsandboon

 millsandboonuk

 millsandboon

t might just be true love...

MILLS & BOON
Desire

Indulge in secrets and scandal, intense drama and plenty of sizzling hot action with powerful and passionate heroes who have it all: wealth, status, good looks…everything but the right woman.

MILLS & BOON
MEDICAL
Pulse-Racing Passion

Set your pulse racing with dedicated, delectable doctors in the high-pressure world of medicine, where emotions run high and passion, comfort and love are the best medicine.

Eight Medical stories published every month, find them all :

millsandboon.co.uk